Under a
Marbella Sky

Roly Quesnel

May 2006, Estepona, Spain

Blue. Deep, incandescent. A perfect canopy. Spanish sky. Wincing, vision blurred, I'm on my back. Try to move. I fail. Too dizzy. Smoke. Grey plumes funnelling upwards. Grey on blue. Mushroom shapes pulse, embers flee like a hoard of maddened fire-flies, a random, swirling chaos of orange tails, fizzing as if some clumsy giant had disturbed their nest. Then the frenzied crackling sound imposes itself on the buzzing in my ears. From the explosion. Did anyone survive? The fire is close and moving, waves of heat wash over me. Blood seeps from various wounds, from my left ear, which is numb and worryingly deaf. The sun and blue are now fully obscured by the brown-black heart of the plume.

Flames rear up only meters to my left. I lurch forward, smoke blast stabs my eyes, tears stream and my throat rages against rasping vapours. Run. Limping frantically, without thought, direction, away from flames. I plunge through harsh, thorn-infested scrub. Clothes and flesh yield in chunks, a spastic stigmata of flailing limbs. Why is Spanish countryside so murderous? A vision of a green field jumps unbidden, surreally, into mind. I feel the squelch of sodden lumpy turf, the rain leaving little pools with iridescent sheens in the abundant cowpats. Holidays in Wales, picking mushrooms in the morning, the smell of barns and hot animals. I must be close to death, is this that moment when your life flashes before your eyes?

Panic drives me forward and I plunge further and faster, flaying myself alive on the predatory foliage. With a violent jolt, I miss my footing and sprawl forwards, pitch head over heels down a bank and land on my back on the flat earth of a dirt road.

A fire engine skids to a halt before me, not crushing me by the narrowest of margins. Two figures in heavy clothing, enormous boots and strong gloves appear, wordlessly pick me up bodily, hurling me into the cab of the truck. I feel the comfort of the seat, the air-conditioning, smell the strangely sanitised air. The roar of fire is replaced by the sound of crackling radios and the comforting sound of heavy Andalusian accents.

'How do you cope in that outfit in this climate?' I ask the inhabitants of the cabin, blinking at me in confusion and surprise. I don't hear the answer, whatever language it comes out in. Delicious unconsciousness envelopes me. Finally, release.

2

October 1982. Warrington, England

It is the glass that is most shocking. It rains in tiny shards all over us, catching the light, laying an instant, random mosaic over the old carpet. The bang has stunned us into catatonia, but as the smoke storms the broken windows, panic and self-preservation propel us downstairs. My eight-year-old brother Gary is crying helplessly. My mother's face is ashen white, her eyes wild, she grabs our hands and drags us after her. We emerge onto the street below through the shattered door, coughing in the black smoke, then stagger back far enough to turn and behold the hell that has befallen us.

Flames belch lasciviously from the blasted window of the chip shop. My mother now starts to scream uncontrollably, and Gary buries his face in her, trying to blot out the horror. I sprint toward the flames, searching for a way in, scanning for a trace of life. The intense heat singes and forces me back. Desperation rises, I run aimlessly, frantically, in front of the fire, striving for some possibility of action. Flames. Only flames and searing heat. I scream, tearing my throat, vainly competing against the roar devouring all before me, hoping for some response, some miracle. I don't know how long goes by; time is suspended. Someone grabs me, and returns me to my mother's side. They are both whimpering still.

Hoses play water into the inferno, and all turns to steam and billowing whites, greys and blacks. In no time the flames are quenched. It was so easy! Why weren't they here in the first place? I seize my chance and run again for the interior. Strong hands grab me again.

'Get back there, lad! Are you trying to get yourself killed? There's gas...'

I try to fight them off, but they are too many for me. My energy, my will, fades. Hopelessness creeps over me, and I can only stand and stare, trying to process the unthinkable.

3

March 2006, Warrington, England

Freedom. A loaded word. Prone to misuse, abuse, misinterpretation. My current experience of it is not measuring up to any traditional expectations. I walk through the intense drizzle of a late winter's morning. Drizzle so fine, drops are almost undetectable; a suffocating, freezing aerosol that penetrates the inadequate old coat I am wearing. I am shivering when I enter the dingy little cubicle, the venue for my weekly session with my probation supervisor. The freedom I have is tainted, illusory. Mr. Ian Watkins, probation officer, holds it in his greasy little hands. The hand that giveth is the hand that taketh away. It's not real freedom they have granted me, it is a legally binding form of bureaucratic penance. The conditions of my licence state among other things, that I subject myself to his supervision; he will sanction any jobs I may get, where I am able to live, what my movements may be. I have thus been condemned to live with my mother. In our dreary house, that we moved to after the gas explosion, where we set up camp, the three of us, to nurse our wounds, to attempt to raise life anew from the ashes. A prison of the spirit, haunted by spectres of regret and self-loathing.

I am jolted out of this reverie by Watkins blathering on.

'Eugene, it never ceases to grieve me how you seem to have wasted all the talents the genetic lottery has bequeathed you. Not to mention the gifts society has squandered on you. You are naturally intelligent, articulate and educated, and yet your efforts to find work thus far have been lacklustre at best. You've been given a second chance, you have our support, the state is paying your benefits to enable you to reintegrate, and your attitude appears to be entirely uncooperative.'

5

This is in part true, of course. I have merely the vaguest interest in finding employment. Day-jobbing, predictable routine is anathema to me. I have simply never done it; it is a culture and set of assumptions I do not understand. The trouble is I have no alternative proposition. The employment opportunities Mr. Watkins will accept on my behalf very much correlate to exactly those which I am least capable of, or interested in.

'Mr. Watkins, with all due respect, I've applied to dozens of businesses, the vast majority of whom have not even condescended to reply, and if they have it's to tell me I'm over qualified. What use is someone like me to a supermarket, or a pizza delivery company? There's a queue of enthusiastic immigrants out there gagging for any one of those jobs, who will do it much better than me. Every job I have seen is a low paid piece of shit that-'

'-Mr. Phillips, I would remind you that that sort of language is as unacceptable in this office as it is in the workplace.'

'Sorry.' It's an easy word, but I squeeze it out purely through a herculean effort of will.

'Chin up lad, it's not all doom and gloom. We are makers of our own destiny, and the buck stops with each and every one of us.'

And so on. He's trained in talking in clichés, above all else. Ahead lie twice monthly meetings for, how long, two more years? More? It is a purgatory only politicians could have invented. The thought, that this weasel man can, at any time, with adequate justification, recall me to the warm embrace of Strangeways prison, is a debilitating reality that further clouds my daily life.

Mercifully, his case load is heavy enough for these tortuous sessions to be short. I am given further spurious targets that bear no relation to the actual job market, or my rather limited aptitudes, and sent forth. I trudge out into the dense, all embracing rain and midday half-light, and start to shiver my way home. Bile invades my mouth unbidden. The pavement is a mire sucking at my legs, pulling me down. The tentacles of these endless, formless days ahead creep and wrap themselves around me, tightening on my throat, squeezing the last dregs of life from me. Home with Mum; a sentence to be the bystander at someone else's slow, inexorable decline to an undignified and un-mourned death; forever held in the grip of her cataclysmic depression since that day.

I am aware of, somewhere deep within, a dim light, flickering, its milky flame struggling to illuminate the dark. I am powerless to give it fuel, to strengthen it. The mire is not merely existential, but a living, breathing dung heap of bureaucratic obligations and surveillance; topped with the fresh excrement of social prejudice against ex-cons, their recidivist inevitabilities and self-fulfilling prophecies. Most essentially, it is a mire of crippling, inescapable failings and inadequacies; nihilistic, self-pitying cauldrons of emotional and social dysfunction, a gloriously dark collection of personal baggage.

I am stopped and dragged out of this hopeless, quasi-suicidal sulk by a shop window, because of its hilarious incongruity. It's a relief. Out of the window of Thomas Cook's, leaping indiscriminately, like a surprise drag act in a seminary, is a collection of posters and brochures resplendent with images of palm-fringed azure beaches, verdant tropical paradises, sophisticated European city streets, their cute cafe terraces basking in the warm sun. I turn round to better compare the reality around me, the utter lack of light, the uniformity of redbrick and gunmetal grey buildings, the endless chain-store monotony of the street. It elicits a bitter chuckle, one tainted with a hint of desperation. I resume the chilly trudge, the mire beckons and embraces me, and I return home to float, alongside my mother, in its languid, odorous lagoon.

Once I am dry and the shivering has stopped from the sodden walk, I am slumped at the kitchen table, regarding Mum. The light has faded, gloom envelopes all, the inclement weather heralding night even more ridiculously early than usual. Conversation is impossible. She has nothing to say, and I have little to offer either. Uselessness

7

hangs in the air, stale as the bacon fat and margarine that cling to the aged, grubby surfaces of the kitchen. Historical unpleasantries haven't made our cohabitation easy at the best of times, and my mother's ever diminishing grasp on real time and space means our interaction is minimal, devoid of much more than the immediately functional and necessary.

I return to the daily conundrum, of how to pass my remaining sentence in this house. As the licence is, effectively, another form of sentence, transposing one soul curdling web of restrictions from a gaol to a more familiar but equally debilitating venue. Like the one old lag said to me, shortly before my release, 'If you think this is hard, wait till you get out. It's just keeps getting harder.' Too right. He'd shake his head wearily and roll a parsimonious, smelly little cigarette. For me, just risking a crafty spliff could be a return ticket to the clink. All the freedom of teetering on a precipice in a hundred-mile gorge, with one distant, tenuous path out along its rocky walls.

I could watch telly. If there was something to watch. Nothing inside the insidious box holds any interest or relevance to my life, formerly, or currently, a life that withers before my eyes on the vine of my impotence. I could read a book. If there were any in here. I no longer own, nor can afford, any video games, whose mindlessly addictive vitality has been a useful solace over the years. Go to the pub with friends. I have none. They were all lost, far back, along the way to here.

Here. Now. My own private, self-inflicted, customised perdition.

~

A strange calm settles, once the flames are vanquished. Blue, sluggish, oily-looking smoke meanders upwards, steadily melding into the grey sheen of that universal sky so familiar to residents of the North-West of England. Blue on grey. I'm staring at the blackened frontage of the building, its familiarity is horrendously, heretically abused. The sign, Phillip's Fish and Chips, is barely visible, but for the negative impression of the words in peeled, scorched paint. The window of the chip shop has been blasted outwards, the building opens like some volcanic beast's maw, gorged on tar and basalt. Charred fittings, broken glass, and swirling, blackened pools of water evidence the scale of the destruction.

'Suspected gas explosion, get these people back!' I hear a policeman yell.

Firemen drift, cartoon-like in their blobby yellow hats, obscenely jolly as the colour shouts over the chorus of dirty grey and black. Red hoses, oversized Spanish liquorish, coil everywhere in sinuous latticework. People step amongst it, in strange lumpy movements, boots crunching in the slush and pools of filthy water. The stink of burnt oil and charred plastic is overwhelming, seeping through my nostrils, leeching through my sinuses, into my brain. It starts to fill my eyes; the vindictive, murky patina grows and the whole scene becomes distant and recedes. Another policeman appears, with the absurd, tit-shaped helmet tucked under the arm. A face, featureless, floats before me. No eyes, just a mouth moves, making words.

'You need to come with us now. There's nothing you can do. I'm very sorry.'

More figures arrive. A stretcher is taken into the interior. A long sheet is placed over something inside. The meaning of the scene before me comes into focus, pinpoint, in punishingly clear relief. Police officers throw blankets around us and a policewoman guides us away, anxiously trying to protect us from the stares and rubbernecking, as the scene is surrounded by what seems the entire neighbourhood, gawping with mock concern and barely contained, voyeuristic excitement. Ahead of us, behind the cordon, stands a gaggle of faces I know too well. Jimmy Kavanagh and his mates, slouched and relaxed, beholding my family approaching with sardonic amusement. I read it in their faces, I see the great smiles behind their eyes. Jimmy Kavanagh; bully, braggart, petty criminal,

9

a walking teenage Exocet missile, primed with contempt and cruelty, the son of his father in every sense.

''Kinnel Eugene, maybe the food'll taste a bit better after that. Couldn't get any worse.' To which his acolytes giggle contemptuously.

'Watch it sunshine, now move along,' says the policewoman, and we are whisked forward as the day starts to fray at the edges and the light slowly drains away through an invisible hole in my vision.

'It's my fault, it's my fault,' I repeat over and over to the policewoman. She shakes her head, but as much with bewilderment as with conviction. My mother and Gary are both looking at me, searching my face for something, some sliver of comprehension, hope even. Mum's stare leaves my face, and steadily settles somewhere else, far away.

4

A cursory glance at my boarding pass and passport confirms my entry to the boarding lounge, a delicious point of no return. A roll of the dice. I am fully committed, but somewhat ill prepared. My remaining possessions in life are contained in my favourite battered black holdall. I carry the passport, about sixty pounds, and little else.

Ringway's lights recede in the early dawn, as the plane lifts up, revealing the flat expanse of England: its copious piles of red Lego bricks and grey tops, everywhere intense lines of roads like so much discarded nylon fishing line. Small, polite fields and abstract clumps of trees fight half-heartedly with the endless encroaching brick and concrete, tarmac and glass. A zillion tiny points of light dust the whole. Electric icing sugar. Greeny-grey, chaotic and ill disciplined: cosmic cat vomit maliciously thrown at the wobbly little island surrounded by the iron seas. We bump up through misty congregations of vapour, a multi-level fog installation, through which the cat vomit appears intermittently.

About ninety minutes into the flight, the land opens up into a broad canvas of ochre, silver-grey, and green. The brush strokes are minimal, bold and powerful. The splotch of a city appears, isolated in endless wastes of desiccated sepia. This, I am informed, by the captain's professional politeness and barely disguised boredom, is Madrid. It looks surprisingly small and compact for a capital city. Ever more unfamiliar patterns slide below me: mottled, random blobs and stains overlaid with a regular endless mesh of black dots, stretching to the horizon, even from this height. Long lines slice and weave through this, knitting together splashes of white Lego bricks this time, like some god's child has cast a bucketful from the sky and tidied them into little piles. Vast haunches of growling limestone leap out of this Arcadian tapestry, to stand in splendid isolation, arched backed, lizard-dinosaur like. Their lower flanks are green and lush. The intensity of the light, the vividness of the world and its unfamiliar patterns holds me spellbound. It slips past, a sleepy, sluggish river of land, ten kilometres underneath, modulating gradually.

'I've always wondered who the bloody 'ell picks all them olives. Look at it, where d'ya start? I'd go nuts. Bet it's a load of bleeding Romanians or summat. Dunno why they bother, it's right greasy that olive oil, too heavy. Can't make a good chip frying in that stuff.'

'Really' I say, to the guy sitting next to me, who has just piped up for no perceivable reason other than maybe his third can of John Smith's. 'So what would make a good chip?' I ask, then immediately regret it.

'Proper Yorkshire fat. Or is it veggie oil, they use these days? Hardly any decent chippies left. It's all kebabs and fried chicken.' He's wearing his identikit perry shirt and shorts, yacht pumps and pork-pie hat, even though it's March.

'Well, you're right in that olive oil is not adequate for making good chips, but it's to do with the temperature at which different fats boil at.'

'Oh, right.' I can see him thinking *smart-arse,* but he doesn't say it. My family has history where such crucial matters are concerned. He turns back to his mates. There is a splash of them seated around me, and, like stray dogs scent the proximity of garbage bag treats, the approaching Costa has awakened the pack mentality and their Pavlovian responses are in full flow. More beer is ordered, songs are starting to be sung, and hostesses twitch, ready for the first one to step over the invisible, and of course, legally enforceable line.

'So, where you off to then mate?' I ask, then curse myself again, for my curiosity.

'Marbella innit, stag do, Jerry over there. His missus thinks he's only going to Blackpool. So did he until he got in the taxi. He doesn't know what he's in for.'

'I'm off to Marbella, I've no idea what I'm in for either. It's a new one on me, this Spain.'

'First time? You'll love it mate, you won't wanna come back, the birds in Marbella are like...' and his face convulses in an expression of hyperbole. 'But half of 'em are hookers mind.'

'Oh? Right. Still, no harm in looking ay?'

'Careful what you look at down there, mate, they like fresh meat. You won't know who's a hooker until you get the bar tab and their hands are down your pants and your wallet's long gone. The African ones, they'll have you on the street, they're just not bothered. I tell yah, it's the bleedin' Wild West there, I love it.'

'Horses for courses, I suppose.'

'Well you could always go to Torremolinos, play bingo with OAPs, if you can't take the pace. What you going for?'

'See me brother, he lives out there. Haven't seen him in a while.'

'Oh nice, he'll sort you out. You don't know what you're in for, hahaha.'

Don't know what I'm in for. Never a truer word spoke. And that is a much better feeling, a vastly more encouraging vista than any I have surveyed in a considerably long time. Just not knowing anything about what will happen next. With zero expectations.

It was an impulse. To each and every action there is an equal and opposite reaction. School physics. The travel shop window with its sacrilegious offerings of distant happiness put the hook in me. With what little money I had from my stingy benefits, I was able to purchase a flight to Malaga. If I returned within a couple of weeks, I could get away with what is technically breaching my licence, the consequences of which could regenerate the whole cycle of incarceration, release, supervision. All of these deadening implications ran through my mind, while the travel agent waited patiently, trying to fathom my distant stare and angst-ridden face.

'Will that be one-way sir, or do you have a return date in mind?' She had to prod. Force the issue.

Fuck Watkins. This place. Home. My life. Fuck all of it. What was it he said about being makers of our own destinies?

'That'll be just one way, please.'

A decision made. Loaded with consequences. It felt, and still feels, truly liberating, exploding everything with one small payment. I've led a life characterised by indecision, by fecklessness, a debilitating inability to seize the day and change things. To act instead of be acted upon. To be the piano player, rather than just be another piano. So this is momentous. I feel it. My destiny. Watkins might actually be rubbing off on me.

~

We land, and a ripple of applause arises. It's the Spanish looking passengers who are the perpetrators of this unlikely public exhibition of gratitude. I file along the narrow aisle, surveying the detritus of abandoned tabloid newspapers and airline magazines, the flight attendants nodding and smiling methodically at all who pass, their make-up just about hiding the strain of a 4 a.m. start, four days a week.

Once inside, I blindly follow the herd of trundling hand baggage. Inside the terminal, the floor is of polished stone. Like a fancy hotel. Everything is loud and cacophonous. The few airport staff around seem to talk unnaturally loudly, and the whole world appears to have the volume control on boost and the treble control to max. Back home, sound is sucked out and smothered by furnishings and carpets, and curtains of rain. Big pictures of fairy-tale white villages, clinging to crazy hilltops, are placed regularly along the wide shiny corridor, with names that to me sound equally fanciful: Almuñecar, Ronda, Competa, Frigilliana, Mijas, Benahavis, and then Marbella. I stop to behold what is my first idea of my destination. It's not on a mountain, though there's a huge one lowering over it. All is white and appears charmingly picturesque, with potted red geraniums all over the place, iron railings on windows and an outrageously deep blue sky. It doesn't look like anything I've ever seen. It doesn't look real. Any of it. Where's the hookers, I muse to myself, and move along to the passport cabin.

I hand over my passport to the uniformed officer. He passes it through some kind of reader. His eyes flicker up to me momentarily, taking in this atypical tourist. Absent are the holiday shorts, bright new clothes, the optimistic attire: he sees lank, uncut hair, shapeless hoody and baggy, stained jeans. I think he is confirming something to himself about me. If only he knew the half of it.

Watkins thinks he knows. I had hoped I might be assigned some rambunctious old Marxist. This cute fantasy was modelled on a former buddy from Uni, one my few friends from that peculiar time. Bruce was a strident working-class lad from the East End, a sociology student who would regale me with his paean to a better world. A socialist utopia. The last of the class warriors, I used to tease him. Most of it washed over me, as we were usually smoking the hash I had sold him on occasion. But he was infinitely better company than the identikit kiddies on the degree conveyor belt, who thought ten pints of lager and drunken sex was the height of rebellion. He went on to be a probation officer, but I soon lost touch with him. As I did with anyone who didn't move in my immediate circle of need and indulgence. How ironic it would have been if my case file had landed on Bruce's desk. He would have commiserated with me, over a pint, off the record. So, I didn't get the cynical old Marxist, I got the self-righteous, small minded, conformist, bourgeois, holier-than-thou, God fearing, patronising pain in the arse.

It's easy to assume the world is all the same: shops, supermarkets, cars, buses, jobs, houses, Coca-Cola, beer, Mercedes Benz, Ford, mobile phones, good guys, bad guys, the wankers, the idiots, the ball busters, the bread heads, police and thieves and the Mr. Watkinses and the rest of the poor sods grubbing along trying to survive. Having been to France, Germany and Holland I know other

15

countries are different, with their other language and not quite right food, but essentially life is all the same. Why should Marbella be any different? People do and want the same old stuff, only the language and the label changes. Standing at this cabin, I am poised to leap blindly into the void, and praying to land on something soft. Or be dragged back, ignominiously to Watkins and the retribution of the system. Computer says no. The police officer has to repeat loudly 'Gracias', to get my attention, and hands me back my passport. I am indeed free. I breath again and enter Spain officially. So here it begins.

~

How to get from Malaga airport to some bizarre address in a town I've never visited, to find a brother who doesn't even know I'm coming, is the task before me. A brother who I haven't seen since a last, painful Christmas, six years ago. Who I haven't communicated a word to, in most of those. It's not that we don't get on, it's not that we weren't close. It's just that things became complex after the fire, it was hard just being yourself, to reach other people, to share what was inside, to know what you felt, never mind share that with a brother. And it got harder. We evolved different versions of what we wanted from life, common ground all but evaporated. Things didn't go as anyone might have planned, wanted or imagined. And here we are. This is where I start. Again. Fresh. Close the door on where I've been and who I was. In this land of fairy tale mountain villages, without the faintest idea of what this country, this place, this Marbella, is all about.

The bulky black holdall appears on the luggage belt. Eighteen and a half kilos it weighed in at. My entire worldly possessions in hand, I'm standing at a bus stop under a huge concrete roof connecting the parking to the terminal. The echo of horns and diesel motors resonates, and the fug hangs thick in the surprisingly warm air. A taxi is out of the question, eighty euros for a ride down the coast, no thank you. Bus it is, the common man's transport. Pretty much everyone clambering on is Spanish, which I further understand when the driver charges me a mere six euros and twenty. Who are these people who can afford taxis I wonder?

Airconditioning holds me in its frigid embrace, a fairly novel experience, and an unexpected one in March. I'm hunkered down in a window seat, to see this new world as it rolls by, to see what of its secrets it will reveal to me. If I can see that is. All is viewed through a headache inducing squint, such is the brilliance of the sunlight in what is still, in fact, winter. Sunglasses will be required, which doesn't cheer me up; the pointless fashion item of choice for a certain brand of poseur, or over entitled nitwit. And saxophone players. Goes without saying.

Everything shines brilliantly, as though I have fallen into some kind of hallucination. Real Ultra High Definition TV, a supercharged, crisp, full colour reality that bears no relation to the smudgy gloom of most of life in the UK, or anywhere else in the north of the continent I had been. I am entranced. To make matters worse they have painted pretty much every building here white. White! Seriously?! And they aren't filthy! No red brick, no grey-green ambient fluff of hedges and shrubs, there's palm trees and yucca plants and other verdant jungle type stuff everywhere. They're spectacular. They run in rows along the sides of the dual carriageway between dozens of blocks of flats, all with balconies, many of which appear to have been glazed in by glass, like everyone wants a giant fish tank attached to their lounge. I'd have thought with this climate you'd want a nice balcony.

I am passing through Torremolinos, the name being familiar from a Monty Python record my dad had. Torremolinos, Torremolinos, and bleeding Watney's Red barrel I say and catch myself smiling. Nostalgia has crept through the dark carapace that holds most of my memories of home and family in its tomb. Somewhere back there, back then, we had been a family, there had been normality, and I have to come to bleeding Torremolinos to remember it. Something lifts momentarily, a space in my head forms, admitting light, fresh air.

I relax and watch this bright white, pseudo-tropical, jungle-urban mash-up roll by. The road follows the coastline, a jugular vein connecting the capillaries of all the flats, hotels, bars, and streets coming down from the densely packed blocks that march in ribbons and clumps, up the sides of the mountainous, shaggy landscape. Steadily, concrete appears to be devouring the brute force of geology that has preceded it. Cranes loom up, trying to compete with the palm trees and winning as they clutch at the sky in their dozens. High up, the mountains bear vast scars, revealing their white innards. Presumably the source of the cement that is growing, fungus like, up every available slope.

To my left, beaches of various lengths and depths plie their way between rocky outcrops and hotel complexes. The brochure blue sea twinkles and grins back at me. Even in March, swimsuits are visible, though not in numbers. The sand is a grimy greyish-brown, washed by some half-hearted waves. The sea is so flat it could be a vast reservoir. My concept of beaches had been formed in North Wales as a kid in the late seventies, where sand was golden and stretched hundreds of yards to an inevitably freezing, growling Irish Sea. This resembles a dusty parking lot for septuagenarian bodies, more or less everybody on the sand is a pensioner, resembling in body and complexion nothing less than a prune.

At one point I stare up a construction resembling an entire new town, block upon block in white, pink, ochre, and terracotta march up, the world's biggest concrete layer cake. It sprawls up the mountain, obscuring the peaks, and amidst it all flutter endless banners on long poles. Rather than the flags of nations, the brand names of developments, each one a kitsch version of an imagined Spanish paradise, pollute the sky. Billboards blare out the slogans of aspiration, of luxury, all writ in the jargon of square meters and mortgage deals, peppered with the adjectives of affluence.

18

Another crop of developers' flags arise, in a great long line, next to the highway. Billboards scream about golf and 'first line'. Pictures of buggies and swimming pools mingle with computer graphic realisations of the dream homes being constructed all along the jugular.

And then I see it.

At first it appears to be just another billboard, a self-satisfied, surprisingly young man with a silly double-breasted suit, and worse, braces. Two shapely, not very Spanish looking ladies, drape themselves off the big man's shoulder.

'Welcome to Holmeland, where we weave your dreams', it proclaims. Behind them peeps Gary, fifty foot up, and twenty-five-foot-wide, above a busy motorway. I laugh in disbelief for some time. So, baby brother has made it. I suppose that must be making it, splattered across a billboard, in a country miles from home. This is the new Jerusalem my brother Gary had escaped to, to make his way in the world. And maybe his fortune.

I always wondered why he'd bothered to study Spanish along with his business studies, or why he wanted to be an estate agent, but he clearly had a vision, an actual plan. He saw a way out to somewhere far away from Warrington. I nod to myself, in recognition of a kind of aspiration that has been alien to me all my life.

~

The bus deposits me in the bus station of the town called Marbella. An enormous mountain frames everything, a lump of rock more gargantuan than anything I have ever seen, anywhere. It climbs in vertical ridges, bright and magnificent, spattered with the green of trees and shrubs, and rent occasionally by the long slides of fine white loose rock. Dizzyingly high, it hunkers up behind the town, pressing it to squat at the water's edge. Towards the sea, the town appears, typically, to be made of white blocks of flats. A taxi is now definitely in order and I hand the driver the address I'd found in one of Mum's drawers at home. It's shocking to think without this happy oversight,

19

I wouldn't know where Gary is, and getting information out of Mum these days, is next to a hopeless quest. *'Urbanizacion Sueño del Mar'* it says, *'bloque 3, 4B'*. A block of flats, probably. Near a place called San Pedro.

Minutes later I stand before low blocks along a quiet road. What are the odds he is still here, years later? I push what appears to be block 3, 4B and wait. A female voice answers with a strong Essex accent, which surprises me initially, familiar yet odd under the glare of white walls and palm fronds. My heart sinks, he's moved on.

'Hi, my name's Gene, I'm looking for Gary Phillips. This is his address, right?' A pause. 'I'm his brother.'

This provokes a response. 'Oh, well yeah it is, erm... it's just he's not living here now, I am, but yeah, it's his. He never said he 'ad a bruvva.'

Relief mixed with confusion.

'Well I was his brother last time I looked, but I've been away, and we haven't been in touch for quite a long time.' I inwardly wince at my choice of phrase, but she doesn't seem phased. 'Is he still at work?' I prod.

'Yeah... yeah, he will be...' she processes this simple statement for a long time.

'I've just come straight from the airport, so maybe I could leave my case here and go off and meet him, for a beer, you know, catch up an' that?'

'Yeah ok, I'll come down, won't be a moment.'

Bingo! Found him. I might have ended up searching for days, on reflection. A face appears through the grill, pretty, but over made up, though she appears to have just got out of bed, or that could be some kind of swimwear, I'm not honestly sure. She looks me up and down, appraising herself of this strange new revelation; Gary has a brother! I'm slightly taller than Gary, my hair is mousier than his darker, almost Mediterranean look. I'm a paler imitation of my better-looking brother, not that I've ever got hung up about it. Least of my worries.

'Yeah,' she says, 'you do look like 'im. I don't believe it, Gary's l'il bruvver.'

I let this particular false assumption pass, Gary is four years my junior, as the door swings open and she stands aside for me to walk through. She shows me into a moderate, sparse looking apartment, with the obligatory terrace, minus fish tank, furnished bachelor style, with a few feminine touches: discarded bikinis, make-up-stained tissues, fag packets, and not a few empty vodka bottles.

'Scuse the mess, I just got up, I had some mates round after work.' She half-heartedly moves one or two bottles to new places, where they still equate to being untidy.

'Long party.'

'Oh no, we don't get out till about four or five, later even in summer, so yeah I'm basically nocturnal for half the week, innit.'

'Blimey, where do you work?'

'Y'know, down the port', as though this explains everything.

'So, if it's alright with you, I'll just leave this here till I can locate Gary, and I'll pick it up later. That'd be neat, very kind, thanks. Where does he live now?'

'Oh, he's got a penthouse, Playas del Duque. You can walk it from 'ere, just about.' Again this is meant to be self-explanatory. 'But maybe you'd better go to his office.'

'Where's that?'

'In the-'

'-Port, yeah I see, of course.' Silly me. I am going to learn all about this port.

She gives me directions scribbled on the back of an official looking envelope which hasn't been opened even.

'Don't you want to keep that, it looks important?' it seems obvious to ask.

'Naaaah, I won't be here long enough for them to catch up wi' me. Chuck it when yer done wiv it.'

'Er ok, thanks er, sorry…?'

'Frankie.'

'Ah right, thanks Frankie, you're a star.'

'No worries, anything for Gary's bruvver.'

Her smile is just a bit more than friendly now. Obviously being Gary's unknown 'baby' brother conferred on me some kind of cache I am not aware of, it could be social, sexual even, such is the coquettish smile that has crept across the orangey made-up features.

'So I'll, er, catch you later I guess.'

'Yeah no worries babe, see you then.'

The spherical, superhuman swell of the bosom in its nightgown cum bathing robe, or whatever it was, entered into my consciousness fairly rapidly; only surgery could have worked such wonders. The girl is a caricature of herself, but paradoxically, still exceedingly attractive.

Following the back of the official threatening letter envelope map, I walk toward the port called Puerto Banus. I have heard the name somewhere, in connection with some news report on the Costa del Crime, or something of that ilk. My Spanish is so non-existent I hadn't connected '*puerto*' to 'port'. So far, my monolinguistic feebleness hasn't proved much of a handicap, and I've learnt one word at least. The envelope map is duly dispatched into a litter bin as I stand in front of a kind of pastiche of Spanish village architecture, when really, it's a row of shops and cafes. Much of the architecture around here conforms to that premise. Still, it is prettier than Torremolinos. BMW Series One sportsters emblazoned with the legend 'Holmeland' line up in their own parking slots, and in a bay all of its own is a Maserati Quattroporte, according to its signage. Someone wants to be noticed. Being conversant in the names of ludicrously expensive sports cars is a stamp needed on one's social passport in Banus. Yes, just 'Banus', or 'port', as the local expats refer to it, and they are most of the people. But none of this is known to me at this moment, as I stare at a very swanky office with lots of swanky cars around, which you wouldn't find too often in Warrington. Wilmslow is reserved for that.

Nervousness thrusts its sweaty hand into my intestines and gives them a squeeze. The sun is fading and shadows creep across the white condos. For the first time this day, the air cools to something more familiar to a Brit, and the humid scent of salt and sea is detectable. It doesn't have that pong of traffic, of mud, heavy, carboniferous vegetation in varying states of decay, that the damp air in the north of England has. A perfume still floats on the air, like a faint old-fashioned cologne. I breath this new place and its sensations in and out for a while, poised perfectly, immobilised, between my past and the future.

The receptionist inside the huge office window is casting me curious glances, so I make the move toward a meeting that has been a long time in coming. Inside, the air-conditioned environment rules, a kind of plastic atmosphere, free of the extraneous odours and temperatures, that the world outside is full of. Background music of some laid back jazzy lounge is leaking out of ceiling speakers. The foyer of this office says 'minimalist interior design studio' rather than 'estate agent'. A couple of huge, backlit aerial panoramas of Marbella glow, the enormous jagged lump of limestone sporting all manner of the white Lego bricks crawling cancerously up its lower flanks. Other than that, low, wide sofas and little else completes the decor. There's a statue of a nude woman made from some unrecognisable, tortured metal; some oversized clumsy stainless-steel vases containing a form of dead roses, and instead of magazines, electronic picture frames that have photos of vast villas fading in and out. This is a company that wants to set itself apart, to confound expectations, to deny it is merely in the business of selling houses.

'Can I help you, sir?' comes the request from the predictably groomed beauty behind the enormous smoked glass desk that only has an Apple computer on it. Nothing else visible that might suggest work.

'Er, yeah, is Gaz... erm, Gary Phillips in at all?'

'Do you have an appointment, is he expecting you?'

'Oh no, he's definitely not expecting me.' I laugh nervously, like I am standing in one of those dreams when you find yourself in an unfamiliar place full of people, but you've forgotten to put your trousers on, and no-one is noticing you are just wearing underpants. But you know you are.

'Well, I'm sorry you will have to make an appointment, as he's terribly busy. What would it be concerning?'

If she is Spanish her voice exhibits no trace, but she certainly looks Spanish. She sounds accent-less, no trace of anything, which is unusual. You can always tell where an English person is from, regionally, or economically. There's nowhere to hide with an English voice, so I thought.

'It's concerning that I'm his brother and I've come to see him. It's been a while and we've not been in touch, so he wouldn't be expecting me.'

'His brother?' The professional veneer slips for a nano-second, and she struggles to disguise the surprise in her voice. The twitching of her eyebrow shows she is processing multiple interpretations of this unexpected information. 'Oh well, I'm not sure... er, let me see if he's free. Please, take a seat. Could I get you anything, water, a coffee?'

'No thanks love, I'm alright, it's fine.' I'm conscious that my own accent sets me apart, in this strangely placeless place that is Gary's office.

'I'll just see if I can get through to him, he has someone with him right now.'

The ensuing conversation is purposely inaudible to me, takes longer than the simple exchange requires, leaving no doubt that the news has caused some considerable reaction at the other end.

She puts the receiver down, seemingly trying not to smile. 'He'll be with you in a moment'.

Such a simple, innocent phrase, an ironic counterpoint to the culmination of years of absence from each other's lives. She glances over, and smiles professionally, as she would, but you can hear the gears meshing inside that pretty head. This new revelation will no doubt light up this cool office in the morning. I almost feel sorry for Gaz, as I know him. 'Gary' was not something your peers called you back home. It does seem out of place, a Gaz doesn't fit with the white walls, the oh-so-modern decorative items and the cool, soulless air.

Minutes creep by. The stasis is broken by a door opening and a gaggle of voices approaching. They are jolly in a business-like way, suggesting deals done, mutual benefit and acquisition. One of the voices is unmistakably Gary's and yet it sounds so strange. It's not just the sound of his voice, but the words in his mouth. When I'd last seen Gary, he was still a cocky little runt, fresh out of Uni, full of bullshit and ambitious talk, dissing everything about England, me, our family, our world we thrashed around in, drowning in our anger and self-pity and self-loathing. Now he sounds polished, confident and grown up. Barely a trace of his regional accent remains. He sounds exactly what he said he wanted to be; successful. He appears, ushering a middle-aged couple down the steps into the reception; silvery hair, deep tans and quasi-American clothing, so formless and casual is it, but still obviously expensive. He glances toward me for a brief moment and raises a finger as if to say 'don't move, wait there until I have finished', well no, it is to say *exactly* that. The expression in his eyes says it more than the finger, but the mask of the professional smile does not crack, only I can see through it, because he is after all, my baby brother.

The final handshakes are barely dead on the end of his arm, before he turns to the receptionist and says, in a falsely studied and calm way, 'No more calls Rafaela, and cancel my seven o'clock, or see if you can't move it maybe to, I don't know 8.30, would you, *gracias*.'

Then he turns to me. I hold my breath, literally and metaphorically, and appraise myself of the man before me; no longer the baby brother. Wherever it is he is, he has definitely arrived. The clothes are smart but not square, expensive fashionable, his body is trim but hard, suspicions of gym membership, and his hair well cut, slightly greased back. He looks handsome, properly Mediterranean, and for a moment, very confused. He runs his hand through his hair as he approaches, stands in front of me, hands on hips, checking the vision is real. Then the mask cracks, Gary really smiles, his body softens, and he takes a step forward and envelopes me in a gentle but long embrace. Neither of us speak for a moment. He steps back and starts into the appraisal routine again, this time with an ironic smile on his face.

'Alright mate,' I say, when I can't stand the stalemate any longer.

'Alright? Am I alright? How the bloody hell are you, what... when, I mean, God, Gene what *are* you doing here? ' He is still smiling, surprised but not angry, quite. All I can do is shrug, my eyes welling up.

'Thought I'd take a holiday, just, needed a change.' I laugh as I think I might cry if I don't do something with my useless self, hanging there, not knowing what on earth to do next. A firm hand behind my shoulder steers me toward the corridor.

'Come on, let's go to my office.'

I settle down into a comfy chair, the soft, leathery-type surface slipping around making squeaky sounds and sit, like a schoolboy in front of the Head, the ingenue at his first job interview. Gary is behind the gleaming glass desk, which again only has an Apple computer on it, looking like the cat who got the cream.

'Rafaela, bring in some cold beers would you,' he intones towards the silent screen of the Apple. I can't even see a telephone.

Rafaela appears with a side table, on which is a champagne bucket full of beer bottles, and retreats noiselessly, leaving a waft of her perfume and hair. It smells like something I want to dive into and drown in. I am sitting, still not saying anything, just absorbing this minimal new world with its smart young prince.

'When did you get out, Gene? You never said anything, I had no idea-'

'I came out a few months back. Automatic release for good behaviour.' A fib. I'm wary of divulging any details of my precarious legality.

'Crikey, and...' he pauses, probably trying to compute what or who I might be running from, what I have brought with me, what is my special kind of baggage that the last few years has saddled me with.

'Yeah, I've been staying with Mum. I stayed with her up until I left for here.' Gary nods pensively, absorbing all the implications of that simple statement. 'She's the same, the social keep a good eye on her. She's kind of happy with what she has, I guess. It's not a life, but I think that's what she wants. The wonders of daytime TV, and the medication. I reckon the pills will do for her long before her time. She sends her love.'

Another fib. There's a snort from Gary. Dealing with our mother is always complex, fraught. A minefield. He places finger and thumb across his eyes, draws a breath.

'Christ, I need a beer.' He bounds out of his seat, cracks the tops, hands me something in an old-fashioned shaped bottle with no label. I'm scrutinising it, nonplussed, when he says, 'It's the Reserva.'

'What! Wine?'

'Noooo,' he laughs, like a spring has been released, 'it's the Alhambra Reserva, best beer in Spain.'

A couple of slugs of the cold, malty, dry liquor and I'm feeling a bit more uncoiled myself. I do rather have some explaining to do.

27

'How was it in there for you?' It's a refreshingly direct question, for which I'm grateful.

'Boring' I say, and laugh. I keep laughing, my face creases up and I struggle for wind. The laughter running in waves over me, washing off the stench I have carried with me for so long; of prison slopping out, of stale sweat, fear, suppressed anger and hate; of all the bodily fluids imaginable; of semen and shit and piss, blood, bile, spit, and the stink of cold recently deceased bodies, the inevitable suicides that permeate prison atmosphere like nerve gas. All this runs off of me, as I slurp the cold beer, and laugh, tears running down my cheeks.

I've waited for this beer. I haven't been near a pub or an off license since I came out. All I have wanted to do is keep low, turn my back, close the door, pull the chain and wash the whole shitty mess of these last years down the forgotten sewers of regret. And now I'm sitting in this swank office being served beautiful cold beer by an angel and it's all too much for me. Eventually I collect myself, and Gary hands me another slim, green, label-less bottle.

'Looks like you needed that.'

'First one since I got out, worth waiting for.'

I explain to Gary about the tedium of prison life, the aimless hours, the constraints, the sufferance of all manner of bigotry and vindictiveness, the eternal vigilance, the inevitable fights. Don't challenge anyone else's status, don't assume you know anything about anyone, keep schtum at all times, give nothing away, be *invisible*. Or try to be. Until someone else's hate comes looking for you regardless, and you have to defend yourself, or forever be a whipping boy. I have learnt to not be afraid of violence, but to embrace it, channel it. Avoid as much damage as possible, nurse your wounds, and wounded pride, in silence. Curl yourself into a tight little ball, and hide it in a far corner of your mind, and show nobody anything, lest they gain an advantage or further ideas about your vulnerability.

Not a word about the license. He doesn't think to ask, mercifully. Prison hadn't treated me too badly, all things considered. I was lucky enough to have a cell mate who wasn't a sociopath, someone stupider but more vulnerable than me, who did far less dramatic things but nonetheless ended up with the drug dealers and murderers. I sought refuge in the prison library, rekindling my interest in the social anthropology I had all but failed and ignored at Uni. Anthropologists were usually known as tree huggers or hippies among the other students, but I carved myself out a special infamy, as the Trip Master General. I arrived at college already well acquainted with the virtues of marijuana. It had been my teenage crutch, in preference to beer and cider, as was the local norm. For those three years I was king of the stoners, the fastest, hippest groover, always off to the best, most secret raves, always able to find the purest pills, the best trips. On graduating, narrowly, it was this expertise that led me to believing my own publicity, that I couldn't get caught, that I was just too cool, top, sorted, to have to think of things like the legality. Taking drugs was as normal as having a cup of tea, according to some rock hero or other, so no big deal. I was able to get frequent, and often lucrative work in the semi-legal world of rave promotion, of clubs and the star DJ's of the time. I lived in a world beyond laws and social convention. I rode a roller coaster between the particular high and musical stimulation of the up days, the rave and journey around it, and the inevitable crash out; the downer days embroiled in sweaty, stale sheets in whichever bedsit, slugging water and gobbling bad takeaways until the next round of flying high came by. Mercifully, I didn't take to the hardest drugs. Ketamine was too frightening and numbing, and heroin made me puke so badly I couldn't do it. I passed the crashes by eating and sleeping through them, watching rubbish TV and playing video games badly. This nihilistic, navel gazing treadmill would lead me to the sentence of six years for aiding and abetting the trafficking and sale of controlled substances. My endeavours to teach some of the foreign prisoners to speak English, and even one particularly damaged soul to read and write went a long way to ensuring my earliest possible release, helped also by the chronic overcrowding in Strangeways. It was also fortunate none of the others arrested with me, went to my prison. None of the big boys went down. Just the foot soldiers like me. The drivers, gofers and misguided good timers. I don't think of myself as a drug dealer, merely a good timer, who became too involved.

Gary disavowed my teenage dope smoking. He knew about my escapades as a student, and my subsequent extra-mural activities when I was working with the club promoters. He'd been afraid and disapproving, like an ambitious clean-living young student might be expected to be. He'd distanced himself pretty thoroughly from me, by the time he finished reading business studies at Loughborough, and I hadn't been too offended or even aware. In my self-obsessed way, I'd merely assumed he was just too square to get what I was about, to understand the lifestyle and the music, to connect to the scene that to me, seemed a world in itself. By the time I was becoming actively involved in the movement of class A substances on a personal level, he'd packed his bags for the Costa del Sol, in 1998. From then, our awareness of each other was limited by distance and disinterest. We'd catch up at Christmas every year, where we sat in semi-silence with Mum, who was drugged on telly and Temazepam and later Thorazine. Every Christmas became more of a strain for all of us, especially Mum who apart from putting up with our squabbling, was less able each year to prepare any food or understand what might need doing and organising. Which left things to us two under-domesticated young northern males to cobble together what we imagined might be a family Christmas, like before Dad had gone. The resultant tensions between Gary and I, my general apathy, and his disdain of me, made for some pretty desperate unfestive festivities. Each year the whole sojourn would last less time, finishing up with 2000's epic Indian takeaway thirty-six-hour non-xmas. Nothing happened but the usual televisual tripe beamed out relentlessly, as Mum would get too anxious over anything more. We spent the entire time sulking silently, simmering with angst and resentment of each other, of fate, of the hand that had been dealt to us that day back in 1982 when the gas explosion incinerated the world of our family. Not that it was much of one by that point. I'll never know if my father's premature and horrible death precluded some gruesome divorce, how they would have dealt with her affair, what exactly the fallout would have been had fate not intervened. Never know what that convulsion left her with, no absolution, resolution, just a gaping hole. What did that do to aid her slide into long term depression? Gary and I would be forced to sit through this each year, this legacy, just waiting for the whole awful pretence to dissolve, so we could flee back to our separate corners of existence. Me to the road, the highs and the oblivion of a totally chemically managed consciousness and he to the Costa, fairy land in the sun, sangria, *señoritas* and squaredom, as I saw it.

'Bloody hell, Gene, sounds like you did well to come through all of that unscathed', says Gary when he's digested the details of life in Strangeways. 'Ironically you look better for it, compared to last time I saw you, I almost didn't recognise you, once I'd got over the shock of the news from reception. Christ, don't pull a surprise like that again anytime soon.'

I sigh, looking across the glass expanse at the baby brother who'd escaped and made it work, who had achieved some kind of happiness.

'Yeah well, it's not likely', I smile thinly, 'I don't plan on any of that happening again, ever. I've had time to see just how messed up things were for me. I'd have ended up dead before much longer, and not through the drugs either. Being around those kind of people, the stress of doing the shipments, it starts to get to you eventually. You know it's unsustainable, but how do you escape it? For me, going down was worth it, it broke the cycle. I can start from scratch.'

31

'So how is Mum?' The eternal question that hangs over us, daily, twenty-four seven. One neither of us has answered effectively throughout our lives.

'I've been there all this time. I don't have anywhere else to go.' Economies of truth. Needs must. 'She didn't know I was being released, she hadn't opened any letters, she didn't pick up any of my calls in the last couple of months. She keeps her routines, sleep walking through a TV show or scribbling the details of the telly shopping offers. I had to clear out several notebooks about crap for sale. Was she doing that when you last saw her? When did you last see her? She couldn't even tell me.'

'About ten months ago', Gary kneads some kind of designer stress ball. The aura of cool and style has leaked away, and Mum's shadow of decay and despair is leaching through the aircon. 'She was, well, you know how she is... It was hard. Ana was shocked, I probably shouldn't have let her in for that. You'll meet Ana, my partner.'

'What, business partner?'

'No, my girlfriend.'

'Bugger me, you must be sure she likes you.'

'Well obviously. We must have dinner soon, all of us' he says, though I am not convinced he thinks that is something he is looking forward to. Does she know I even exist? I seem to be an understandably well-kept secret. 'Mum was getting into repetitive things, compulsively tidying some things, and other rooms totally messy.'

We both stare silently into the middle distance for a while.

'She didn't have any idea of how long I'd been away for. Never visited. Not surprisingly. Think it would have flipped her out, that place. Didn't have many visitors. Bit of a blessing really.'

'I... I meant to... I was going to.'

'Piss off Gaz, you didn't need to. I'm glad you didn't. It's behind me, it's history. I needed it, it stopped me killing myself or getting myself killed. Gave me the space to see where I was, what I'd become. It was scary waking up to all of that. The prison psychologist was pretty good, he helped me through a lot of stuff. He was kind of my only friend, the only one I opened up to.'

The second beer has wriggled down into me, strong and crisp, and I am twitchy now. I'm not sure at all of where we go from here.

'So,' Gary slams his hands on his arm rests, 'what next? Sunny Spain, Marbella... I mean it's great to see you, I'm surprised obviously you're here, I'm also quite flattered. I thought I'd lost you, which would have been just as much my fault as yours...' he is biting his lip a bit, not sure where to lead the conversation. My presence is obviously something he has never had to countenance. It's plainly not on his radar. It hadn't been on mine until two days ago. 'What's the plan, big brother? How long are you going to be around?' The hand goes back to massaging the stress ball.

'The plan, ah yes, the plan.' I feel Watkins' gaze, his patronising pomposity. I haven't fully formulated an idea about the potential pickle I am getting myself into by breaking the terms of my license. I must be careful not to let any cats out of bags. 'Well, I hadn't planned to come. I had been at home for a while. Looking for work, you know, they help you to. But nothing's changed back there, everyone is just doing more of the same, more shopping, more watching telly, more drinking, more drugs, they're all the fucking walking dead, it's just... just... '

'Hey, calm down Gene.' Gary evidently isn't used to raw, nihilistic angst in his office environment. I've had half a lifetime of it and am still searching for a clue as to how to deal with it, that isn't drug based at least.

Deep breath.

'I just had to walk, I had to leave. I need a job, but I don't know what I can do, I don't know Spain, I don't speak the language, but for fuck's sake it can't be any worse. It's a living death back there, I need a new place, a clean slate, just nothing to do with all of that.'

'Yeah, sure, I get it Gene, I do, I get it.' He seems genuinely sincere. 'You got a place to stay, your luggage, it's at a hotel?'

'Ha ha, Gaz, I've got my world in one bag, which is sitting in your flat with Frankie. It was the last address Mum had. It took me hours to find it. She really is losing it.'

'Oh. Okay. I see. Well let's start there. I'll call Frankie tell her you'll be staying a few days. She doesn't actually pay rent, so she can't argue, it's my place. She works in a club I have an interest in.'

'You? Into clubs?' I raise an amused eyebrow.

'It's not like that, it's an investment, high class place, table service, high net worth punters, a long way from your raves, mate.' He smiles. I can see why Frankie is in awe, he looks good and has it all going for him, and he is in club land to boot.

'Thanks Gaz, I appreciate it. I can start to try and put things together. I want to try it out, I got nothing to go back for.'

Despite Mum being on her own, back in Warrington, Gary can't argue with that sentiment, but I have dropped like a stone in a calm pool, and the ripples are spreading outwards through his consciousness. The half of his family, his kin, who had wasted his education, his potential, and the prime years of his life, has landed in his backyard in his sub-tropical dreamscape, and he is trying to process it to make the next move. Just as he beckons me toward the door, a quick brusque knock hits it, and it opens. I recognise the man instantly: the bulk, the shiny suit and braces, the preternaturally perfect white teeth, slicked back hair. Unmistakable from the billboards all along the coastal motorway, the Holmeland himself.

'Gary... Oh hi, you're in a meeting, so...' he spies the beers in the champagne bucket, changes tack. 'A friend of yours? We need to run over the pitch to Sorzano. Have you got ten? How do you do?' He extends his hand which has two heavy rings and an oversized, expensive looking watch on it.

'This is Gene, my brother. Gene, Mike Holme, CEO.'

'Hi, pleased to meet you.' I had clocked the slight beat between the 'my' and 'brother', but the reaction on Holme's face isn't hiding his surprise. Or his annoyance.

'Well hello Gary's brother,' he continues pointedly, 'nice of you to drop by. But you'll have to excuse us, I need our Gary right now. I'm sure you two can catch up later, Ok? Gary pull up those plans and the costings and sit yourself down, we've got work to do.'

Holme places a polite but firm hand on my shoulder and moves me door-wards. Gary looks like a naughty boy caught nabbing sweets in the tuck shop.

'I'll catch you at the flat later Gene, thanks for coming over,' he says faux nonchalantly. Holme has closed the door before he's finished his sentence.

From inside Holme is emphatic enough for me to overhear, 'Who the hell was that? Since when have you had a brother?' The answer to which should be fairly self-evident, academic even. I wonder what Holme wanted to hear as an answer.

I wander back down the air-conditioned corridor which is subtly lit, slender shafts climbing up the walls, which seem to be of some kind of textured fabric. The whole place, and now Holme, has given me a pretty clear picture of where Gary has arrived at in life. And I have gate-crashed the party, but the fact that my existence appears to be a well-kept secret can only mean I was never going to be on the guest list, no matter what.

As I appear back into the lobby Rafaela hands me an envelope.

'Here, Gary asked me to let you have a set of keys for the apartment in *Sueño del Mar*, he'll see you there later.'

'Thanks, that's great, I'll be off then, nice to meet you.'

'Very nice to meet you, quite a surprise. *Buenas tardes, hasta luego.*'

I smile back and retreat, wondering what she'd said to me at the end in what sounded like proper Spanish. This angel appears to be half English, half Spanish. Makes sense in this real estate game.

The darkened street is still fairly populated. I'm over dressed, the long-sleeved denim shirt and worn out hooded sweat top, plus my heavy long jeans have been suffocating me since I arrived. Few people are dressed in much more than a sweatshirt or light top. Tourists conspicuously wear much less. There's none of that inevitable look of people wrapped up, buried inside layers: dark blue, brown and black armour against damp, cold, smelly air. Everyone appears to be loose and relaxed, it's like that rarity, a nice summer's evening in England.

The always scented air is heavier and there's a new extraordinary perfume. Literally. It's a perfume, like someone has gone down the street spraying something as a demo of their new product, it's so all pervading. The low trees that line the pavement have oranges on them. Big, decidedly orange looking oranges. I reach up to pick one, I mean why not, who the hell would imagine you could pick oranges on the street? Why hasn't someone come by and nicked them all, like would happen back home? The little bunches of white blossom, growing around the ripe oranges, are the source of the magic. Orange blossom smells like that, who would have believed it? I'm entranced, and as I move through a branch to grasp a juicy specimen, I whack into a huge spine that penetrates my finger to a considerable depth.

'Fuuuuuck!' I shout in surprise and some discomfort, withdrawing my hand to see a good deal of blood emerging from a visible hole in the end of my middle finger. I pop it into my mouth. A passing Spanish woman with two unbelievably noisy kids offers me some advice, which I cannot understand. The kids stare at me with an expression of incredulity and pity, like only a tourist would be so dumb as to do that. I gingerly go back to extricate my chosen prize, I'm determined to eat an orange off a tree in the middle of the street, it's just such a bizarre thing to find myself doing. This morning I was in Warrington and now I'm in a Jaffa Cake advert. I get the orange orb out of its crown of thorns with no further injury, and get on with trying to peel it. The skin is super thick and as I break it, the pungency of the citric blast is gobsmacking, it actually stings my eyes a bit. It's like oranges on steroids, monster alien fruits come to earth to blast those puny little things in the supermarket to oblivion. I get through the pith, and break the pieces out, hungrily popping a good chunk into my mouth, biting down for that fat juicy taste explosion I know is coming. After all of that cacophony of amazing smells, it must- bang schlooooooooooop. My cheeks are sucked inwards, my eyes smart, my nose and gums threaten to tear themselves off the bones that support them, as the last shreds of moisture from inside my mouth seem to evaporate through my lips. I spit the great clump of pithy flesh out onto the pavement and stand there champing at the air trying to get some saliva back into my mouth. The bitterness is overwhelming, my mouth is metallic and numb. I'm dumbstruck, like someone has played a really sick joke on me. First the perfume, the cute flowers, the big juicy looking orbs, then the psycho thorns and then finishing you off with orange scented drain cleaner. I'm so absorbed in the injustice of it all I fail to notice the angel, Rafaela, standing next to me, giggling.

'You're not supposed to eat them', she admonishes, smiling sympathetically.

'What the hell are you supposed to do with them then?', I laugh back, trying to see the funny side as my mouth starts to moisten again, I regain my composure and my eyes stop watering. 'They should have a health warning!'

'They're for decoration, we have them everywhere, and for the perfume of course, it's beautiful in spring. And you English make marmalade from them. We just let them rot usually.'

'You English? So, you are Spanish not English?'

'Weeeell' she says coyly, 'I am Spanish nationality but my mother was from England, and I did go to an English school for a long time.'

'Blimey, you're a Spanglish mongrel' I quip, then think, shit, I've insulted this beautiful woman I don't know.

'Si Señor, I am Espangleeeesh', she says in an obviously cod Spanish accent, still smiling, her white teeth glowing in the dusk. Her chestnut hair is shiny, and the street lights catch glints in her almond shaped, light brown eyes. I'm transfixed, smiling dumbly, and I catch myself. I'm fifteen again, gawking at pretty girls without realising and not hiding my awe.

'You know where you are going? Have you been to Puerto Banus before?'

'Never been to Spain, love' I reply, then decide to shut up. I don't want to put any more information into the mix that has been decidedly shaken up by my appearance. 'But I'm good, I came down from there earlier, thanks.'

'Ok, night then, nice to meet you.' This time she looks like it isn't just a professional courtesy.

'Yeah sure, you too, see you next time.'

With a last dazzling smile and flick of chestnut waves, she turns and her heels click clack up the street. I watch her go. The hips swinging gently, accentuated by the heels, and the calf muscles jumping out that bit further. After three years in the slammer, it is a truly uplifting sight, a vision of the loveliness and beauty that is the complete antithesis of everything I have lived through lately. Cells festooned with pictures of gynaecological gymnastics and silicone super surgery makes you forget what the real thing is actually like.

I glance toward the port. Cars and people move in and out. It must be a yacht marina; it certainly doesn't appear industrial. I decide to head to the apartment and rest. It's been a day of head frazzling unfamiliarity, and I find I'm tired and hungry. I've got bugger all money, and no idea what to do about food.

At least Gary spoke to me, he could've just denied he knew me, shut me out, I wouldn't have blamed him in some ways. It can't be easy having me show up, having to explain my existence, which he has patently not acknowledged in this parallel universe of orange blossom and white condos. I can only retrace my steps to the apartment and wait for him to show up. I'm sure this exchange will be different. He'll be on home turf, without the constraints of the carefully manicured world of his office, and he'll have Holme's words ringing in his ears. How *do* you explain a brother like me?

~

I manage to let myself into the apartment, meddling with unfamiliar keys, that turn the way you don't expect them to. Frankie is still here, but she's changed into what I imagine is her work clothing; a tight fitting short black dress that shows plenty of her leg and thigh, and its strapped, plunging neck line outlines the spectacular curves of her breasts and highlights the two half-moons of flesh. This is a cleavage that demands attention, the whole effect is alarmingly close to the pictures on cell walls in my recent home.

'All dressed up and nowhere to go' I say by way of conversation. Her tone towards me hasn't changed, though she's been informed unilaterally I am house guest for a time.

'I wish' she replies, while applying some form of colouring to her already heavily coloured visage. 'Just anuvva night keeping the rich and famous 'appy, so they treat us nice and we get those lovely big tips.'

'What is it you do?'

'I'm an 'ostess'

'Oh aye?' My sardonic smile is intended to provoke her.

'Bugger off, I'm not one o' them, I deal with the clients, keep them 'appy, make sure they've got everything they want, give them somefink nice to be seen wiv, innit.'

'I see.' I don't, but at the edge of my mind is the more lurid interpretation of this job description, which she must have read on my face. The kind of clubs I have frequented in Amsterdam were less nuanced about the concept.

'Oi, it's not like that, cheeky bugger.' She doesn't seem offended, as though this assumption was merely an occupational hazard. 'Proper hostessing means looking good and taking care of the clients in the club, that's all.' Pause. 'Well it can be more, but only if that's what you wanna do, and it doesn't do you any favours in the long term, and the bosses don't really like it. Most of them have got interests in the putty clubs as it is, so they don't want to cross wires, if you know what I mean.'

'Putty club?' I'm bemused.

'Some clubs 'ere in Spain are like a broffel, innit. It's got a bar, and you can buy drinks, and you can go to a room with a girl or whatever, and it's all perfectly legal an' that. I know some of the girls make a bloody fortune that way. Not me though.' She shudders involuntarily. 'We make good tips on the punters in Sparkles.'

'Sparkles?!' I guffaw. Seriously? 'You mean Gary is running a club called Sparkles?'

'Naaah, he don't run it, he just put some of the money into it and he takes the clients there, wevver it's the buyers or the town hall lot.'

'Doesn't sound very Spanish, Sparkles.'

'Naaah course not, the only Spanish who come are like friends of Holme, lawyers an' that, and town hall of course. It's mostly Brits, Dutch, lot a Russians, Ukrainians, Arabs, whatever.'

'Sorry, town hall? Like councillors?'

'Yeah, course, they're like royalty round 'ere, you know?'

'No I don't, I know nothing about this place. I'm a virgin.'

She appraises me coyly, disbelieving. 'Awright, well you ask your bruvver, he'll explain.'

That looks to be all I get, and Frankie heads out to a waiting taxi, although as far as I can estimate it's a ten-minute walk. Ten minutes in those heels is a lifetime though, for sure.

So here I am, my bag has been placed in one of the rooms, and a clean towel is on the bed. Nice hostess touch. It's past nine, and I haven't eaten since the stodgy sandwich in the airport abused my severely deprived gastric pathways. Prison food is almost preferable. I flop down on the sofa in the lounge, flick on the vast flat screen TV on the wall. It's a Sky TV box, all your British staples, home from home. Christ, where does Spain start around here? I only realise I've nodded off when I am woken by Gary kicking my feet to wake me up.

'Shit, what time is it?' I'm so bleary after the journey and the change of place it could have been morning.

'Quarter to ten. Change your shirt or something, we're going out for dinner. Come on, it'll be nice, you probably haven't eaten anything half decent in years I bet,' says Gary, looking like he's come straight from the office.

'Too right. Slop, sludge and roast dried-out dead stuff for three years. Her Majesty's a la carte poison. But it'll be shut, it's too late.'

Gary laughs, 'Now's dinner time for the real workers. Change, put something smartish on.'

'Gaz, I've got a bunch of shitty five-year-old t-shirts and tops in the bag. I don't own anything smartish. Never have.' With a shake of the head and a snort, Gary disappears from the room and reappears momentarily with a 'smartish' shirt, I suppose it could be called.

'Try that out for starters.'

Minutes later I'm sitting in an Audi, a big one, with a deep sounding engine. 'Nice wheels, very nice. Go with the job?'

'Sure does, about the only perk though. The rest is just run run run, meetings, plans, shows, more meetings. It's non-stop.'

I'm not sure why or where we are heading out to, if it's just Gary's generosity or there's another agenda. Said agenda appears forthwith.

'We're going to eat with Holme and Rafaela'. Well that much at least is a bonus, being able to behold the majestic Rafaela for a

41

couple more hours makes me feel decidedly chirpy. 'He wants to get to know you.' This hangs in the air, like a threat.

'Uhuh? What does he want to know about me, I seem to have been a well-kept secret up until now. Not blaming you or anything, it's up to you, but I have obviously surprised a few people.'

'Holme is...'

Gary pauses to choose his words, and I can't help but drop 'A bit of a twat?' into the space provided. Gary laughs, shakes his head, and his fingers tense and release on the steering wheel. If Gary has been at all put out by the situation thus far, he's doing an excellent job of hiding it. After so long with nothing to do with each other, we can't exactly be described as close, or as having a relationship, so I'm naturally apprehensive.

'Holme is one of the most powerful men on the coast right now. I'm his number two person, apart from Garcia-Sterling, our lawyer, but I'm not actually a partner. Holme's my boss and when he says jump, I jump as high as I can, whatever time of day and wherever. It's just how it is. His reputation and the reputation of the company is hugely important because of how we have to do business here. We're foreigners, *guiris*, and we can only do what we do with the cooperation and goodwill of our hosts.'

I'm wondering what a *guiri* is, but I figure such local details can wait for another day.

'So, you have to keep the local Spanish politicians and business people onside, right? The town hall, yeah?'

'*Correcto*. Everything here is about who you know, who scratches who's back. And then you pop up, so naturally Holme wants to get a handle on that, and make sure nothing can compromise our business reputation.'

'Fuck me' is all I can think of to say.

'Due to your recent activities, if that were associated with us, that would not be helpful, and so that risk is something he wants to take care of for you. If you mean to stay, that's how it has to be. I don't have a choice in this. Given your record, it puts me in a compromising situation, and we have to protect ourselves.'

'From me. Nice. But understandable I guess.' If they knew the full story, I think I wouldn't be so indulged.

'It's nothing sinister Gene, it's a good thing. You'll see. I think you'll like what he has to say.'

I'm praying he's not eager and pedantic enough to do some kind of checking up back in the UK. 'OK, let's hear what he has to say. It's not like I've got a lot of options on the table. I haven't got a pot to piss in. If I had a CV, it would be full of dodgy club promoters and sound companies and a nice record for trafficking class A drugs. And, I'm on the Costa del Crime.' I laugh at the absurdity of it all. 'You couldn't make it up!'

Gary is at least smiling, amused enough. The car is climbing on a dark road, the town has disappeared.

'Where are we off to? Somewhere discreet where no-one will find my body?'

'Piss off' Gary says, chuckling. 'We're heading up the mountain you see behind town, there's a steakhouse up here Holme likes. It's discreet, and people don't bug us there. In port, everyone is in your face, wants to be your friend, be seen with you. The price of success in a town full of wannabees and bullshitters, I'm afraid.'

'Cool. Steak. Bloody hell, when was the last time I had one of those. Beats meat pudding and chips, I never want to eat that again.'

'Do you want gravy with that?' Gary adds, in the Warrington accent of our childhood.

'Peas, no gravy' I add in the same accent, that even I have mostly lost.

'And no bloody vinegar!' we both add, echoing the refrain of our most hated customer from back in the days of the chippy. It's a shared moment of memory, a chink in the armour of wilful amnesia. It's a reminder we are flesh and blood, we lived through it together, forced to witness the super slow-motion car-crash of our family, until

43

we found ways of evading and running from it. Whatever works for you, whatever makes it bearable. The car is silent for the rest of the journey.

We pull under a tree filled with out of season fairy lights, and beyond is a wide terrace, with plastic windows folded down and designer patio heaters shooting jets of bluey-orange up glass tubes. It's decidedly cooler up here, and the scent is strongly of pine trees.

Gary comes round and takes my shoulders in his hands, and draws in.

'Just be cool, listen to what he has to say. Don't mess things up for me, not when we are about to win it all. And, Gene, it's good to see you, really.'

'Thanks Gaz.'

'And do *not* call me Gaz, or I'll go back to calling you Eugene, you daft sod.' And in this state of apparent reunited brotherly jolliness, I make my way formally back into the real world, to have dinner with Marbella's most powerful real estate agent.

I'm curious, wide eyed. I have barely eaten in a real, proper restaurant. Take-aways, transport cafes, fast food, all night diners, tick. By the hundreds. Not through choice, it was just the life I lead dictated that's where I fuelled myself. Fish and chips shops, never. Not since the fire. This place is the Spanish equivalent of an old-school, posh country restaurant back home. It has antique artefacts hung everywhere that have an agricultural appearance about them. Planks of wood with sharp flint inlaid into it, metal farming tools, and horsey looking apparatus abound. Several stuffed animal heads hang off the walls: a goat with oversized horns, a couple of stags, and a bloody great bull's head, whose neck is as thick as a tree trunk. Weirder still, rows of what appear to be legs hang from the ceiling. They all have hooves, and are covered in grease and fungus, an abattoir gone mouldy.

As we pass the kitchen, I catch sight of an enormous charcoal grill where surly men are turning great hefts of meat. The place smells variously of beef fat, the musty, greasy waft off the rotten legs, and expensive male cologne. It is full of fairly plump, red-faced, middle-aged people. The men wear a uniform of fawn or blue blazers, with check shirts, ties or cravats. Their hair is uniformly slicked back and is collar length. Their wives have, what I presume, is the Spanish equivalent of the blue rinse; intensely coiffed and dyed blonde curls. Fur and fake leopard skin are much in evidence. At least I hope it's fake. Heavy gold jewellery and earrings, pearls and ornate brooches. I have never seen creatures like this on planet earth. They cast a cursory glance at Gary, then all of them switch to me, appraising me. The wives' eyes scan me up and down, reading who knows what signals, and turn away having decodified whatever it was they needed. We sit at the end of the long room, in the shadow of the forest of hooves. No sign of Holme

'What's with the dead legs,' I ask as soon as I can, 'what is that all about?'

'Dead legs?' Gary blinks uncomprehendingly. 'Oh, right,' he finds it funny, 'that's *Jamon Serrano*.' I stare back nonplussed. 'Ham, Gene, you know, ham sandwich.' Strange idea, leaving pig's legs dripping fat onto your guests. 'We'll have some, it's amazing stuff, you won't believe it.' I certainly am not believing it at the moment.

People arrive, the wives' head's turn to scan the newest entrant; Holme, with Rafaela behind him. This time the reaction is completely different. The heads twerk with approval, with shared nods and cocked glances of admiration. A couple of the gents stand up to shake his hand as he walks through. As they do so, they place their other hand on his shoulder, and slap it firmly, the proximity of the whole exchange seeming to me very intimate.

'Holme lives locally, in La Zagaleta, so a few of these are his neighbours' Gary offers by way of explanation.

'I believe you've met Rafaela' says Holme as he draws up to the table. Gary kisses her on both cheeks, and she turns to me and her head is about to lean forward expecting the same reaction, but I

45

clumsily proffer my right hand, keeping the usual arm's length, and my rigidity is received with a smile of recognition. She looks even more stunning than earlier. She's changed to a simple red dress, high necked, but figure hugging, cut to reveal her shoulders which are angular and coffee cream coloured. She appears to float in front of me, like she's superimposed on our more ordinary world. Her smile lights up the table. I sit down and clam up, offering as little interaction as possible as we do the intros, receive menus, order drinks, everyone speaking in fluent Spanish. I feel like a silent smelly fart at a wedding ceremony.

A plate of wafer-thin red meat turns up.

'Have some dead leg, Gene' invites Gary. Ham should be pink, I say to myself. I slide in a slice, waiting for that salty, porky sensation familiar from a million sandwiches and buns over the years on the road. Instead, I'm eating a greasy but succulent peach, sweetness and creaminess, balanced with deep piggyness. The thin fat melts like butter. The flavour runs around my whole mouth even after I've swallowed it. I'm stunned into silence as the table laughs at me.

'I love to see people try *Jamon de Bellota* for the first time, it's always much more than they expect it to be' Rafaela says.

'*Jamon* what?'

'The *Bellota* is an acorn. The pigs live in the forest and forage for acorns, that's what gives it the special creamy flavour.'

'Yeah that's good' I admit, 'really good. I must get some of that, take a leg home with me, ay?' I glance up to the suspended pigs' legs, my idea of a joke.

'Well it'll cost you three hundred quid if you do' adds Gary. My wide-eyed surprise is the next cause of hilarity. 'Actually, that particular one we just had is around five hundred a leg.'

'The rewards of hard work eh, Gary' puts in Holme. He has a slight head twitch when he finishes his sentences I've noticed, like a flick, as though he's saying 'there, cop that, that's what I say'. His

46

cheeks are full and flushed, his lips strangely and sensuously pink and fleshy, and he purses them when he's listening to you, and before he speaks, he moves them slightly around as though chewing up what you've just said, before flicking off another of his own pearls of wisdom. He does indeed appear to be a bit of a twat, as we'd say back home. However much he's worth. 'So, Gene, welcome to Spain,' he starts, speaking at a slightly exaggeratedly slow pace, to make it sound profound and demand my singular attention. I find the effect both irritating and condescending.

'Gracias' I respond which produces yet another round of polite hilarity at my expense, though I know it's well meaning.

'Gary here is a very important person to me, and to my business. He'll forgive me, I know, if I say he is my protégé, and I have invested a great deal in his development and his success. A success that is a tribute to both his ability, and my judgement in bringing him up from the hordes of hungry junior realtors, scurrying like rats around the coast.' I catch a slight wince in Gary's face, but otherwise his mask is perfect. Rafaela leans her exquisite chin on her hand and gazes dutifully at her boss. Holme continues at that same irksome rhythm.

'Our success is dependant, among other things, on our scrupulously clean business record and reputation. We are a Marbella brand. The customers, and the powers that be, without whom we cannot trade, trust us. We are a shining beacon of transparency, professionalism and excellence in a market that is riven with sharp practice and commercial shoddiness. We are highly visible. Our brand is the most recognised brand in its field in the south of Spain. We play a significant part in the community life of the town, sponsoring events and mentoring aspiring, local young businessmen. Protecting that image, safeguarding our brand, is of prime importance.'

He pauses, as though I need any time to understand what he is trying to get at. This guy is plumbing new depths of pomposity. I'd met a few record company people in my time, some real egos, often total coke heads, but Holme makes them look amateur. It isn't so much what he is saying as the way he says it, the pace, the intonation, and the fact he is looking slightly above my head as he addresses me, only occasionally making eye contact. I wonder how much of this I am going to have to sit through. Moreover, how much of this has Gary has had to put up with in his time? Holme is what Watkins might have been, if he'd been in real estate.

'When I met you earlier today, I was most surprised to understand you are family of Gary's. I pressed him on this immediately we were in our meeting, as he had never mentioned you, so I felt a little let down, an unusual occurrence with regard to Gary. He explained to me, albeit briefly, the story of the fire and the death of your father and the effect that had on your mother. This is all new to me, and makes Gary's achievements all the more impressive. He also explained how you came to be at Her Majesty's disposition these last few years.' Jesus, how that phrasing pisses me off. Why not call it like it is, as though he can't say straight ordinary things lest he's dirtied by the words, pompous fucking ass. I think mercy has arrived in the form of the starters, but he waves them away without glancing at the waiter. I haven't eaten now for fourteen hours, unless you count wafer thin dead leg meat, and my tolerance of this clown is in serious danger of evaporating. As a result, I start to munch through the bizarre pessary shaped bread sticks in the little bowl. The cracking and crunching of these tasteless, dry snackettes is profoundly audible, but I am desperate.

'Let me get to the point, as I think we are all hungry.' I stop crunching as I'm struggling to hear over the noise in my head. Who invented these pointless bombshells of biscuits? 'Gene you've had a difficult time, for reasons I can empathise with. Gary has been able to overcome those same issues and turn them to his advantage. Gary is a key player in our company, and he is part of our brand. And being part of our brand means being everything we stand for, twenty-four seven. At home, when you're out, wherever you are, whoever you are with, you represent us. Your appearance here with no warning, and your unfortunate recent history, while entirely your own business, does nonetheless pose a potential problem for us. Curiosity would be piqued, people may dig around, searching for an angle. There's nothing some people won't do to knock us off our perch. To minimise the risk of this, Gary and I have decided to bring you on board. Give you the leg up you so obviously need after being released, as all ex-prisoners do.' Put that way, it really stings, but I can hardly object to the description. Come on then you smug bastard, finish it off so we can eat some fucking food already.

'You are going to work for us, Gene. In the furniture pack division, where the logistical element of your previous experience will be useful, and you'll be able to build your life back up again. You will, however, have a story to go with it. The story is the official version of your life for the past few years, and that's what we will stick to should anyone ask, and the story you will keep to as well. Any instance of deviation by you from that line will result in instant dismissal, and withdrawal of whatever perks and benefits may or may not have accrued. Only because Gary is so special and important to us, am I willing to be so magnanimous. We'll have our lawyer draw up an agreement, integral to your job contract, and you can start your life over again, clean sheet, no-one need be any the wiser. Only the people at this table need know otherwise, ok?'

I'm silent for a moment. 'Wow, I don't know what to say' is the rather pale cliché that drops out of my mouth eventually. I could of course go into detail about having to get this approved at probation level, getting new license conditions accepted, probably making frequent visits to the UK for supervision interviews. That is one course of action I could pursue, and drag Gary into all sorts of bureaucracy and intrusion. Or do nothing and risk being rumbled, deported, who knows.

49

I have no real idea of the full implications of any of my actions, so I'm going to go with the flow. And anyway, I'm starving, and the only thing I've swallowed so far, is my pride.

'Gracias!' I burst out, which feels appropriate. There's a laugh all round, the tension lightens, drinks are poured and the evening heads in a normal direction, sort of. I get to eat the best meal I have eaten in at least ten years, in the company of the most beautiful woman I have ever seen. Holme's plan is a small price to pay, as much as I resent his tone. I am who I am, and I did what I have done, and now I have to dance along in some kind of charade to protect the good name of an estate agent. What crass, anodyne little fairy story is going to become the explanation of my recent life, and do I even get a say in it? It seems not, as it appears to be a fait accompli, to be sealed up by lawyers.

After dinner, once the obligatory handshaking, back-slapping and multiple cheek kissing has been completed, I'm back in Gary's Audi feeling fairly benign, courtesy of the exceptional steak and wine.

He's the first to speak. 'Well done Gene, you took that really well. I wasn't sure you wouldn't kick off, it's not how I like to do things.'

'Whose idea was it?'

'It was mine to give you a job, as I think it's an amazing break for you, and just what you need, and I figured Holme would feel less antsy if you were in-house, so he knows what's going on. He came up with the whole back story idea and the lawyer. It's how he rolls. Everything is always nailed to the floor, no loose ends. There's a lot of cowboys on this coast, so he tries to stay ahead of the game by being ruthlessly legal and watertight on anything. You've just got a taste of that.'

'OK, who have I been for the last three years?'

'Well, I've come up with something, as he isn't going to waste his time on the details. You can look over it back at the apartment, check names and places, to see if it scans well and hangs together. You've been a DJ in Goa and Thailand for three years, didn't you know? You had a great time, pity you missed it.'

I can laugh at that, there's an irony to the idea, as it's something I had mused about doing, but the hold that criminal gangs have on you creeps up and surprises you. You think you're being clever; you think you insulate yourself, that you're not beholden, and that the choice is yours to live that way. But it's a mirage, and the minute you rattle the invisible cage bars, the menacing hints and friendly advice loaded with threatening innuendo come thick and fast.

After Gary and I have read over the 'story' and changed some superficial details for things I can more easily remember, he readies to leave.

'Listen Gene,' he's struggling for the right tone of this, I can tell. 'You really threw me a curve ball today, that was a pretty weird situation to be put in, especially with, you know, the whole business we're in and the pressure. It could have been messy.'

'It wasn't my intention. Sorry.'

'No, it's not your fault, it's just the context, don't you see?'

'Yeah, well I never imagined this is where you'd be in your life, did I? Did you?'

Gary snorts, 'Christ no. It's like chasing the dragon, to coin a phrase. My job is to hold onto Holme's tail and do the heavy lifting, be the clearer upper, the deal maker, the deliverer of good and bad news, and sometimes I have to shit on people from a great height. It's actually really tough. Sometimes I think it's only Ana keeps my feet on the ground, and she understands the whole scene fortunately. She gives me perspective. It won't always be like this; I have different plans long-term.'

'Can't wait to meet her',

'Oh, you will very soon. Let's get you settled in first.'

'Well so far, I have a new identity, a nice flat, been for a great meal, and I've got my baby brother back. What's not to like?'

Gary hugs me long and hard. 'Welcome back bro, I'm glad we made it back together again.'

'Yeah, who would have thunk it eh?'

'So, don't go and fuck it up.'

'Shit Gary, why-'

'Ok, ok, you know what I mean, it just didn't come out right. Sorry mate.'

'I'm done with fucking up Gaz. I'm not going to be chewed over by people anymore.'

'Good to hear it. I'll check back tomorrow. Someone will come over with the papers and stuff to sign, and we'll see about getting you down to the warehouse to suss that out, ok?'

I may have already committed my gravest fuck up yet. Time will tell.

'Done deal. Thanks. Grassy arse.'

Gary grimaces at my distortion of the Spanish word, waves and disappears toward his Audi.

~

Numerous bottles of vodka lie around, so I pour myself a tall one, find some ice in the fridge and sit on the terrace. It's two in the morning, but I can still hear life outside, the drone of scooters, occasional car horns, dogs barking here and there, an owl hooting. Even seagulls fly over in the dark, evidence of how close to the sea we are. It's warm enough to sit here in what I'm wearing. I notice the absence of police sirens, part of any city's soundscape. I breathe this new world in, savouring its ever-varying aromas. In one day, I've erased years of indifference to each other, I have a job to go to and what may be something approaching a normal life being offered to me. I just have to play the silly game of pretending I'm a goody goody to spare Holme's and Gary's blushes. I resign myself to considering it a price worth paying for the moment. I think about calling Mum, then remember how late it is. If she picked up the phone ever, anyway. Would she notice I've left even? I'll let her know later in the week, put her mind at rest, or so I tell myself, knowing her mind is far beyond that.

~

I'm woken by a crash, and some giggling. It's still dark, maybe I've been in bed a couple of hours, who knows. Voices, female, but also a male. Shuffling, clinking of glass. A phone rings inadvertently occasioning a rush of 'shhhhh' and more giggles. I'm slipping back out of consciousness when I'm aware the door is opening and a figure moves in through it. The vague light from the corridor reveals a familiar curvature in silhouette. Frankie slots in under the light duvet and breathes champagne vodka fumes over me. Hands envelop me, and I can feel the bizarrely firm shape of her breasts against my chest. It isn't unpleasant, but doesn't feel completely human. Something about the density brings to mind a volleyball.

'Ello darlin, baby bruvver, 'ow was your day?'

'Interesting. I learnt a couple of Spanish words. Met the legend that is Holme. Nice dinner, yeah, it was okay. And you?' I'm not sure where the conversation is leading. I am also painfully aware I have not felt the caress of female flesh in a great many years. Even the comfort of my own five fingered ministrations had gotten old long ago, so I am as celibate as I could ever have imagined being. Frankie is starting to caress my chest and nuzzle into my neck, and I have my hands running up under the clothing on her back. I am transfixed by the texture and consistency of her flesh. She's not a gym body, she's what might politely be called slightly plump, making this lovely fleshy cuddling. Her flesh gives softly, no hard muscles or edges, just smooth squishiness and a mingling of perfume, alcohol and sweet perspiration. I find myself drowsily being lulled by the sensations, and am aware my retired member is responding to this unexpected visitation. It's an unfamiliar sensation, like a long-forgotten dream that comes back to you one night, vivid but just out of reach. Her breathing changes rhythm slightly, shorter, impatient.

'D'ya fink Gary likes me?' she asks. I'm a bit nonplussed and search for something neutral and diplomatic.

'Well, he must do, you live here for free, don't you?'

'Yeah, spose so, he must do. Wish he didn't have her, it could be like old times.' The rhythm of her breathing slows, becoming relaxed.

'You go back a long way, yeah?' Her lips nuzzle into my neck, behind my ear, she breathes more slowly still.

'Oh yeah, we were good for a while, he's lovely, inni…'

Her breathing settles to a steady slow beat, and she shifts her weight to my side, pulls me to her, and falls fast asleep. I've ended up the day as this girl's teddy bear. In not much more time, I'm gone as well.

5

I wander drowsily into the kitchenette that opens onto the lounge, staring around me, trying to make the unfamiliar familiar, reorienting my existential geography. No cell walls, no dank semi in Warrington reeking of stale cooking fat and TCP. It's bright and sunny, the glare illuminates the interior. The sliding windows to the terrace are open and warm air drifts in with its perfumes. It's funny how it's the thing I notice most and fixate on, the scent of the environment here. It's so radically different and full of layers and different traces of things, it's so… fresh. Sounds hackneyed, but it smells just that, fresh, like it was made today.

A tall, elegantly thin Spaniard hands me a coffee, and says in effeminate accented English, 'Hola, I'm Nacho, nice to meet you.'

'Yeah hi, Gene, how's it going?'

Frankie emerges and comes into the lounge in a hotel style bathrobe. She has one hand pressed to her face, half shielding her eyes, and regards me sheepishly.

'Ello babe, you alright? I'm sorry about that last night, we was well pissed. I hope I didn't…'

'No, no, it's cool,' I say, wanting to spare her imagination overworking, and avoiding too many reminders of the befuddled frustration of the occasion. 'Where had you been, just working?'

'Yeah but it was a bit of a party. Holme came in with a bunch of clients, and they cracked like eight magnums of Crystal, it was madness.'

Nacho sees the incomprehension on my face.

'Crystal is de best champagne, iss very very expensive,' he elucidates for me.

'Right gotcha. Like how much?'

'Ohmigod, iss like fuckin eight hundred euros a bottle!' It is decidedly surreal to hear someone swear fluently in English with a heavy, camp, Spanish accent. But more surreal is the simple maths of eight times eight hundred.

'Excuse me, Holme spent six and a half grand on champagne?! I was with him last night, when did he do that?'

''E came in about two with a couple of guys from the town hall and their mates, that Sorzano bloke. He's always hangin' around wiv the politicians, it was Sorzano, yeah. Gave me a nice tip an' all.'

I remember the suave Latino guy backslapping Holme in the restaurant, they did leave together before Gary and I drove out.

'Is always de same, *son puto ladrones los políticos²*. Thieving bastads dey are, but you know we gotta live and we make good money las' night.'

'Was Gary there?' I ask

'Naaaah babe, 'e's not really the type for that. Only when he's needed. Holme usually comes in with the top clients, just him an' his lawyer, that toad Sterling Garcia or whatever, and the bitch.' Frankie spits the word out.

'The bitch?'

'Alexandra Campos de Theunissen. She's his like girlfriend, but she's like ten years older than 'im. She's had loads done to her, I mean everyfink.' Frankie has no sense of irony. 'She's so fucking plastic, she's only wiv 'im for what's in it for 'er.'

'And what's in it for her?' I'm already intrigued.

'I've 'eard she's married to a Russian who don't live here, an' he's not bovvered if she has flings like, cos he's got a mistress. She's really well connected, brings Holme clients, so they're all in bed togevvah, Sorzano an' all the rest of 'em.'

'Why's she such a bitch?'

---

² They are fucking thieves those politicians

'She 'ad my mate sacked just cos of the way she looked at 'er. She lords it over everybody.'

The conversation carries on in this way with all manner of vindictive half-truths, gossip and wild rumour being chewed over thoroughly as Frankie and Nacho faff about trying to get some kind of breakfast together. A further girl appears with tousled hair and smudged make-up, with similar looking medical/aesthetic enhancements to Frankie. She says hello and slumps on the sofa, and no-one thinks to introduce her. There's an insistent beeping and Frankie retrieves a mobile from somewhere in a pile of discarded clothes.

'Oh fuckinell babe, it's Gary, he says you're supposed to be down at the office at 10.30 and it's nearly eleven...'

~

It's three in the afternoon and the last few hours have been a whirlwind. I have signed up to my fake life of the past three years, I've given over passport and documents, I've been to a lawyer's office and signed some kind of social security application, and now I'm sitting listening to a stocky, muscular Ukrainian man who is explaining to me my new job: orders and deliveries, how the loads are put together, how to keep the records, check with the main office for access times and dates. Suffice to say I have entered a highly ordered universe, all computer managed and humourless. Gary insists I'm being done a huge favour, all my paperwork to make me legally employable in Spain, done in a day, for free. He assures me this would have taken me weeks on my own. I've no reason to doubt him. Now I'm trying to keep track of the mind-numbing detail of this job. I am to be paid the princely sum of about eight hundred and fifty euros a month, the equivalent of five hundred and fifty of your English pounds, which strikes me as a staggeringly low sum for back-breaking and tedious work. I also have to be at work at eight in the morning, I have a half-hour break for breakfast, go figure, and I finish at three thirty, which is the silver lining in this otherwise mysterious and dark cloud. I am thirty-six years old and I have never worked a regular job in my life, let alone pretty physical work. I am in a warehouse with various happy go lucky immigrants encompassing Poland, the UK, Ukraine, Morocco, Senegal, Colombia and Argentina. No Spanish. Not one. My job will be to help put together packages of furniture and home decor that are installed into houses that people have bought off Holme, to deliver and install them, under the careful eye of Dmitri, the surly Ukrainian.

After my induction, I head out for a social bonding session with some of my new-found workmates. We are in a cafe, on a street on the industrial estate where the warehouse is located, and inevitably I am asked who am I and where I'm from. I reluctantly spill out the bones of the story I have just signed up to, so my new identity is now official and public. The common language is English, and it's a new experience to hear it spoken in several different ways and accents, and none of it particularly well. Apart from Darren, who is a scouser and proud of it, but come to think of it he doesn't speak it any better than the others. He's much younger than me so no danger of us having crossed paths before. Darren is curious.

'Say, wack, how come you're doin' this with us if you're a DJ. DJs round here make a fortune, you wanna be getting' some of that mate.'

He has a point, and it's the weakest element of my story. I have DJ'd but not in any great capacity, and I didn't stick with it and build a reputation. I was making more money helping arrange shipments of ecstasy around the country, concealed in speaker systems.

'Well, I've just got here y'know, and I need to suss it out. It's only March anyways and the season hasn't started properly, so this is filling the gap.'

'It's shit round here anyway' he counters, ever the contrary scouser, 'you wanna be in Ibiza mate.'

'I know, but I had a contact here, and it's kinda convenient this job, short term. Then I'll look for something before summer.' I have no idea what I am doing beyond tomorrow as of yet, and the job *is* convenient.

'He's fucking Gary's brother; this is who he is.' I turn, stunned by this statement. It is Dmitri. The others make way around the table for him, and it's clear he has their respect and deference at least. I flush a bit and wonder what I've done to be on the end of such an aggressive intervention.

'Yeah, that's true. He's helped me out, give me a job. I'm a bit short, and got nothing on for a few months so you know, this is good for a while,' I say, trying to be neutral and justify my luck. No-one responds. Dmitri drains half his pint, then turns to face me.

'Listen Eugene, I don't like be told who working here when I have no idea about it. You walk in here, thank you to your brother and think you one of us. I don't need any more men, I have good team here, these guys work hard, we look after each other.'

'It's Gene' I say dryly. I have never tolerated being called Eugene, it caused me so much grief in my childhood in a place like Warrington.

'You fucking Eugene, I have it on papers, so you get called Eugene. If one of my guys lose job to make way for you, I come looking for you, you understand me?' His body tension makes it perfectly clear these are not idle words. I must have upset some delicate ecological balance among the warehouse workers, though I picked up no sense of it from the rest of them.

'Give him a break, he might be alright.' Darren attempts to diffuse the situation. Ibrahim, the tall silent Senegalese guy shifts uneasily. Dmitri isn't done yet though.

'You see Ibby here,' pointing to Ibrahim, 'he walk across desert and nearly drown on boat from Morocco to get here. He will get paper and passport soon, and if he lose job, he can lose all of that. You know what that means? You understand this? And you shut your

59

mouth Darren. This serious business.' Darren shifts in his chair and sips slowly. It's clear who runs this show.

There's a silence. Men stare into their beers, as Dmitri glares at me imperiously. I have no heart for a fight and nothing to fight about.

'Dmitri, I didn't ask for this job, it was offered to me. I came here yesterday from Asia with very little money left. I got ripped off by the last promoter, and I'm a bit desperate. I don't want to be doing this any longer than I can be okay? As soon as I get myself a gig, I'll be out of your hair.' I try to sound reasonable, but it sounds a bit pathetic. I wasn't ready for a scene like this. It's too close to prison, with the old lags who throw their weight around, trying to maintain the status and reputation they held outside. 'OK? Seriously, I don't want anyone's job. I could always talk to Gary if anything was to happen, sort it out so everything stays the way it should be.'

To my dismay, this doesn't assuage the Ukrainian, on the contrary. He leans over the table and says menacingly, 'I don't want spy in my warehouse. You do job, do what you are told, you don't talk to your brother about nothing, or I will break your fucking knees.' He downs his glass and leaves, and the table is left looking at the floor, scratching beer mats until Claudio the Argentinian pipes up.

'My friend, do not take this personally.' I laugh in disbelief. 'Dmitri it is his way, he's very proud of us and he protect us. We all come as immigrants, people here can be very bad, very untrustworthy. They make you work, they don't pay, they call police to check your papers, they can have you in police car, drive you three hundred kilometres and leave you in middle of the *campo*[3], my friend. Or worse. Marbella is full of many people with money, and comes many criminals, and gangsters, and the politicos they are the kings of the party. It all happen with their permission, these men are the kings of the castle. Marbella belongs to them. So we who have come here

---

[3] Countryside

60

with nothing, we have to stick together. And you my friend are different. You are one of the bosses, Gary is your brother. You must show Dmitri you can be one of us, and nothing happen to nobody's job here.'

'Shit man, I would have happily had a job emptying the bins rather than cause all this grief, I don't want to put anyone out, I just need to get on my feet, you know?' My pleading isn't an act at this moment. This antipathy and resentment are enough to make me return to Watkin's bosom. It's not worth the trouble. But the situation relaxes, we have another beer, and they all say goodbye in a friendly enough way. When I leave the bar, I have no idea where I am, have no way to get back to Sueño del Mar, and I don't have a mobile phone. It's at this moment Gary's Audi swings into view. The guy is a genius, extra-sensory perception. The car pulls up to me, but with the tinted windows I can't discern the shape inside and to my surprise a woman emerges from the car. Yet another lithe, coffee cream coloured beauty. And as if to complete the set, she has green eyes, black hair, and a more angular Semitic looking nose than Rafaela. She appears to be a thoroughbred southern Spaniard. My studies in anthropology, the few bits I was unstoned enough to absorb and remember, had enlightened me as to the surprising mixture of races that went into making up the Spanish population. Perhaps a quarter of the population were of Jewish origin and certainly in the South here, many Spaniards were little different in appearance from people of the Punjab and Persia.

'Hi, I'm Ana,' says this new, darker angel. She is maybe too dark and exotic to appear angelic, she's a veritable Persian princess from a Thousand and One Nights sent to rescue me. I am gawping again. Of course, Ana, Gary's sustaining force. 'He warned me you might be abandoned, and I have a nice long lunch break so I've come to rescue you.'

I climb in gratefully. Niceties and introductions exchanged, I ask, 'Gary has no lunch break so he sends you on errands?'

'Lunch breaks don't happen in Holmeland unless its business. Those people never stop. I worry for your brother; they will burn him out.' Her English is mildly accented but grammatically perfect. 'I can take you back, I'm free until five thirty.'

'How does that work, you go *back* to work then?'

'It's siesta at this time for most people.'

'But it's not hot now, who needs a siesta?' She laughs at my bald logic.

'It's the rhythm of life in Andalucía. European businesses think we are backward and some of the government want to change to British hours, but this will be difficult to achieve. The Spanish mentality is very *cabezota*[4], it is very stubborn. Old ways don't change fast, despite nearly thirty years of democracy. Look at our politicians,' she adds as though this is self-explanatory.

'I've been here less than forty-eight hours and I'm not getting a good impression of your politicians.'

Back at the apartment, I am flattered Ana is wasting her lunch hours getting to know me. The sun sparkles alluringly a kilometre down the hill, the perfect complement to the fizzy water we sip. Frankie is not in evidence. Perhaps conveniently, if past history is to be believed.

'I'm glad I have finally met you. I thought you would be forever mysterious. I'm sorry for your troubles, I hope Gary will help your life get better.' She smiles, and her hand pats the back of my hand. I'm again a bit discombobulated, being in the company of such overwhelmingly attractive young women, on friendly terms, out of the blue, after all of the months of... I try to concentrate.

'You mean Gary actually told you about me?' I had started to think I was a figment of my own imagination, everybody dropping dead with surprise that Gary has a brother. 'Is it true you've met Mum?'

---

[4] Stubborn

'Yes, last summer. I understand everything, really I do. So naturally, Gary took me into his confidence like that, he told me all about you. He loves you, he missed you in his way, and he really wants to have his brother back.'

I sigh, and remain silent for a while, tired of apologising for myself and my past, even to myself. Mostly to myself. 'Well, we have a lot of ground to make up, but I think we are going to do it. I've got to find my feet, but I think I'm going to like it here. It's not what I expected, I'm just a bit freaked out still by how... different it all is.'

'To England?'

'No, to everything. Well, all that I've seen, in Europe, on the telly, whatever. The whole place resembles a film set, the trees, the sky, the mountains, it's like a kind of sexy Mediterranean California. All you need is some big yankee cars on the streets.'

We idle away some time on laughing at our respective countries and their people's idiosyncrasies. I am warned five minutes in Andalucía can mean anything up to two hours, so when someone says I'll be with you in five, I need to be a bit flexible. People never say they are late, they are just 'on their way'.

'Yeah, a bit *mañana* is it?' I say, quoting one of the few clichés about Spain I had picked up in the UK. She slaps me half seriously, but smiling.

'Don't say that, I hate that expression, it's not true. We have a different sense of time here. Up until a generation ago most people were very, very poor, and life went slowly, at the speed of the sun in the sky. There was no money, and people owned nothing, so there was no hurry. What matter when you are hungry, and can do nothing about it. My grandmother used to gather roots in the woods to eat sometimes. If an animal was killed on the road, they would take it home. Many people left for Argentina and never came back. You have to understand where we have come from, and how violent the changes have been. Especially here in Marbella. This town is thousands of years old, in the centre there is an Arab castle with the

63

village houses built into it, the streets are as wide as a donkey and a basket. The past is all around if you look, in the names, many of which are from Arabic. And now they are building over everything, people come in with their suitcases of cash, and buy our land and our history and turn it into concrete and fill their pockets, and the politicians queue up with their hands out.'

'But that's what Gary does; he sells that dream.'

'Yes, I know' she says this without qualification and fixes me with her greeny hazel eyes.

'And you're a lawyer, so you must be party to all of this, it's your business too?'

'I know what you are thinking. It's a contradiction, it's ironic. I make a very good living helping foreigners carve up and exploit our land and our heritage. They make it into their own version of Spain. But this is the story of everything here since the seventies. The tourists are our bread basket. But maybe now it is going too far, too fast. Ordinary people cannot afford to live here, we are pricing ourselves out of our own world. But the politicians make it worse. Instead of controlling it they tear up the rules, and take bribes to let people build where they want. If you break the planning laws, you pay a fine, you put the fine on top of the price of the property, you get your documents, your profit, the tourist gets their apartment, villa or whatever and everyone is happy.' Ana is slamming her hand into her other palm, and is quite flush, her eyes flashing with disgust.

'If that's the way you see it, how do you feel about Holmeland, do you approve of it?' I'm taken aback by her frankness.

'I did at first. I come from a normal Marbella family, generations of us. We were probably Jewish once, I am not like you, light skinned north-European. I am not one of the *pijos*[5], I am *pura Andaluza*[6].' She sees my incomprehension. '*Pijo* is what I think you call posh in English, that class of entitled people who have always

_____

[5] Slang for posh people
[6] Pure bred Andalucian

64

had everything their own way. Especially under Franco. I am not from this class, so for me it is a big thing to make it to be a lawyer, but yes, then I have to deal with the contradictions of the corrupt system I now find myself in.'

I let out a long breath, as all of this has washed over me in a torrent, and she now looks somewhat embarrassed. 'Wow, feels like you've had that bottled up for a while.' Her expression remains intense.

'I am glad you are here, Gene. I think it will be good for Gary. He is so dedicated, and he works terribly hard, and he believes completely in what he is doing. It is his dream to be successful in this way. But there is a lot of pressure, and the people here now on this coast are not trustworthy. Everything is about money, what is my percentage, my commission, where is my piece of the action. Gary must turn the deals Holme makes into reality, but some of what is happening makes me worried. For Gary.'

Her concern deep and genuine and I'm moved, but also confused and ill at ease. I have made a career of avoiding serious relationships, and seriousness in general. Such is the path of the inveterate stoner. But in this new place, this strange filmic world, I am aware of how all my old certainties and evasions are not applicable, at all. I have to work out a way of surviving meaningfully and not going back to the existential shroud of chemically induced proto-happiness. But the only person close to me has a serious life, with serious responsibilities and serious people. Despite what it looks like round here, it sounds like serious business.

'With my baggage I'm not sure what I can offer him, I'm a bit of a passenger, a burden really', is all I can proffer as a response, as indeed I feel ill equipped to offer anything right now.

'You are family'. My expression says what I think of that. She knows the mess of my family. She contradicts my silent assertion. 'Family is everything, you are the same blood and that counts for a lot. You would know this if you were Spanish.' She cracks a bit of a smile and appears to lighten. 'It will be good for Gary to have a brother here. Here, everyone is your friend, but not really. Everybody drinks, party, yeah yeah good times, we make a lot of money, but they are not your real friends. Your real friends look out for you. Here people only want you for what they get for themselves. This is the brave new world we are building in Marbella and the Costa.' She looks at me, at my rather stunned expression. 'Hey, come on, it's not all like that. Soon you will come to meet my family, you will see the real Spanish way. Marbella is not real Spain. At least not the one Gary works in. He loves to come to my mother's house. It's like a holiday from his reality. For me it's normal, it's the base of life, and all of this,' she waves an elegant fine boned wrist and hand with immaculate nails, at the vista of palm-fringed realty fantasyland below us, 'this is just business. It's good.' She shrugs. 'I make money, I have a great career, I support my parents and my younger sister, but it's not good. It's good but it's not good.' She smiles at her contrariness, stands up, kisses me on both cheeks, as everyone does here, and leaves.

I sit for a moment, as the scent of her lingers on my cheeks, and those eyes still flash in my mind. Gary is a lucky boy. My head is spinning though, trying to compute the various currents and tensions I am already picking up in the narrow, intense world I have dropped into. Well, what did I expect? Absolutely nothing, so it's all food for thought.

6

'What's for tea Mum?' I've got Doug with me, as his mum has had to work late and his dad is on a shift. He's come over for tea, but Mum has forgotten this arrangement she made only yesterday on the phone to Doug's mum. She's applying lipstick in the mirror by the front door, evidently on her way out. Perfume hangs in the air, strangely exotic and other worldly, masking the smell of frying fat from the chip shop below.

'Get your dad to send something up, I haven't got time.' She checks herself intently in the mirror, making sure the lips shout their shape loudly. She looks like someone out of a film. She's dressed up, like she's going out to something special and it's Wednesday tea time. The sight is odd, it clashes with the banality of the day and time.

'Where you off?'

'Bingo love…' she throws my way as though it's obvious. 'I won't be late. What do you want from the shop, I'll call down to your Dad.'

This sounds odd, as though she's a customer ordering, not his wife, my Mum. I shrug.

'It's alright, me an' Doug'll go down. Come on, what d'ya fancy Doug?'

'Cor, can I choose anything?' Doug's eyes are wide with expectation.

'Course you can love' says Mum as she walks out, placing a kiss on a finger that she pops on each of our foreheads, leaving a faint cosmetic scent on each of our bonces.

'Thanks Missus Phillips' he says after the figure clacking down the stairs on strangely high heels. 'Flippin 'eck your mum is like…' And he stops himself.

'What?' I'm embarrassed and indignant at his tone.

67

'Well y'know… she's sort of alright, in't she…'

'Fuck off ya dirty bastard' and I thump him, less playfully than he'd like to think.

'Ow, fuck off I don't mean like that!'

'Like what then?' He looks sheepish.

'Can we get curry sauce?'

'Yeah, guess so' I shrug. I leave it, not knowing where I would take that line of questioning, the thought is too confusing. We enter the chip shop where my dad is doling out orders to customers, aided by old Mrs Braithwaite.

'Ooh, look what cat dragged in' she intones in a scrambled sort of way. Her dentures are famously ill-fitting. My mother frequently berates my father about why he employs this 'old battle wagon', claiming she puts customers off, and is too slow.

'It's like a bloody working man's club in there with her' she would say, 'brings the tone down. We need to be modern, show a better face to the public' and so on, to which my father usually replies something like 'you can criticize when you're prepared to get up to your elbows in chip fat and batter instead of blowing my bloody takings down at the bingo.'

The way he said bingo was always like he thought it was beneath her, or a bit stupid, or that bingo was maybe something else but he wasn't saying what. A standard reply from her was something along the lines of 'at least bingo is fun' or 'tell your poker friends, they should try a bit of bingo, they might like it.' It is a regular field of battle, how they choose to spend their free time with friends. They don't seem to have a common thing anymore, except when they go to Kavanagh's dad's pub, and then they always come back arguing. It is late enough for me and Gary to be able to escape to our bedrooms and avoid the verbal brickbats that will fly across the kitchen. Tea mugs slam, occasional doors, and the ensuing tense silences are filled by a telly that stays on for long after I've gone to sleep.

'What d'ya fancy then young Eugene, the choice is yours' intones Mrs Braithwaite. I can never tell if she's being respectful to her boss' son or taking the piss. Probably both.

'So, your mother couldn't sort any tea out for you?' says my dad, flatly.

'Nope. Bingo.'

'Bingo' repeats my dad, with the same flatness. Doug strains to pick up some kind of subtext. 'So what you havin'?'

Doug goes overboard, having chips, mushy peas, a cod fillet and a steak pudding, with curry sauce. Mrs Braithwaite frowns disapprovingly.

'Oooo, you'll know about that later on laddie' and she chuckles away to herself.

'What about Gary?' asks dad. I hadn't even thought.

'He's upstairs.'

'Well yes, but doing what?'

'Reading I think'. My younger brother can be solitary. He finds ways of avoiding the crossfire of my parents' skirmishes. My cover is always Doug, thanks to his boundless energy and inquisitive recklessness, I can always hatch some scheme of madness that distracts me or keeps me completely away from the house, if need be.

'Right, we'll get him the same as you're havin' then' orders my father.

We adjourn to the small kitchen over the shop.

'Gary, come and get ya pudding and chips!' I yell to a closed door. Gary emerges, indeed carrying a book.

'Bingo again?'

I nod, mouth full of pudding, gravy dribbling down my chin. The good thing about living in a chip shop is you always have comfort food on hand, and your mates think it's Christmas every day.

'Flippin 'ell' mumbles Gary, picks up the paper wrapped package and heads back into his room.

69

'Bit of a miserable sod your brother inni' says Doug eventually.

'Naaaah, he's alright. He's a bit brainy, you know, a real swot. Gets way better marks than me. He's already deciding what 'O' levels he wants to do. He wants to go to a University.'

'University?! What's he gonna do that for? You've got a chip shop, that's good money that is.' Doug is plainly affronted by such vaulting ambition. *'If my dad had a chip shop I'd work in it tomorrow. Fuck school, waste of fucking time, I hate all of them wankers.'*

'Don't think my dad is that enthusiastic about working in one.'

'Really?' says Doug, genuinely puzzled. He's silent, wolfing through his overflowing plate, plainly confused by the complexities of business. Doug and I waste time defacing some comics we have bought, drawing obscene appendages on Star Wars characters, until his mum picks him up. I watch some telly, while Dad comes up from the shop and busies himself with a cup of tea and a sandwich.

The sound of the latch goes and Mum arrives, this time the whiff of perfume is mixed with cigarette smoke and booze. She hangs her coat up silently, pulls off her heels and slumps onto the sofa, letting out a long sigh. She doesn't say anything. I can feel my father tensing, readying to say something, and I decide to head for my bedroom. I know some form of row is coming, it just remains to be seen what sort. A silent stand-off, a ping-pong of sarcastic one-liners or an all-out firefight.

Before I get a chance to reach my air-raid shelter Dad says quietly, *'How was your bingo?'.*

The way he says bingo is sarcastic in itself. Mum doesn't answer immediately.

'Knackering'. My father's neck muscles spasm. I retreat to my room, to the welcoming distraction of my record player and Dad's albums, and lose myself in the music.

Days go by, and I adapt to work. Real work. I know it's real work because at the end of the day I am exhausted, muscles I didn't know I have are aching and complaining. I sleep a deep sleep, dreamless but for visions of chestnut haired, coffee-cream enchantresses and roomfuls of big men in big suits all braying at each other. I purchased a bicycle off Darren so I can get to the warehouse. It cost me a hundred euros but is potentially worth much more. Its provenance is entirely dubious, but who am I to ask? The guys treat me better as the days roll by. Only Dmitri remains taciturn and hostile, a mood he definitely reserves especially for me. He is fairly expressionless on the whole, doesn't give much away, other than barking orders and insulting people in his clunky English if they don't meet his expectations. The other guys are what I would expect, they spar verbally all the time, trying to outdo each other in testosterone obscenity and ridicule of all and sundry. It gets a bit wearing, but it's also refreshing in a bizarre sort of way. Having worked in the druggier fringes of the music business, it's a contrast to the self-obsession typical of people who spend much of their time high and cultivating an aura to better promote themselves with. Here in this shed, if you can't hold your own against the stream of daft insults and wind-ups, you won't last a day. Ibrahim keeps himself highly aloof from it, merely smiling at the jibes and jokes. I hear some visiting Spanish delivery drivers refer to him, apparently in all friendliness, as '*el negrito*[7]', which I recognise as definitely not kosher. That would have ended nastily back home nine times out of ten, but doubtless, in this environment at least, political correctness only extends to the correct observation of the morning break and treating the waitresses in the

---

[7] 'The little blackey'

local cafeteria with something approaching respect, be they Spanish or East European. I have yet to come across a business here that isn't overwhelmingly cosmopolitan. Ana's comment that it isn't real Spain is not over-dramatizing it. I'm still waiting to find out what real Spain is though.

Habitual, but discreet, smoking of weed is practiced by the crew. Darren and Ibrahim rarely miss an opportunity for a quick puff, but occasionally incur a threatening rebuke from Dmitri. More than once I see him partake in any case before resuming his bossing and chivvying of us all. Thus far I've ignored the offers. I don't want to go near memory lane just yet, and weed just feels like a backward step. I don't see Gary for days on end, he is perpetually glued to a mobile if I do see him, or snatching a quick call to me between meetings he runs to, all day, every day.

Two weeks in, late in the day, Gary's Audi brakes dramatically to a halt, dust spurting from irate wheels. The shirted figure, his mobile sizzling at his ear, makes a bee line for us, the aura of impending problems preceding him like film titles. He's off the phone and yelling for Dmitri, who duly appears from his office up on the mezzanine floor of the warehouse.

'Alright Gary, how's it going, you okay?' I offer tentatively.

'No I am fucking not' he rasps without making eye contact, 'where the hell is everybody? I want everybody here now! You too Gary. Dmitri!' he continues, pacing and checking his mobile, before taking Dmitri under the arm and all but marching him over to us. Once he has our attention, he starts in on whatever it is that is burning him up. I've never seen this Gary, not surprisingly, I can't imagine it's something clients would ever see. 'Which idiot spoke to Gonzalez and Garcia? Which one of you clowns spilled the beans about them not getting the contract to fit the interiors on the El Angel build?' Nervous looks flash between the crew; shrugs, mumbled denials and general vacantness. 'Did anyone here know the Swedes were getting that contract?' More wagging heads, the warehouse is a forest of question marks.

'What is problem, Gary?' asks Dmitri. 'Nobody here know nothing about contracts and things like that. This I know. Except maybe your brother.'

All eyes look at me, but Gary just shakes his head in disbelief. 'Dmitri, Gene just got off the boat. The only way he could know that is if I told him, and *why* would I, *of all people,* do that? Are you accusing me of that? You better know what you are saying Dmitri.'

'No, of course not, I mean he's new so maybe he…'

Dmitri doesn't appear to know where he's going with this.

'You got a problem with my brother working here? Do you want to talk to Holme about it?'

'No, of course not.'

'Good, then.' Gary and Dmitri are locked in a staring match, and despite Gary's evident seniority, Dmitri is playing some kind of weird game, some kind of agenda I don't get. I just know I have to watch my step with him. 'Right listen up everyone. Whether it came from this warehouse or somewhere else doesn't change anything. They got wind they weren't getting that contract, and as you know they've been building the stand for the fair in Madrid next week. We paid them in full upfront, so they've just decided to keep the money and walk off the job leaving us with our dicks hanging out, and a stand to build and deliver to Madrid in time. Naturally we'll sue their arses all the way to Gibraltar, but that doesn't help us now. Anyone has any bright ideas where we can get ourselves some labour? Carpenters, painters, shopfitters, those kinds of guys?'

'Yeah,' pipes up Darren, 'I know a couple of English guys who work on the film sets and that, it's the same kind of thing. They're used to working long hours and fast, I see them do it often.'

'Get on the phone to them now, find out their rates and I'll double it if I need to, but get them in here tonight. Dmitri, get this place ready to do this, make space, get all the tools we need. You'll all get paid for the overtime, but nobody goes home until it's finished, understood?'

There's a general groaning, but Dmitri is already marshalling everyone, and making everyone aware of his feelings about it. Gary indicates for me to follow him out to his car.

'Is there something going on with Dmitri? He seems to have an issue with you, or something.'

'That's putting it mildly, Gaz.'

'Well what? Tell me.'

'First he accused me of trying to take one of the other's jobs away, then he said he didn't want a spy in his warehouse.'

'His warehouse? That's nice.'

'He's a bit of an arsehole, but he hasn't given me any grief since that first day. Where did he come from?'

'Lebid, one of our main investors, wanted him running this side of things. And Lebid gets what Lebid wants, when you're paying for most of it, especially.' Gary seems uneasy about something. 'Just keep an eye out, let me know if you see or hear anything… iffy, odd.'

'So, you want me to be the spy Dmitri thinks I am. Great.'

'Shuttup, you'll live,' he laughs, 'Anyway, you've got work to do. Help Darren get the crew. See you in Madrid.'

'What?!' but he's already tearing off in his sleek white Audi.

~

The next few days can only be described as a sort of hell. Darren and I manage to corral a mixed bag of people, who all work in what they call the art department of a film crew. I agreed to pay them over the double Gary offered even, figuring we had little choice, and it was less than that prick Holme probably spends on Crystal in a week. In the end, no-one queries my insubordination, or even notices probably. The weekend disappears in a fug of angle grinding and welding fumes, drilling, hammering and painting. I end up being a sort of gopher, running around shops and ironmongers picking up all sorts of supplies and materials, floundering along with lists of

74

Spanish words I can barely pronounce. I am struck by the patience and generosity of the people who serve me, in getting to the bottom of what the order is. It isn't just because of the money I have in wedges in my bumbag, they genuinely appear to take pride in solving it. The art department crew are the best workers I have ever seen. Talented and innovative, they solve problems calmly and matter of factly. They work without cease, fuelled by beer and later in the night cocaine and/or Red Bull starts to appear, and seems to do the trick as we work till around four or five each morning. Sleep is fitfully grabbed on the multitude of beds and sofas in the vast furniture warehouse. After three days of virtually no sleep, the full stand, in its component pieces, is finished and ready for loading. Holme makes his inspection, strutting pompously around, picking at faults, cursing publicly the previous contractors, and slagging off some of the shortcomings of the final build, while skinny men and gym hard women in tight fitting suits from the marketing department tut and um and ahh. He looks about him, at the hollow faces staring blankly back at him, dirty jeans and bloodied, bandaged fingers on more than one person; at the level of sawdust, dirt, filings and all-round detritus, the piles of empty pizza boxes and beer cans. He stops, stares up at the ceiling, and then does something unexpected, something close to humility. He thanks everyone kindly and sincerely, takes out a wedge of notes and says, 'Now go and have a party you filthy fucking monkeys. Get some sleep, and see you in Madrid,' and he and the other management, Gary, Rafaela, the lawyer and accountants and the various marketing goons applaud, and then pick their way with designer shoe-clad feet through the mess, and off into the dawn.

Two hours later I am in the local cafeteria, which I have already come to appreciate as a national institution, the absolute backbone of the working nation, where a quiet breakfast on a Monday morning has turned into an unexpected bacchanal. The four hundred euros left by Holme is disappearing surprisingly rapidly. Serrano ham, pork fillet and roast green pepper toasted bread baps appear in great piles. Jugs of beer arrive continually on our table, and a couple of bottles of Jägermeister circulate. Various sweet delights are unpackaged from boxes and cabinets, and stranger alcoholic combinations are offered around. The camaraderie is genuine and welcome. Exhausted bodies cram as much fuel and tranquilising liquids into themselves as possible. The combination of gruelling hard work, endless hours, the filth and stench of machinery, chemical sprays, paint, glue and solvents has made my body into an aching, trembling shell, while my head is filled with helium, such is the effect of sleep deprivation. Into this has gone an enormous blast of carbohydrate and protein, alcohol and gas. I feel elevated, flattened out, light as a feather and heavy as a rock, barely able to move out of my seat, as I crease up in guffaws at the latest obscene story from one of the crew. Nothing I experienced in the music business was ever this intense or exhausting, and the high was always purely chemical and coalesced around beats of the music. Now I experience, through all of it, a kind of satisfaction and a sort of epiphany. Like I have arrived somewhere different, and despite the exhaustion I feel renewed and part of a group, who, despite the mickey taking, abuse and winding up, hold a simple affection and respect for each other. It is then, that I receive a thumping slap on my shoulder, and Dmitri grabs my chair and spins it around to face him. The group falls quiet. A suspense imposes itself on the gathering, no-one being sure what is about to be expressed. Dmitri is profoundly drunk, but still has an air of control, and still that ever present hint of menace he reserves for me. He raises his arm then points directly at me, drawing everyone's attention.

'You!' he intones ominously, 'You... are... a wanker.' His face is a mask, his arm is still, there is a collective intake of breath, and not inconsiderable sniggering. I am frozen in my seat; the first hints of adrenaline and fear are fighting through the porridge that is my blood. 'But you done good.'

A huge smile breaks over his face as he empties his vodka glass over my head. This is the cue for all the remaining drinks on the table to fly, and soon the manager has ushered us angrily out into the street, and the waitresses wearily tidy up, exclaiming and rabbiting on with the upturned palms gesturing in that already familiar way that represents so much here; exasperation, acceptance, intolerance, impatience, amusement. They bid us farewell, their annoyance only temporary, an occupational hazard, an indulgence like that of a mother toward her raucous young.

8

The Madrid fair is a different type of ordeal. Bodies have only added a hangover to the oppressive symptoms of exhaustion. Loading, travelling six hours and a further six hours of installation in the cavernous halls of the Madrid trade fair complex have drained what little was left. It is relentless. Once the set is built, the marketing people show up, turn on their plastic smiles, the lights go on, and a different world takes over. I am in the toilets, washing after having finished the final clearing up. The spacious, gleaming toilet area is full of two kinds of people: those in dirty workmen's' clothes, and those in the uniform of selling, the suits, the jackets, shirts, ties, and braces. There's a tension and brittleness about the suits. Their ordeal is about to begin, that of the manual labourers is over, until the break out in four days, when the hundreds of thousands of euros worth of lights, wood, plastics, steel, wiring, photos and carpeting all ends up in the enormous skips at the back of the vast hangars of the exhibition park. At least a couple are busy tapping and wiping their noses, trying to mask the incoming rush of the cocaine they need to propel them into the competitive hurly burly on the exhibition floor.

My crew are headed home mostly, but Gary has insisted I stay on and has booked me into his hotel, to help him out 'with a couple of things'. First though we have been summoned to the prayer meeting, as listed on the itinerary. Only on my arrival in the hired conference room do I understand this is a euphemism for a sort of team talk. I actually thought they might be doing some kind of praying! One never knows with business people. All the sales and PR staff are there in their suits and twin sets. The air is charged. Everyone is sat on the anonymous looking chairs these rooms always have, the world over. Conversation is all at an unnatural volume. People gesture robotically, exaggerated emphasis, like a room full of

Tourette's sufferers. Twenty plus people are present, waiting before a platform with a microphone at the front. It could easily be a modest little chapel, a church of the Gods of Realty. Holme enters from behind us, accompanied by Gary and the usual suited acolytes I recognise, but have no idea what their function is. What surprises me is that the sales people as one leap to their feet whooping, hollering and whistling, applauding their leader.

As he reaches the dais, he raises his arms for silence. He scans everyone in the room, with a half-smile, he nods approvingly at some of the clothing, and hair-styles among the women. He draws a breath theatrically, then starts in.

'What are we going to do?'

'Seeeeeellllllllllllll!!!' comes the roared response in unison.

'What are we going to make?'

'Loads of moneeeeeeeeey!!!' comes back the unified response even stronger.

'Who are you?'

'We are the stormtroopers of Holmeland!!!'

At this I want to explode into a great belly laugh, but Gary's glare from behind Holme stops me in my tracks. I am truly in an irony free zone, witnessing what, I thought, people only did in eighties movies. These guys just sell holiday apartments as far as I can gather.

Gary now steps up to the podium, to fill us in with the details of what the specific goals are of the event: who to target, who to ignore, how to discern the genuine leads from the fantasizers and wannabes. He mercifully lacks the preposterous theatricality, which makes his spiel all the more disturbing because he is completely sincere and committed to what he is saying, and its floridness is in contrast to Holme, but chilling in that he has an almost spiritual intensity about it.

'... we have the power to take that ordinary, everyday, humdrum reality and mould it. We create the spark that sets off the fire of their true, hidden desire. Where we fertilise in their mind the embryo of total fulfilment, of that nirvana of modern lifestyle. We peel away the scales that the endless dross of ordinary real estate publicity has layered onto their eyes, and reveal to them their own potential. How, thanks to us, thanks to our development philosophy, thanks to our structured, shared ownership payment plan, they can find that holy grail of our optimum life quality concept…'

The pauses are filled with shouts of agreement and enthusiasm. All that's missing is an organ and a choir in this new temple of property development. When I am in the warehouse, I see only bland collections of sub-Ikea, minimalist tat being shipped wholesale into the identikit golf boxes gathered around swimming pools in gated villages of sterile pseudo-Spain. But these guys are genuinely convinced this is the new Jerusalem. Gary is reeling off statistics on conversion rates, lead generation, margins, discounting policies, and who knows what else. It is double Dutch to me. He is a bubbling geyser of hard commercial information.

'You, what's your name, Gilchrist is it? What the *fuck* are you doing taking notes? These details are in your action pack, you'd know that if you'd looked at it on the train up here, you should have already memorised this. You look and listen to me, you listen to the mantra, you suck up every ounce of the power I am giving to you, and you believe it, and you can't do that with your head stuck in your palm pilot! I'll be watching you on the floor this morning, and if I don't see that hunger in your eyes, if I don't feel the heat of belief radiating from every pore of your body, you are walking back to Marbella with no job, right?'

The ritual humiliation is doubled down on by the others. 'C'mon pussy' 'Get it the fuck together Gilchrist', 'Come on man, sort your shit out', 'Don't let us down now…' and so on until Gary raises his arms for silence, a la Holme even.

'Go forth, and sell. Weave the dreams of these people's lives. Raise them up from the mundane, the predictable and sell them a life they haven't even learnt to contemplate yet. See you on the other

80

side.' The room erupts in more whooping and cheering, before quieting again, as Gary continues. 'A few administrative details. Expense vouchers are now available from Rafaela, who'll be on station in here each day. Do not exceed your personal allowance. If you need a client allowance, make sure we have their profile, and it better be a bloody good profile, because trust me I will scrutinise every last one of them back in Marbella. Anything I consider to be unjustifiable or misjudged will be doubled and deducted from this month's commissions. Rafaela will be very busy, too busy to deal with anything else, which is why we have Gene over here.' I look up, the gaze and scrutiny of the room makes me squirm. 'Gene will be your runner. If you need to send out for something, need a reservation or anything to do vis-a-vis clients, he will sort it out for you. He'll also be based in here for today at least. He's my brother so be nice to him, you ruthless bastards.' This gets a self-satisfied round of laughter, and looks of amusement.

'So, I'll have the cocaine snorting off the stripper's tits, please', pipes up one particularly tall square-jawed type as he saunters over to me.

'Are you being funny?' is my repost, as I can't bear to flatter him with laughter and I can't summon up anything bitterly sarcastic or satirical in time either. He leans into me, and pats my face with both palms of his hands, stooping to my height.

'You'll know when I'm being funny, Gene baby' he says and saunters out with the rest. I wait for Gary, once the room is quiet.

'Who the fuck does that tosser think he is?' Gary stares calmly at me.

'He's salesperson of the year, he cleared one hundred and twenty-eight K in the last twelve months. That's who he knows he is Gary, that's what we do here, we sell the dream and we make real money doing it.'

'So he hasn't realised he's a complete wanker yet, then?'

'Haven't you realised what this company is about yet? What I'm about?' He shows actual irritation for the first time in my short sojourn under his wings.

'And what's with being a goffer for the masters of the bleeding universe, I work in a warehouse.'

Gary slows his speech a bit, like I'm a child. 'You work for us. This is your job this week. Your boss is Holme. He pays your wages. That's what he wants you to do. Fill him in on everything, Rafaela. Give him three hundred euros in expense vouchers, on my account.' He turns back to me, a bit more human this time. 'Get over to that shopping mall across the service road there, and get yourself some decent clothes, you know, shirt with a collar, trousers, a belt, two sets. You gotta look the part, this isn't the warehouse Gene. Onwards and upwards.' He manages to squeeze out a smile, picks up his shiny brown leather attaché case and strolls out to marshal his troops.

Two hours later, I'm showered, smelling soapy and dressed as required. The clothes are non-descript and alien to me. I have consciously avoided anything in my life I perceived as 'straight-dom', whether socially or in employment terms. I have declined wedding invitations of some friends before now, purely on the basis of a dress code I didn't want to conform to. I have, in all my wobbly journey through life thus far, believed clothes don't maketh the man, but reveal his soul. If you dress in a suit, or corduroys, or torso hugging shirts, then you are merely conforming to an imposed agenda from whatever idiotic section of society is trying to crush you into its desired pigeon hole. Or worse, simply a corporate whore. I was able to get away with this world view in the rave scene. I had the luxury of wearing exactly what I wanted in all its slack-arsed, baggy, non-figure revealing, a-sexual, ripped up, washed-out, fabulously non-conformist, scruffy gloriousness. This nonetheless carefully cultivated and maintained aesthetic signalled my tribe: the 'I'm not part of the straight world, man' club. It afforded me a certain anonymity. Maybe that's all it was, just complete anonymity. I'm feeling anonymous right now though, and maybe that's a good thing. I'm embarrassed by how much psychic anguish I'm putting myself through just because of some clothes. No-one else cares or notices, as I fit seamlessly into the environment. If I was dressed in my usual fashion, I would be garnering disapproving and curious looks from all and sundry, as though a Big Issue seller had wandered into the halls. Would you buy a condo off *this* man? Horses for courses, as in all things, and for the first time in my adult life, I decide to let it go.

~

The stand itself, that we laboured on in a beer, pizza and drug fuelled frenzy for three days and nights is impressive, if ludicrous. Unlike most other stands around us, which rely on the time-honoured tropes of photos, slogans, branding, models of imagined houses and comfy chairs for clients to be wooed in, Holmeland is on an altogether different level. It is by far the biggest stand in the entire hall as far as I can see, and it occupies the central position at the apex of the two main avenues of access, so the confluence of people is optimum for sure. While most companies around us have opted for models, and videos of computer-generated real estate, Holmeland is a Disneyesque mini-world of golf, swimming pools, tropical palms, and Polynesian style beach huts. The whole thing wouldn't be out of place on the side of a beach. There's a water feature with real fish, a fountain, and copious tropical vegetation we trucked up from a garden centre in Fuengirola. The clients are delivered from the entrance to our portal via branded golf buggies, driven by cutesy girls from an agency, dressed up in golf attire, albeit sexy golf attire as the skirts are super short, and the polo shirts deep cut enough for a cleavage to make its mark. Holme certainly wants to be the Alpha male of the real estate world. Given how much cash went through my own hands during the build, and what they must be paying for the plot in the hall, it represents a humongous investment, especially when you add in the lavish expenses extended towards clients, and our own hotel bill in a four-star place of astoundingly stylish blandness.

I am busily occupied fetching coffees and refreshments, keeping publicity materials replenished, right down to sticking childish looking Holmeland stickers on all and sundry. The reps buzz about with their fixed smiles and automated hand gestures. Thanks to my close proximity to all of the hubbub I get an insight into what Holme actually sells. I realise my naivety, having assumed they just sold houses other people had built. No, Holme really is selling a brave new world, but one that doesn't yet exist. I am astounded, when the penny drops, that all of it, the golf courses, swimming pools, tennis courts, condo blocks, beach clubs, etcetera ad nauseum, are being sold 'off-plan' as the phrase goes. None of it has yet been built! The plans are more than that, they have lustrous colour brochures, portable mini laptops playing sophisticated computer-generated fly-throughs of this wonder world. I hear the reps spinning their webs of virtue around the financing, exclusively through Holmeland, who are privy to special mortgage rates, thanks to their own financing arm. It's exclusive to them. Which allows them to offer various fractional ownership packages, and woe betide anyone who utters the phrase 'time share'. So they, more often than not, are selling a shared property that hasn't been built yet. You owe the money not to a bank, but to Lebid Holme Finance Corporation SL. Plus you have to buy your furniture and fittings package directly from the catalogue. In short, he gives you everything and you are completely his child and client thereafter, and even when you've paid off the finance on your part owned building, you are still paying ground rent and services in perpetuity, but look what you get for it! The reps weave fantastical scenarios of an exclusive, inclusive lifestyle, untouched by the grubby realities of mass tourism, hermetically sealed away from the hoi-polloi behind twenty-four seven gated security. The social and sports club facilities, the creche, the on-site delicatessen, restaurants, lifestyle shopping. It's the *mot du jour* for sure, lifestyle this, that and the bleeding other.

The other word more in evidence than 'lifestyle' is 'investment'. It peppers every sentence and part of the business, to the point where I overhear at least two reps selling not the place, the property, but simply the purchasing of the first commitment. The financing deals are in instalments, and it appears perfectly kosher, and in fact actively encouraged, to sell on your non-existent fantasy lifestyle part-owned flat on a golf course, before it has even started to be built. Because that's where the maximum profit is available. At current inflation rates your 'investment' will have accrued at least 25% before you have to cough up the second instalment. Which of course you could re-invest in phase two, 'flipping' those purchases to allow a bigger investment still in phase three, and maybe other Holmelands due to come on stream in Bulgaria, Morocco, Cape Verde, Barbados, Brazil and even South Africa. I have a ringside seat to watching ordinary, retired or middle-aged couples with a certain amount of middle-management, company pension affluence, being spun into global property investors with an extensive portfolio on three continents. And it is actually happening, the papers are being signed in front of me. A firm of lawyers, Ana amongst them, beaver away at the back of the stand with ready prepared documents for various national jurisdictions. Successful signees are whisked away on Golf carts, with the rep clutching a handful of high value expense vouchers from Rafaela, no doubt to crack a bottle of Crystal and some special *jamon* in a nearby *bodega*.

Gary dives around, polishing off rep's pitches personally on occasion, the evidently senior person flattering the client's sense of importance. He is ceaseless, his focus total, his sincerity seemingly genuine, no signs of help from Mr Charlie, as I pick up from others.

I watch the money-go-round from within myself, outwardly doing the fixed smile and completing the mundane tasks demanded of me. The whole thing has been fascinating, as well as horrifying.

As someone with zero personal assets, partner or family to please, and no desire to live a self-contained, neutered existence in a golf bubble in a country whose very existence is rendered down to the level of an amusing, scenic backdrop, I cannot relate in any way to what is being sold. Even the naked appeal to greed of the process of borrowing, flipping, speculating and cashing in leaves me cold, as that naked profiteering appears illusory or highly risky at best. I at least have a clear picture now of the full machine, and how my job in the warehouse is a tiny cog down the bottom near the exhaust pipe. In my own smug way, I pity the people trooping in. I can't imagine why anyone would arrive at the point of wanting a Holmeland shared rabbit hutch to live in. It completely escapes me, but, and this makes me laugh out loud to myself, the entire system, around Marbella at least, appears to be devoted to this. I incur a couple of warning flashes of eyes from the reps close to me, and bury my contempt a little deeper.

The day winds down, the last handshakes are made, the last backs are slapped, the last papers slip in and out of attaché cases. Reps are busy poring over paperwork, deals and contracts, choices of furniture packs, module numbers on actual plans of the imaginary world. Gary comes over to me as I'm tidying up the detritus of plastic champagne flutes that were in increasing evidence as they day wore on.

'So what do you think?' he beams at me.

'Er... yeah, amazing. Very impressive,' I manage to piece together something approaching positivity. 'It seemed busy, and I kind of have an idea what it is you are all selling now, it's beginning to make sense, so to speak.' I laugh a little too falsely to hide the fact I'm glossing over what I really think.

'We sold 26% of the first phase of El Angel, and have pledges and pending deals for another 18%. Lead generation is also going way above projection. And the good thing is we don't have to hang around for the various banks in umpteen different countries, we can get that financed directly, and that means we can pretty much start construction within a month. Just a few loose ends to tie up,' and he bites his lower lip as though the loose ends are more than metaphorical. 'So, seriously what do you think?' He's matter of fact this time, he's clocked my fake enthusiasm. I think for a moment and decide to tell him like I see it, up to a point.

'Well, I'm amazed you can sell shit that hasn't been built yet. And I don't understand the whole thing about golf and lifestyle, to me that's like, no style. I mean, golf! What is it with golf?'

Gary laughs at my frankness, indulgently. 'Yeah, it's a bit of a closed book to you I imagine. Golf is the most significant driver of the economy on the coast. Golfers spend more per head than anyone else, golf developments are easier to sell, hold their value better. The profits on the golf properties pay for the construction of the actual golf course, it's a win-win. Basically, golf is the new golden goose.'

'Do you play? Don't tell me you play golf, please don't.'

'Well of course I play. When I can, which isn't often.' I'm bemused. 'It's a business thing. Social… business thing. When in Rome…'

'Bloody hell, you live the life, act the part to the last detail, right?'

'That's about it. Once we've wrapped this development up though, I can take my foot off the gas. We're nearly there with it. There's a lot going on right now and,' he regards at me, with an expression that's half apologetic, uncomfortable, 'this affects you as well.'

'How do you mean? I'm gonna get rich as well, hahaha.'

'Yeah, ok, joking aside. This is a big push, this development. We have a co-investor, without whom we'd never get it off the ground. He's Lebid, the Ukrainian owner of the warehouse, very big in oil and gas, like so many of them, you know the story.'

'Chelsea football club type story?' I semi-sneer, my disgust for football knows no bounds, especially since its elevation to an over-moneyed quasi-religion.

'Not quite in that league, but yeah, thereabouts. He's here, and we have to show good sales, we wouldn't want him to pull out. His entourage need entertaining tonight and we have to look after them. I'm going to need you around, and for a couple of other errands.' He has his hand on my shoulder and his proximity is close, Spanish style. To a Brit it feels invasive, over intimate, but I see Spaniards in this hall, back in Marbella, doing the hand on the shoulder intimate personal space thing all the time. It's unusual Gary is doing it as I haven't seen any other Europeans work that way.

'Shit Gaz, it's time for a beer, aren't we done yet?' I sound like a whiney child.

'The client is always right and money never sleeps. Two clichés for the price of one, brother, c'mon let's go. Leave all of that for the cleaners, we're out of here.'

'Okay, you da boss,' I mock but follow dutifully.

~

I'm in a taxi with Gary somewhere on a busy, hellish spaghetti of roads heading toward the centre of Madrid. After the light and fresh air of Marbella, Madrid is a stocky, grubby cousin, with a forty a day habit. The weather is decidedly chilly, the traffic intense, and the taxi driver swerves, brakes, honks and grumbles his way through the mayhem. We tip out and enter a cramped tapas bar, Gary ordering a string of incomprehensibles as we are taking our seats at the short bar. A layer of tooth picks, paper napkins and general detritus litter the floor. The waiters weave and dive amongst each other, serving the constant hum of customers, the coffee machine screams and snorts, the clash and clink of cups, saucers and cutlery is constant, as is the shouting and confirmation of orders. Everyone seems in a hurry, and the staff oblige with a rhythm of service that is frenetic and consistent. It's remarkably different from down south I say to Gary.

'Ahh, you've noticed. Yeah Madrid is another planet to Andalucía. You know the Madrileños say Africa starts just south of here. That's their way of saying the Andaluces are really Moroccans and a bunch of lazy, thieving, work-shy lay-abouts.'

'Oh nice, a bit racist don't you think?'

'Yes, that kind of chauvinism is still rampant, especially amongst the *pijos*. They've all got their Philipino domestics, their Latino gardeners and cleaners, it's the same the world over, mate. The Spanish are just a bit more open about it. It's the same in Kensington, trust me.'

'I've noticed the locals address Ibrahim in the warehouse in ways that would get you in deep shit in south London.'

'Yeah, more than likely. I couldn't live in this town' continues Gary, 'It's great at night but the weather's hellish, either freezing or baking hot. The people are uptight until after 8pm, and it's like a frantic version of the rest of Spain with the space and the fresh air taken out. I still prefer it to London, mind.'

'The people look different, more European, like us actually' I observe.

'Bang on again. Much less Moorish influence here. Down south we stick out for sure like the *guiris* we are, but here we could pass as locals. Maybe Africa really does start down the road' he laughs.

'What is this *guiri* thing, I've been called it plenty of times and I don't know if I am supposed to be offended.'

'A *guiri* is the Spanish slang for a foreigner. One that sticks out for being obviously foreign and oblivious to Spanish ways. Your average tourist in Marbella. I think it's a historical name that was repurposed to deal with all the foreigners who make no effort to adopt the language or customs. It's really so they just remind you, you are not one of them. Spanish. I wouldn't take offence at it.'

'OK, I freely confess to being a *guiri*, can't speak the language, haven't a clue what's going on, but I can do a bit of *mañana* if required. Comes naturally.'

'Daft bugger. Listen, we've got fifteen minutes before we go to meet Holme and Mr Lebid. Nice to have a breather.' His phone rings, but Gary checks the number and ignores it. Fifteen minutes is as much time as I've had alone with my brother so far, apart from our first day.

'What's the score tonight then,' I ask.

'Ok, so Lebid is the principal co-investor in El Angel. He's also the supplier of the mortgage financing. But as he's such a ball breaker, he demanded a percentage of certain revenue streams within the development, as a sweetener, to come in with the finance.'

'Which was what?'

'The furniture package operation. He insisted on having 50% stake, and all future sales should have a binding clause to purchase the furniture packs. The profit is locked in.'

'But that's a bit of a bummer if you don't like our furniture, and let's face it, it's bloody awful most of it, so soulless- ' and I stop myself, realising I'm probably not supposed to say that.

Gary laughs. 'I know, I know, it's pretty bloody awful, but it's got the best margins of anything we do. If the client doesn't like it, we offer a buy back policy, which keeps them happy, and keeps Lebid happy.'

'I've never seen any of that stuff come back in,' I counter.

'No of course not. We have a subsidiary doing that completely on the side, no contact with your department. It's our liability, so Dmitri doesn't care.' The penny drops again. I'm having plenty of pennies drop these days.

'So Dmitri is actually Lebid's man?'

'Yup, now you're getting the picture.' I'm not sure whether Gary's genuinely flattering me or being patronising, I'm so clueless on the grand scheme of things. He's being remarkably tolerant of me all things considered, as he's no idea how I'll perform, if I'm reliable or not, and the stakes are pretty high. I'm about to find out just how high. 'However, I convinced Holme to make a counter demand, as we were putting so much money into his pocket. I mean he stands to make way more than we do even.'

'You played hard ball with your biggest investor?'

'Of course. Only way to get respect. We have to have the planning signed off with the Marbella politicos, and it's Lebid's job to make them happy. This fair, this whole development is a template. It will be fairs in all major Ukrainian, Russian and Eastern bloc cities. We'll be selling Holmeland like hell to the whole of Eastern Europe, and beyond that China, if we fully sell these three phases. The sky really is the limit, so you can see how the pressure is on us.'

'Christ, I'm surprised you want me around in all of this. I'm not exactly qualified.'

'Actually', Gary punches me on the upper arm 'Holme likes you. He's impressed, how you rose to the challenge of the set build, how you got down, fitted in, and didn't come a cropper with Dmitri. Not everyone has got on in there. The current crew seem stable and unified, which is a first. I like to be in control, and know everything about what we do. Dmitri and the furniture are the one area I don't have a one hundred percent comfort factor with.' Yet another penny drops.

'Hence spy in the warehouse. Why would Dmitri be unhappy with that? Has he got stuff to hide?'

Gary regards me expressionlessly. Matter of factly he says, 'It was Holme's idea, not mine. I didn't want to put you into that position, but I thought I'd at least let you have the option. And there was nothing else to offer you, so it's not all bad. And as for Dmitri? If there is something, I don't know what it is.'

'What's the next step?'

'We have a couple of issues to wrap up with the town hall, and once we have the building permits solid, Lebid and Holme will lock down the mortgage financing, which gives us a massive competitive edge. A buyer doesn't have to worry about how to get the money from a bank, we are the developer and the bank.'

'Doesn't that complicate things?'

'Yes and no. Lebid has massive cash reserves he needs to use in profitable ways. So he's gone into mortgage finance, via his part owned bank in Hong Kong. By going in with us, he gets a steady stream of clients for his loans.'

I've never seen beyond the economies of concerts and raves, hire of sound equipment, plus my side-line, the profit margin of which turned into several years in Strangeways. It's alarming, my younger brother on the bridge and at the wheel of this vast ocean liner of property speculation.

'Are you comfortable with your business partner? Do you trust Lebid?'

Gary let's out a long breath and pulls on his beer. 'Well, I figure he has as much to lose as we do, and he can't do it without us, so it's a bit like the cold war, if one of us falls out and goes for the other it's a case of mutually assured destruction. And anyway, I don't get much say.'

'Seriously?' I'm surprised at this admission, but also the slightly deflated way Gary expresses it, it's the first chink I've seen in the otherwise supremely confident front he puts up daily.

'Yeah, Holme isn't one for sharing or listening to junior opinions. He is, unlike myself, absolutely one hundred percent convinced of his own invincibility in this. Which, at times, worries me.' I'm actually surprised by the frankness Gary is suddenly displaying, and my rapt interest and surprise tone waken his discretion again. 'Anyway, forget what I just said. Anything I ever say to you is because you're my brother and is in complete confidence. Apart from Ana, I don't have anyone else close I feel I can talk to. Marbella is a goldfish bowl, and we are the biggest fish in that wee small bowl, so it's difficult to let your guard down, ever.

The whole world is peering in all the time; the press, the competition, the government, the police-'

'The police' I interrupt, 'why would they be interested in real estate? I thought Holme was completely kosher, that's the spin, right?' There's a creeping alarm within, being somewhat over-paranoid, since my initiation into the club of the criminally convicted. Gary's reaction surprises me. Maybe it's the anonymity of a crowded bar in a side street in Madrid, out of the goldfish bowl for a minute.

'Marbella is the most corrupt town on the planet' he says emphatically but quietly. 'Everything we do has to be approved by the town hall. They have no planning regime that is legally approved by the central government. Jesus Gil ripped it up years ago, and they make it up as they go along. If you want to build, you pay the man, and the lawyers and the whole system goes along with it and pretends it is business as usual. It *is* business as usual. Every town in Spain is the same to some extent, except Marbella has been doing it for so long and for so much money…' he trails off staring absently at the bubbles sliding up his glass, as though for a minute he is outside himself, gazing at the goldfish bowl and seeing all of it, for real, maybe for the first time.

'Ana said something like that to me. About how the whole system was on the take.' I try to console. Gary snorts in grudging recognition.

'She's right. Half the properties she's conveyancing are probably illegal in reality. But the system turns a blind eye. The government tried to get Gil a few years back, but that was for football corruption when he owned Atletico Madrid, rifling taxpayers' funds to prop it up. He got six months but never served a day, and died before they could ever force the issue. He left his proteges behind and they have basically carried on the same regime, but of course everything goes into their pockets.'

'But who is Sorzano? Everyone mentions him when they complain about the politicians. Have I seen him?'

'Yes, you saw him first night in that restaurant. And you'll meet him.'

'Eh?!' My concern is genuine, I have no desire to be around this style of high-class criminality, it's something I can't get my head around, which makes it all the more threatening.

'Errand number two.' Gary eyes me directly, unblinking. 'Holme has instructed me to send you to Sorzano's Finca with a delivery, accompanying Darren. You will map read and just be there to make sure all is fine.'

The alarm in my stomach has turned to a sort of hi-tempo drum and bass track, thrashing cymbals and multiple beats punching up to my rib cage and trying to find a way out through my throat.

'Why me? Why the fuck me? I'm not doing anything illegal, Gary, you *know* where I've been.'

'Whoa, it's okay, it's not an illegality that you need to worry about. It's just business. Marbella business.'

'What the...' but I don't find words to express the shock, fear, and indignation of this imposition, by my own brother. It feels like a betrayal.

'Gene, let go of my arm', I'm back in the room, and I have Gary's upper arm in a fierce grip. I draw a deep breath and try to collect my thoughts. This vast business, its dubious legality of a nature I don't fully grasp, with partners of suspect origin and credibility, swims before me. 'I need you on this,' continues Gary, 'I need to know I can rely on you. You turned up here unannounced and I made it work for you, I put you back on your feet.' I move to protest, but Gary puts an index finger to my face, as though to stop my lips right there. 'You put me in a spot, you did, and you rattled Holme at a sensitive moment when adverse publicity, ammunition in the hands of the wrong people, could have been difficult. Like it or not, Holme has wiped your arse and now he wants to use you as he sees fit. Quid pro quo.'

'He doesn't fucking own me.' I growl back. The finger again.

'He *does*. He owns all of us. As long as you take his money, that's the deal. This isn't an ordinary job, or an ordinary company. Marbella has its own logic. Dirty money brings all sorts with it. It's full of gangsters, shake down artists, and of course ruthless businessmen, who use the lack of proper fiscal and planning regulation to make themselves exceedingly rich indeed. We have to deal with the world as we find it, not as we'd like it to be. Here, we have to play by Marbella rules, and there's only another couple of hands to play until we have the game sown up. We come out the other side. Rich.'

'You mean you get rich, I-'

Gary grabs my shoulders and his face is right in mine, his forehead leans on mine, 'Gene, this is good for all of us. You're on the inside, you're one of us, I've got your back, and you will do well out of this. If you stay on for the ride, you'll do very well, trust me. If you decide to bail next week, you'll walk away with a bit of cash in your pocket, but to what? Next step?' He draws back, sees the confusion and anger in my eyes. The swamp and its clammy hold is sucking me towards its dark heart. I have to be still, calm, try and see things clearly, for if I thrash and flail I will sink without trace in the mire.

'Gary, I appreciate everything that's happened, just don't try and get me to run before I've barely stopped crawling, ok?'.

'It's just driving down to Sorzano, and delivering a present for him, then he works his magic, and we all get rich. Simple.'

I'm aware of an attractive woman looking at us with her head tilted, as though amused. 'Catching up on some quality time, brothers?' It's Rafaela. 'The car's outside, let's go, Lebid is heading for the club.' And we are off.

Gary, Holme and I are driving to a rendezvous. Through the dark windows, a dense, unfamiliar cityscape rolls by. I climb out of the black Mercedes 500 series. It's a narrow street I now see, in an older part of the city. A discreet door in an anonymous facade opens to us. A second dark Mercedes pulls up from which climb four fairly straight looking, but burly business men. One of them I recognise now, fooled momentarily by the smart suit. Dmitri. My insides flip involuntarily, and the swamp pulls at them. Gary and Holme greet the tallest of the men who I assume is Lebid. No one makes an attempt to introduce me. I stand further back from the group, trying to melt into the wall. I'm far enough back to not hear their conversation, but at some point, I am obviously mentioned as heads turn toward me, and two of the Ukrainian party nod in obvious acknowledgement of something pertaining to my presence here. Another car pulls up, a rather tatty saloon, and to my surprise Darren is at the wheel. From the gesticulations of the group of men, I figure some kind of arrangements are being squabbled over. It's not angry but neither is it casual. Gary is on his phone, and scribbling something onto a card or paper scrap, I can't tell. Holme hands him an envelope, then he makes his way over to me. His face says all is well, he's happy, it's a good night out, but I can see the unusual rigidity in his body. He's on edge.

'Gene,' he says giving me a good slap on the shoulder, like all this is perfectly normal, 'You are going to take these two gentlemen, Mr Lebid's assistants, to the address on the paper. Show it to the driver. Here's some float money to meet their expenses, I don't need any receipts. Put this number into your mobile. Any trouble on the journey, call this number. They will deal with any problems you might have.' He looks at me meaningfully. 'When they've had their fun, you and Darren will go with them to collect the present for Sorzano. Darren has all the details. He's already picked up your stuff from the hotel.'

'Gary, if this 'present' is what I think, why doesn't Dmitri take it to Sorzano?'

'Gene, think. Your previous business.'

'Thanks, I know, that's why I asked.' Darren and I are pawns. Nobodies. Expendables, at the bottom of the pile. I reluctantly place the envelope and note inside my jacket, and Gary gives me a casual pat and heads back to the group. I am raging inside, a mixture of fear, indignation and disbelief. I am being forced onto a stage in a dingy theatre I don't recognise, playing a role in a scene I didn't audition for, and I haven't learnt the lines or been shown the script. I'm sucking it up, biting my tongue, because I don't know what other options are open to me, in a strange city, surrounded by people I am dependent on, and forces I have no control over. I dearly want to just be back in the hotel with a club sandwich, mini-bar vodka and bad German pornography. Which is sometimes rather good, I remember from the previous night. I have to snap out of this momentarily pleasant dreamscape. Two Ukrainian men head for the Mercedes, I climb in the back and we move, apparently following Darren. 'Hola' I say, not knowing what language to speak 'I'm Gene'. They nod politely, smiling.

'Yevgeny.'

'Vladimir' comes the reply.

So that's the formalities done and we settle in silence into the journey to who knows where. I put the number Gary gave me into my mobile. I can only dread the circumstances under which I'll need it. I have no idea whose number it might be.

In about fifteen minutes, we pull up outside a carbuncular office block on the edge of an industrial estate. It would look like any dull office on a trading estate, but for the huge red neon heart sign on the roof, flashing, and the various pink and green neon tubes framing the blocked-out windows. It's a brothel, one of the more glamorous commercial kinds, rather than the smaller local ones. We enter through a lobby of dizzying, flashing lights to a security desk and scanner. This triggers much beeping and Yevgeny and Vladimir, after a short conversation with the doorman, take out and hand over their handguns. Back slapping and jokes follow, the doorman is Ukrainian, but this goes no way to appeasing the fear that knowing my guests are armed has induced. We proceed through to a cavernous, ordinary nightclub with its booths, balconies, tables, swirling lights, pounding techno and long bar. It could be anywhere in the world. What sets it apart perhaps is that the females are all of one sort, scantily clad, voluptuous and provocative. It's not unlike some of the clubs in Amsterdam I remember from the bad old days, except for the scale and number of girls around. We are seated, at a table at the edge of the dance floor and my friends order, to the waitress who also appears to speak Ukrainian. Or it could be Russian, I have no way of telling, but certainly they are doing more communicating than I am. Who is looking after who I wonder? I am greatly relieved when Darren appears, grinning like a Cheshire cat, and barely able to contain his excitement. My guests nod approvingly and we settle in. Girls circulate constantly, swaying past us, stretching and posturing to the music in various ways that produces yet another stress on my already overloaded system. A bottle of some fancy vodka I've never heard of appears, along with mixers and ice bucket, plus a small silver box. The waitress, topless and wearing some kind of bizarre fur fringed bikini bottom with a head dress of some forest animal hands me a check. It's for six hundred euros and I feel a stab of alarm, then remember the envelope in my pocket. I hastily rip it open and to my intense relief find a good number of one hundred-euro notes, and I peel off the requisite amount.

We make a toast and drink a couple of stiff shots each. I'm aware of a pain coursing through my neck and shoulders. I am so tense; I try to release my torso and hunker down into the chair a bit. Darren is jumping up and down with excitement, to the great amusement of Yevgeny and Vlad. They open the silver box, revealing about two grams of white powder, obviously cocaine. They both calmly chop a line each and look at me expectantly. I am confused and stare blankly back at them half terrified of giving the wrong response, but I'm lost. Darren leans over and bellows in my ear above the din.

'Give 'em a fuckin' banknote ya dickhead'. With a colossal sense of relief and pitiful fumbling I hand over a note. Once they've finished, they chop the remainder and offer it to us. I decline, but Darren looks at me, as though asking permission. When he sees my face, staring back, clueless, he laughs and snuffles it up. He gives me a good-humoured punch in the ribs, as though I'm the dumb, speccy, uncool kid of the class. Yevgeny leans over and retrieves the note from Darren's hand and waves it at the waitress who sweeps by, placing it into her hairy bikini, mouthing '*spaceyba bolshoi*[8]', that much Russian I have picked up in our warehouse. A short word in the ear of the waitress and moments later an African girl with magnificently generous hips, in a ludicrous Tarzan type of outfit sways over, accompanied by a tall, pale, thin Scandinavian looking girl, who conversely is dressed as though going to a garden party: straw boater, short white summer dress under which protrude white fishnet stockings and gaily coloured suspender belt. The attempt to dress up the obvious, and dramatize it with cheesy costumes, makes an already lurid and seedy performance spill over into the surreal, as the girls attempt to play out their chosen characters, turning on the routine of faux attraction and arousal. Tarzan/Jane adds some hip gyrations and afro-ized erotic dance moves, while Alice in Wonderland stretches her skinny long legs into contorted positions, a bizarre rendition of ballet dancer lost in the wrong hallucination. I stare literally open-mouthed at this other-worldly display, the absurdity of which is completely bypassing my new friends, as their hands search around and over the merchandise, whose smiles all the while are wide, but the light in their eyes is off.

After a brief display, the waitress reappears and they nod their approval. They get up and, arms around their conquests, they head for

---

[8] Thank you very much

99

a door at the end of the dancefloor that has a great garish neon heart glowing around it. There must be several floors of rooms above the dance floor. Another check appears, and the waitress waits, fixing me with a blank stare. It's for four hundred euros this time, and I fiddle with the envelope. I'm such a dork when I least need to be. Darren doesn't hide his amusement. Gary must have checked the prices of his guests' desired wishes in advance because the money is bang on. He knew that girls are cheaper than vodka in this madhouse. Darren and I settle in to finish the vodka, watch the girls go by and wait.

After a few short, bellowed exchanges in each other's ears above the din, I give up bothering to converse and settle down to endure the unexpected and unwanted sojourn. The effect of the noise and the lighting, and the strange half-hearted erotica being acted out to further incoming clients is disorientating. I find myself very much a spectator of myself, highly conscious of being within my own head and skin, staring out through a pair of eyes that are someone else's, but distant and detached as the exaggerated stimuli around start to meld and mush into something indistinct and primeval. It's a vision of hell as a strip club, a suburban post-industrial Hironimus Bosch painting, complete with multinational gargoyles, the up-lighting of the low tables making garish and Halloween-like ghouls of the faces around them. Everything seems so crass, so desperate, so tawdry, and yet so familiar. A dissonance I can't fathom until it dawns on me, with some embarrassment, I am experiencing this sober, straight. Seeing it without the aid of narcotics. Without the intermediary of MDMA or ecstasy there to channel the sounds and lights into the heart of my brain chemistry. Swirling the two into a tight embrace, whirling incessantly and parasitically into a warm throbbing mush, sending its fizzing tendrils through all of my nervous system, winding my muscles and limbs around its childishly repetitive beats. Without that chemical crutch which I have leaned upon all of my adult life, until Her Majesty intervened, the whole experience is completely alien and inexplicable. The music is metallic and repellent, the

100

characters around me, mere grotesques in a squalid sexual pantomime. Darren suddenly swipes me, bringing me back into the real time.

'What the fuck you laffin' at?'

I have a dumb disbelieving grin all over my face. I drain the vodka and tonic and prepare another one.

'Nowt. It's just funny that's all. It's a freak show, completely nuts.'

Darren looks at me askance, he's too hooked on the flesh show to be able to take even a slight step back.

Now my mind goes back to the actual last time I was in a club. *That night*. It must be nearly three and a half years, what with the time spent on remand before they got around to the tedium of the trial. Plea bargains aplenty, some people sang like canaries and got protection and all the joys of the state's gratefulness. It meant that it was much easier for me to avoid incriminating people, as several of my associates had sold out anyone they could. I just had to fess up, 'it's a fair cop, guvner' and do my time.

That night I think we'd done ketamine, after the usual feast of ecstasy and Dutch weed, and maybe I had taken a trip as well, hard to say now. It'd been a successful run we thought. We were celebrating in the only way we knew how. Our road crew are in some evil smelling club, lost in the Essex hinterland holed up in the chillout dive bar where the DJ's and the liggers hang out, conspicuously taking drugs. In come the uniformed plods leading the way, truncheons waving, yelling, their stab vests strutting, their belts encumbered by the apparatus of repression and detainment. I remember laughing. Laughing fit to bust, I thought I was watching a movie, I thought it was a convincing but extravagant practical joke using actors, because they were so good at it. I laughed on, even as I was screamed at to stand up against the wall, and I carried on laughing up at the plods in the funny costumes and big sticks. When the baton hit my ribs, then my upper thighs, my knees, I remember the pain at first was like slow motion. It was deep, muffled and uncertain, like in a dream when you run, but your legs are like treacle. The nervous system was hiding, snickering behind the tree in the park, and then the adrenalin came running up and started banging me on the back of my head and wham, whole waves of stomach churning pain welled up as if the whole club had been dropped into a cold, flooded quarry and the waters came slooshing in, horribly engulfing everything.

I remember lying on the concrete of a cell floor, vomiting, my body reacting to the contradictions of ecstasy, adrenalin, pain, fatigue, dehydration, confusion and then, properly, in full gleaming high-definition technicolour 3D letters six miles high, there it was. Fear. I remember slumping over the interview table, trembling, comedown freeze up, blubbing like a toddler, tears and snot streaming out of me as the detectives handed me Kleenex, laughing in disdain and contempt. I blurted out as little as I could get away with, and they didn't seem to press me. I was more a subject of amusement, as the awful realisation coalesced through the tears. This was real, serious shit. What started as a laugh, a dare, a distraction, the logical extension of consuming copious amounts of recreational drugs, had led me to this pathetic puddle of humanity in a police cell. Scared shitless. And the horrible realisation, that the party was unquestionably, definitively, over.

The traumatic flash back hovers, superimposed in my mind's eye on the current scene. My heart is racing and I'm trembling. Darren is looking at me again, but worried this time. Well, more worried about me than for me, as he glances around, trying to get the measure of my transformation. The silver box on the table catches my attention again. I flip it open, there's a good line left, and I calmly wipe it onto my forefinger and rub it all gently into my gums and slump back. Darren stares, not sure what to make of me now. I feel the surge of positivity, my mind lightens and the smoke clears. The beasts of paranoia and fear, their thrashing tails, lolling tongues and saliva dripping jaws, are dragged backwards, sucked into the floor by the power of an alkaloid extraction of a common South American shrub. But even that is not enough to disguise the elephant in the room. The swamp. The one I thought I'd escaped. The bad people, the scary people, the people who are not fazed by hurting others, the people who have ice in their hearts, nine millimetres in their jackets and cocaine on their mirrored coffee tables. I offered my humility, I ate my pride, I came back to ask forgiveness, to start again, to mend what was left of our fractured family, to try and find calm, clarity, to clear the grey smoke that infests my life and my soul. Hi Gary, long time no see, and in a few hops, skips and jumps, I'm sitting with Ukrainian armed gangsters, taking coke in a freaky brothel somewhere in the arse end of Madrid. Thanks to the cocaine the incongruity of this state of affairs doubles me up with laughter. I am a whole lot better now. I'll trade a bit of cocaine to lay the fear to rest, at least for a few hours. Then who knows, I might get to go back to a warm bed and a telly, and fuck all this crazy shit. Darren still appears confused and nonplussed and is about to say something when the two Ukrainians lumber up.

They show no signs of having had any form of experience at all in the preceding half-hour, indeed they look as though they might have spent the time reading the paper on the bog for all the difference it makes to their demeanour. A jerk of the head signals us to follow, and Darren glances at me to check I am going to be normal, a hint of anxiety telling in his slightly jerky, over enthusiastic movement. He appears boyish and young, out of his depth. Glad it's not just me.

We follow them out, uncertain of what will happen next. As we turn away from the cars, and start to head behind the building, Darren and I exchange glances. We don't need to say anything, our eyes say it all. The lumbering figures lead us between a high mesh fence and the steel cladding of the block, security cameras peering down from corners and posts at us. A door appears in the side of the building. Yevgeny punches a code in and a series of locks open. Wherever we are, someone has spared no expense to protect the place.

We are beckoned down the stairs into a basement room to nothing more prosaic than a fairly ample underground office, which calms me slightly.

'Sit. Wait' intones Vladimir. The pair of them disappear through another security door, with yet another code and multiple locks. The office isn't empty. A middle-aged woman sits disconsolately in front of a computer monitor. She lifts her gaze momentarily, then returns to whatever absorbs her. I have no idea if she speaks English, so I maintain my silence. Darren and I sit, basically staring at the ceiling in anticipation. After how many minutes I don't know, such is the cacophony of thoughts and static noise in my head, they reappear, each carrying a holdall. We stand up. Yevgeny opens each one. Inside are bundles of used notes, euros, of all amounts, even some purple ones, the mythical Bin Ladens, five hundreds. He lifts out a bindle. The paper wrapping goes around it, in both directions, so one can't remove a note without breaking the seal. It is stamped and numbered.

'See. Numbers. We check. They check when you deliver. Understand?' he says in the heavily accented monotone, that is as chilling as it is comical.

'Understood.' And then some reflex idiotic curiosity prompts me, 'how much in total?' Yevgeny leans forward slightly, looking me in the eye.

'Not your business.'

'Shut the fuck up!' hisses Darren as quietly as he can.

Vladimir laughs, then regards me, 'Like he says, shut the fuck up.' He opens the bags up fully to reveal the wads of notes. Yevgeny meanwhile has taken out a tiny digital camera and takes several shots of us standing next to the holdalls. And a close up shot of each of our faces. I'm not sure what purpose this ritual serves, other than to intimidate. I curse my brother deeply for placing me in this moment. The anger produces a solid knot in my throat and allows me to forget how plain scared I am. 'You drive. We follow, we watch. You have details of address?' He is addressing Darren.

'Yeah, sure, it's all sorted. Got it.' He's managing to sound normal, but his darting eyes say otherwise. Yevgeny has put the camera back in a drawer, and in its place puts a cardboard box on the desk. It has a red ribbon around it. Incongruous to say the least.

'Present for Señor Sorzano. Pick up, let's go.'

Both of us stare at it, immobile, each thinking the same, what the fuck is in the box!? All sorts of possibilities career through my mind. I can't move.

'For fuck's sake, you wet streak of piss' hisses Darren again, and picks it up. Yevgeny smirks at this, adding humiliation to the rich smorgasbord of negative emotions for the evening.

We follow the pair out again, and I'm lugging the surprisingly heavy bags, while Darren gingerly cradles the little box in his hands. Holdalls go in the boot. Darren is about to bring the box into the car. It's my turn to hiss at him.

'Don't bring that in the car! It could be anything.'

'Like what?!'

'Like…' my overheated brain races around to give from and clarity to my paranoia. 'I dunno, a grenade maybe?'

'What?' says Darren in disbelief. His contempt is clear on his face, but I can't press home my theory.

'You drive!' comes a bellow from Yevgeny, and we leap hastily into the car and head off.

We are making our way through the suburbs of Madrid gradually. It's just another urban jungle like so many others. I definitely prefer the coast and its mountains, the sea always close, the palms. I'm sitting rigid, with the box on my lap. Mind racing.

'Are you still shitting yourself because of that box?' Darren is laughing, humiliating me further.

'Well, what is it then?'

'None of our fucking business that's for sure.'

105

'Bollocks, I'm having a look.'

'Your funeral, mate. Dickhead.'

This is stupid. I untie the silly ribbon and I thrust my hand in, impatient, as though the contents of this box are the summary and definition of my fate in this mad, beautiful land. I pull up a large ornate jar, with a ceramic lid, wax sealed, with a shiny black goo inside. Beluga Caviar, it says on the label. I stare at it. Ok, it's caviar, what did I expect. It's just caviar, *of course,* and I start to laugh. Darren regards me with scarcely veiled pity.

'You are wrapped way too tight Genie boy, take a fucking chill pill or I swear I'm gonna kick you out the car down the motorway, you are doing my head in.'

We drive on in silence. Behind us, somewhere in the darkness, in the sleek, menacing Mercedes 500 SLE, ride our two comrades in corruption.

~

'Here we go, motorway coming up in a minute, then it's easy', I say, head deep in the fat map book of Spain I have been given. It's late, the roads are quiet, but we've got a good four hundred kilometres to cover. 'What's that?' I say, seeing a uniformed person waving a yellow illuminated baton. A group of cars, police cars, loom up on the curve of the roundabout of the motorway junction.

'Shit. Traffic stop.' Says Darren. 'Should be okay, I only had one vodka. Sit tight and say nothing.' We pull up to the kerb, directed by a police officer. 'Should be just a routine breathalyser.' He rolls his window down.

'*Donde vais, chicos?*[9]'

'Almería' replies Darren.

'*Identificación, por favor*[10].' Darren pulls out a driving licence. The officer waves it away. It's a British driving license. I now realise I have no identification whatsoever. '*Pasaporte.*'

---

[9] Where are you off to, lads?
[10] Identification please

'Haven't got it.' Darren looks blankly back at the officer.

'*Has bebido? Por favor, una prueba de alcolemia[11].*'

A phone sized digital machine with an attachment is proffered to Darren and he breathes into it. A bleeping sound. The officer nods. We wait.

'*Pues negativo, pero justo.[12]*' So I figure Darren isn't over the limit. Maybe we can carry on. There follows a barrage of questions, all in Spanish, the officers having no command of English, or care not to use any if they have it. Darren's stumbling and irritation with his inability to communicate properly starts to sound slightly panicky. I am simply rooted to my seat, staring ahead. The body language of the officers changes, and not subtly. They step back a bit, bodies braced. Four officers now surround us. While this happens, we notice the Mercedes pass, ignored by the officers. I can't see the reaction within due to the strongly tinted windows. Mercifully. It continues on its way. They beckon us to step out of the car, open the boot, the doors. An officer peers inside the back. Another pulls out the box and inspects the caviar curiously, then places it onto the roof. We are standing back ten feet away from the car now. An officer pops the lid of the boot open, and says something, the result of which is an officer immediately places himself in front of us with a hand held up, and the other hand on the hilt of his gun. I have said many, many things about policemen in the UK, but at this moment I wish it was the unarmed version that we were dealing with, not these paramilitary plods who can't understand a word we say.

Sweat starts to bead on my forehead, running in a trickle down the small of my back, mouth dries, heart thumps. The oozing, filthy quicksand of the swamp wraps its lascivious embrace around me again, sucking, sucking. My computation of the possibilities in this moment all lead to one of two places. Back to prison, or being shot. As if to confirm this, I hear the zipper on the bags, a command, and

---

[11] Have you been drinking? Alcohol test, please

[12] Well it's negative, but only just

three revolvers are raised directly at us. I try, literally, not to piss myself.

Further babbling in Spanish. Darren looks at me. His face doesn't read panic, merely a weary impatience. Is he inured to guns being pointed at him?

'I hope our insurance policy works' he says to me. I assume he means the phone number Gary gave to me, but it only adds to my rising panic. Darren calmly extracts an envelope from his pocket, unwraps the note inside and wordlessly holds it to the officer's face. The officer scans it, his face goes from irritation, to surprise, to indignation in the blink of an eye.

'Make the call.' Says Darren.

I dial and the phone starts to ring, but the officer snatches it off me. He turns away taking the note, and my phone, obviously exasperated. Darren glances at me with a slight smile. I think I am still exhibiting rabbit in headlights face, and I'm definitely relieved it's not cocaine in the bags. It's the sole comfort.

Someone has answered as the officer is now talking to them. He walks away, too far away, and my Spanish is not good enough to grasp even a bit of what passes, but from the tone of the officer, it appears some kind of negotiation is going on, haggling even. Darren smiles at me, which evinces scowls from the other officers, still watching us, whose guns are still pointing at us. Another car comes onto the roundabout and slows, the passengers staring in disbelief, but one of the officers breaks away, furiously waving them on, brandishing his pistol. The car accelerates violently away. I am in a movie again, against my will.

The officer on the phone beckons the other three over. A heated argument starts, and while they try to keep it from our hearing, the officer with the phone is being quite forceful. He goes to the boot and comes out with a wad of the cash, peels some off and pushes it into the hands of two of the others, while the last officer, evidently furious, throws his hands up in disgust and stomps back to his patrol vehicle. He's not accepting the cash, but can't prevent the other two from doing so. The scarcely credible pantomime unfolds before our disbelieving eyes. The officers appear to settle it between them, and the main one comes back over to us, hands Darren the envelope, and me my phone.

'*Buenas noches señores, buen viaje*[13]' and he turns back to the others, waving us away. Darren and I leap into the car and head off, breathing heavily, letting the tension slip away, the sound of the even revs of the engine on the open motorway soothing us. Darren now starts to giggle quietly. I remain bemused, but my sense of relief is a cool breeze rustling up my legs and finding its way into my stomach and intestines.

'Pull over' I say, after about five minutes.

'What the fuck for?'

'I need a shit'

'You are joking, right?'

'No, seriously, pull over now!' Then the inevitable question, to pile on the humiliation. 'Darren, are there any tissues in the car?' Darren's giggling turns into full on hysterics.

~

Around 3 a.m., we appear to be at our destination. Given the general stress and fatigue of the last several days, conversation has been the minimum necessary. The knowledge of driving several million euros around in bags is not one that is easy to relax with, on an empty open motorway, with two armed thugs somewhere behind us in the dark. There has been not a little of glancing nervously in mirrors, and edginess surrounding any car that lurks too closely to us. Eventually, we are here facing a huge green industrial gate, in the heart of flat, featureless agricultural land. The Mercedes reappears and pulls up a few meters behind.

---

[13] Good evening gentlemen, have a good journey

'Tweedle dee and tweedle dum are with us again.' I observe flatly.

'And this doesn't look promising' says Darren.

'Well it's the only thing that meets the description, on this road at this kilometre point.' I'm too tired and frazzled, and I just hit the horn, impatiently, with a long loud burst.

'Jesus, shuttup! There's probably a bell, dickhead.' Darren gets out and searches around the gateposts, and sure enough finds some kind of buzzer. He speaks to someone. Our chaperones simply observe from the Merc.

The imposing green gate starts to slide open and we drive through, down a long drive lit with twinkling embedded lights, and the dark lines of citrus plantations run off in either direction. The Mercedes mercifully remains outside. The scent of blossom pervades everywhere. Soon a lumbering figure appears out of the gloom walking towards us, a shotgun leaning over his arm, and some Labradors bounding around insanely, barking. He beckons us to follow him. We come out onto a gravel forecourt facing a peculiar long, low farm house, with an ostentatious three-story square tower with crenelations bang in the middle, dwarfing the rest of the building. It's not particularly glamorous or stylish, on the contrary, it's dreary apart from the preposterous ostentation of the tower.

'What does Sorzano do exactly?' I ask Darren, just so I know exactly who we are supposed to be meeting.

'He's a lawyer. Sort of. Not officially, because he's Venezuelan, so he can't practice here. But he's Mr Fixit. You want something to happen in Marbella, you go to him.'

'Well he's no architect that's for sure. What a waste of money, out here in a flat orange grove, miles from anything. Very odd.'

'Yeah, nicely hidden though eh, who would know what goes on here. Conveniently far from Marbella, innit.'

The main door opens and despite the late hour, several people appear, similar to the types I see in the restaurants in Marbella. The blazers and trousers, fuddy-duddy check shirts, cravats, slicked back hair on high foreheads. It's the same uniform of the older Spanish business class I have seen Holme moving among, very un-European for sure.

We climb out of the van, escaping the reek of vodka, stale farts and chorizo sandwiches. The man I recognise as Sorzano from the restaurant comes over to us and embraces, smelling thickly of fancy cologne and cigar smoke. He waves and grunts orders at some minion who goes to the boot of the car. He beckons us to follow and we do, as we are the object of much back slapping and greetings from the expectant gaggle of men. Once inside, I slip into a peculiar movie again. We turn down a long corridor that is more like a museum. Myriad chunks of ornate, grandiose furniture abound, and higher up the wall the dead glass eyes of hundreds, literally hundreds, of beasts stare down upon us. All forms of deer, goat, boar and bulls, some birds, even gazelle, antelope maybe. African game of some sort. David Attenborough would have a cardiac in here.

We reach the end of the corridor and come out into a big, high ceilinged room, wooden beamed, with opulent sofas, a grotesque chandelier hanging in the middle, thoroughly incongruous among the dead animal heads. And what heads. In here we suffer the morbid gaze of several lions, pumas, leopards, zebras, buffalo of various kinds, hyena, and most disturbingly of all, a pair of huge Rhino heads given pride of place on the main gable end of the room. The sense of scale of death is overwhelming. Such beauty slaughtered for sport, indiscriminately, and shown so callously, ostentatiously, on their mahogany plinths. I have never seen anything so obscene and I am stuck, gazing open mouthed. Some grinning middle-aged lothario slaps my back and presses a generous crystal beaker of whiskey into my hand and shows me to a sofa. Darren and I perch, like ingenues at a coming out ball, bemused by our lack of comprehension of Spanish, and the death show looming over us, and all of the grinning, yabbering, middle-aged, smug bastards all around us. It's three in the morning but they are all in good song and rosy cheeked with whiskey. The log fire sputters merrily in the huge fireplace. Suddenly, surreally, a dinner gong sounds, and everyone gets up and goes quiet. At the end of the room a rougher looking man, the gamekeeper type who met us, comes in hauling the two bulky holdalls and drops them in the middle of the low table between the banks of sofas. Sorzano is behind him walking slowly, arms aloft like a self-satisfied preacher. I see him properly for the first time. He's probably about fifty something, but looks younger. Wealth can buy you youth, if you are careful. He looks fit, gym fit, well groomed, his greying black hair swept back, tonight fastened into a small pony-tail, which makes him appear decidedly louche. He could have been a fifties matinee idol with those looks. But here he is, enormous cigar in hand, his idiotic golden smoking jacket tightly belted up, standing like the emperor of backhanders, his arms aloft framing the two bags, as he takes in the admiring, expectant, ruddily gleaming faces of his mates. The men's attention in the room is already off us, as they have turned to worship at the altar of the Euro. The men pass the bundles around, feeling and smelling and pawing them, then tossing them at each other, slapping them around each other's faces and guffawing incessantly.

'Fanguverimush, my goo frienz from Inglan and Roosiya, hahaha', and he chortles away pleased at his preposterously bad English, with a bizarre hint of an American accent. He peels off a few notes and walks over to us, stuffing a wedge of notes down our shirt fronts, like we were strippers.

'*Y ahora, por fin, ¡el espectáculo!*'[14] The phrase is greeted by an enormous roar from the men and they make, as one, through the open patio doors into a court yard. They form in a small reverential semi-circle in front of a lone horse, held in the dim light by a groom. The horse suddenly starts, neighing, and the groom struggles to keep it still. The source of its concern is duly revealed as a groom leads

---

[14] Ánd now, finally, showtime!

another horse through a gate. This must be a stallion, judging by its larger size, thicker neck and tell-tale swinging penis a couple of feet long. Our guests variously gesture and signal us to be calm and attentive. They fall silent, expectant.

The groom leads the stallion, his arousal perfectly visible despite the light. Snorting, hooves chomping on tiles, the chiding of the grooms, the flexing equine muscles, the musky potent scent of horse sweat, is counterpointed by the rapt attention, the salacious grins on the faces of the audience of greedy old men. The stallion mounts the back of the mare, and surprisingly deftly penetrates her. His neck arches over, and he gives three gargantuan thrusts. At each thrust there is a reflexive, empathetic gurgle of pleasure from the assembled men. The stallion flexes and tenses further, nostrils flaring, and to my disbelieving eyes he visibly trembles and gasps as he comes into his mount. The horse's climax induces a great lusty cheer and guffaws from the audience. All kinds of phrases in deep guttural accents are uttered, but coupled with their gestures, it doesn't leave much to the imagination. It occurs to me that maybe this is a form of ritualised Viagra for these ridiculous old buffoons. Although it was only horses, I feel scandalised by the intimacy of it all. Being forced to watch any creature having sex, for the viewers pleasure, seems to be one step too weird. Darren and I exchange a glance of bewildered disbelief and wait, resigned to the fact that nothing much else could possibly surprise us this night.

A pretty, petite and coffee skinned maid in the traditional black dress and white pinafore addresses us, and beckons us to follow. Probably Philippine, who appear to be the chosen nationality for domestics with these people. We follow, gratefully, exiting as quickly and discreetly as possible from this theatre of the obscene. We can barely look at each other, no words can portray how completely outlandish is the spectacle we have just witnessed. We have been rendered utterly speechless.

We are shown down some other long corridor, mercifully free of taxidermized death, to two comfortable suites. Comfortable, apart from the visceral shock of having the mounted head of a polar bear standing sentinel over the enormous double bed. A polar bear?! With a quick '*Gracias*' I direct the maid swiftly back out of the room, remove my shoes and trousers then tip myself into the bed and gratefully allow unconsciousness to claim me, which it does in barely a minute.

9

I awake with a shaft of warm sunlight rousing me out of the deep. My body attempts to respond, feeling like plasticine, needing giant, strong hands to warm it into pliability and life. The surroundings are unfamiliar and I'm alarmed for a moment. I start, a reflexive disgust at the fact I am staring up the nostrils of a polar bear. Then I remember the flaring nostrils of the stallion. I fear that vision is going to haunt me for life and I'll never be able to have sex with a human again without *that* image intruding.

The room is somewhat opulent, antiquated and fusty, although everything is painfully new. I have no sense of time, just that day has progressed. I pull myself vertical and hazily waddle to the window, pulling back the curtains as the sun blinds me, and I sway about, grabbing the sill for balance. Outside is a perfect day, that now familiar potent, deep blue canopy and super high-definition texture stares back at me. Long rows of fruit trees stretch away from the window, the regularity and featurelessness broken only by telegraph poles, topped with some kind of vast shaggy nests. They are so huge it looks like a flying dinosaur might be surviving in, where the hell are we? Almería or something. The details click into place, the drive, the fair, the money, horses... I lurch over scrabbling wildly around the bed until I find, creased and slightly dampened with night effusions, the wad of euros. There's a few thousand there. Dirty money. But still money. It all comes into place, and I sigh in sheer disbelief at the spectacle I witnessed last night.

The strength of the light and its warmth on my still fatigued body is hypnotic. I never knew it was possible to actually not think about anything. Just to breath in the light, be there, but not there. It occurs to me I have spent most of my life thinking. Though the purpose of all that marihuana and ecstasy was to not think, to erase the trauma of what happened and how it was after, conversely it didn't make me stop. I spent *too much* time thinking, even though I can't remember huge swathes of what and where and who for the last thirteen years. None of it has felt like this moment, sitting in the light, in the spell for a minute, floating in nothingness. And then it's gone, it's too late, all of the inescapable narrative that brought me here, barges through the door in my head. The players and their multifarious plots demand the show must go on. Money, golf, apartments, more money, guns, drugs, whores, golf, bags of money... I stare vacantly at the gleaming bright light and the blue void. The warmth slows the consciousness, I close my eyes, and keel over back onto the bed and drag the sheets over me, I'm gone again.

A rapping on the door slams consciousness back into me, and I sit up quickly, aware this time the intermission is over, the story is definitely about to roll on. It was just a moment, a resting point. It was nice. I am calm and ready. Darren pushes in.

'Come on Gene, let's get the fuck out of here. It's full of strange old men, seriously.'

'Whoah slow down. I need a shower. And some breakfast.'

'Well hurry up, I'll be sat over by the pool. It's just on the other side here, very nice it is too.'

'Be right with you.'

I go into the bathroom which again is ostentatiously appointed with silly gold taps, rococo style fittings and chintzy fabrics. This place is ridiculous. There's an ample corner bath hot tub type thingy, with a shower attached, but not hung up. Bugger, I really want a shower. I pull off the fetid clothing from yesterday and sit like a baby in the bath and use one hand to shower over myself. An array of unctuous soapy stuff, violently over perfumed tries to tempt me. I stand up to better access the smellier crevices of my midriff and find myself staring at a painting hung over the bath. I'd not clocked it initially, as hotel rooms are always full of pointless prints of something or other. This one is an abstract sort of painting, funny

116

suspended shapes, very arty. I study it closely, the textures are real, a wee drop or two splashes up and lands on it. I flick them off with my finger and the canvas actually wobbles.

'Who the fuck would hang a painting over a bath?' I say out loud in amused disbelief. There's a signature, 'J.Miró' it says.

I'm dressed and out by the pool, where it appears Sorzano himself is holding forth to Darren, who nods in mock empathy though he patently hasn't a clue what Sorzano is talking about, his Spanish being nearly as bad as mine. Sorzano greets me with the obligatory handshake and shoulder squeeze and we are beckoned forth. The next thing I know we enter a spacious, predictably opulent dining room, with only a few dead things gazing down on us, and a sumptuous breakfast has been laid on. No sooner have we stuffed ourselves gratefully on breads and omelettes and meats and coffee and watermelon and some thick sweet custardy type of stuff, than Sorzano whisks us off on a tour of his empire, this time in his hilariously accented English. It's like a compulsion, everyone, no matter how lowly or insignificant must be led to understand the wealth, taste and status of Anastasio Sorzano, former Caracas lawyer to the stars, until Hugo Chavez made his life unbearable,. He wastes no time informing us of where his political loyalties lie, somewhere to the right of Attila the Hun. He's like a child who is still excited by having his own sweet shop long after he should have got used to it. I've never seen so much pointless stuff in all my life, why would you fill your house with stuff that's boring even in a museum? Antique guns in gilt edged cases, dozens of ornate horse carriages, vases and sideboards and clocks and kitchen ware and more paintings. Sorzano mentions several names of artists I have heard of. Helicopter pads, stables with dozens of splendid horses for their midnight shows, quad bikes and more shooting equipment, but for actual use this time. Sorzano is sitting on an incalculable fortune we had just enlarged to the tune of a few million in cash.

117

'I have three more finca like dis one. *Mucho trabajo*[15] eh?'

Three more?! Maybe that's why they were all so flippant and silly last night with the bags of money. It literally is small change when taken against the totality of the wealth this slimy gentleman has amassed. Amid all I have seen, the excess and opulence, the ridiculous taste and obscene trophies, I can't see the point in having any of it. A vision of life so decadent and pompous, and yet he has replicated it four times in different parts of Spain, if what he says is to be believed. And this man, this pumped up, posing middle-aged lothario, holds the keys to the kingdom of Holmeland. You couldn't make it up.

~

We resume the road gratefully after an hour of this showing off and head for Marbella, still five hours away. Our Ukrainian shadows have evaporated, content the money arrived at its destination. They might have enjoyed the scenario more than we did.

The motorway stretches far ahead, mercifully in daylight. Driving at night in Spain is like journeying across The Void. Near total darkness, with barely a light visible at times, civilisation appearing every few kilometres, only to be swallowed back into the blackness again. I had no idea Spain was so enormous. It goes on and on, and there's hardly any traffic on the roads, not counting the insanity of Madrid of course.

Darren is quiet, if not downright taciturn. I can't be bothered to delve or raise a friendly conversation. I slip into my own thoughts, the light and space of the open road pulling out wisps of memory and reflection, unfurling like the long lines of fruit trees and meandering dry gullies in between. The memories are composed of feelings and atmospheres, states of mind rather than events and places and people. Much of what has happened in my adult years has been lost to substances. Little remains of the nights spent surfing the waves of

---

[15] A lot of work

118

beats and noise in countless clubs and raves. My more vivid memories are of the days in between, the grey outs of weather and mood, the avoidance of my family and its woes. In these conditions the emotions of my father's death metastasized into all manner of pathologies; of guilt, and inadequacy, as somehow, we should have done more to save him, or have been immolated with him, not surviving to replay it all and live the consequences. Of resentment, bitterness, directed towards the people who turned their backs on us, and anyone happy in general. Why did so many of our friends and family ostracise us? Since I have been old enough to formulate such questions, my mother has never had the emotional stability and clarity to answer any of them. The feeling of being cursed, infected, and discarded, transmuted itself into a low level contempt for normality, for friendship, for human warmth. What friends do I have from my youth? From Uni? Who did I want to catch up with after getting out, have a beer with, who was waiting for me? Not even Mum, lost in her haze of antidepressants, anger and denial. Her condition is the direct result of her grappling with the internal chaos. Doctors willingly collaborated in her medicating the trauma out of sight. What's the difference between her medication and mine? Only legality, as far as I can see. They are just symptoms of a condition we both share. Gary has escaped this family disease. Ambition, dedication, and willpower have given him a life, and a sense of himself I am obviously light years from achieving right now.

The country broadens out with not much to change the view from white villages, agricultural buildings and fruit trees, or burnt, featureless, arid scrubland, a dramatic semi-desert. All is barren apart from where the hand of sprinklers has scattered its liquid gold and the plants jump in the stony shale soil, searching for expression to be met with rigid authoritarian control; linear, uniform, monotonous, forced by banking, wire, trellis, spikes and poles into the rigidness desired by productivity demands and mechanical harvesting techniques. The only signs of spontaneous nature are in the scattered cacti and scrub that have a desperate and natural beauty to themselves. They clutch to gully sides, eroded sand banks and the borders of the manicured estates. Amid them, struggle red poppies, winking in clumps, enjoying their brief moment in the limelight. Gradually, long, hideous, filthy plastic sheds start to appear, held in place by more wires, hoops and posts. They huddle close to each other in packs, the opaque, sun blasted polythene piled on in layers like so much drying, flaking skin. Agricultural eczema.

The ugliness and harshness of contemporary food production is a shock. It dawns on me, seeing the trucking depots and vast amounts of packaging, storage materials and facilities, that I am travelling through the green grocer of Europe. Frequently we pass wandering bands of impoverished looking Africans, both black and Maghrebin. Sometimes huddled around a brazier, hanging out by a shack, with some barely surviving ancient bicycles, or literally huddled under tarpaulins strung from low thorny trees. These must be the migrants who service the demand for labour in what must be hellish working conditions. After the lush glamour and neo-Hollywood opulence of the surroundings of Marbella, its aquamarine seas, azure skies and sub-tropical generosity, this Spain is tawdry, dilapidated and oppressive.

'Jesus, who would want to emigrate to this' I say, to break the spell of disinterest in the cab. Darren snorts contemptuously. My surprised stare elicits an explanation eventually.

'You should talk to Ibby some time,' he says referring to our Senegalese colleague from the warehouse. 'He walked *across* the Sahara, scraped together money by begging and doing nasty jobs all through North Africa, to get on a boat to the coast down here. Ask him how many human skeletons he walked past on the way. He worked in one of these places for three years. Some of the growers here, they are worse than the old slave owners. They'll happily have you killed if you try and rock the boat. You've got no papers, no rights, you run from the police. So if you disappear, no-one really knows, and no-one cares. Sometimes the locals get pissed off, say if someone crosses the line, robs a Spaniard or worse, then you get a full lynch mob situation, it's fucking medieval, believe me. Ask Ibby. To you, it's just a badly paid job in a warehouse your brother got for you, and no doubt you think it's a crap job, as you've got a college degree an' all that, but for Ibby, he's made it, won the lottery, died and gone to heaven.'

He says all of this without looking at me. He doesn't even disguise his contempt. It does kind of put my situation into perspective. I remain silent, mulling over my relative position in life. Hell, I've only been out of Strangeways six weeks or so, and I already am leading a life I couldn't have imagined or planned for. I do have a job, I do have a roof over my head, people who care about me, and I have my dignity and my self-respect, all things considered. Though even that has felt challenged by the events of the last two days. How much have I seen in this short time of those for whom that is a luxury, a meaningless bauble as they float around the edges of existence, discarded or contained and exploited? The sex workers in the countless clubs we pass on the road, the migrants and boat people littering this landscape, those I see wandering around scavenging in the bins in the wealthy areas of Marbella, like so much human flotsam left at the high tide mark of society's beach. I've spent years hiding behind a chemical blanket of excuses and evasions, leading a life of such unique selfishness, that it's only now, out here, when faced with the multiple absurdities and inequalities of this raggedy arsed country I've come to, that my own sense of ennui that has been my great crutch and badge, is now looking woefully flimsy, and very much past its sell by date.

Darren is eyeing me, curiously, something is eating him.

'Why are you spinning everyone that crap about being a DJ?'

'It's not crap. I have worked as a DJ.'

'Oh yeah? Well, beats working in a chip shop. But you never did that, though, 'cause it was long gone by then, ay?'

121

I'm stunned into silence. What the…? I haven't rehearsed a response to this scenario. I stare ahead, sheepishly. Darren continues after a time.

'I'm from Huyton. My Nan lived in Warrington. My dad would get her a fish supper from your chippy back in the day. Everyone round there remembers the story. It was a big deal. In a small world. I remember hearing about the bust in the club an' all. The one that put you in Strangeways.'

I'm disturbed now, that Darren would have had an ear to the ground on such things. Who does he know, who did he run with back in Lancashire? I let out a long sigh.

'You must think I'm a bit of a twat, all that stuff about Thailand.'

'Naaaah mate, everyone here has a story, everyone here is runnin' from something. You come to reinvent, to forget who you were back home. If that works for you, I'm not gonna say 'owt. It's your business, wack.'

'Thanks. Actually it was Holme's idea. All of it. Protecting his image and the good name of his company, because they have a reputation to maintain, respectable businessmen. I was a liability, showing up unannounced, fresh from Strangeways.'

'Straight up? Fuck me, what a cunt.' Darren's directness is a fair verdict nonetheless.

'Yeah, complete hypocrite. Same old story, one rule for them and one for the rest of us. Should've ripped off that bag and fucked off to Thailand for real', which makes us both have a good belly laugh. Darren now smiles broadly across at me, in a way I don't understand. I look quizzically and he raises his eyebrows in a cheesy knowing way.

'You didn't?!' I say, an idea forming in my head

'I fucking did.'

'No waaaaay!'

'Way mate, every fucking way. You saw those coppers just pulled off a bunch of notes from a wad. They weren't counting. Everyone gets their slice. That's the Marbella way. Sorzano and them don't care, they've got bags of the stuff, every time something gets built in Marbella that wanker gets another bag of cash, while the likes of me, and Ibby, have to eat shit from the likes of Holme for eight hundred and fifty euros a month.'

'So?'

'So I lifted a couple of wedges.'

'How?'

Either Darren is a great bullshitter or a hell of a thief.

'After the coppers finished with us. The broken wad. Nobody knows what the coppers took. I figured there was a bit of slack there.'

'Spectacular.'

My admiration is genuine. The balls, the presence of mind, the sheer chutzpah of this chippy little scouser, barely twenty-five, ripping off bundles of mob cash from the most corrupt politician in Spain. He is obviously more than he appears. I'm surprised by his honesty. Then he further surprises me.

'There you go Gene ol' boy, that's your share. For being a good oppo on what was a pretty fucked up expedition. Glad we all came out of it with something eh?' and he drops a wedge of notes into my lap. I stare blankly at first, willing my frozen mind to engage with the fact, then meekly, with trembling fingers I count through the crisp, slightly odorous new notes. Seven thousand euros of mob cash in my hand. It buzzes, like it has a life of its own. God knows how much he lifted for himself. I find myself asking myself the question, should I accept? And simultaneously answer it with the palpable justification that it's filthy money, and they deserve to be relieved of it. The usual thieves' self-justification, but they feel especially valid and noble given the venality I have been witnessing for days.

When I look up again, Darren is regarding me meaningfully. And I realise generosity is two sided. Honour among thieves.

Ensnarement in a web of secrets and liabilities. A bargain made, forced even. I also realise it has probably bought Darren's silence. He has no interest in betraying my secrets now. But I also decide quite definitely there is much, much more to Darren than meets the eye.

'Thanks' I say, but curiosity won't leave me alone. 'So what's your story? How come you end up here. You don't seem very Marbella, if you know what I mean.'

Darren laughs, but it's a nervous laugh. I wait. He sees me, expectant, it's only fair, I figure.

'Came on holiday with some mates, to Benidorm. I liked it. Decided to hang around a bit. Met a bloke in a bar, said he was setting up business in Marbella, and needed some lads to help.'

'What sort of business?' Darren's face is a picture, his nonchalance is so forced, the wheels behind his eyes turning, trying to find the right words, to his own bogus script.

'Errr, you know, markets and that. Market stall. Second hand furniture. That's how I got the job in the warehouse, like.'

'Right, cool. And you're still here.'

'Yup.'

Stalemate. No sense of pushing further. I could fill in any number of minor criminal, dodgy details, and most of them would probably be close to the truth. I let it rest. It's a truce for now.

~

We play out the rest of the long journey in silence, which is actually a relief. The present appears much more complex than I have admitted to myself. I have a sense of perspective that has eluded me, even in Strangeways. As we pull off the motorway and run toward the warehouse, the swaying palms and greenery, the white condos, the people jogging along in their bright sports gear, all glide by. It's the sunny, super high definition light, giving everything that hyper real look; gorgeous in its way, with the Mediterranean glistening off toward Gibraltar, and even Africa clearly visible, peeping over the Straits. I smile to myself, I am genuinely glad to be back in Marbella, after Madrid and Almeria, whores, gangsters, police, and fat, smug middle-aged politicians. The whole edifice is too beautiful and unreal to resist, it's so perfectly formed and made and marketed. It spreads out before you every time you drive the east-west artery of the Costa del Sol. It belies the utter corruption and venality at its heart, so dazzling and alluring no-one dares tell it like it is. I smile at the contradictions, I have a warm feeling, I am looking forward. My anger at Gary has moderated. It's just how they do business. Nothing personal. It's done now. I'll get over it.

10

Laser beams ply through the air, bouncing off the steel rafters of the warehouse. The visual assault of strobes, lasers and projections is matched by the denseness of the music. The speaker system is physical in its impact, the bass beat lifts you, bounces you, from somewhere inside your stomach. The heat is human, moist, thick with the scent of a thousand young, sweating, bobbing people. Dougie and I are entranced. It has been an elegant subterfuge to get out all night, playing one parent off another. Thanks to my mum's lacklustre interest in my comings and goings, I know there's little chance of Dougie's mum finding out he's not actually staying over.

We push through the crowd, hoping to see a face we know, anyone who can point us in the direction of a known contact. The quick joint we smoked furtively outside, in the ugly truck park on the edge of this Runcorn industrial estate, is wearing off, and is not making the music sound the way everyone said it is supposed to sound. We need that mythical pill, the one everyone talks about but hardly anyone I know has tried. MDMA. Ecstasy. The name is enough to make me want it. Flavour of the month, summer of love, the myths surrounding it have run like typhoid through the local youth. It kills you, drowns you, drives you crazy, turns you into a vegetable. We have heard of deaths, seen the hysterical tabloid rantings. They would say that, anything to stop us having a good time, escaping from the drudgery and oppressive expectations of being a grown up. I'm off to Huddersfield Poly in the autumn, leaving Doug to catering college. We intend to suck the marrow out of this summer, to get high and laid, in equal measure. So far, we have failed resoundingly on the latter count.

Slowly we push through the throng, circumnavigating the main crowd, trying to spot likely dealers in strategic areas. The toilets

126

are too heavy on burly security men, despite the illegality of the entire set up. The promoters don't want to take a chance on aggro bringing in the fuzz. They have too much to lose. Doug jabs my ribs, and bellows in my ear, trying to beat the noise.

'There's Baz Anderson, look at him, I'm sure he's on it, let's ask him.'

Baz. He'll know for sure, and he knows us, he was in our class for years. No problems. When we get over to him, he doesn't so much greet us as smile all over us, his head shaking from side to side with the incessant rhythm. We mime pill popping and shrugs, signing away like deaf people until he gets the message. A bellow in my ear.

'Outside, round the back, behind the red removal truck' and he's gone again, bobbing off into delirium.

We make it round the back of the warehouse, and evidently business is brisk, there's a queue snaking round the side to behind the lorry. We bide our time, twitching with anticipation, as we edge steadily to the back. At the corner of the truck we come up against a huge guy, boxer's nose, green bomber jacket, eighteen-hole Doc Martens. A proper looking Nazi.

'Wait' he growls, as a huge hand stops me. We wait. 'Alright, go on through.'

Emerging into a space between the two parked lorries, silhouetted figures lurk, hands in jacket pockets, legs splayed.

'How many do you want? Smileys five quid each.'

'Two please.' I place ten pounds in an anonymous hand.

'That guy there.'

Doug and I approach a dark figure, whose face I can't see but I have an awful creeping sense of recognition, making my knees go a bit jelly. Doug tugs my jacket urgently. Then I hear why.

'Fucking Eugene and that fucking Fenian McCaffrey. You can piss off, I'm not giving no pills to a fucking Taig.' The voice is clear. Jimmy Kavanagh.

127

'What do you mean, we just paid for it' responds Doug. 'Just give us what we paid for. It's just pills, not fucking church. And I'm English, I was born here.'

This earns him a punch, and he doubles over holding his mouth. Kavanagh lands a kick on him, and I grab Doug, dragging him off before the whole bunch set on us. We sprint away, between parked lorries, trembling with anger, frustration and naked fear. Once we have put enough distance between us and caught our breath, I turn to Doug.

'What was all that about? What did you do?'

'What did I do? You heard him, he's a fucking Orangie, a soup taker.'

'What the fuck are you on about?' I genuinely have no idea what Doug is talking about.

'His dad is an Orangeman. Belfast. The fuckers burnt us out of the Falls in 1969. My mum was pregnant with me. You know my folks are Irish, but that's why I was born in Warrington. Because bastards like his dad burnt down our houses and we fled for our lives. And they never let you forget it, the fucking, evil, stupid, fucking bigots.' He thumps the side of a truck with each expletive, panting, seething with righteous indignation. I'm stunned into silence, awed and humbled by this revelation. Doug has always been cagey about his parents, who are both Irish as hell, thick Ulster accents. The North of England is full of Irish. I'd never given it much thought that some of them might actually have fled here. Not counting the potato famine of course. The Troubles is a constant rumble of background noise, mostly perceived through the news. It has never impinged on me personally. Though both Kavanagh father and son cast a pall over my family in general, I had never associated them with this real world politick. As we gingerly make our way back toward the warehouse, we resolve to make the best of the bit of hashish we have left, and cut our losses. On another day, Doug will tell me the quick history of the civil rights movement and how his young parents were caught up in

128

a conflagration that the rest of us Brits still know barely anything about, and understand even less. And it consolidates my fear and loathing of the Kavanagh clan. Losing our ecstasy virginity has to wait for another day.

11

Two days later the sales team return to Marbella. There is a fair amount to do in the warehouse, with stuff coming back from Madrid and a sudden rush of stock and orders due to the successful sales effort at the fair, presumably for stuff that has already been built. The place is palpably abuzz. No one says it, but everybody assumes the big deal is done, that the golden goose has chosen her nesting spot and everyone is going to get fat and happy. I don't see Gary or Ana, or anyone from the offices, as they are all in meetings, whizzing around, being important. Rumours feed back to the warehouse Sorzano was seen coming out of the offices and driving off with Lebid. Holme reportedly hasn't left the building for three whole days, and they've been ferrying in food and clean clothes.

On the Wednesday morning I am just getting myself together to head off on my push bike to the warehouse, when there's a jangle of keys in the door, and Gary let's himself in. It's obvious straight away he is in a high state of something. Whether good or bad I can't yet tell. He has darkish shadows under his eyes that tell of the recent frenzy of hours, and he's jittery, showing slight symptoms of grinding teeth and a sniffly nose. I suspect the Colombian marching powder has been helping the current flurry of business developments. I didn't expect this of Gary, but it appears to be par for the course for so much of what passes for normal business practice and everything else. I suspect if I wanted to head down to the beach or up the mountain for an acid trip I'd spend half my life searching the Costa for a tab, but right now I could scrape a line from the surfaces of the flat, what with Frankie's crowd's general way of cranking up for their work and pleasure. He takes me by the arm, steers me onto the terrace and pulls the window across behind, not that Frankie and whatever other stragglers are anywhere close to consciousness yet.

'Gene, the deal's done' he starts in excitedly, and I try to cut him off with a 'well, yes I had kind of...'

'No, it's done, but there's been developments. It's different.' He's pacing with a contained smile pulling at his face. 'There's a conflict of interest between our existing business, the new foreign developments Mike is leading and the Lebid development, El Angel, the big one.'

'Conflict? Where's the conflict, everyone is making out nicely from what I can see. You didn't ask how the trip went.' Gary observes me nonplussed.

'The trip?'

'Yeah, it was an interesting evening. Especially when the police pulled us at gunpoint outside Madrid.'

'You were pulled? I didn't know that.'

'You didn't ask.'

'All I know is Sorzano was very happy. He got us the building permits. It's full speed ahead. There weren't any problems, were there?' I shake my head, as much in disgust at the whole charade, but Gary doesn't see that. 'So you made the call. The police were cool?'

'After they'd helped themselves to a few thousand, on the instruction of whoever was on the end of the phone. Three officers had their guns trained on us while they argued about the size of their bribe. That was a first for me, I must say.'

Now Gary actually looks alarmed. 'Jesus, I'm sorry, I had no idea.'

'Who was on the end of the phone?'

'Someone high up, in authority. You don't need to know.'

'But it's all okay right, you can build your golf condos?' I'm trying not to sound sarcastic, but it isn't easy.

'Well that's what I'm trying to say, if you'd let me.' Yes, Gary is definitely cranked up. 'Lebid demanded a separation of this project from existing developments and other projects abroad as he considers it distracting and diluting the er... anyway the point is...' he's gabbling

131

and I think he's actually done a line before coming up here, 'that we have created an entirely new company, separate in every way from the core business, and it needs a completely different CEO. No conflict of interest or distractions. Separation of responsibilities. Holme wants to expand worldwide, his ambition is truly global, so he's stepping aside from this.' I know what is coming and it chills me to my core, but Gary is seized by evangelical fire. 'Holme has made me...' he pants, he's staring at me, searching for approbation for this moment of triumph... 'the CEO of the new Holmeland. He's given it to me, I'm the boss, I'm going to launch this ship on the world, the skies the limit. I've made it Gene; I've finally made it. And this is just the beginning.'

He goes on, and he's telling me all the usual stuff from the marketing plans with the extraordinary profit margins and commissions involved; he's blinded by the money, because the sums are colossal, even by the standards of Sorzano's gargantuan bribe. An entire mountain side, thirty hectares, three golf courses, twelve hundred units at an average retail price of four hundred and fifty thousand euros. Over half a billion in retail value. I say nothing, it's outside of my comprehension. He stops and eyes me expectantly. First, I take him in my arms and give him a long, close hug. It's good. Then I address him.

'I am really pleased for you Gary, it's no doubt what you deserve and I hope you'll make a huge success out of it.'

'Thanks Gene. But...?' I have to laugh, he can detect the subtext to my congratulations.

'I have seen things these last few days that I wasn't prepared for, or expecting, or even imagined were possible. It's a big dragon whose tail you are clutching Gary, how do you know it isn't going to turn around and burn you.'

He pauses momentarily, 'Um yes, the Ukrainians, the money, I know, all very weird, but not really, it's just how business is done here. I don't like it, I don't, but it's done now. We had to do that to get where we are, and now it's just business. Normal, legal, good business. Trust me, I have it all under control. I know exactly how this works and what is going on. I always protect myself. I have an insurance policy.'

He's obviously strung out on fatigue, stress, charlie and adrenalin, but still there's something about this Gary makes me think he's now believing his own hype. That the natural cynicism and caution of someone like us, brought up in Warrington, that suspicious, resentful, northern attitude to huge success and wealth, has been scalded away, that last layer of protection from the bullshit merchants has evaporated in a hail of self-belief, colossal profits, and an apparent impunity to the law in this very unique Marbella stylee.

'Gary, do you trust Holme? Do you seriously trust Lebid?''

There's a beat of a second or two before Gary says, 'It's not about trust. We are partners, mutually co-dependent for the success of this. We aren't going to turn each other over. We can't. I have it all under control. Don't worry.' There's a flicker in his eyes that betrays a shred of doubt, a subconscious, suppressed mistrust still alive back there in his real self, and I am pleased to see it

'And Holme simply walks away, with nothing? '

'No, course not. I'm just CEO, he owns 50% along with Lebid.'

'So what do you get out of it!?' I still don't understand business.

'A fat salary and even fatter commissions. Why do you think I sell it so damn hard?'

Now it makes sense to my profit averse brain. 'Well done, you are going to be the king of Marbella. Should be quite a ride.'

'Yeah it will be, come to the coronation.'

'How do you mean?' I'm acutely aware of the proximity of this to my life, to me personally, to the limited sphere of calm and lucidity I've recently managed to pull around me.

'You're part of it Gene, you can do this, there's a place for you in all this. You've really impressed me this last week. We had some, how can I say, sensitive transactions to handle, which needed a steady nerve and a calm, competent operator, and you came through for us.'

Ha, that's funny. 'Well I'm not so sure about calm. Or the rest.' Thinking about the future, planning, assessing options and making decisions about my life, is new territory for me. Ambition is not a page in my psychological A-Z street map. 'I haven't thought about that, I haven't really thought at all, just finding my feet, you know?'

'No worries, don't say anything now, plenty to think about. We are having a press launch on Friday, and a reception at night, at my club. Get some more glad rags, this is going to be a celebration. All the local and even national press will come, TV, Marbella society. This is when people see we aren't just arrivistes, cheeky *guiris*, fast operators, we are developers, serious business people with a plan to make Marbella more prosperous and attractive than ever before. Get off to the warehouse, there's lots to do, the club needs to be ready for the launch.'

A slap on the arm, and he's gone.

I sit down on the terrace and stare over the palms to the sea. Today it's overcast, wisps of splenetic grey and white twist in and out of the mountains, layers of messy vapour march up from the Atlantic beyond Morocco, the air is fresher, damp smelling, of rain. Something doesn't sit right with me. It's too good, too convenient. Gary's elevation has the feel of a move being made, that he's being played. Why do I think this? Because that's all I see here. Everyone is playing everyone. It's all plays, it *is* still the Wild West. I don't know why he isn't more cautious, more qualified. The cocaine. Not a welcome or constructive addition to the cauldron this deal is steadily becoming. Time to get to the warehouse. After a couple of calm days, the dragon is again lashing his tail, this time at all of us, and we have to tighten our grip.

~

The next two days pass in a blur. I am careering around in one of our trucks picking up supplies of all kinds. Tables, dressing, chairs, lighting, bar equipment, crates and crates of champagne, glasses and god knows what else. My phone constantly rings with ever more stressed people making changes of plan, requests, asking where this or that is, who told you take those, get that now, don't get those ones, they were supposed to be here hours ago and variations and combinations of this ad nauseum. The stress and white noise in my head and everyone else's are compounded by my inability to speak Spanish with half of these callers, so pidgin English meets accented northern English to no great effectiveness

Then, it's party time. Gary and Holme have been busy all day with the more formal press conference and publicity circus, so I haven't seen or heard anything of how it went. Everyone here has been non-stop. I'm standing, beholding the finished spectacle, as the dusk grows. The venue is the night club, part owned by my brother, on a first floor of a long building facing onto the main square of Puerto Banus. It's not a square like in a cutesy village, this is a plaza of concrete and shiny cement and tile, wedged in between ranges of condo and office blocks of no discernible architectural style or beauty. They have, judging by the colours, shades and expanses of tinted mirrored glass, been designed to shout 'money' loudly at all who pass. This is the Spain Ana's family don't understand, and she does.

The entrance is a grand stairway ascending to the first floor, and the circus erected resembles Oscar night on the telly. A red carpet, flows from out in the plaza up the stairs. Ugly cylindrical steel and concrete candelabra-like torches flame languidly. Lights shoot up the front and a great plasticky sheet draped across the facade of the building simply states the legend 'Holmeland', and a new corporate logo I haven't seen before. Someone has been busy. When I first arrived with a delivery this morning I stopped and laughed my head off at the red carpet. It seemed to be a joke, like it was ironic, aping the films and shots from the celebrity TV spots. A slim, severely coiffed, young effeminate Spaniard turned around to see who was guilty of this disrespect and glared at me. He was evidently in charge of the design and was gesturing intensely at various people holding bunches of flowers and decor and stuff. There were a lot of people running and looking stressed, and noise and demanding and ordering and gesturing. And I had the nerve to stand there, not actually hysterically busy, and laugh. After a raft of other filthy looks joined the designer's disapproval, I shot off to get on with things and reserve my opinions and amusement. It was going to be a trying day and so it proved to be.

It is strange being involved in something so unfamiliar and hyperbolic, something so apparently shallow and ridiculous. Every effort is being made to invest the evening with status and cache, to create a golden glow of affluence and effortless success. Its desperate artificiality and contrivance are so palpable that, to me, it seems to send itself up. Do people really feel they are important when they get to walk along a red carpet? Can they be that shallow? Don't they know it's just a carpet we bought from Leroy Merlin DIY Superstore for only 4.99€ a square metre? They could have one at home if they wanted. This edifice of money, success and status they have thrown up, this temporary shrine to their own hubris, strains and trembles under the weight of its own ludicrous contradictions. By commandeering every possible signifier of that status and success, it appears little more than a derivative pile of dreadful old clichés that every night, somewhere in the world, are worn to death by the 'successful'. Whether it's yet another self-serving, vainglorious award ceremony or some other vehicle for uninhibited self-congratulation, no-one ever decides to stand and laugh, to walk away, head shaking in contempt and dismay at the fickleness of human vanity. No, the whole world bends its knee and worships at the altar of success, puts it on TV, comments, reports and analyses it, without actually being critical, or reflective, or even objective. This process is culturally lauded everywhere, by the politicians, the commentariat, and us ordinary folk with our addiction to celebrity. We daily partake of the endless soap opera of pointless tittle tattle of the life of the 'beautiful people'. And what is this one about? Selling houses. It's not brain surgery, it's not feeding famine starved children in some third world hell hole, it's not discovering a cure for cancer. We are not the heroes. What is work for most people but a means to an end? A path you slog along with little control or real autonomy, dancing to the idiotic tunes of economy and employers, to put a roof over your head and food on a table. The surplus money then becomes your means to fabricate your persona, construct your lifestyle, negotiate its language and currency and trade it with similar people.

Fuck them all, really.

Evening. Party time. I am stood alone, gazing up, the abbey where my brother shall be crowned king of Marbella. I laugh to myself, as I have already overheard today, that very phrase I coined two days ago. I am washed and scrubbed and wearing yet another new outfit that is completely alien and ludicrous, but the disarmingly attractive shop assistant in the Corte Ingles insisted it did the job. She was practically wetting herself with excitement when she realised the occasion for which I was shopping. She pumped me for information on every aspect. What brand of champagne, the flowers, lighting, who was the DJ, what celebs were due to come. I must have been terribly disappointing to her. I would have gladly handed over my invitation to her, it would have made her year. But one must be loyal to those to whom one is beholden, and show appreciation and support. Yet another example of the endless series of departures in form for me; conforming to these expectations, partaking of a ritual and lifestyle that is as uncomfortable as it is unfamiliar. I am the Fish out of the Water.

A hearty slap on my back breaks my reverie, and it's Darren, grinning.

'Alright, calm down, calm down,' he's mocking his own scouseness. 'Are you goin' to a party? Can I come, are there any nice birds there?' He's taking the piss.

'What you doing here, don't tell me you're going in there as well?'

'Fuck off, that's only for the wannabes, mate'. He looks at me, daring me to be offended. 'I'm off down the port with some mates. I'll stick me head in later when all the real wankers have gone home. They're total lightweights, but they know how to waste money alright. Enjoy the champagne, tara, see ya tomorrow' and he saunters off, emanating a kind of mischievous self-satisfaction at being able to mock my position.

'I'll wait up for you' I say to the retreating figure. He returns a straight, single, middle finger without turning round.

I survey the scene trying to find a reason to go in there, other than rare familial duty, being present at Gary's coronation. I should feel happy for him. It's a hollow sort of pride though. Everything he's achieved leaves me feeling belittled, but conversely, I am unsullied and beyond the shallow, grasping materialism it all represents. Or at least I like to think so.

The crowds of guests are now coming thick and fast. All the different ants run around, fevered and hyped up, scurrying for attention, cavorting, preening and sucking in the rarefied air of the event.

This cynicism buoys me to an extent, allows me to feel aloof, immune from the neurosis that compels people to strain and preen and measure themselves by these arbitrary social standards. I congratulate myself for not being fooled, sucked into the fantasy of success, status, worth. But something niggles, some familiar ennui tugs at the back of my mind.

Freshers' ball, Huddersfield Polytechnic. Eighteen, but still maladjusted and introspective from the trauma of the fire, plagued by insecurity and self-loathing, I throw myself into this first week with a committed, suicidal level of hedonism. With no Doug to support or control me, to play off, I am a megaphone with no volume control, a runaway train. I stand, in the centre of a hall, by myself within the milling crowd of hormonal, social, teenage chaos around me. I am stoned. Really very stoned indeed. The aural distortions elevate me away from normality, as conversations become abstract soundscapes and words take on new meanings, or simply colours and dynamic traces of light. It was that lovely sticky Nepalese black hash that the rich Iranian guy, Faizal, scored somewhere in London. We connect in halls instantly, the stoners always pick up the vibe of the other stoners. The several bong hits have transported me on an undulating magic carpet into this room where I am invisible. But I see all of them. I see their frantic smiles, I see their awkward body language, the anxious glances, the reflex tics of biting lips, moving hairs, pulling at clothing, flexing underdeveloped, inadequate muscles or busts. People stare nervously, searching for friendly signals, or blather excitedly and inanely like squawking sparrows in a bush. Meanwhile from my cave, the whirlwind revolves around me and I see it all clearly. They are all so desperate. They do not understand, only in here is stillness, wisdom, understanding. They just don't get it. I get bored of the band who are playing nasty, rehashed, clumsy electro-pop music. I can't bear the inadequacy anymore and head back to my room where I spend the rest of the night listening to the Stereo MCs. Once I'm not so high, I am aware I am alone. I have missed the evening. Nothing happened, there was no actual epiphany. The transcendental knowledge I thought I had brought back to my room with me has now transmogrified into the close walls, the nasty coloured curtains, the stale tea cups, and the detritus of joints, bongs and bitter residue of rolling tobacco. Where is the exalted state from earlier? Why do I feel deflated, cheated, like I misjudged something, missed something somewhere?

I repeat this routine every weekend, before every social interaction in the students' union. Then it becomes more than weekends. As the distortion of even the best Nepalese hash becomes monotonous and disappointing, I seek out stronger transportation and otherness. LSD becomes habitual, only increasing my ability to hide away in the psychotropic citadel, believing I am safe from the mundane inadequates trying so hard to party and have 'fun'. I don't need fun; I am on a search for truth. It doesn't help the essay deadlines. Gradually LSD becomes too demanding, too complex, philosophically overloading my frail ego, making the citadel into a prison on a vast empty plain. I find a better balance with ecstasy, and ever trustworthy marijuana to relax the come downs. It gives me back my citadel, which I fill with beats and rhythms and repetitive sensations. It doesn't ask or demand or confuse me anymore. It becomes the place to be, and a place I can actually share with everyone else. Or at least those ravers who similarly seek the rush and escape of the beats each weekend. And thus the pattern of the greater part of my adult life is cast.

Doug visits me for one weekend, but is appalled at the juvenility of everybody, the aimlessness of the partying. His desire to get out of it has waned, in the face of real work, the hard, uncompromising graft that is catering. He sneers at what he calls 'middle-class self-indulgence.' We steadily lose touch. I believe this is commonly known as growing up.

This sense of perspective is bizarre, standing where I am now. I am not elevated. I stand, slightly paunchy, thirty-six years old, in smart but characterless clothing, alone, as a totally over the top event unfolds in honour of my brother and his boss and mentor. I am only what I am, nothing more or less. I lay aside the contempt and cynicism for the hordes of excited party goers passing me and being sucked up the red carpet. I only feel… amusement. I am amused especially that

I am here, dressed like this, heading friendless, sober, into an event that actually just intimidates me. I smile now, in realisation and bemusement at how deeply I was able to disassociate myself from the norms of society, family and friends simply by taking the drugs of my choice. I engineered my entire adult life simply with narcotics. They determined when I slept, what music I listened to, what and when I ate, the company I kept, and ultimately the tragedy of slipping through the cracks of civilised society altogether.

So, I have to do this. Time to grow up and cast aside the useless crutches of my former habits. It's just a fucking silly party after all. When I'm bored I'll just go home. In the meantime, let's see how Marbella rocks. Something gives me a spring in my step and I am striding now toward the carpet, leading, vulva like into the great concrete womb along the side of the plaza.

Photographers duck and bob, regaling the prettier girls and VIP types to pose for them. Flashes pop incessantly. Couples and groups pose in front of a large board festooned with the iconic logos of affluence; Moet et Chandon, Holmeland, Ferrari, Swarovski and other names that are lost on me. Hordes of lookalike smart girls, spooned into tight dresses and irrationally high, clunky heels are greeting and checking invites. People on stilts with flowing clothes are juggling half-heartedly, posing for photos, smiling and grimacing in expressions of who knows what. Go-go dancers with huge angel style wings of white feathers wriggle lithely between the crowds, their muscled torsos and amplified cleavages, bejewelled and corseted like supercharged sex bombs. They would be striking on a normal day but like this they ooze eroticism. It's potent and vivid, yet an invisible, unspoken electric fence hovers around them. Lose your composure and caress one of these nymphs and the enormous security men are discreetly everywhere. Their trademark coiled wires and earplugs ape the cinematic spooks, but with much added muscle. Sure enough, one likely lad finds himself lifted bodily and removed swiftly to who knows where, for attempting to grind with one of them. She

141

shrugs off the disturbance, ignores the kafuffle and continues sublimely as though on auto pilot, smile fixed, writhing steadily, languorously. Is she stoned I wonder to myself? It might actually help.

Around the entrance a steady stream of people who obviously have invites are being directed upwards. Fringing them are gaggles of younger women and men, hanging around expectantly, searching for faces, asking for favours, trying to prise an invite, an excuse, anyway of grabbing some of that rarefied air, being part of the event, being one of *the* people. And here am I, strolling up for want of anything better to do in my department store togs that still feel like someone else's clothes.

I stand in a long queue waiting to have my invite checked. To my left is a gaggle of English looking girls, judging by the golden blondeness of most of them, the rounder faces, the slightly less slender appearance than the more Mediterranean types around. One of them swings her head toward me, her great golden mane sends a waft of luscious scented hair, a smell that can only come from a woman of a certain age, a fullness, a seductive human odour, rising over the artificial scent she employs. Her eyes are hard crystal grey and her fine brows frame a long angular nose and too wide mouth. The full lips on the oversized mouth verge on ugly but she is all the more attractive for it. She's young, probably twenty, twenty something. She shoots me a delicious smile, and her hand finds my arm, slides down to meet the invite held there. Coquettishly, provocatively, she lifts up my arm and inspects my invite.

Her eyes light up as she announces to her group, 'Mr Gene Phillips and guest' which raises a good-hearted half mocking 'ooooo' from the gaggle. Then keeping the melodramatic fun going she asks, 'But where is your date dear Gene, surely she hasn't abandoned you?' This coupled with the exaggerated batting of her eyelids and pouty lips, although deeply insincere, is still entirely seductive. Her accent is unlike many of the youngsters I run across on the coast, it shows

142

no signs of a regional source, decidedly mid-Atlantic. Given how expensive her figure-hugging dress and the sparkly necklace are, I suspect she is an actual little rich girl trying to gate-crash the party with her mates. As she regards me expectantly, I am smiling dumbly as I do every time I behold a beautiful woman, and she drops the faux coquette routine, and a wave of recognition flashes across her face.

'Oh my god, Gene Phillips? You look… god, you are Gary's brother aren't you!' and a triumphant smile now lifts through her features, she pulls herself up to an impressive height, taller than me on the heels, hooks her arm through mine and with a smirking, victorious, backward glance to her friends, marches me up to a waiting hostess. I appear to have been adopted for the night.

The hostess is Frankie. She does a double take, but maintains composure.

'Awright babe, you look great, lookin' forward to it?'

I nod, smiling dumbly, as Frankie's eyes swiftly run up and down my newfound friend, with barely disguised hostility.

'Let's check your ticket. Mr Gene Phillips and guest' she announces a touch too loudly, and bizarrely the arm through mine pulls me to her protectively, possessively. 'Straight on up, cloakroom is on the left, mind how you go, darlin, awright?' Her smile is slightly strained now.

'Thanks Frankie, maybe see you later for a drink, eh?' A duel of eyes ensues between the two women momentarily.

'Yeah maybe, whatever, have a nice night, awright.' She turns her attention to the next customer.

As we climb the stairs my kidnapper asks 'Who was that? You know her?' She sounds faintly worried, as though her catch maybe isn't up to expectations or has dubious taste.

'She's my flatmate. She's Gary's tenant, and employee, and I live in my brother's old flat, hence she's my flatmate.'

'Oh nice' she says, unconvinced.

We are heading up the stairs in a queue of people. Everywhere, tight, expensive looking fabric glistens. Shoes are eye-catching, there's nothing chain store, everything around me has been chosen and thought about and put together for an effect. Older women sport fur of various dead animals, and shiny suits are preferred for older Spanish men. The air is a veritable soup of aromas, with sweet and sharp and flowery and citrusy notes fighting against each other, producing a heady, cloying atmosphere. Arriving at the top, we file through yet another pack of paparazzi; this lot must be the approved version, as they beg less and are more authoritative and demanding.

'Over here love, give us a smile, best foot forward, hand in front, shake your hair, just the two of you please, behind the lady please sir, this way Hello Magazine, Mail on Sunday, can I get your name...'

Photographers zone in on us instantly as my friend is taking all the attention from the other females around. She shifts instinctively into poses, head back, hair trailing, forward fringe hanging over, hips swivelling, hanging off my arm, draping herself around me. I stand bemused as per usual, smiling vacantly, not sure what attitude is expected of me. Commands are shouted, requests, chivvying. All for nought, I give them nothing for I know not what to give. Some of them turn away disgustedly, shaking heads, 'what a waste, no idea, what's he all about...'

The arm propels me forward yet again toward the table with the Champagne I had so dutifully delivered only hours earlier.

'What's your name?' My brain stops freewheeling and engages. I am going to have to converse and partake, again an unusual departure from past form. Standing around stoned at a do like this would be pretty bizarre, I admit to myself. Waste of good gear even.

'Britta' replies my friend.

'Is that English? You look English, but I'm not sure you sound it.'

144

'I'm Swedish, but I lived in the UK for a long time before coming here.'

'What brought you here?'

'My father's work. He's in Gib, banking or something, or maybe it's a casino now, online kind of thing. To be honest I don't really know. I don't ask, and he doesn't say. I never see him, he's usually away on business, if not he's out on his boat. I've been here for five years already.'

I have finished my first glass of bubbly and I reach for another, something to keep my hands occupied. It also seems to fortify me, the bubbles bring the alcohol to bear agreeably rapidly. The effect is not at all unpleasant. I have never drunk champagne before. Would never have been seen dead drinking it.

'You don't sound too wild about Spain' I continue, opting for small talk. What other talk is there to a stranger fourteen years your junior who is using you for a free night out?

'Well it's not exactly Notting Hill or Neuilly is it?' I don't know where Neuilly is. Something European for sure. 'I mean it's lovely, you know, but god the Spanish are so just not with it. I mean if you can find decent shops, they're only in Banus, and the assistants are so clueless even if they can speak English. Yeah there's the beach, and some good parties, and the weather, you know. That is better than Stockholm, totally, but it's just all a bit tacky.'

'Tough life, I guess' I can't help mocking this rather insular view.

'Don't be mean,' she slaps me playfully 'it can be hard for a foreign girl here, with an asshole of a father and a mother who would rather be shagging her tennis coach and lunching with the ladies every day. I don't know why they bothered having me, really.'

'Sorry, I didn't realise, it's just...' and I have to admit I know nothing about little rich girl's ennui. It's a new one for me. All the time she is talking she is scanning the crowd, searching out who

145

knows what, friends? '... that it appears a nice place to be. There's worse places, trust me.'

We carry on in this vein, tittle tattle, she complaining about the hardships of bad parenting, over entitlement and excessive lifestyle choices without the right people to deliver them, and me gently poking fun. The champagnes are sliding down, and I'm wondering what this kind of generosity costs. A whole truck load of Moet, leaves me giddy and very jolly. It's not like slugging JD and cokes or necking pints, which leaves one roiling for a fight or a long sleep. I feel like dancing!

'Bloody hell, my brother is generous with this stuff ay?'

'Well of course,' she purrs like I'm dumb 'you have a gold VIP ticket, not everyone is getting this treatment.'

'Do I?' comes the deadly honest reply. This naivety reduces her into fits of giggles, that and the bubbly.

'Where are you from, have you just got off the boat from Morocco or something. Are you sure you're Gary's brother?'

'I never said I was Gary's brother.' I am being mischievous now and enjoying it. 'You assumed that, from my name and a coincidental likeness I have to the gentleman in question.'

'What?' she cocks her head, looking askance, weighing up if this is a good or a bad thing, whether I am worthless or good for a free pass anyhow. 'So who the hell are you with a gold VIP pass if you're not his brother?' She sounds genuinely exasperated to my growing amusement.

'His cousin maybe? Twice removed' but the smirk on my face I can't contain isn't convincing. 'If you aren't happy I guess I'll just have to let security know you're not actually on the guest list.' A shadow passes across her face, and her teeth clench momentarily. The bluff is at stalemate, broken by a slap on my shoulder.

'Gene there you are!'

It's Gary with Ana. We exchange obligatory kisses all of us, and Gary appraises my partner for the evening.

'Well, it's pleasure to meet you I'm sure. I had no idea Gene had made such interesting friends so quickly here.'

'I'm Britta' and she twists self-consciously and coquettishly, lips slightly apart, looking for all the world like she'd eat him up right now. Why do all women want to fuck my brother?

'Come on,' says Gary, 'let's go and get some Crystal, stop drinking that muck.' Britta's face lights up, Gary is talking her language. We follow Gary and Ana to the back of the VIP area where all is back slapping, kisses, nods, mutual adoration and plastered on grins. Everybody's eyes constantly scan the room for who's who, people nod with approbation as certain other people hove into view. I'm standing back from conversation, absorbing the milieu, still with a broad grin on my face. The Crystal slides down even better. Dare I say it, it lacks the acidic edge of Moet, and I start to giggle at myself. Seriously, comparing champagnes on my freebie VIP ticket with my rent-a-girlfriend. And of course, it all fits. This show, this giant splash of hedonistic exhibitionism is all part of the illusion, the dream being sold in the form of condos and golf memberships, and this is its apex. Oh, and one would have to add in the surgically manipulated body image as an essential supporting prop as well. My companion is indeed young enough and genetically fortunate enough to look hot as hell with barely any effort but for her generous clothing allowance from Daddy, but the range of intervention around me is spectacular.

I notice a tall, slim, handsome young man staring at me intently. He looks Spanish, or maybe Persian, probably wealthy; he's not dressed like a thug, or local happy go lucky lad about town. So why is he sending me these aggressive looks? I tend to respond to it unpredictably. I've had my fare share and it usually causes me to overreact, which means I frequently come off worse, as I lack any ability to control aggression, once triggered in me. It's never pretty.

'Oh Christ, that's all I need' moans Britta suddenly.

'What's up?'

'That's my ex over there. He hasn't got over me yet. He can't stand to be dumped; it's never happened to him. Arrogant prick, just wish he'd get the message. What are you laughing at, what's the big joke?'

'He's giving me the evil eye, trying to psych me out. This is too funny, and I don't even know you. What a plonker, as we say up north.' I am laughing but anxiety prickles underneath, as I am never comfortable in such a situation, it's such a waste of energy to get into this macho silliness. Britta marches over to him, and he straightens up, slightly intimidated. I don't know what she says, but it has an effect, and a slightly contemptuous smile spreads across his face and he turns away.

'What was that about?' I ask as she returns to my side, stiff of face.

'Nothing, all sorted. He knows where he stands. Get me another drink, let's celebrate! Your brother's king of Marbella and I'm free of that idiot.'

We stand, champagne flutes in hand, plucking the ever-circling canapes off passing trays, carried by the younger, lower paid fringes of Marbella society. The youngsters who are presentable. Strictly no fatties I notice. I am at the centre of a swarm, guests flap like moths to the flame to congratulate Gary, to fawn, to be photographed with the golden couple. I try to edge to the back, but Britta is not having any of that and manages to drag me into several shots. Her social cache must be ramping up big time, standing next to Marbella's new king. She glows, grins and looks the part, and I make an effort to at least seem like I haven't fallen out of the sky and landed here by accident. Too much champagne helps, and my dumb grin is probably getting wider and dumber.

Around us move the great and the good of Marbella. Many a stretched face, robo-boobs too numerous to mention. If one of these sirens, a mature cougar, doesn't have a boob job, it's more noteworthy than the actual ubiquity of breast enhancement here. It's

148

like seeing a familiar old classic car, with all its quirks and variations of shape and curvature, at the mercy of gravity.

'Come on, let's get in the mood shall we?' Britta has a cheeky expression on her face.

'Okay, then, and how shall we do that?' Though I think I know what she is referring to. She leads me by the arm, like I'm her little sister, heads straight for the toilets, and without hesitation drags me straight into the ladies, into a cubicle and locks the door before slumping down on the seat collapsing into hysterics. She hitches up her skirt to reveal a long bronzed, muscled thigh clad in a sheer stocking which holds itself up miraculously. From inside this nest she withdraws a plastic bag with the inevitable white powder. As good a place as any for a stash. It would be a brave or foolhardy security guard who searched that one out. I am filled with admiration, and for the first time this evening, naked desire.

The make-up mirror comes out, the gold, no wait, a *platinum* Amex card chops up two neat lines. With a conspiratorial smile she leans into me, her grapey, warm breath enshrouding me, mingling with her hair and perfume, offering the little mirror. I thrust a hand into a pocket for a bank note. Snuuuuuuuurf. The rush hits, and her face starts to enlarge and pulsate, her lips take on a more pregnant pink hue, and her eyes deepen. She may be a little rich girl, but she has some interesting contacts. The purity of the charlie is above anything I'd ever come across in Holland. My lungs dilate and draw in breath, the heart speeds up and all parts of my body are energised. For a moment I check my paranoia, my new found suspicion of all things narcotic, but it doesn't stand the test. It can't resist the powerful surge of faked dopamine release, it withers and dies, expiring somewhere on the tiled floor of the cubicle.

She looks me square in the face and asks,

'What is it you do Gene? Who are you? Who is the real you, Genie boy? Gene Genie.' She punches me in the chest in mock aggression.

'I was a DJ for a while, I was always working on raves, in clubs.'

'So you know how to dance then?' She demands, her respiration raised and expectant.

'I can certainly say that that is one department I am-'

'Right then, take me dancing, now.' She grabs my head and plants a long, determined kiss across my mouth, her tongue probes and flickers and jabs at me, as she half giggles at this torture. She pushes me back against the door and looks me over, eyes twinkling in the rush. 'Mmmm, that was nice. Ok, Genie, let's dance.'

However, it looks like our desire to cut the rug has been curtailed by the main event of the night. The final ritual of corporate self-congratulation and Gary's coronation are about to begin. The DJ has put on some corny fanfare and lasers are projecting the Holmeland logo around the ceiling. Smoke effects kick in, as people make their way en masse to the dance floor. The free champers has done its work and everyone is pretty hyped up. It's a strange mix. Square business types and their wives in stolid Spanish bourgeois garb, the younger sales crowd in sharp fitting clothing, lots of tight backless dresses and high heels, flowing manes of hair and orange perma-tan, more middle-aged lotharios and cougar wives in overly flamboyant glittery shiny combinations, trying hopelessly to compete with the younger set and be distinct from the other mature party goers. These are the buyers, potential clients being wooed and dazzled, sold the dream of the endless long fizzy Marbella party that will be yours if you live in this dreamland.

The music reaches a crescendo and stops and Holme appears on the stage, alone. I just now realise it's the first I have seen of him tonight, he's not pressing the flesh like I would have expected.

'Good evening Marbella!' The habitual American style whooping and high-pitched squealing errupts, which has somehow wormed its way into every aspect of modern life since I was last circulating publicly.

'Tonight is a very special night for us,' and amazingly he goes into the same long ponderous kind of self-aggrandising sales speak he usually does in the few times I've seen him. This is evidently well appreciated among the few politicos and members of the business community but the younger crowd and buyers are getting twitchy. They want a show and a party, a celebration. A slight air of ennui creeps over the crowd, and Holme's lack of real charisma risks killing the vibe the champagne has worked so well to build.

'-but tonight is not my night. I've done what I set out to do. To put Marbella back on the map, to make it a byword for luxury living, and for successful investment. This night belongs to the man who has done so much to make this possible. None of this would have been achievable without him, and without our team, so it's only right I hand it over to him, as I am called to pastures new. I have great plans to bring our vision of luxury lifestyle investment development to many corners of the planet. For this reason, I shall be leaving Marbella soon, and it gives me great pleasure to introduce to you the new CEO of Holmeland, Gary Phillips.'

A hiatus trembles momentarily as the crowd processes this unexpected information; a ripple of surprise and hesitant comment, then a higher pitched noise builds, as Gary steps onto the stage, Ana by his side. The younger crowd now get it, it is indeed true, the king is dead, long live the king. They start to whoop and yell and applause build and keep building. It's as though the beautiful people have won, one of their own is king of the hill, top of the heap. Young, tanned, good looking, successful, driven, a perfect couple, the icon of the younger, cooler, upcoming, multinational Marbella. The adulation is bordering on hysteria, several girls clamber on stage in their ludicrous heels to plant kisses and hugs on him. One of them loses balance stepping back down and twists awkwardly, causing her over-enlarged breasts to pop out of the inadequate anchorage of the shiny stretch fabric. This just whips the frenzy up further, as some wag now returns from the bar with several bottles of unopened bubbly which are hastily passed around and let off. A sticky, yeasty rain comes down on all and sundry. The older guests dive for cover, the respectable grand dames of respectable Marbella tut and fume, desperately trying to maintain some dignity and shield their coiffed hair from disturbance. Gary and Ana attempt to retreat from the stage but are besieged by well-wishers, as someone sprays the crowd from on the stage. The DJ brings on a pounding track with high vamping keyboard, and techno delirium ensues. Arms flail, fists pump the air and the place explodes into energy and abandon.

The evening has divided into two distinct groups, the party crowd on the floor with spray and music, and the rest retreating to more dignified calm and canapes. Britta has been riding the crest of this wave of adulation all the way, and is now leaping and grinding with me. I don't see Holme, but I do catch sight of Lebid and our two friends from Madrid staring at the mayhem. They melt away, as do a few of the more business types. Now it's just any other party going off in the Marbella style. I'm bouncing up and down, swaying and gyrating, elbows pumping and dodging, head bobbing and ducking. I've rediscovered something I'd forgotten from way back. Dancing is fun, it can transport you, lift you up, to the otherness where all the mundanity of humdrum life doesn't matter. It's been forever. The club scene had for so long been about business, about evasion, strategy, hustling and watching one's back, as the deals became bigger and the stakes got higher. And now I have tasted again what it used to be like when we were still innocent, when we just sweated and got high, let the ecstasy wash us in its warm rhythmic embrace, rolling along for hours. Britta is yelling and jumping on me, energised by my odd but committed groove. A crowd is forming a circle around me willing me on, and I'm lost in it. It's a release of a kind, one of many that I've needed. It reminds me it used to be good, it wasn't all stress and criminality. There used to be fun, and I'm having fun now. It's short lived though as I am furiously out of breath, gasping for air. I'm not fit enough for this.

As I start to flag, Britta looks at me with a knowing smile, takes my hand and leads me away again, back to the sanctuary of the ladies' loos. Another couple of lines appear on the mirror, and I stare not at them, just at Britta now. I'm unconcerned about the class A narcotics, the commonplaceness of it here in this scene has cured me of the paranoia I had until recently experienced. And anyway, I'm too buzzed up, and the edge is coming off it so I can't wait to get another hit. Snuuuurfaroo. I'm holding the plastic bag of charlie which still has some left, so I unthinkingly drop it back down and place my hand high up on Britta's thigh, where she is sat on the seat of the loo still, and I lean over her. My head leans into hers and I connect with that smell of hair again and nuzzle my face into it. My head races with the rush of the excellently pure drug, and my skin feels sensitized, my nerves tingling and all the energy of the dancing transforms itself into pulsating tiny points of light all over my body. She pulls her dress up her thigh and guides my hand to replace the bag under the sheer tights. The touch of skin is a shock, a lightning bolt of sensuality. My hand lingers, stroking, and I am transfixed by the sensation. My throat has a lump and my mouth goes dry with anticipation and desire. She stands up, her arms around my neck and pushes her face into mine, her tongue launching deep into my mouth hungrily. I am slipping overboard into a sea of languorous textures and drowning in the aroma of her skin, her sweet mouth all grapey with drink. Strings of golden flax coil around me as we writhe in an embrace of tense desire. Her arms are so smooth, long, elegant wrists and well-manicured delicate fingers. She raises them up to let me kiss her neck, and swim around her, gobbling up her scent and texture and the lines of her chin and neck.

We are hardly in the right place, discreet or comfortable. I pull away and stare at her, taking the picture in and just checking it's real. There are probably so many things not quite right about this. Those grey eyes and the open, upturned mouth, heaving breath, her head lolling and a wanton smile breaking out across her ugly beautiful mouth. Oh, I remember one now.

'How old are you?' I ask, giggling, with what is probably rather a creepy smile.

She simply looks directly back at me and says, 'Old enough Gene' and in one swift movement her arms take the hem of her dress and peel it clean off her slender body. Her hands dart inside my shirt and it too is peeled rapidly off and I plunge onto her torso, the satiny sweet surface glides around me. I am giddy and breathless, as my lips peck and probe at the slight indentations along her collar bone and her cleavage. She undoes my belt and my trousers slide cooperatively to the floor, and she has now grabbed my penis, which has overcome the alcohol and is bone hard in a way I can't remember experiencing before. She looks at me with a smile that says she is no stranger to this outré coupling in an odd place.

'Now that's what I was hoping to find.' I'm not sure what to do now, as I am not used to sex at all, never mind under these circumstances. Everything is pulsating and swaying and I'm hyperventilating. She picks up one leg, places it onto the toilet seat which with her heels places it fairly high. She takes the front of her tanga and slides it to one side, then gently, expertly, tenderly, guides me neatly inside her. The heat and wetness enclose around me, drowning me, filling me up. I close my eyes and bury my head in the hair around her neck and gradually start to find my rhythm. Steadily we clench and hold and inhale, hands on backs, licking the growing saltiness off each other. Around us is the noise and banging of doors, toilets flushing, taps running, the gabbling of drunken girls gossiping and hooting with fun and abandon. In this Formica cubicle, in a nightclub in Puerto Banus, I heave a huge breath and my body rigidifies as I come into her. I am draining out, deflating completely, and I fall limp in her arms, my breathing easing down and I am spent and freed and cleansed and released and made new.

154

'Oh, well that wasn't quite what I expected,' she says, leaning back, appraising me. 'Been a long time has it?'

'You could say that,' is all I can say. I'm not offering excuses, I'm practically a stranger to relations with the opposite sex. There's a slight kick of incipient humiliation in her comment, which just now reminds me how complicated this sex stuff is. And a reason I have avoided it for a very long time, though not solely through choice, obviously. 'Guess we better finish this off then, see if you can't dance me to a climax, ay?' She smiles sardonically, unwrapping the remainder of the coke. Duly snorted up and fizzing nicely again we adjust dress in order to leave the cubicle as inconspicuously as possible. But there's a loud smash on the door, a concerted fist bashing, obviously intended for us.

'Get the fuck out of there you slut!' comes an angry male voice. 'You fucking slag, bitch...!' And a kick lands on the door, which is threatening to jump off its hinges now.

'Oh Christ' groans Britta, looking genuinely distressed and fearful. 'That's my ex, Karim, you know, we saw him earlier. He's *such* an arsehole.'

'Yeah, just a bit,' which doesn't fully summarize my confusion and fear at this moment. Coked off my gourd, recently freed from jail, misbehaving publicly at my brother's coronation, and now staring down the barrels of moronic testosterone and wounded, young male pride, which only an entitled, chippy little ponce like the guy I saw earlier could properly do justice to.

'Let's just wait for him to go away, he'll get bored soon.' This wishful thinking on my part is sadly dispelled by an elevated level of banging, insults and general unpleasantness. It sounds kind of distant, an echo, a delay effect in my head, and I'm playing a part, it's not actually me. Must be the coke.

'Shit, just get me out of here. You don't know him, he'll really cause a scene, he's a nasty, spoilt little shit. Why do you think I left him. Please.' A palpable fear takes hold of her, she's not posturing now. I wonder what kind of history she has had with this person.

'Ok, I suppose, what can happen, I mean, I'll talk to him, I won't let him hurt you,' I say with a kind of flaky smile. I'm decidedly light headed, disoriented, not fully cognisant of the actual seriousness of a crazed younger male on the other side of the door, who may well be even more off his head than the two of us.

I ease off the lock, and swiftly open the door, filling the doorway, blocking access to Britta. Karim blocks the doorway, panting, looking the worse for champagne, swaying a bit but very charged. Girls are exiting the bathroom in fear. I stand, just blocking, not knowing what to do next.

'You fucking whore, you humiliate me publicly like this! Fucking this clown in the toilets?! Everyone knows, right. Nobody does this to me!'

He's wondering whether to try and get past me or not.

'Look mate just leave it alright, she doesn't want to know, just leave her alone and there'll be no problems.'

He looks at me, as though seeing me for the first time.

'Who the fuck do you think you are?' he says, 'Keep your filthy fucking hands off my girl, you pathetic fucking los-'

I think he was going to call me a loser, which is not the worst thing anyone has said to me. But tonight, I don't feel like a loser, which is good, after so many years feeling exactly that. I'm not sure what I feel, other than rather elated, and confident even, and like I don't give a shit what anyone else thinks anymore, and actually like I've run out of patience. I don't feel like being the butt of insults anymore, of being the failure, or the inadequate, or the unnecessary burden, or the person people put up with because I've got the best drugs, but they don't like me or know me, because they can't see past their own stoned out self-regard to even know who I am or what I want or don't want or what I really would like to be and why I don't give a shit about them either, they're just a client, a customer, another nobody in the banging noise of another hedonistic night of self-destruction. I don't want to have to listen to other people's dissatisfaction and arrogance, or delusion, or their obsession with their social status, their appearance, their chicness and coolness and their lifestyle choices, or how well they eat and work out, and how they buy the best clothes and the go to the best clubs, and how can you be seen in that place, and did you see that *aw*ful show on TV the other night and why is he going out with her, and what car do you drive and don't you think Man United are wankers and are you going to the festival next weekend and haven't you got any better pills than that mate, it wouldn't get a fly high, I'm not paying five quid to smile for three minutes and can you get any coke, pills are for losers.

Loser. Yes I think that was the word he was going to use, but he doesn't finish the word as while I am thinking this, in the less than half a second it takes me to think all of this, my back muscles stiffen and my abdomen contracts strongly propelling my forehead forward, making contact with a simple but concentrated force around the bridge of Karim's nose, which utters a slushy cracking sound, a bit like an egg being dropped on a granite kitchen floor, causing him to gasp in a high pitch and collapse onto the ground, clutching the now deformed nose from which is issuing a not insignificant amount of surprisingly crimson liquid. I contemplate this figure on the ground, this prostrate form, who has somehow, without invitation, taken up the focus of so much of my disaffection and ennui, and actual deep resentment. I conclude that he deserves it, and that I now have a rather tricky situation on my hands. These fast slow-motion thoughts unravel in front of me, as though coming over a teleprompter somewhere in an indeterminate space a little way in front of my eyes. Britta tries to pull me forward away from the carnage as girls shriek in dismay at the handsome young man so vulgarly and bloodily dashed on the sparkling tiles. Yes, the tiles have an ingrained, bluey iridescent sparkle to them. The effect becomes the sole focus of my attention, the noise around me receding, until this reverie, which

157

probably lasts only half a second as well, is broken by another lurching tug on my arm from Britta, and we make for the exit of the now chaotic bathroom. As I start to try and focus on what will now happen, and how to deal with the uncertain aftermath, things focus for me, as two huge security guys arrive at a run. The first one, a huge African guy with a bizarrely angelic face and the body of a gladiator, puts a flat hand on my chest, and fixes me with a stare. I stop. The second guard, a stout, barrel chested, shorter white guy with a dense crew cut, pug nose and wide Slavic cheeks and eyes, presses past me and inspects the damage to Karim who is whimpering on the floor. I pity him and am curious at my uncharacteristic behaviour, and would rather like to take it back, as it wasn't personal, but I think it is now too late so I shut up and stay with the giant hand poised on my chest. The guard returns, and a hard, strong hand wedges itself under my armpit and half lifts and pushes me forward, as he breathes into my ear, his east European accent making the words somewhere between TV comedy and downright menacing.

'You fucked up, this is to police, because he injured, now you come with us,' and I am propelled forward as the gathered crowd of rubber-neckers parts. Now it's my turn to be humiliated again, properly this time, as I am dragged like a common thug through the extravagantly dressed crowd, the heels and Botox and bosoms and slashed back dresses and shiny make-up and champagne flutes part and nod disapprovingly and tut and grimace. Through the press of the crowd Gary appears, and the two guards stop.

'What's happened?' He looks aghast, as though some long forgotten nightmare from the north of England has risen afresh to taint the sweet, orange blossom scented air, to shatter the aura of genteel, young and modish success and affluence. Which I suppose it has. I am pulled aside out of view while Gary converses with the guard. After a moment he steps over to address me, without meeting my eyes.

'Whatever happened, I'm not interested, I don't want to know, no excuses. How could you? To me? Tonight.' He pauses, looking for words, breathing deeply and powerfully, trying to contain his rage and disappointment. He collects himself and continues, 'I think I've got you off. I'll sort out the other guy, we can stop him going to the police. The last thing we want is the police to show up now. You can imagine how that will look.' And he fixes me with his eyes for the first time, to let that sink in. How it will look. Ah of course, it wouldn't look good. The illusion of clean fun, wholesome, trouble free lifestyle and safe profit doesn't square with the blue flashing lights, the questions, the voyeurs peering at the drama, sucking its veins for whatever salacious thrill and detail that can be extracted. Right now, things do look indeed rather dramatic. Not good. Two leviathans stand guard over me, Gary fumes and fidgets in a contained kind of way. Karim appears with none other than Ana, trying to sooth and deflect his justifiable ire. He shoots me a look that is nothing less than palpable fear. The tissues pressed to his face are spattered scarlet, which, no, isn't a good look either. The rubber-neckers are continually shooed away by the security guys. Britta is some way off, being consoled by friends, staring at me as this Jeckyl/Hide

transition has brought her down with a bump. And it is I at the centre of this not-good-looking drama. I the spiller of blood. I the bringer of disharmony and fear. It's not a 'I' I recognise, and I find myself strangely disconnected, as all of these sensations are so unfamiliar. As is the manic coke high I've been on for what feels like hours but is probably less than one. And everyone is still looking at me. Not directly, it's all sideways glances, stolen stares, like some wild animal has been brought to heel and they're waiting to see what the captors will do. I stare around me, aware of the continued pumping behind my eyeballs, whether it's adrenalin, champagne, coke or all of it, I can no longer tell. I want to stop, slow down, jam the brakes on and screech to a halt, get out of the car, sit in a cosy chair and have a nice cup of tea, but the engine is still running full tilt. Gary pulls me back to him to get my attention.

'Go back to the flat, pack your things. You're done in Marbella. I want you gone by tomorrow afternoon.'

He turns and goes over to Ana and Karim, placating and schmoozing. Karim doesn't appear to be too hurt, just suffering unfamiliar indignities. They move him along and make to go back to the VIP lounge with him, all concern and caring.

'Come, you heard Mr Gary said.'

It's the Security guard, looking at me, his jaw slightly tense and the muscles in his cheek flinching occasionally as he waits for me to respond. There really isn't much else to do but comply with his request.

Outside I breathe in, tasting the sea scented air, still mild and vaguely fragrant. Orange blossom leaching in from nearby. It's a bizarre contrast, all the usual nonsense of a bad night out, drugs, violence, noise, and instead of damp and cold and traffic and kebab fumes, it's orange blossom and the sea. I'm standing alone in the middle of the square where I started only a bit earlier. Still people stroll up, wrapped tight in the clothes and heels of hedonism. Young bodies honed, hardened, or cajoled and plastered into emblematic forms; older bodies disguised or scraped and strapped behind ostentatious or shiny creations. The synthetic adrenalin effect has long subsided. The sullen damp cloud of the down insinuates its long fingers into my frame and my consciousness. Gradually, real emotions start to return. My sense of self, with all its usual negativities and inadequacies starts to settle down like the dingy veil, dusty from years in a cellar, ripe with mould and cobwebs, that it is. I stare at the edifice of the club, the Holmeland logo still dancing about its face in laser light. I watch the people moving in and out, suck in the whole atmosphere of the place. I start to walk away from the club, toward the smell of the sea. I need some space, as the shroud is growing and threatens to smother me. I still haven't set foot in 'port' as it is called.

I find myself walking along a narrow sea front with a low-rise row of pokey, boxy shops, restaurants and bars. It isn't too busy, it's late March after all, but there's no lack of groups of people, couples sauntering. It's a cutesy, pseudo-Spanish village in style, but fails on most levels as the overlay of neon, signage, garish decor and slightly grubby appearance of the buildings is utterly tawdry. Gigantic boats bob and sway, ornate plastic pigs; fat, globular and bloated with ostentation and hubris. Extraordinarily expensive cars line every inch of the quayside, and most people appear to be walking the quay simply to gawk at them, the ultimate in envy tourism. No fishing boats, just floating gin palaces, fibreglass status symbols. Toward a tower at the far end of the port are several gigantic motor yachts, the like of which I have never seen. Locked up, covers on, windows shuttered and darkened, this opulence is obviously a part time trifle for someone busy making, or sitting on, piles of money elsewhere.

Despite the obvious wealth dripping over the ropes and off the rails into the water, the place still has the tone of a cheap holiday resort. Pizza restaurants, music bars, cheesy mock Irish pubs and sea themed bars abound, steak houses and curry houses and shops selling handbags and shoes and scarves and all the usual stuff at truly obscene prices, run cheek by jowl.

I stare into one shop, the place devoid of customers, various bags and trinkets standing sparse and alone on near empty glass shelves, bright white banks and slivers of light creating geometric shapes. The whole place is a study in harsh, minimal design, dedicated to merely everyday items. The assistant stares blankly out onto the quay, her eyes tracking the couples and gawkers outside, bored out of her mind. At the side of the shop is a narrow passage and the sound of voices and music travels down. I follow it and appear on an inner street, with the building and its higgledy-piggledy blocks of Spanishized concrete rising up high on either side. Stucco and

161

shutters and Roman tiles on the higher floors battle acres of flashing neon at ground level. Music throbs out of every premise, each one designed in its own way to press some button in the minds of the gaggles of tottering girl gangs and paunchy, sauntering golfers. Security personnel are stationed everywhere, all with that same inscrutable air, poised and wary, eyes working fast, scanning and tracking from within the gargantuan, still frames. A veritable United Nations of muscle. Africans, Moroccans, Arab and Asian, white guys looking variously European, Slavic, Scandinavian. The street is flooded with all sorts of nationalities too. It's funny how I can easily pick out the Brits. It's something about the way they move around in packs, echoing each other's dress codes, laughing as one, reacting to goads and jokes from others as one. It's familiar from the hen and stag partiers I remember filling Amsterdam and Hamburg, familiar from the Saturday nights in Warrington or Wigan or St Helen's.

A slight air of menace drifts subtly, just enough noise and alcohol, people and abandon, for it to flip at any moment into something less than jolly holiday. All this, just meters from the floating palaces of the super-rich. It's bizarre.

'Watch out guys, here he comes, the terminator.'

A bunch of likely lads are grinning at me, and I realise this comment is aimed at me. I pick out Darren from amongst them, who is grinning at me, shaking his head.

'What the fuck have you been up to, you naughty boy. Spoiling baby bruvver's party isn't the way of advancing your career prospects now is it eh?' he adds, clearly thrilled by the news, which obviously has travelled ahead of me the few yards from the square. 'What happened mate, I heard you got fired an' all.'

'Well, I think I blew it pretty much. Gary told me to leave by tomorrow afternoon. It's over for me in Marbella apparently.' I say this matter of factly, as I haven't reached an opinion or even an emotion on it yet.

'I heard you smacked some little rich kid. Doesn't seem like your style, that, Gene.'

My expansive mood and the fact I have nothing else to do means I give the assembled group a blow-by-blow account of the entire evening thus far, which obviously entertains them, judging by the whoops and guffaws. A pint is thrust into my hand, and the general theme of having fucked up the beautiful people's night is worked over and celebrated and relished by the assembled lads. I've obviously come down to the lower reaches of the Marbella social ladder, and they take me to their bosom as one of their own. Temporarily at least. The shroud is lifted as pint after pint plus chasers eats it away, alcohol fuelled moth grubs, freeing me from further introspection, a welcome blind anaesthesia.

'You remember Jonno, Gene, don't you?' Darren leans in conspiratorially after a while. 'He was on the job in the warehouse for the show in Madrid remember.' God, it feels like years ago already, not just the few days it has been.

'Yeah sure, aright Jonno' I slur, 'you was a chippy, right?'

'You should try working with him on them film shoots they do,' continues Darren 'Long hours but it's good money, he might be able to get you in.'

'Yeah sure no worries mate,' Jonno says raising his pint to me, 'to the Terminator,' and this generates another drunken, appreciative roar. Neon, noise, roaring males, alcohol, holding forth, playing to the gallery, slagging off, shouting and arguing about something, politics, preaching, losing my thread in a haze of chasers, sliding onwards to memory loss, giddiness, splashes of clarity; crossing roads, falling over, something with kebabs, shouted insults and ribaldry across a square, chants of 'Holme is a wanker na na na naaa' in football stylee, local policemen brandishing torches and veiled threats, then lonely walking through scented streets, rustling palms, and a bright moon in a cloudless sky, a fumbling of keys, cursing hard marble steps meeting insufficiently anaesthetised shin bone, door open, falling, soft, cool cotton, oblivion.

12

A crack in the blackness, dim shapes coalescing, sounds tapping at the edges of consciousness. Eyes open, squinting in strong, unexpected glare of a day. Painful, misty stiffness sits, epoxy strength, on my awareness. Pinpoint throbbing, cranium-piercing horror, a nauseous robe of pain and incomprehension. Some indistinct, primeval self-preservation urge forces the unwilling body into spasms of movement. No real coordination possible, swaying motion bouncing off door jams and walls, noisy clattering into panel doors, swirling light and strange room angles crowd the partial vision, until the familiar and brutal goal of the quest materialises and coalesces as a clear image of a physical object in real time and space. The toilet bowl. All non-necessary internal liquids are violently expelled. Acrid vapours and tacky bile glue up my mouth and head again. I slump groaning to the floor, relieved, but sinking back into oblivion.

After an unknown interim, I regain consciousness properly and try to extricate myself from the gymnastic way I have wrapped myself around the toilet. Lurching into the shower I deluge myself with cold then hot water, and, equilibrium having been regained, I stand on two feet and assess the situation. I am alive, this much is apparent. The body in front of me is hunched, the head drooped with dark shadows under the eyes. I have a thick lip and a cut on my eye brow, some scabbing on my forehead. I must have bumped into something, or someone. The nausea is present, but manageable, but the pains are significant. A sharp tender bruise yells from my shin. My forehead has definitely taken some damage and is likewise tender and sore. My hands are grazed, skin missing also from elbows and knees. If this is what my body is like, what happened to my clothes I wonder and half crack a smile at the thought. The smile freezes on my face, as the clothes establish the memory link to the evening before. I was wearing them because I went to a party. I met a young girl, got hammered on cocaine and had unprotected sex with her in a nightclub toilet, and then assaulted her ex-boyfriend. I was thrown out of the party, probably got sacked, and then got blind drunk with… was it Darren and… who else? I'm staring at this broken, naked disaster in the mirror, piecing together the carnage of the night before gradually, its implications taking on a monumental aspect. Yes, that was it. Now it is clear, as the day itself, as this sad sack in the bathroom, breathing heavily, trying not to be sick again. I've blown everything, my job, my credibility, my brother's respect, and not to mention my license. I've pissed a ton of people off, embarrassed them and myself and narrowly escaped a charge with the Spanish Old Bill. Pretty good for one night's work. Now I am fully back in the room, so to speak, I decide to get dressed, asking myself over and over again, how did I get *to here?*

Coffee in hand, I sit gingerly on the chair on the terrace and gaze out toward the sea over the roof tops and palms. It's slightly chilly, but the air is fresh and sharp, penetrating my lungs and clearing my head a bit more. Three enormous paracetamols have yet to hit home so I'm grateful for any extra help. I find my mobile and search for any texts. Sure enough, from Gary: 'let me down. think we both know that u dont fit this world. wanted to give you a chance, can't have this kind of liability. stakes way too high. will get you flight sorted. sorry has to be this way.' 0315am.

I stare into the distance, head empty, thoughts suspended, allowing the breeze to play the clean air over me, letting the sounds of the day fill up the scene. Palm leaves rustling rubberlike, scooters screaming away in the distance, the seagulls, sparrows chirruping, a hawk whistling somewhere high up. The feeling I have forming is familiar. It's been around forever. Of not being part of the world around me. I'm the piece of the jigsaw left at the end, I don't have a place in the picture. I'm not angry, I expect this of myself. Here was a new puzzle. All I had to do was put the pieces together, fit myself in, and complete the picture. Instead, true to form, the puzzle is all over the floor, and I've lost many of the pieces. I was just starting to see what a nice picture it was.

Frankie appears, looking sleepy and hungover. Her body language says she is sad, but pitying of me. She doesn't even have to say it, I've fucked up royally.

'So, what you gonna do babe?' she asks, head sympathetically at an angle, eyeing me from under a flop of tousled hair braids.

'Gary's pretty much told me to go back home. Says I'm a liability, can't have me around.'

She doesn't respond initially.

'Well, it was a bit messy last night. Not good, you was lucky you didn't get nicked.'

'It was just a fight in a pub really, no big deal' I say, trying to take a point of view I am not wholly convinced of. But it would work for some.

'Well yeah, sort of, but y'know, Gary's such a big shot, and it was like his night, the whole of Marbella is like looking at him, and you, like…' she doesn't need to finish, she spares me the full verdict.

'Well, it was nice while it lasted. Good to catch up with him, but I better be getting back to England, you know, things to do, people to see.' I say, sarcastically.

'S'at what you gonna do?'

'Well it's kind of tricky to stay here given I completely live off Gary's benevolence.'

'His what?'

'Kindness. Same thing'

'Oh right, course I forget you went to college an' that dincha, funny cos you don't seem like one of them.' She says this without any apparent malice or irony.

'One of them?' and I smile in surprise, intrigued as to what label I am the beneficiary of. Smiling feels good. I must smile more on this dark and cloudy morning.

'Well y'know, clever like. Gary and Holme, they're always trying to sound clever, like they know what they're doing and you don't, it's a secret and you can't never know it. The way they go on, always makes you feel they're above you, they belong to a different class and you're never gonna be able to join them.'

I'm intrigued by this, Frankie has never expressed opinions in my company, possibly for good reason, but this morning is plainly different. I've been dumped to the bottom of the heap so she's able to say what she likes as she's still in the club and I'm on the plane home.

'I suppose that's just business, it's all smoke and mirrors, selling illusions and dreams, you gotta talk the talk, walk the walk. To me, frankly, it's all bullshit, it's just selling houses, it's not rocket science.'

Frankie's face is a picture of surprise. Then she bursts out laughing and we both laugh like drains, and when it subsides, I feel lighter, like the travesty of last night is only a relative blip in the grand scheme of things, and Holmeland is merely another miniature world of no consequence.

'I think I got you all wrong,' says Frankie. 'You're actually really different from Gary.'

'Different?!' I laugh, 'Let me tell you how different.' And I tell her what I've really been doing for the last ten years, and about our family. Because what the hell does it matter now anyway. When I've finished, she's deep in thought, like she sees everything differently. She breaks out of this reverie, slightly embarrassed at having this new knowledge, about me, about our family tragedy, about the baggage we trawl behind us. About the cloud Gary escaped, and the one that still threatens to engulf me.

'Aren't you supposed to be leaving today then?'

'You gonna buy me a plane ticket?'

'Piss off, no way.'

'Looks like I'm stuck here then.'

We laugh again, enjoying the tragicomedy which is but a storm in a teacup on a southern European shore.

I revert to type. After the night before, the day passes in what is politically incorrectly referred to as 'monging about'. Listlessly hanging around watching TV and not doing anything at all in particular. Frankie and I. Whiling the hours away. Eventually, in the evening, she pulls on the glad rags again, straps herself into a dress and heels and heads off for another night of servicing expensive hedonism.

Alone now, I'm aware of the voice yelling at me somewhere in my head, reminding me Monday is my appointment with Mr. Watkins. The license terms will be irreversibly broken. While I know they won't actively come looking for me, I'm a nobody effectively, they will recall me to Strangeways for a minimum of four weeks if they do catch up with me. Gary is unwittingly proposing I deliver myself back to prison. More Mr. Watkins. It feels very distant from here. Not quite real. And that suits me. I crash out in front of the telly, and at some indeterminate hour I fall into bed, having found myself asleep on the sofa after who knows how long.

~

A whole Sunday rolls by, in pretty similar fashion. I chastise myself momentarily for not venturing out, exploring this new country outside my window. A combination of fatigue and mental indifference persuades me to stay on the sofa. I am inevitably joined by Frankie, dressing gowned, recovering from yet another long night of forced smiling. We pass the time laughing at the inanities of daytime television, surfing the waves of trivia and lifestyle obsessiveness available on a zillion channels. Being older and vastly more cynical than Frankie, I attack pretty much everything on offer, and she tries gamely to defend a whole range of celebrities, game and lifestyle shows. Once we start on the vodka mid-afternoon, this

169

process deteriorates rapidly into general childish slagging off. It's a nice release after the seriousness and pressure of working for Holmeland.

Occasionally I check for texts. None are forthcoming. I'm still here, I think. But jobless. Darren's cunning has at least given me a safety net for a while. Breathing space, time to figure out a way to avoid a return home. There, only further intense, stressful trouble awaits me, at the hands of the probation service. I'll talk to Gary tomorrow. I'll leave him alone. Do my own thing. This fabricated positivity makes the future seem less bleak. Frankie goes out to work at the club and I settle in to dig up some favourite old films. A proper lazy Sunday, but with a sense of ease and humanity I can't remember in, well, ever. Since childhood anyway. Frankie's company has the benefit of being unpretentious, and free of agendas. She has no axe to grind, she lives day to day in the Puerto Banus bubble, and takes it at face value, with no particular expectations beyond the routine and immediate gratifications. I admit to myself I spent years sneering at people like her. In my drug inspired, warped sense of individual specialness, I imagined I was above banality, I was not beholden to the lowbrow obsessions of the herd. After three years inside, sitting here now with my non-future in my hands, I see it clearly for the laughable, self-indulgent chimera it was. It's decidedly shocking, actually, Gene. What have you got to show for all of that? Nowt. Exactly.

13

'Goaaaaaaaaal!'

Doug wheels away triumphantly from the forlorn goalkeeper. Little
Gary. He hasn't stopped sulking since we stuck him in goal. Being
the smallest and youngest he never chooses teams or what he gets to
play, which inevitably means he gets the short straw. Doug and I pick
from the gaggle of kids, the jumpers are plumped into discernible
markers of the goals, and Gary is inevitably condemned to a role his
size and temperament barely equip him for. This self-defeating
selfishness is remarkably short sighted. We always lose when Gary is
in goal, though there are several kids who would make better keepers.
Conversely, we all think we are Kenny Dalglish.

'Four-nil, four-nil, four-nil, four-nil...' sing Dougie's entire
team, ecstatic at their trouncing of us.

Gary stomps up the field holding the ball, fury and self-pity
battling across his features. 'Someone else go in, it's not fair!'.

The team glances around each other, expecting me to take the
lead, as I am more or less the oldest and Gary is the junior. The
prospect of Gary playing outfield is even more unpopular. He's my
problem. As the weakest link, here by order of Mum who insists he
should be able to play with the rest of us, I have the responsibility of
employing his limited talents in the least damaging way possible.

'Gaz, get in goal.'

'No!' He is clutching the ball tightly, his face a reddening
rictus of determination.

A brotherly battle of wills, the kind that frequently dissolves
into petty violence between us, one that usually ends in my favour, is
precluded by the arrival of two figures on their souped-up push bikes.
Familiar figures. Buddies of Jimmy Kavanagh, who, to everyone's
relief is not with them. The game halts as we stand as one, wondering

171

what this visitation implies, unwilling to continue. We outnumber them considerably, but their hardness is not in dispute, and they have the ultimate protection of thug-in-chief, Jimmy. They circle our group in a wide arc on their bikes.

'Slapper.' Says one.

'Slag'. Says the other.

They stop. One of them mimes dick sucking at Gary, who stares in fear and bewilderment. He hasn't any idea of what such a gesture means, but the rest of us, in the first throws of puberty, know only too well. The other starts up a sexual panting. He starts thrusting his hips. Pant pant. His mate joins in with female groaning.

'Oh Frank! Give it to me! Fuck me Frank. I want it hard.'

We are all transfixed with disgust, and confusion. This visitation of adult explicitness is too beyond our relatively innocent minds, more preoccupied with football and pop music.

'Oh yes Irene, yes, yes, yes, ya slapper. Slapper, slapper' he yells as he pants to a mock climax. They dissolve into hysterical laughter, looking at me and Gary.

Irene is my mother's name. Everyone here knows who Frank is. The Frank Kavanagh, Jimmy's dad.

'Your mum's a fucking slag.'

This shocking sentence drops onto the wet grass. Stinking, like fresh dogshit. They cycle away leaving everyone twitching, avoiding our eyes, not knowing how to react. It's too invasive, intimate, too out of our pubescent comfort zone to be dismissed, joked about, forgotten. Gary drops the ball and runs for it. Heading for home. In tears. I follow, leaving wordlessly, aware only of the embarrassment and discomfort that has smothered our football match.

I am about to enter the chip shop, to tell my father as discreetly as possible about this act of emotional terrorism, to plead for some kind of justice, retribution. But his expression stops me dead. He won't meet my eyes. His face tells me he is crushed, fuming, roasting alive inside, all while trying to serve customers. Mrs Braithwaite does the talking, trying to cover for the silent volcano bashing the friers, trying to hold on to some semblance of composure.

I enter the flat upstairs cautiously. Gary is in his tiny bedroom, his face buried in a pillow. From the bathroom I hear a harrowing sound, that of low animal sobs, distraught, inconsolable. My mother. And I know that the horrible pantomime I witnessed on the football field was not a fiction.

14

Monday morning, that dread moment, for millions, as they drag themselves toward unwanted hours of work, school, responsibility, drudgery. I stay in bed. Mulling over whether to call Gary and see if maybe he's backtracked on his demand. The prospect of returning to England is nothing short of miserable. It means going home, to accompany my comatose mother, it means looking for some demeaning job they still won't give to an ex-con anyway. It means navigating the judgmental and humiliating benefits system. All of that once they decide to let me out again. It means living in Warrington until I have means to do otherwise. It's a gloomy, soggy, suffocating cul-de-sac of an alternative to this.

Lying in bed. I could do this in Warrington. Outside is a world I still barely know. Ridiculous. I bound out of bed, shower, and put on some of my newer, straighter clothes. I decide to leave aside the baggy trousers, dirty trainers and shapeless t-shirts for once. They feel too… Warrington.

Frankie is up and about, just.

'Morning, what you up to today? Same old same old?'

' 'aven't thought about it yet. Why? Got itchy feet? Cabin fever already? Mind you, you should be used to it, shouldn't ya?' She laughs, at my expense, but not maliciously.

'Here I am, barely out of jail a month, and I'm lying around watching daytime telly and scratching my balls. My life is wasting away before my very eyes! Save me Frankie, what am I to do on this lovely Monday morning?'

'Well I've got a day off. We could go out.'

'Out! Good. And then what?'

'Dunno, we could go and get some lunch for a change.'

'Frankie, you're a good man in a tight spot. Let's do it.' It's the line uttered by Robert de Niro, in my favourite film, Brazil. I love the dystopian flip side of the grotesquely shallow society. How many times have I seen it?

'Where'd you wanna go?' she says, shrugging.

'Why don't we go to Marbella. Real Marbella, the old bit. There is an old bit isn't there?'

And so, after much cajoling and a hilarious faux fashion show, where Frankie tries endless dresses and outfits, and I mercilessly take the rise out of her, we are ready to depart on our adventure. I'm trying to get her to wear something where she doesn't look like a ten-dollar hooker. Her wardrobe is obviously focussed on her professional needs, and the predilections of the fancy clients in Gary's club, all of which is much too OTT for lunch in the Old Town. We don't want to stop the traffic. Through much good-humoured bullying I manage to get her to tone it down to some fetchingly distressed Levi jeans, a yellow halter neck top and a shiny bomber jacket. Her impressive synthetic breasts are still impressive but not shouting from the rooftops as most of her outfits make them do. So off we go to the real Marbella. This will be a change to the plastic, golf-addled Andalucía I have been used to thus far in my sojourn.

Old Marbella is a revelation; touristy, but nonetheless genuinely old and authentic. The age of the place is apparent in the long narrow streets, the wobbling walls and undulating roofs revealing the ravages of time. Much of it is still residential, the houses being not unlike old terraces in the north of England, two up two down mini dwellings with a front door opening straight into tiny lounges. This being a place where locals live, and it being lunchtime nearly, the aromas that waft out of many windows are rich and seductive. Garlic by the truck load, endless variations of stocks and sauces, saffron, bay, pork and fried fish, stews and soups. Maybe we should just knock on a local door, rather than bother with some touristy restaurant, so good are the smells coming from every other house. Frankie and I run around like kids on a school trip, both childishly excited by so many new sensations. The orange blossom is heavy in the air, when not competing with garlic, and every so often we are stopped dead in our tracks by a sprawling bush of Jasmin spilling over an ancient, distorted courtyard wall. Frankie, disgracefully, after five years in Spain has never set foot in real Marbella either. I wonder how many other Brits never get beyond the beach clubs and the bland condos.

Sticky toffee almonds, fried doughnuts, some delicious ice creams, a couple of coffees in quaint plazas so cute you could film an advert in them. Indeed, we trip over a film crew doing just that. Some gorgeous Spanish girl leaning out of a window of an old cottage, serenaded Romeo and Juliet style. I have no idea what the product is, and I marvel at the amount of equipment piled up, people running around with tripods and cables and god knows what.

'Oi, can't you see we're working, out the way,' and the speaker digs a fist in my ribs. I turn around and it's Jonno, one of the crew we dragged in for the Madrid build. 'Keeping out of trouble?' he smiles.

'So, this is your proper job?'

'Ha, yeah, you could call it that. Blimey, she with you?' He has clocked Frankie.

'Erm, yeah, friend of my brother's.'

'With friends like that-', but he's unable to land the punchline as an officious person brandishing a walkie-talkie shoos us aggressively back along the alleyway.

'Come on, let's get down on the seafront, find somewhere nice with a view for lunch' asks Frankie. She hooks her arm through my elbow, and leads me off toward the sea. We pass through a luscious tropical glade, which is actually a park, but could be a jungle, and emerge onto an esplanade of new blocks at the end of which is the sea. The Old Town is set back a good four hundred meters from the sea. And it is old, as witnessed by the construction materials on some of the derelict buildings, snapshots of a bygone society, with its lime wash, adobe walls, cane mesh roofing and Roman style tiles. In amongst this, as Ana mentioned, are the remains of a modest Moorish fortification on a rocky promontory. Weirdly enough it has a school built into it. I found it fascinating and am sorry we are heading back into modern Marbella. However, the sea front is not without its charms. The buildings are condo blocks lining the beachfront, a hotchpotch of seventies and eighties pretension. But the prom is pedestrianised and lined with a double row of splendidly tall palm trees running for as far as the eye can see. Restaurants, cafes and trashy shops line the front. Still only March, the temperature is in the twenties and the place is full of couples and groups strolling, eating, chatting and watching the world go by. All sorts of languages are heard, from all types of people. Scandinavian tourists stand out like sore thumbs with their luminous white skin from a lifetime of endless dark winters.

Eventually we settle down in a bistro of some sort, where the menu comes in a language we understand and the dishes are vaguely familiar. It's a mash-up of North African and Latin cuisine with obvious Spanish staples. We wash it down with Cava, which it turns out is Spanish champagne, and much more affordable. The sun glistens on the sea. The palms rustle, and we order another bottle. There's no hurry to get up and go anywhere, the view is lovely, the temperature perfect, and a curious, unfamiliar sensation overwhelms me, that of wellbeing. This is really nice. I gaze down the long promenade. Countless people doing just the same. Drinking in this lovely... I stop and have to laugh at myself, this lovely *lifestyle*. Yes, I'm doing lifestyle! Not merely existing, or working, or getting out of it, I am at this moment experiencing a lifestyle. Kicking back, chilling out in a committed, constructive way I would have avoided like the plague in former days, but something has seduced me. Holme and Gary are all far away, such is the power of a lovely afternoon and lots of bubbly. I glance at the mobile phone. No texts. Yeah, maybe he's not that bothered after all. Who cares anyway? It's just selling houses.

'Oh look, it's Declan and Nadia.' Frankie sounds a bit perturbed. 'Oh gawd. They're gonna see me.'

'Is that a problem?'

'Well no, it's just like, he's a client, from the club, but it's not the same is it.'

'Hahaha, so you can't talk to them in real life?'

'You know what I mean…'

She's looking toward a couple approaching. Declan is a shortish middle-aged man, with a slightly comical, rapid walk on his short legs, and Nadia is easily half his age or less and is a full foot taller. She wears frayed jean shorts cut short, revealing extraordinary long, svelte legs. She looks fairly Mediterranean, with full lips, and black wavy hair, though they are still a way off. Not a few people walking turn a head as they pass to marvel at the sight, if not Nadia's legs, then the comedic contrast between the two.

'Oh heck, they've seen me.'

Indeed, their faces light up when they spy Frankie, and they make for our table. Frankie does introductions in a slightly embarrassed way, but they both appear perfectly comfortable seeing her outside of her usual role. Nadia, it transpires, is Bulgarian. Declan is Irish. Obviously wealthy, as evidenced by his bulbous watch, a Breitling he tells me, when he sees me scanning it. Plus the obligatory Ralph Lauren Polo clothing. Golf chic. That must be the shortest oxymoron ever. But they come over as jolly and very fond of Frankie.

Yet another bottle is ordered, but Declan doesn't do Cava, only the French stuff for him. And it is nicer, I have to admit. Inevitably the conversation gets around to mysterious me. Frankie just introduced me as a friend called Gene. I've been waiting for this, trying to frame my story in light of recent events, how best to hide in plain sight. Then I think, why bother? I'm hardly a freak by local standards for sure. Having burnt the only bridge I had, I am beholden to no-one now. So, in answer to how I ended up in Marbella, I tell him straight. It's a story he appears to relish judging by the expression on his face. Declan, it turns out, knows Holme as they move in the same uber-wealthy crowd, drink Crystal in the same clubs. And they are competitors. Or, more strictly, a part competitor. Declan doesn't reveal too much, other than that he's in kitchens, kitchen fitting, supplies, en masse. Whole complexes. He complains how out of date and substandard the local stock is, and how he's hoping to revolutionise the business here, by bringing in quality materials, designed in Germany, but manufactured in China. By going for enormous bulk, he reckons he can undercut anyone on the coast. I'm not sure I'm interested, but he rattles along. I've noticed this here; people will talk about business at the drop of a hat. You'll be ostensibly relaxing, drinking, eating or kicking back and people are on about business non-stop. Come to think of it, a certain type. Rich people. That must be how they get rich, never switch off, just keep on doing business.

It's not long before I realise there's a reason for him talking about business. I'm on the inside, or was, at Holmeland, in Lebid's warehouse. I find myself giving out information, filling in some blanks for Declan, he's building a picture and a plan. He sucks me dry for information. So as not to lead him on, get his hopes up, I tell him I'm probably not working there anymore.

'Ahh, yes, now would that be at all connected to a bit of a hoo-ha at the party last week, would it now?'

'It might very well be, it's a fair cop guvnor. You got me bang to rights,' I try to say in my best Essex accent, making Frankie squirm with horror. Everyone thinks it's a hoot. We carry on in this vein for some time. Nadia says not much at all, as she speaks little English. She gazes dotingly at Declan, who, while not exactly an Adonis, is certainly good company, and is genuinely affectionate, not patronising, as older rich men can be to beautiful young women.

Declan regales us, often hilariously, with tales of sharp business practice on the coast, the scammers, the ruthlessness, and how Spain's sclerotic justice system leaves businesses hung out to dry, due to the lack of any fast or efficient means of pursuing non-payers. He hints at other methodologies, with a cheeky grin and a wink. He's extremely affable, but is obviously pretty damn shrewd and a tough nut when it comes to business. The most surprising revelation is who the worst payers are. The town halls and various levels of government make up a vast market for the thousands of services and suppliers, and it turns out they are the slowest and worst to pay. Whole companies live and die by the whims of *concejales* and bureaucrats, who gets paid when, if at all. The vicious circle of bribes, kickbacks, favours and mutual interests goes on and on.

'You know who the biggest criminal gang in Spain is?' asks Declan rhetorically. 'The fecking government!' This evokes laughs of recognition even from other tables, but he's not finished. 'You know how to make a small fortune in Marbella? Come with a big one!' More laughter.

Evening is approaching, everyone is slightly sleepy but decidedly content. The waiter brings the check, and I lean over to see the damage. We've been here a while, which could mean uncomfortable amounts of money, but Declan has snatched it and passed it back with some notes he peels off a thick wad in his trouser pocket.

'But most of that is ours, Declan', I protest, but he waves me off.

'Feck off, you silly beggar. You deserve it after what you've been through.' Then his face changes, becomes serious. He looks me in the eye and asks, 'What's your next move, son? What are you really gonna do, now?'

'Well, my brother wants me on a plane out of here. I really don't know. It's all been a bit of a whirlwind, as they say.'

'Come and work for me.' He's deadly serious.

'Really? But I-'

'But what? You're not stupid, I can see that. You're educated. I think you've got something in yer, you've just been playing silly buggers too long. I'll give you a chance, and if you mess it up, you'll be out on your ass in twenty seconds', and he laughs like a drain again, as do we all. As we get up to leave, he passes me a card, and shakes my hand warmly.

'Come by the offices tomorrow, around eleven. Unless you're busy that is,' he says with a wink. And they're off, he with his fast little strides, and Nadia sashaying gracefully along at half the rhythm, the giraffe and the warthog. Frankie and I look at each other in disbelief, and we hug in sheer joy at this unexpected turn of events. I am elated. It's only kitchens, but frankly I don't care what it is. It's something to fill the vacuum facing me, put a shape and a structure onto the future. Because the future is right there, smack up against my face, and I no longer want to evade it the way I have been used to. A job, for me. Not standing in my brother's shadow. A way forward. A way of not going back.

'Let's go and celebrate' I say to Frankie. She gives me a withering look. 'Only joking. I'm knackered, and somewhat pissed. Take away pizza and a film, I reckon.'

She smiles up at me, takes my arm again as we head off along the prom in the late afternoon sun. 'Sounds nice. Count me in.'

Back at the flat, things don't go to plan. I am stood, still pretty tipsy, staring out toward the glow behind the distant mountains. A dozen different pastel shades vie with each other, silhouetting the palms and mountains. It reminds me momentarily of that Eagles album cover, Hotel California. I laugh to myself, and turn around to share this thought with Frankie. She's just behind me. She's staring at me, with a look I haven't seen before. I draw her towards me, and her breasts press hard against me. They have nowhere else to go after all. It's slightly peculiar, but I don't mind. We are kissing before we know it. Deeply. Something releases in me. Some last knot of regret, of shadow, a bitter nugget of solidified memory dissolves in the delicious tastes and sensations of Frankie and I wrapping ourselves tightly around each other. Wordlessly we head for her bedroom. A soft, wide bed, the glow of the dusk slanting in, making Frankie's pale, full flesh glow deliciously, as she peels off her clothing, looking at me all the while. I do likewise and we fall onto the bed and lose ourselves completely in each other. For a long time.

~

At some point in the night I wake up. Thirsty as hell. Dehydration from alcohol and physical exertion of an intensely carnal sort. It must be late. I take a drink of tap water, leaning down to the tap, like a schoolboy. I have a long, well-earned pee. I stand and stare into the mirror at the strange face peering back at me. I mean, it looks like me, but I don't recognise him because of what he feels like inside. Physically different, yes, and existentially as well. I smile at myself, a great big broad grin. I inhale the odours of bodily fluids on myself, of sweat and intimacy, lust and satiation. It's great. I don't even bother to wash my hands, I want to crawl back into that warm pit and preserve this for as long as possible. And that's what I do.

Sometime around dawn, the light breaking wakes us both up. And we start all over again, and then fall back into a deep slumber.

~

'Oi, wake up, aren't you supposed to be down at Declan's place?'

'Oh shit, yeah.'

Frankie collapses into giggles as she watches me clumsily and chaotically trying to get myself respectable and ready for what appears to be a job interview, though I'm not actually sure.

Forty minutes later I am standing in front of a warehouse in a part of Marbella I don't know, delivered by taxi, to my new destiny. Declan greets me warmly and gives me a guided tour of everything they do. It's clear there's nothing anymore glamourous or remunerative than the warehouse I have so recently left. My job is going to be pretty hands on and manual, yet again, but a job it is, and they appear to have much work to do, with people visibly running to keep up with things in there. Trucks wait outside and there's yelling and gesticulating between various people, forklift drivers, carpenters, labourers and people dressed in office clothes holding clipboards and yelling out lists from them. It already seems like a money-go-round, and Declan is looking to dramatically scale this up judging by yesterday's conversation. Once we sit in the office, his agenda is made perfectly clear.

'Now, you're gonna have to get back in your brother's good books somehow, I don't want you to burn any bridges, alright?'

'Well he's not returning my calls at the moment, and he's said he wants me out of Marbella.'

'It's a free feckin' country last time I looked, Gene lad. All I'm saying is your brother is sitting on the largest pile of unbuilt properties on the coast. Potentially twelve hundred plus kitchens, if that bastard Lebid doesn't keep it for himself, and he knows feck all about kitchens, right?'

'Yes, I get it. But I can't promise-'

'Of course not, Gene, I know, I know. But we've got time. They haven't even started the build yet. You can get settled in here, learn the business and then by the by you'll hopefully be getting along with your brother, and we'll see if we can't be of mutual benefit, all of us to each other.'

'Yeah, that makes sense. I'll have to tread carefully, behave myself,' at which we both laugh, 'and if he sees me getting along well here, and not getting in his hair, I'm sure his attitude will change.'

'Exactly!'

Declan appears to be happy with this premise, enough to offer me a six-month contract at a better wage than previously. The real potential is in the commission I can make if I deliver orders. I am having to learn this unfamiliar mentality, that of the commission, the slice of the action, the kickback. The back scratching and apportioning out of favours and cash oil the wheels of absolutely everything here. Declan says business is conducted in exactly the same way back in Ireland. He loves it here because he claims the Irish are to the UK and the US what the Andaluces are to Spain; a tight knit tribe with old-school catholic and familial values, where you look after your own, and reward the people who look after you. They like a craic as much as the Irish and have a flexible, sometimes disdainful attitude to the protestant work ethic. Maybe that's why he has thrived here. Either way, I know I'm going to be happier for not working with a threatening thug like Dmitri looking daggers at me the whole time.

Once back at home, I try to phone Gary yet again. The number goes through to the office, and I'm fobbed off with the 'he's very busy' platitude for the umpteenth time. A short time later I receive a text: 'got you a flight for Friday to Lpool. I give you a lift to airport. Pick u up 0830. Sorry. Too much on my hands to have to deal with old family issues'. So that's what I am, my behaviour, my presence, an old family issue. Nice. He could have spun me that line when I arrived and not even opened the door. I did bring this on myself, which simply confirms his long-held perception of me, as an inveterate loser, a slacker, a liability, a lost cause. But I do not concur. I'm feeling different, about myself, and about everything. I'm not running this time; I'm not going to be the self-fulfilling prophecy of the ex-con. I will show him, slowly, carefully, but I will change his mind about me. Why should he get to be the only one to escape the awful cloud of our youth? I send him a text back: 'have found myself a job start monday. sorry for all the bother. will sort myself out and leave you alone. staying in marbella and making a go of it. see you around sometime.' I receive no reply. How long that will remain the case I don't know. At some point the fact I am staying in the flat will become moot. And that's another unexpected aspect of life to materialise. I appear to be in a relationship of sorts, I think. I'm not sure. Frankie's eight years younger than me, and I have no idea if that kind of sex is a sign of casual kicks or an actual need for something more rewarding. My history with relationships is even more haphazard and dysfunctional than my working life, if that were possible.

Frankie appears, she's been to the gym, though what she does there I'm unclear on, as she has no detectable muscle tone, I now feel qualified, happily, to affirm. She greets me with a big cuddly hug. I tell her about the day, and she's pleased, excited for me. She doesn't mention or ask about Gary. That's tricky territory certainly. Her sort of employer, sort of landlord, maybe sort of ex-boyfriend, there's who knows what history between them. So long as she doesn't start giving me comparison notes with Gary.

When she leaves for the club, dressed in the more provocative style required, she gives me a lingering, possessive kiss, saying ironically,

'Now you be a good boy while I'm out working away.' I'm left on my own, like most nights, pondering on all of this. And I have that peculiar sensation again. Wellbeing. A qualified wellbeing. For when I reflect on Gary, and everything he's engaged in, his partners, the investment at stake, and the business practices they take for granted, it makes my guts tighten. Frankly, it would terrify me, but ironically, my stupidity has inadvertently put a distance between myself and all of that, all of them. I feel much better all-round about where I am, than I felt merely a week ago, heading up to the fair in Madrid. I sigh, long and deep, ending with a slow, exasperated chuckle. I have, in three weeks, been through more emotions, made more decisions, experienced more new sensations and possibilities than in the last ten years, at least. And that makes me sleep well, so well Frankie's arrival in the early hours barely impinges on my consciousness.

15

I am awoken by my mobile ringing constantly. Through my early morning foggy brain, various anxieties try to assert themselves in the mist. Why is someone phoning me so early? Is it Gary, what does he want so early? Is it Declan, was I supposed to start work today? This latter is the worst, as I am convinced as I stumble out to find my phone in the lounge, that I have messed up before I've started. I'm sure we agreed to start on Monday, but now I have a horrible sinking feeling; Declan's number. There's only four in the phone's memory as it is. Gary, Ana, Declan and someone unknown in a position of power in the Marbella police.

'Hi Declan, what's up, I wasn't starting today was I?'

'What? No... Listen, something's going off in Marbella. I've seen it on the news, the police have raided the town hall, they're saying everyone's been arrested! It's feckin' Armageddon over there. Get over to Holmeland, see what you can find out. People are already saying everything's getting shut down. Call me. Bye.'

I'm trying to process what I've just heard. It sounds overly dramatic, but it was on the news. He's sure spooked by what he's hearing. I dress quickly and grab my bike and head down to the offices.

I'm at the top of the street leading to the port. Something is plainly awry. People, quite a few, congregate outside the office, but the body language is not positive. It's anxious, desperate even. Some press arrives, at least two camera crews, but people are not talking, and the crews hustle for someone to cooperate. I try to approach discreetly, not being sure how much a persona non grata I am around here. Everyone is deep in conversation. I recognise the sales crew, a couple of the legal people, various others unknown to me, all with the same air of distress and tension, and bewilderment even. For a moment I think somebody might have died. I edge closer, everyone ignores me. Which in some ways is a relief, I'm not the story around here anymore. So what is? The question starts to rattle me inside. There's a security guard on the door keeping out the press and unwanted, and it's only because Rafaela recognises me the guard allows me to pass. Once I'm through the hubbub outside, the quiet tension inside is palpable. Rafaela's face is a mask of confusion and fear.

'Erm, *hola*, I've come to see Gary, is he in?' I ask for want of anything else to ask, it's what I'm here for.

Rafaela looks at me nonplussed at first, then the penny drops, 'Gene, haven't you heard?'

'Only that the police were over at the town hall, why would that…' her expression makes me give up saying anything facile.

'I think I better let Gary explain, wait, I'll see if I can get you in.'

There follows a short, quiet conversation I can't pick up, then it's a curt 'Ok he'll see you'.

I enter his office, and Gary is staring out of the window, and doesn't react to my entrance. I sit down in the same squeaky plush chair of a few weeks back. There's a silence. I attempt to fill it, to at least see where we are going with this.

'Gary, I just came to say, like in the text, I'm staying here, I've got this job, see, and I'll be completely independent. So it's okay, I won't be around, I'll get out of your hair.'

'Fuck my hair!' he suddenly explodes into life, but not facing me, still facing out of the window, 'get out of my hair, what the fuck has hair got to do with anything now?'

He returns to silence, staring ahead out of the window, his back three quarters away from me, so I can't properly see his face. He is chewing a finger, breathing deeply. He pulls away from the window and turns toward me and his eyes come up and meet mine. It's a shock. His eyes are red rimmed, his face has lost its colour, and his jaw is set hard, grinding a bit, muscles tensing and flexing and flinching, and his breath now comes in fits and pants as though he is trying desperately to contain something welling inside. Silence again, he's just staring at me.

'What's happened?' I ask, might as well get to the point, as I still can't piece together what is going on.

Gary breaks into an ironic smile, and as best he can, given the tension in his face he says, 'The game is up. They've decided to kill the golden goose, burn down the house and we are all going to hell in a handcart. We are, to use the vernacular, completely and utterly fucked.' Minute spasms continue to run around his face and his eyes actually rim with tears.

'Jesus, are you okay? What the hell is going on,' I ask, bewilderment and fear both rising within me. I haven't seen anyone look so thoroughly devastated, not since our own tragedy all those years ago. So it's all the more awful to see Gary in this state again, as though we've been dragged back for a replay of our most awful emotions. He rubs his face with his hands and collects himself. He places his hands flat on the desk and begins in as matter of fact a way as he can muster.

'This morning at 8.45 a.m., members of the national police and the state anti-corruption judge's special Guardia Civil task force arrived at Marbella town hall and closed it down, detaining everyone inside. Simultaneously, all *concejales* not in the building were also detained. Currently all *concejales* and the mayor are under arrest and have been taken for questioning. Employees are being detained, questioned, and then some released, while others are being remanded in preventative custody. The town hall has been officially dissolved as the responsible body for the administration of the municipality under some lost ancient legislation still in force. It means Marbella now falls under direct rule from central government in Madrid, and all its affairs are under investigation by the *Fiscalia Anti-*

corrupción.[16] All business passes to the state authorities. We understand all permits and concessions relating to construction specifically have been frozen, indefinitely, pending full investigation.' He stops to let this sink in. I am stunned into silence. 'That's the official way of putting it' he continues 'and what it means in practice is that everything we do has been stopped. We've been taken out. All the permits are null and void, all work, construction, monies, everything to do with the development of Holmeland, the whole of El Angel, is dead and buried, and they are coming for us sooner or later. Sorzano is nowhere to be found They have seized and frozen his assets, where they can find them. *Policía* are in his properties in Caceres and Almería, Seville, Madrid, wherever.'

'Ho-ly-shit' is all I can think to say. It's stunning, it's a massive body blow, the ramifications of which send my head spinning and I can only begin to appreciate what it means for the business whose office I'm stood in. 'So that means...' and I can't even begin to finish the sentence, 'What does Holme say? Where is he?' I ask as his presence is very much lacking, surprisingly. Gary's face resumes its minute spasms, and after a deep breath he continues.

'Holme left the party early the other night, as he told me he would, as it was, as he put it, 'my show'. So he missed your little drama, but that indiscretion, as deplorable as it was, really is meaningless now. We are going to lose everything. I might be the one going to jail, I'm half expecting them to come through the door now and arrest me. Holme drove to Madrid that night, and left on a flight to Caracas early on Saturday morning. On legitimate business ostensibly, as that is where his new project is based.'

'Sorzano's from Caracas...they fucking knew, didn't they.'

Gary slumps into his seat, trying to combat the pressures racking through his mind and body.

---

[16] The special magistrate charged with investigating political corruption

'That's conjecture, but I find the timing remarkable, especially as he hadn't actually confirmed he was leaving, just that it was planned in the near future.'

'He stitched you up.'

'Well, that certainly could be one possible interpretation.'

I don't know what to say, what help or succour I can offer. None, really. Silence. Gary continues, more quietly this time.

'Ana has been arrested as well. Most of the main solicitors who deal with the conveyancing have been hauled in. Ana has been as she was heavily involved in all the legal aspects of legitimizing El Angel.' He is staring fixedly at the table in front of him, his hands wringing steadily.

'But if it's legitimate, what's the problem?' I ask, probably naively.

'Well, legitimate in the sense the paperwork is real and done by lawyers, it's just the whole issue of town planning isn't technically legal, as I explained to you in the bar in Madrid. The planning is approved at Marbella level, but the overall urbanisation plan that applies to every municipality has to be approved by the Interior Ministry.' Matter of fact, no hint of judgement or exasperation, or emotion even. 'Marbella hasn't had a PGOU, that's the overall plan you see, they haven't had one approved for well over fifteen years. It's never really been a problem. Everybody is happy so long as business gets done and everyone gets their cut.'

'Well, Sorzano has been getting his cut alright, I know, I can vouch for that one.' This isn't intended to be sardonic but sure sounds it.

'You may yet have to, to the fraud squad.'

'Jesus, seriously? I told you I didn't want to get involved in that, but you said it's all okay, it's just business. I told you we got pulled, so now I'm implicated directly in all of this. The police saw us with... how many million was it actually Gary, in those bags?'

'Three million. If that makes you feel better. Three million so we can build a half-billion-euro development. That's how it works. But now, Zapatero in Madrid is riding around like a knight in shining armour trying to nail down everyone involved in this way of doing business. What has been taken for granted in Marbella, and Spain for that matter, for as long as anyone can remember is currently disapproved of in government. Can you believe it?' he starts to get animated and the indignation flushes his face with colour. 'And those politicos and ministers and their business pals and their friends in this and that Junta and their judges and notaries and lawyers and bankers and every single fucker in this sodding, backward, shithole of a country with their filthy fucking snout in the trough, and their expense account cards and family holidays and the wife's minks and the mistresses' cosmetic surgery, think they can send their useless coppers to bust our balls for doing the one thing that makes this fucking country work' -by now the phone has flown across the room and detonated against the arty wallpaper- 'and ruin everything we've achieved, and make us the scapegoats for their stinking rotten system' -a well-timed swipe of the hand sends the iMac crashing onto the floor- ' and hang us out to dry with our bollocks flying in the breeze while they carry on with their fucking hypocrisy the length' -smash goes the chair on the desk- 'and breadth' -smash again on the desk- 'of the fucking cunt tree!' which is said with such force that the enormous glass desk top disintegrates into tiny chips, and crashes down onto the wreckage of phone and iMac and chair, like a Skittles ad gone wrong. Gary stands looking at the carnage, breath heaving, and I am glued to the spot. Rafaela and some others behind her gingerly open the door to find out what on earth is going on.

'Get the fuck out of my office!' Gary screams in a not very appropriate way. They beat a hasty retreat. Gary continues surveying the rather expensive rearrangement of office furniture, and smiles to himself, a desperate, bleak smile, the smile of someone watching Rome burn but without violin to play.

191

'Gary' I try to say when I think calm has settled.

'What!??' is the abrupt and aggressive reply. 'What is it, big brother, what do you want to know, what can I help you with on this fine sunny morning in beautiful Marbella, hmm?'

I regard the man who a week ago stood in shiny slacks and expensive shoes towering like a colossus over the beautiful people of Marbella in his moment of triumph. He looks half despairing and half insane, ready to explode in ways I can't imagine, as he has always been a fairly placid and easy-going guy. This volcano is unsettling and shocking. Clenching and unclenching his fists.

'What is it?!?' he demands again, anger flashing over his face, mingling with the bewilderment and exhaustion that are consuming him from the ground up.

'Well, what the fuck are we going to do?' I ask, and it does sound rather pitiful in the context.

'We?' He almost laughs.

'Yeah, I want to help, if I can.' Pathetic.

Now Gary does laugh. 'What are you going to do Gene Genie? Get the PGOU approved, drop the charges, pay back the bribes, legalise all the dodgy title deeds, pay back the investors who've been misled, the ratepayers who've been stuffed, what, what…. WHAT Eugene?'

'Fuck, I dunno, just…' and the sentiment flounders and drowns in the sea of broken glass at my feet.

'You are going to fuck off back home, Genie boy,' he continues at the same fever pitch, 'not because you behaved like a juvenile prick last week, not because you embarrassed me in front of the whole world that matters around here, no not because of that, but because I, like a proper prize twat, sent you with three million euros to Sorzano's house to give him Lebid's money, because Holme we should get Lebid to pay him, if he wants his share of the deal, and not our money, even though we could have found that amount of cash probably, but NO!! So now on top of waiting for the Guardia Civil to come and throw me in jail to await a trial that is probably six to eight years away, I have to explain to Lebid how I'm going to get his money back! And you are a material witness to this classic piece of skulduggery, that is just one more nail in the gigantic coffin currently being constructed for us all, before our very eyes. What a bunch of idiots we are! No plan B! No idea that maybe one day, someone with the power to do so might say, enough of this bullshit, I'm in charge and we are not having a bunch of *Andaluz* peasants running around cocking a snook and making billions while we're still taking pissy bribes to afford nice holidays, serrano ham and a few Rolexes. And Holme, well he's the smart one, because he put it all in my lap and fucked off! Genius!! Pure unadulterated genius!'

There's a pause, sulphur evaporating.

'So okay, I'm leaving. I got that part.'

'Gene,' he's calmer, serious in a concerned way 'you need to get out of here, it's not really safe for you. You know stuff that the police will be interested in, if they stopped you, they know the money was transported, to whom, and by who. It's only a matter of time. Go back to the UK, get your head down and forget all this.'

'What?! I can't leave with all of this going on, I mean...', I mean what can I realistically do? I run out of steam. It seems to be hopeless and terrifying. I can't bear the thought of the kid brother who made good, who escaped the mire, being immolated on this bonfire of vanities. That bizarre, unique, welcome sense of wellbeing is already turning rotten within me. Turning back into the mouldering, slow, evil smelling poison that has sloshed around the bottom of my psyche, since that day. And I have nothing realistically to offer. We both stand in silence for some moments.

'Take the plane on Friday. This isn't your fight Gene. You didn't nail yourself to this particular crucifix. I did. Willingly, and now I've got to take what's coming.'

Tears come. What seemed so beautiful, so pregnant with redemption and promise only a few weeks earlier, now looks just like the desk, viciously deconstructed on the floor. We embrace. There's a knock on the door and Rafaela cautiously opens it.

'Gene, I've got Lebid on the line and I can't keep fobbing him off, you've got to speak to the guy. I can't hold him. He will be over here in no time unless you speak to him now.' Her tone makes that sound ominous and Gary makes to leave.

'Stay at the flat, don't go out, I'll catch up with you later if I can. Speak to no-one, understand?'

'Shit, right you are.'

I'm back in the street dodging through camera crews, ignoring proffered microphones and snapping paparazzi. I break into a swift jog and after a moment they abandon the half-hearted chase and return to the stake-out. I decide to ride over to a cafeteria close to the warehouse in San Pedro. Around Banus there's nothing but trashy, touristy eateries and overpriced franchise muck. I need comfort food, but one has to travel to where normal people live to be able to find something a self-respecting Spaniard would eat.

I'm struggling to get my head around the situation here. I've never heard of an entire municipality being taken over, it sounds like something out of a dictatorship. What does it mean for a town that thrives on tourism, and spins its image into gold the whole time? What will it do for all the businesses who hustle to sell to the incoming buyers? The little world I know, around the warehouse, the suppliers and workers, the sales people, the printers and builders' merchants, plumbers and sparks, all the people I have rubbed shoulders with in the past few weeks, have had the rug pulled from under their feet. Every golf club, retail park, restaurant, estate agent, letting agent, car rental, kitchen and furniture stores, all feed on the fuel of realty money flowing in. My new friend Declan, like everyone else, is going to take a huge hit. He, like so many here, even the firms of lawyers, and all the great herd of swine that have their snout in the great golden trough of real estate speculation, are doomed. To freeze it, to knock it dead with one fell swoop, it's quite awesome, it's Greek tragedy, it's a rise and fall of imperial proportions.

Who knows where the damage will stop, how far the ripples of corruption will reach out over the society, who will be consumed, drowned and who will wash up on the sand, gasping, sodden but alive, to pick through the debris and carry on? I don't envy anyone here, frankly. The dreamy image, its ultra HD gorgeousness is hiding a stinking, rotting corpse underneath. Gary is right, it genuinely is time to go. It's a bitter, bitter realisation. Rats and sinking ships. I didn't run the last time my instincts told me to, back in Amsterdam, being as they were, numbed with chemicals and my own stoner brand of hubris. Everything I thought I just had, is but a castle in the sand, and the storm tide is coming in.

I slide into a wall seat in a cafeteria and order the Spanish equivalent of a full English. No baked beans and the sausages are of chorizo. I am watching the screen in the corner which is beaming news of the events downtown. TV crews throng outside the Marbella town hall, in its pretty orange spangled square. I can't catch what's being said, but the tone and faces of the interviewees, soundbites from the ordinary folk of Marbella, leave an unmistakable impression. They, the politicos, had it coming. Like anywhere in the world, under the brilliant party dresses, is a petticoat of exploitation and poverty, drug addiction, unemployment and delinquency. You don't have to look far to see it, just look closely enough. And they know what the story is at the top of the pyramid. The TV is running a feed of texted comments from the general public at the bottom of the screen. It runs in a similar vein, people from all over the actual country texting in their anger and disgust at politicians.

Around me heads nod in empathy, but the strain is noticeable, as the writing is on the wall for many of the people in here. I'm terrified for Gary, all the forces ranged against him now. It's odd, all this hoo-ha is something you normally see solely on television. It doesn't happen to people like us. I get to do low rent crime with dodgy

195

Essex geezers, and pay the price for my stupidity. Fair enough. But this white-collar crime malarkey is different. Gary's not a crook. It's just business gone wrong. No-one's been hurt. It's the politicians who make the system that way, profit most from it, so they should take the rap. I'm indignant that my oh-so-successful brother should be implicated in this, that it should affect him. All he's done is work his balls off for a better life and now it's all blown up in his face. And I'm powerless to help.

I call Declan, and without mentioning any of the incriminating specifics, I outline the state of things. That much of the un-licensed property development has indeed been shut down, and there's no clear vision of what the future holds, even if a future exists for the Holmeland development.

'Jesus, they've really fecked it up. Nobody saw this coming, that's for sure' opines Declan. 'But you'll be coming in Monday. There's plenty to do here still. It may blow over, they'll do a deal, they always do.'

'Well, let's hope so. They didn't think so down at Holmeland, it was like a funeral.'

'Alright lad, thanks. See you Monday'.

I don't explain I am probably going to run for it. He doesn't need to know. I will have to explain it to Frankie. Bit of a kick in the teeth. Well, I barely know her, all things considered. Maybe I'm flattering myself. Maybe I had mistakenly assumed I was going to start leading something approaching a normal life, with a real relationship. Maybe I've only been pretending to myself I like her, as pleasant as that has been. Pretending I have been able to let my guard down, and feel close to another human. Maybe it's all a bad joke being played by life on me. Once again. Ah, that familiar shroud of self-pity, drawing over my emotions. Familiar, not all together comfortable, but comfortingly familiar. It allows me to justify all sorts of failure, all kinds of evasion, disregard all sorts of responsibilities. How foolish of me to think I could break the mould, turn over a new leaf, escape who I fundamentally am. Did I honestly think I could escape the curse? Even Gary, despite his effort, ability and drive, is not immune to our particular toxin. Bitterly ironic too, that as soon as I show up, Gary's world is torched to the ground. As ever it's me standing by the wreckage, witnessing the smoke curl up. And here I am, preparing to run, once again, but to where and what end?

How long have I been sat here? Only when I try and muster the enthusiasm to get on my bike and return to the flat do I become aware I'm on my third brandy. Its woolly, warming, anaesthetic charms have fuelled my inward spiral to those familiar, desolate shores of self-indulgent, self-flagellation.

Entering the flat after a precipitous journey home, weaving dangerously, narrowly missing parked cars and moving ones, enduring the honked horns and yells of abuse, Frankie sees straight away something is askew.

'Bloody 'ell what happened to you?' she moves towards me, but I move away, and slump down onto the sofa. It takes me a while to answer.

'Games over. It's all fucked up.' I outline, again, the scenario downtown, but add in the detail of my trip to Almeria, and its implications. 'Gary told me to leave, got me a flight, and I wasn't going to go. I was going to stay. Do that job. Stay here. Y'know?' I can't add the 'with you' because I don't know if I'm presuming. Presuming Frankie likes me enough to be in a relationship. Presuming I like her enough. Presuming a relationship would even work. Because it won't. Because it never does.

'You gonna leave?' She doesn't add a 'me', but I suppose she might have thought it.

'I think so. I think I have to. Frankie, that night, there were guns. Proper mobsters, not like the usual sort, dealers, dickheads. Big Ukrainian guys. This guy Lebid, Gary owes him three million quid, euros, whatever. The police stopped us, they know who I am, what I was doing. So does Sorzano, and he's done a runner. Shit.'

She's silent for a while, perched on the arm of the sofa. Trying not to look at me. I think she dabs her eye, momentarily. Maybe I'm presuming. Again.

'Better do what's best for you, ay? Don't make no sense going to jail for that lot.' She lets out a long sigh, fidgets with her hands. She briefly reaches for mine, holds onto it a while, and shakes it gently.

'Well, it's worse than that. I'll probably be going back to jail anyway. Just by being here I've broken my parole. They could throw me inside as soon as I get back.'

Frankie utters a slight yelping, sharp intake of breath. She shakes her head disbelievingly, searching my face. I don't know what she sees, but she turns away and goes to her room. She is probably familiar with being disappointed. By men. Maybe men from my family in particular.

I sit aimlessly watching TV again. Letting the inanity wash over me. Makeover shows. Chat shows. Quiz shows. A hilarious real estate show about life in the sun, on the Costa, the lifestyle, the bargains, the golf. It keeps me company as I laugh deliciously at the couples being escorted around their dream villas and golf boxes. Living the dream, living the dream.

Later Frankie leaves wordlessly for her work, her mood leaden, crushed. I sit still for a while, not wanting to be alone. Everything is out of my control and coming apart. I call Gary impulsively; to my surprise he picks up.

'Gaz. I need to talk, I don't want to leave like this.' He's silent for a moment.

'I know. Come over, to the penthouse.'

He gives me details, it's just close by his office. It's a relief, to not have to sit alone brooding, with the scent of Frankie's perfume still lingering. Mocking me.

Ten minutes later I am locking the bike to the railings outside Gary's block, when a security guard starts yelling at me. Such is the cache of this block, I am obliged to chain the bike to sign post on the other side of the street. He is mildly aggressive about it, as I haven't the patience to try and decipher his heavily accented Spanish. He patently isn't a local, and he takes this for a lack of cooperation. In Marbella as in other wealthy places, few of the menial drudge jobs are done by natives. The Latin, African, Asian and East European migrants have gratefully scooped up whole sections of the service economy.

I am buzzed in through the main gate and enter a foyer with a reception desk, currently unmanned. Extravagant paintings hang from two walls, in ostentatious gilt frames. An opulent chandelier hangs in the middle, and marble, in swathes of reds, ochres and bluey greens makes up the walls. It could be an Ottoman palace. I enter a lift, which likewise has marble sides, but only a mini-crystal bowl of shiny glass beads, rather than the full chandelier. A cloying automatic scent dominates the air. My steps echo wildly as I walk along the marbled corridor, yet more lights glinting behind sparkling glass encasements. I get to Gary's and it opens before I can reach for the bell.

'Heard you coming, mate. Come in' he says by way of explanation.

'How do you know it was me?'

'There's no-one else resident on this floor at the moment. They'll all be down from Madrid for Holy Week. Who else could it be?'

'Ana?'

Gary shakes his head, tugging on his bottom lip with his teeth. 'Soon, maybe tomorrow.' He offers nothing more.

'Christ almighty, how crazy.' Gary beckons me in.

The penthouse is open plan and enormous, with one wall consisting entirely of glass sliding panels, onto a spectacular terrace

199

which has been landscaped with artistically sculpted plants, cacti and pots, inset lighting in stylish clusters. In fact, all the lighting is from unfamiliar pin-prick little bulbs embedded all over the place in walls, floors, ceilings. Gary explains they are hideously expensive, but are the cheapest to run, and longest lasting lights ever, called LED's. The walls are pale grey and the furniture is exclusively white and low, minimalist and modern. I'm standing in the centrefold of an architectural magazine. The handful of paintings on the wall are fairly abstract, odd and indecipherable but they fit perfectly with the dominant aesthetic. Mercifully, no chandeliers.

'Nice,' is my sincere opinion, 'very nice, I must say.'

Gary comes over and gives me a hug, and I can feel the weight and leaden quality to his otherwise fit and honed physique.

'Thanks. Spoils of war. My reward for the hours of sufferance of the ego that is known as Holme.'

I sit down on a wide low white sofa, worried I might stain it just by being on it.

'Don't take this badly, but how come it's taken so long to actually be invited to your place?'

Gary laughs tiredly, and slumps down into a chair cum beanbag opposite me. He lets the squat designer blob take his weight and he sinks into it, breathing out long.

'It's not a normal home. This is a sanctuary. Ana and I guard it passionately. Our shelter from the storm of ambition and avarice outside. A haven of calm and quiet, free from stress and the madness down below. We never socialise here; this is our private world we guard because you need it. In this town, in this business, everybody is checking you, what you wear, what you drive, where you eat, who you are with, who's invites you receive.'

'I can see the sense in that.'

'Fancy a drink?' Gary's clocks the contorted expression on my face.

200

'After I saw you earlier, I needed a few stiff ones. Cup of tea would go down a blinder Gaz, or is that a bit too proletarian around here?' I tease.

'It's a bloody good idea.'

He struggles out of the beanbag slowly eating him, and heads for a galley style kitchen that appears to have nothing in it, so sleek and white is it. Everything is contained within ingeniously opening cupboards and panels. I hear the sound of water boiling, but can't see the mechanism responsible.

'You've seen Marbella now; you get the idea. It's not real, most of it. Take this building for example.'

'It's a horror show getting up here.'

Gary laughs properly, and the tension slips a little out of him, and me.

'Most of these penthouses are owned by wealthy *Madrileños* who simply have to be seen to have a penthouse in Marbella. They appear for a few weeks a year, go to the same old restaurants, have cocktail parties or just do the party scene and pose about.' He pours tea into two dangerously tall, narrow designer tea mugs. '3.5 million for one of these places, plus about twelve grand a year in community fees, for a quick holiday or two. Most of the big villas you see up the hill there are the same.'

'Jesus, how much? How can you afford a place like this?'

'Ahh, insider knowledge. Friend of a good client of Ana's tipped us off. A Portuguese architect was getting a nasty divorce. He couldn't stop his wife taking him to the cleaners, but he sure as hell could sell his assets for as little as possible just to spite her.'

'So, you got a bargain. You must have spent a few bob doing it up though.'

'Nope. This is how it came. He basically said, how much can you pay, handed over the keys to this extraordinary place and ran a mile before his wife could track him down. Trust me, we had to convince her to go away more than once. She was livid, but eventually got the message, and is no doubt still chasing his sorry ass with lawyers around the world.'

'Nice one.' I sip refreshingly familiar tea in an unfamiliar vessel.

'Well it was until this morning.' I assume he isn't referring to any of my indiscretions. There's a pause.

'What are you going to do Gaz. Any idea?'

'Until Ana is released and we can figure out the way this is going to play, it's difficult to say.'

'She's not going to go down for this is she? Are you?'

'Right now, much of it is preventative detention. There was a robbery at the town hall a few weeks back. Computers went missing. Evidence they would like, now. So they've got a lot of people in a place where they can't do any more damage, and the police can walk off with the computers and files, and then let everyone out on bail. This has been sort of coming for a while and some people on the inside were starting to cover their arses. But to the rest of the world they made out it was business as usual. Like Sorzano, still taking bribes and promising favours just a few days before the state went to war on Marbella. Incredible.' He shakes his head sadly, with a faraway look in his eyes.

'Is the game up, finished, for real?'

'If things had gone to plan, we were going to sell this place this summer, and naturally, with the killing we were going to make on it, we were looking to buy a nice family type house, farther out in the hills. An older place. We planned to marry soon. We felt we could do it, start a family, and all that.' He smiles, but in a way that says he doesn't believe it to be possible, like it's just this dream that seemed so real, but of course isn't. As events have proved, and what a fool he was to believe it. This goal, of just normality, of a comfortable loving family unit here in dreamland must mean the world to him. It's cruel.

'Come on, that's still possible, you can make a bomb on this place and still do all of that, just not with Holmeland. Go somewhere else, start your own thing-''

'From jail?' he cuts me off.

'But you're not a crook, it's just the system is corrupt.'

'It's a possibility.' He's shaking his head again, the indignation and disbelief rattling around inside him. He starts up much more animatedly now, like he's thrown a switch.

'I mean do you know in the office today, not one of those fuckers came in to talk to me, to see if they could help. It was all just me, me, me. What about my bonus, what about my reputation, what will my clients think of me? Our fucking legal team was nowhere to be seen! Only Ana and her boss were arrested, but the rest of them ran around bleating pathetically. They closed ranks with all the other gangster lawyers in town and went grubbing around the politicos from Madrid to get their mates out on bail. I couldn't get one single answer from anyone on the legal side of this company today. Not one! I'm sat there fielding calls from investors who are shitting bricks, screaming at me for their money, threatening me with all kinds of God knows what, and what fucking support do I have?! A bland press statement issued by Sterling, assuring everybody these are temporary administrative hiccups that will be ironed out, and that their investments are perfectly safe. Some of them even believed that crock of BS.'

'God, I had no idea you'd had that kind of shit to deal with today. It's kind of unprecedented, I mean where does it all go from here?'

'Down the fucking tubes, Gene. It's over, period. Everything that has been happening here is gone. It's the end of an era. We are already history. When a government decides its authority can't be challenged with impunity any longer, when the money involved is so grotesque it makes a mockery of democracy, then they will find a scapegoat. Spain is corrupt from top to bottom in its own special way, not like the British old boy network, not dressed up and disguised. It's blatant, vulgar. Bags and suitcases full of cash, minks and holidays for the wife, dodgy expense accounts, I've seen it all. I've watched it happen all around me for years and I just took it as the way things are. You work with what you've got. And now it's all over and Marbella is the sacrificial lamb. I fully expected to be arrested today, but maybe I'm not that important to them. Maybe they are more concerned by their own rotten apples than a few *guiris* trying to make a fast buck.'

'You've probably got more to fear from Lebid.'

'Exactly! He's untouchable, his businesses here are legitimate, and so long as no-one traces back the money from Sorzano, he'll just watch it all fall apart, and probably up sticks and find another town to rape and pillage. Which is why you need to fuck off home and become a nobody again.' There's a stunned pause as I take this metaphorical smack in the chops. 'Sorry Gene', Gary looks at me, mortified, 'I did not mean it to come out like that. Shit. Sorry.'

'You're right. It's worse than that, though. I'm going back to jail. Probably.'

'What, how come?'

'I've not been entirely straight with you, Gary. I was released four weeks ago on license.' Gary shrugs his incomprehension. 'That expressly forbids me to leave the country. My life is entirely controlled by a supervisor, who in this case is a ball-breaking old fart. Once they catch up with me, and they will when I'm back, he could have me recalled to prison, minimum twenty-eight days.'

Gary shakes his head in disbelief. 'Jesus Christ Gene, you never change, do you.'

'Well, I'll be safe in there from your friends.'

'What's that supposed to mean?' he replies, slight indignation edging in his voice.

'The guys in Madrid, Yevgeny and Vladimir. They were tooled up. Hand guns. That money came out of the strong room in the back of that sleazy brothel you sent me to. Lebid, as far as I can see, is just a gangster in a nice suit. Nice business associates.'

Gary remains expressionless. I'm probably telling him what he already knows.

'Tomorrow I'm going to the bank and transferring everything we have over to Lebid. It will probably only end up getting embargoed by the government, accounts frozen, or get wasted on lawyers. I'll just give it all to him, nothing much else we can do with it now. Other than pay it back to the poor suckers who've bought into our ex-development. What will that benefit us?'

'Poor fuckers.' I say matter of factly. Poor fuckers indeed.

'The value of investments can go down as well as up.'

His mobile rings and he jumps, he's definitely wired tight.

'*Digame…*' and a torrent of serious sounding Spanish spews from the earpiece. Gary is nodding and agreeing in various ways. He hangs up.

'Ana is being released in the morning. No charges as of this moment. Some good news at least. All these years of stress and bullshit and licking clients' arses, putting up with their pretensions and vanity and greed, and for what? To have it wiped out in two seconds by a bunch of second-rate socialist politicos from Madrid. Jesus, it could make you laugh. Fuck it, let's have a drink. You're still my brother, even if you do behave like a dick sometimes. Anyway, it's all academic now. El Angel is toast. There really is nothing left for you here anymore. Go home, take the rap, start again.'

Gary picks up a remote control, and a panel in a wall slides back revealing a recessed cocktail cupboard, backlit and glowing like one of his bars in his club. It is stacked with fancy booze. Single malts, brandies, odd novelty bottles, premium vodkas, brands I've never heard of.

'What's your poison?' He asks.

'Gaz, I'm only just sobering up, I don't think I could.'

'Never too late for a hair of the dog. Why have it tomorrow morning when you can have it now? They don't have this in Strangeways, you know.' He laughs caustically as he cracks the seal on an eighteen-year-old single malt whiskey, pours a good two fingers into a chunky crystal glass. It's extraordinary, a pungent but layered blast of peatyness, malty orangey tones, and a hint of salt. 'Finest Islay malt, dear Eugene. Only the best for the king of Marbella' and he clinks my glass.

'You bought all of this' I wonder aloud, it's a small fortune in alcohol alone.

Gary snorts derisively. 'Don't be daft,' he says it with the flat northern ah sound, 'tokens of gratitude from satisfied customers', he adds acidly. It's like his long buried, bitter northern alter-ego has been awoken from the long slumber under the palms of Marbella. I wile away a couple of pleasant hours getting newly inebriated and reminisce with Gary about back home. We avoid the happenings of the fire and its aftermath. We celebrate instead that particular jadedness, that cast of no-hopers, the deluded wannabees, or the frustrated talents and charismatics, who never leave their damp north-western prison on the Cheshire plains, and watch it all turn to mush, regret and self-flagellation. We speculate on former friends, assessing the odds on who managed to escape, how far they got, where are they now. There but for the grace of God, says Gary.

We exchange knowing looks. I know I am not yet free of that particular prison; its clammy hands are reaching for me again.

It's time for me to go, before we get too drunk and open up too many boxes of old memories from back then. It's an unspoken agreement. We won't go there. Now is not the time, if ever. Gary will pick me up, take me to the airport. I have one more day to experience Marbella and all its joys.

16

Amsterdam. I love Amsterdam. I hate Amsterdam. Herman is leaning into me talking loudly and agitatedly, complaining how no-one appreciates his carefulness and cleverness. How we would all be fucking poor without him, because we are fucking useless, and fucking this and fucking that and I glaze over, and his face waves in front of me, bobbling about like one of those silly dogs with a suspended head on the back shelf of a car. I love Amsterdam, the coffee is nice, and the buns, and the space cakes, and the weed is soooo good and you have a zillion types to choose from. The clubs are fantastic, dense walls of sweaty, pulsing people, merged into one on the wave of the beat: into one panting, sparkling, throbbing muscle of euphoria, one giant glistening, smiley face. I hate Amsterdam, it's where we go to bring back those same smiley faces to the UK. Where I have to run the gauntlet of ranting, paranoid characters like Herman. Herman the German we call him, obviously. He's not German, he's Dutch, but he's so overbearing we also nicknamed him the Obersturmgunfuhrer. He hates that.

'I'm not a fooking German, you are the Nazis, you stupid bloody English losers.'

The sleepless hours, the grinding teeth, the getting high long after the high is even high anymore, has made Herman a bit cranky, a bit of a pain. A bit of a complete headfuck to be accurate, and that is putting it mildly. But I have to endure his tirade, and smile and nod and wait for it to subside as he IS the clever clogs who comes up with the speaker cabinets which make the excellent throbbing wall of noise we love, and which carefully and brilliantly conceal the valuable cargo of Smiley Faces, Supermen, or whatever the flavour of the month is for silly names of the pills.

So I'm waiting for the truck to be loaded, with all of its other mysterious cargo, headed for Harwich via Rotterdam. I'll follow it at a certain distance in my van, acting as the decoy, ready for the inevitable searching, questions and general harassment the authorities are so willingly misdirecting at the obvious stoner in the dodgy van. And Herman will travel with me, as the representative of the seller, to see that all goes well, to help us unpack the load as even we can't find the stuff on the other side, so well hidden is it. Herman is tall, skinny as only a fifteen year fan of amphetamines and MDMA can be, his long nose, wonky from a break in some forgotten fight, hangs off a boney face with mean, wide lips, which only make his battered and cracking teeth all the more resplendent, being housed in such an exaggerated frame. Speed will have your teeth eventually.

I didn't seek out these people. I sort of slid into their company. I had been moving frequently between Amsterdam and the UK, working for some of the DJs and promoters, helping with hiring kit for some of the bigger raves. I just started to move a bit of ecstasy in small amounts here and there, when I could see the chance, no-one was any the wiser. And it was easy, and it was more than I needed, and it was good stuff, so people came looking for me for more. So I moved a bit more. And someone mentioned something to someone who thought I was treading on someone's toes, and that was the first time I saw a gun. But it was all gentlemanly, no harm done mate and so on. You work for us now, right? So, here I am with Herman as my regular travelling companion.

I'm waiting to start my purgatory of several hours in his company. We are waiting inside the usual anonymous industrial unit in God knows which part of this flat, featureless, damp, nuthouse of a country. A place where everybody is wonderfully tolerant and relaxed, and simultaneously uptight and officious. What a pair Herman and I make. I'm agreeably spliffed, which enables me to cope perfectly well with the endless whingeing and the inevitable nerves of running the law enforcement gauntlet. Someone passes him a spliff *which seems to calm him down. The doors are being sealed on the large trailer. The buyer from England, who I only know vaguely by sight, one is never party to the actual people behind the deals, comes over. He's with someone I haven't seen before on my few excursions over here. He's talking to the Dutch supplier and Herman and I are skulking out of the way, waiting to be allowed to depart. It's not a particularly social business at this level it has to be said. Everything is just on a need to know basis.*

The lighting in the warehouse is limited, and I'm looking at silhouettes framed by the open shutter of the warehouse. I feel a minor kick of apprehension, like a distant memory is jogged by an unseen hand and falls off its shelf, splat, into your consciousness. But it's a memory, it's not accurate, it's deja vu, it just reminds you of whatever it was that is actually scaring you. The figure moves towards us, and the gait, the splay of the legs, the cocky assured swagger and swing of the arms is unmistakable. The memory has come to life and has achieved physical form in front of me.

Jimmy Kavanagh. A bit older, a bit more weathered, but fit. Like he can still handle himself. Better than ever. A necessity in this game. Despite the rather good Amsterdam sinsemilla, my stomach does an involuntary flip and my mouth dries. He surveys the lorry, checks the back doors, then briefly turns to me grinning, and chuckles.

'Alright Eugene. So college worked out well for you then? Have a nice trip. Look after Herman, he's valuable.' I can barely do more than mutter an acknowledgement, but not form actual words. He looks at me fixedly now, holds my gaze, appraising me, and reveals only contempt behind his eyes. 'And no fucking gravy.' He turns on his heel and is gone.

I'm a statue, staring after the menacing silhouette that, until now, had just been a distant memory of the teenage convulsions of life back in Warrington.

'Hey, what's with you' says Herman, poking me.

209

'Nothing, just thought I saw a ghost.'

'Eh? You know that guy?'

'Yes, I do. We go back quite a way,' I say, trying to be ironic.

'Ha. Unlucky for you' snorts Herman.

I start up the van, and pull off into the long night of tarmac, ferries and nervousness. I shouldn't be surprised to see Jimmy. His dad was always rumoured to be in some Irish mob, had links with the UDA supposedly, some people speculated. Either way, the Catholic paddies hated the family, as they were a certain type of Prods. Very Orange. But they didn't care, they were hard enough to take care of themselves. Jimmy has come a long way since the car parks in Runcorn. It's his natural habitat, the drug trade. It fits his profile perfectly. So what am I doing in it? That little voice that had been niggling at me, popping up during the come downs, creeping up on me on the lazy, dull, sober days, the one saying I should get out of this, it's not good for your health, that little voice has suddenly started yelling at me.

17

I'm sitting in the cafeteria close to the warehouse. My head is thick, I'm dehydrated and a bit nauseous, the result of too much rich, salty whiskey. I've slipped out of the flat early, I can't summon up the courage or motivation to manage my behaviour and emotions around Frankie, even for one last day. What's the point?

As I drink a couple of the thick, creamy *cafe-con-leche,* that have become an essential part of every morning here, I am deliciously aware of the sounds and smells of this environment. The Formica tables and panelling, the posters of Real Madrid and Malaga football teams, sundry trophies and souvenirs of some local sporting accomplishment, and the contrast with religious icons; virgins in haloes of light and flowers, gold filigree, pictures of pilgrims and horses lead by stunning women dressed gaily in flamenco dresses. And weirdest of all, rows of people in what appear to be Ku Klux Klan hoods, but carrying crosses and candles through old Spanish city streets. It looks so completely otherworldly. The screaming of coffee machines intrudes constantly, its force and harshness bears no relation to the hot, strong, life giving fluid in its stubby glass. The endlessly raised voices of the locals yabbering, the shouts of the waiters and slamming and clanking of glasses and spoons. It has already become homely and familiar, and I am brooding heavily on the fact this won't be the morning ritual anymore, or ever again.

Eventually, Darren and Ibby walk in, for their breakfast break, the only break they get in the eight-hour day. But it does mean they are done and dusted at half past three. Not so bad really. There's a few of them, all looking disconsolate. Darren's quiet, and he stops dead when he sees me, like he's seen a ghost. He hurries over.

'What the fuck are you doing here?' It's more fear than surprise or anger.

'Fancied some breakfast, seeing as I'm unemployed, a man of leisure. And also to say goodbye, my holiday is over.' The flippancy of this is not reciprocated by Darren.

'I don't know what you were playing at the other night, but you were mouthing off a bit too much. You need to learn a bit of discretion mate. You ain't got protection like your brother. Not that he's got much now neither. It's a fucking shit storm, man.' He shakes his head in disbelief. This information is unexpected and puts me further ill at ease.

'Like what?'

'You have no idea, have you, you were wasted. You are lucky I was there for you mate, a few of them that night would have knocked your lights out, but I said you was ok, vouched for you, said you'd been turned over by your brother and Holme.'

'What was I saying for crissakes?'

'You were blowin' off about how this was all a mug's game and it wasn't much better than fraud. Emperor's new clothes and something like hegel money, whatever the fuck that is.'

'Jesus, hegemony? I was banging on about hegemony?'

'Yeah and capitalism, and the bosses, and saying how everyone down here was dumb enough to fall for it all, and what they was buying into was a freak show for boring middle-class golfing wankers and on and on. I mean it was sort of funny, but you get people's backs up, people make their living doing this, they've got a bit of pride, so you, being Gary's brother an' all, you sounded like a bit of an arrogant spoilt wanker an' that, you know?'

'Holy shit, I had no idea', yes, I had no idea. All that Marxist cultural criticism I dug up in social anthropology those years ago must have had a sort of flashback. Like post-modern acid, a Marxist flash back. Well that's a first.

'You was on one a bit, but I guess you'd had a rough night already. Don't worry about it now, no matter as you ain't going to be around anyway.'

'I know, I'm out of here tomorrow.'

'You can't leave too soon, mate.'

'What… seriously?' I say with genuine concern.

'Lebid, isn't it.'

'What about him?' my pulse has jumped into my oesophagus and is attempting to strangle me.

'Well he's proper pissed. There's a paper trail leading to him. Remember the coppers who pulled us? They now know we were headed to Sorzano, they also know who the inside man in the Marbella police is. And Sorzano is conveniently hard to find, and Lebid's investment ain't looking so smart, so Lebid is a very unhappy bunny. Does your brother not know about the pull, and the police an' that?'

'Yeah. He's pretty freaked out by it all, and what to do about Lebid.'

'You be a good boy and keep your trap shut, to everyone. Warrington or wherever it is you go to is never far away from here. Every tax dodger, drug baron and dodgy dealer on the planet has got ears here, so wherever it is you go and whatever you get up to, remember, not a word.'

'Thanks for the advice.'

We pass the rest of the time in tittle tattle and commiserations and a good amount of piss taking of the spectacle I created on the night. I am only too sorry I was so smashed I was unable to appreciate any of it. It sounded like quite a performance. Hegemony? When was the last time I even understood what it meant?

The guys aren't hopeful for the future. Most of them are already looking to find new work, believing the whole bubble is about to burst. The knock-on effect is already being felt. Purchases being pulled, deposits not paid, orders for furniture packs dropping to rock bottom. The shock waves are lapping around the ankles of everyone in Marbella and along the coast. The Golden Goose looks like it has been plucked. I make to leave as they head for the warehouse nearby, their mood heavy and disconsolate. Darren turns to face me, as I finish shaking hands with the others. Not too much love lost, I was always a bit of a square peg in a round hole in the warehouse, most of them suspicious, or at least guarded, due to my family status. Dmitri's enmity had never changed, and he would no doubt be only too glad to have me out of the way.

'So, Eugene, dear boy' he says mockingly, delineating that space between us, of perceived and real class difference; he the working class, unqualified scally, and me the lower middle-class college educated drop-out who simply didn't belong in their straight-forward world of day-to-day hand to mouth trudging through the silt of the Spanish economy, 'Just forget you were ever here, walk away. You've got something to keep you going for a bit, so just move on and start again.' He looks at me meaningfully. The meagre wad of notes is still under my mattress, all I have in the world, going forward. 'Take care mate' he says and turns away.

'And you, and thanks,' aimed at the scrappy little figure with his slightly bouncing gait, heading away from me, with no acknowledgement of this last sentiment.

I head for my bike, leaden, confused. The air is fresh and moist smelling, scattered puffy clouds swirling in the stiff, cool-ish breeze. Maybe it'll rain, something I have seen little of, even though we are in early spring. I cycle out from the industrial estate of warehouses and trucks, which could be anywhere. I cycle aimlessly through blocks of flats, then the road starts to take me toward grander villas. It finds me circumnavigating golf courses, with villas and expensive looking condo blocks crouching amid the luxurious vegetation. I'm vaguely heading toward the flanks of the enormous limestone rock they call La Concha. The road leads me over a bridge, and into a pleasant area of eucalyptus trees, their scent is not unlike some kind of cold remedy, yet another flavour to add to the palette of varying aromas I encounter constantly. It's liberating to be moving aimlessly along, avoiding any motion toward the inevitable departure, and the ire of Mr. Watkins.

The mountains in the near distance have several vast gashes carved into them, of roads gouged in layers. They switch back up the blasted slopes ending in nature in the form of pine forest, that stands paralysed, threatened by the developers' cataclysm. Yellow plant vehicles, earth movers, bulldozers, diggers galore, are parked in rows. Vast stockpiles of pipes, concrete constructions for drainage, kerbs, and all manner of infrastructure, stand amid the mud and dust. Nothing is moving. Not a soul can be seen. A frisson of shock and stupidity. This must be Holmeland. El Angel. I hadn't in any of my time here seen where it was, or even wondered. Sure enough, at the entrance to the road that leads inland upwards, are the giant poster hoardings proclaiming the familiar message that I have seen at the fair in Madrid and everywhere around Marbella. 'Holmeland. Lifestyle. Luxury. Investment. Happiness.' I head towards it, a voyeur at a road traffic accident, a dumb rubbernecker of an uncovered corpse, abandoned flagrantly after the crime in full view.

While the distant mountains are complete and natural, with their canopies of green and striations of geological history marked in the crags and peaks and gullies, the closer hills have been deformed en masse. The bulldozers have rendered the landscape to a chaos of texture and colour, geological vomit. Red, brown and purple earth, yellow rock and sand, orangey piles of shale and mud, all manner of textures and lesions wound the vast landscape. It is littered with building materials, ugly prefabricated huts, orange plastic perforated fabric strung from metal poles wrapping the whole ghastly expanse in a messy spider's web of construction detritus. The wind can be seen from the whirling clouds and spirals of dust that eddy upwards here and there. I reach a turning off the tarmacked road and continue along a dirt track, rutted heavily from the trucks, as the full scale of the development starts to fill my vision. The entire side of a what in England would be considered a mountain has been sculpted, re-

215

purposed and smitten as if by the hand of a giant vindictive schoolboy, intent on making his demented earthworks to run his toy cars around, as I did myself in the piles of sandy soil of a Cheshire garden many years ago. The metal fencing, in poles wedged into concrete blocks, lurches and sways in the breeze, and the entrance gates are chained and padlocked shut, with blue and white plastic tape marked '*Policía*' strung all about them. Several official bits of paper, stapled to a board and cable tied to the gate are the only evidence of the catastrophe that has befallen my brother's world. From the models and computer projections I had seen at the fair I am able to superimpose the dreamscape of 'El Angel', the Holmeland mega-project, onto the ravaged topography before me. The curves and textures of nature replaced by the neurotically manicured contours of golf courses, the ribbons of rabbit hutch apartment blocks, the chintzy faux Spanish architectural trimmings of terracing and towers, arches and columns, the splotches of luminous turquoise blue pools in varied kidney-shaped constellations. It resembles nothing so much as a vast, sick joke, lifeless behind its prison bars of fluttering flimsy police tape. Maybe the pines and rock that ring this great, gaping sore across the land are laughing fiendishly, their voice heard in the constant rattling of metal and fluttering plastic, the snapping of promotional flags, and sizzling sound of dust and gravel being shifted violently around by the wind.

It is now, staring at this, that the enormity of what has happened thumps me in the stomach. The size of the kingdom that was to be Gary's, the sheer brain bending amounts of money that must have been committed and already spent, for it now to be lying prone and unconscious, slapped about by the indifferent wind. How long would this mess stand screaming its presence and hubris to the world, a bombsite of ambition and speculation, to be joined no doubt by others around the palm flanked hills of the Marbella fantasy land? The cranes are falling silent, the police tape is going up in more than one place, the promoters' flags flapping and snapping their message, oblivious even while the contracts and deeds and hard drives are being hoovered up by the anti-corruption police running amuck along the coast.

I am conflicted, one part of me chortling and exalting at the fall of such a vainglorious and spurious concept of social organisation. I am a social anthropologist, in theory, on paper, of a third degree. Richard the third, not a Desmond Tutu even. But I can't empathise remotely with this idea of a prefabricated, packaged society you buy off a shelf, in a real estate lifestyle supermarket. Actual societies are organic and unpredictable, usually teetering on the edge of chaos, not mass produced and safe, hermetically sealed behind gates. The other part of me sees the ripped earth spewing its colour and filth out as a scream of despair, a rending cry at the loss of a dream, Gary's dream of success, of meaning and status, of shape to his life, of escape forever from the flat grey embrace of Warrington ennui.

I am aware of a sharp pungent odour, an oily fetid blast, a cheesy slap in the face. What new olfactory madness is this I wonder? The clanking and rattling of the metal construction fence, the cables on still cranes and machinery are gradually augmented by the dull tuneless ringing of bells. Around the perimeter of the site, through the bushes and their yellow flowered fronds appear dozens of goats. They are comical, and cute; brown, black and white, their heads bobbing, padding brightly and nimbly over the rocks and stumps, snatching and wrenching up anything green and succulent in sight. Now behind them appears an old man with a couple of scraggy dogs, his staff prodding the occasional stragglers, his funny whistling and cajoling is like some odd, alien language, part sung, part growled, part yelled. The smell is unexpectedly strong. The goats are mostly laden with astonishingly hefty, swaying udders that practically scrape the floor, with two enormous distended nipples on each bloated bag. It's a bizarre sight, and I can't square the juxtaposition of golf condos, swanky villas, Maseratis and champagne spray with the biblical tones and anachronistic oddity of a goat herd being driven, stinking, bleating and clanking around the edges of the golfers' paradise.

As the shepherd passes me, he nods, and says something that might have resembled '*Buenos días*', but I'm not sure as he doesn't appear to have many teeth. Or he could still be talking to the dogs in his alien Esperanto. The area is now flooded with goats, and I stand, too afraid to move through the herd with my bike, as I have no idea what confronting goats entails, having no previous life experience of the phenomenon. It takes some minutes for them to clear my area allowing me to exit back towards tarmac, safety and fresh air, which I gulp down gratefully.

I ride away from this mausoleum of the property development business. The whole great hunk of distorted geography yells at me to run, to get out, you are out of your depth and you don't belong here, and all of this will consume you, so run away little boy to your damp certainties and familiarities in England. As I pedal rhythmically and robotically away, I am wrenched and tangled by the voices, because the ones inside me are telling me there is no longer anything familiar or certain about England except the dampness, and I know that I no longer belong anywhere. I am placeless, formless, and shapeless. I stare around me as I ride. Overwhelming, raucous affluence and a society bought from a blingy catalogue. I ride along lanes of lush vegetation, vast flowering shrubs swaying and dancing in the lively breeze, while over the tops of the high walls appear the long low roofs of vast villas, each with their collection of huge slender palms, whose leaves rustle in that oddly rubbery way. All properties have enormous gates, many verging on the outright medieval, with heavy wood and faux metal nail heads. Some houses even have ludicrous crenulations. Money and good taste appear to be only uneasy bedfellows, or complete strangers, in this neighbourhood. Video surveillance, for the first time, is much in evidence.

Golf is woven visibly into the geographical and social fabric of this entire place. By design. The golf courses match the gardens and general landscaping of the area in their fastidiousness. The whole is like a set for a giant TV commercial of an idealised version of western life. It all looks too good to be true. So much of England, despite its wealth and highly administered, orderly society, actually looks ragged and messy, ugly and banal. The shapes, textures and structures of its environment reflect only a kind of conformity and utilitarianism, they drip with a pall of compromise and apology. But here in the winding lanes of the suburban end of Marbella, the conjunction of the extraordinarily lush and beautiful vegetation, the abundance of flowering shrubs and riotous colour, and the kind of houses I'd only ever seen in movies, appear as a hallucinatory world of perfection. A place where all that is promised by the system, that affluence, security, sexiness and completeness, all that is implicit and explicit in the all-enveloping commercialism, *that* has all coalesced here. Everything around me says 'I have it all and isn't gorgeous'.

While my inbuilt, northern, resentful chippiness makes my hackles rise and elicits a deep disgust, it is fatally undermined by the sheer seductiveness and beauty of the environment. I remember Faizal mocking what he called my 'plebeian envy' at college. Here I am at once angry and seduced, envious and contemptuous. It offends me and it makes me drool. I picture myself with a drink by the pool, some cool sounds thumping, a sleek babe collapsed in a hammock. To which I raise a huge metaphorical middle finger, frantically gesturing at all of the lucky, undeserving, rich bastards. Plebeian envy indeed.

I am craning my head back as I ride, watching the rows of palms slide under my gaze; a vision I have seen in so many Hollywood films, it makes me giggle. I'm riding through a movie, I'm Nero on a bike, watching Rome burn. How much the convulsions, occurring right now in the lawyers' offices and courts and police investigation rooms, will disturb the sculpted voluptuousness of this other world, is hard to say. Everyone here looks like they've made it already, and will probably chortle at the vulgar, money grubbing arrivistes and their political stooges, while they slurp their premium vodka and tonics; Crystal nicely on ice, the personal- trainer-honed body relaxed in its designer jogging suit, and the state-of-the-art security will keep it efficiently out of sight and mind at the least. These villas are oases of a rare type, and no wonder they huddle together in such a benign and gorgeous place, enjoying the stadium-like spread of the slopes of La Concha, the vast three-thousand-foot-high rock that gives Marbella its micro-climate.

The conflicted swirl in my head and my craning neck mean I only see the vehicle at the last minute, or second. A great yellow lump with chrome shiny bits appears in my peripheral vision and I jam on brakes and swerve, coming to a fairly abrupt halt without balance and tip off my bike to land sprawling onto my side, staring up the highly polished sides of this American penis compensation machine. The beast known as a Hummer. Who actually drives these idiotic machines? What sort of person needs to be seen in something like this? I struggle meekly to my feet, hoping I don't have to engage the occupants of the vehicle. I make to mind my own business and let it pass, trying to be invisible despite the ludicrous two wheeled pantomime I have just given. The driver's window is open, two stocky men sit inside the car. The driver has an expression of deep amusement and incredulity on his face. *The driver.* Time stops, the palm trees cease their rubbery symphony, birds gag mid-warble, I only hear the brute throbbing of the vast engine under the hood of the comedy box on wheels.

'Alright Eugene. Enjoying your holiday, I see. Keeping fit, are we? Good job you didn't scratch my motor Eugene, that wouldn't have pleased me very much.' The voice is more gravelly and deeper, from fags, late nights and high living, the accent is more scouse than the younger version, but the contempt and implicit menace in everything is just the same. 'Sorry to hear about Gary's bit of bother. Never mind ay, he could always open a chippy, not much competition here in that department at least. Mind how you go. Be seeing ya.'

220

This last sentiment is accompanied by a wink and pointed index figure with raised thumb. It's not exactly a gun gesture, but it nonetheless could be. I am like a rod, every muscle has spontaneously frozen, my vision glazes and all I can compute is the face. No. I'm not that surprised to see Jimmy Kavanagh, in this vehicle, here. And it would be bad enough, were it not for the identity of the passenger. Dmitri. Observing me with that same dead expression, only who knows what behind those light blue eyes. One plus one equals too many. Too many combinations of trouble, of violence, of possible implications for what Gary, even I, have gotten involved in. I sprint away on my bicycle, with Kavanagh's cackling echoing in my ears.

My body pushes beyond its comfort zone with the force of the panic induced by the revelation. I'm cycling still, as fast as I can push the bike, back towards where I came from. My lungs rasp, my sides ache from the effort, but still I push on. I try to compute the implications of that equation. Kavanagh plus Dmitri plus Lebid equals what? Lebid plus Kavanagh minus three million euros equals what? What is the relationship of one Kavanagh to one Lebid? One plus one plus one makes chaos. Dmitri plus Kavanagh by the square root of business, part of the same equation, a cancerous calculus, a binary virus spreading from Warrington via the Ukraine and running amok in Marbella. Gary has been an unwitting carrier and has infected me.

I devour the road; I am oblivious to the honks of a couple of irritated motorists as I cycle steadily like an automaton. I try to organise my thoughts, to still the panic, to slow them down so I can read them, but they are still a blur, running from comprehension as I run from my nemesis. Kavanagh. Why him, why now? But it fits. Despite my exertions, I feel saliva in my mouth, bitter bile. I halt to catch my breath, and find a bench, overlooking lawns and trees. It's pretty, La Concha gazing down majestically on this neat bit of urban landscaping. I struggle to pull my thoughts back into perspective. It's so perfect. Holmeland and all of its ambition, status, moving millions, weaving dreams, and when you dig down deep enough there it is, a Jimmy Kavanagh sitting there, laughing back at you.

It is a moment. A moment to which all the other moments stand in relation to. For I have come to nothing. I have reached nowhere. With the ghosts of my past reappearing randomly. I wiped the slate clean and came to Marbella. A blank sheet of paper, with no ink in the pen. To go back is to admit I cannot change. Change me. Change my destiny. This moment, is the logical or illogical sum and result of all those other moments that have preceded this one. All those wasted moments. Staring into the abyss, and finding it empty. An abyss only in my mind, created entirely from it, from the years of bad decisions, elisions and the evasions of a life time.

A whiff of garlic. Behind me, fifty metres away is a clutch of scruffy cafes. Most welcome, for my stomach is screaming at me. I trudge into the restaurant, getting a few curious glances from old couples and a handful of tourists eating, enjoying the day. This is a wake, for my life here in Marbella. I shall miss this; the *'menu del día'*[17]. Unpretentious, wholesome, tasty, as familiar as sausage egg and chips, and as bizarre as pig's stomach in a chickpea stew, and affordable. One thing separates Spain fundamentally from the UK; the *'menu del día'*. The backbone of the nation. If I'd had such a source of ever varying, cheap, brilliant nosh, available in friendly, noisy cafes full of life and character, and the inevitable gorgeous young Spanish waitress (or Romanian, or Latina, or whatever, is it the weather that makes the girls so beautiful in this damn country?), my life would have turned out completely differently. I laugh at the thought. Saved by food! I wish. Have tapas bars reached Warrington yet? I shall reach Warrington. Tomorrow. And there it is, that silver lining in the dark cloud of my broken parole. Kavanagh is in Marbella, and I won't be. Relief seeps into my frazzled psyche.

---

[17] Menu of the day

Holmeland plus Lebid plus Kavanagh equals good riddance Marbella.

18

My minimal belongings, the formless, fashion-less clothes and some equally bland new additions, are packed back into the old black bag cum rucksack, faithful companion of dozens of drug runs and raves and festivals. My life, there, fitting entirely into an anonymous sack, and if it was lost by the baggage handlers, would I even miss it, be worse off?

I have erased my minimal presence from Frankie's/Gary's flat. Maybe a tin of baked beans hides at the back of a cupboard and some other British oddities I purchased initially. That was before I reconfirmed that I have no ability in the kitchen department, and before I discovered how easy it is to feed yourself from the multifarious hostelries that abound in a Spanish town.

Frankie observes this packing ritual disconsolately. We have only exchanged the basics of conversation necessary. She'll be leaving soon, for what's left of her job. The cold draught of recession is already blowing through every corner of the town. Her normally free spending clients in the club have lost their extravagant mood, or are simply staying away. I will be leaving fairly early in the morning, so shortly we'll be faced with saying our goodbyes. It's a fairly brutal change of perspective from only two days ago.

Before long Frankie has changed from the habitual daytime dressing gown to her night garb of skimpy dress, plunging cleavage, and towering heels. She stands before me, looking embarrassed. Aware of the effect, of how efficient it is at stimulating parts of the male id that can only be neutralised by an effort of conscious will. And how wasted the effect is on me now, how little in return will be forthcoming. How something for a moment felt like more than just attraction and convenient casual sex, like we were perhaps closer in spirit than we both imagined. We do embrace. And kiss, cautiously, gently, for as long as it can be born before it becomes a symbol of what is potentially being lost, wasted, never discovered. She tries to pull away, her taxi is waiting. No-one walks to work in shoes like that. I struggle to let her go. To let go of something the like of which my life had never offered me before, or that I had never been in a condition to nurture, to respond to. It just ends up reconfirming swathes of my most negative and self-critical ideas about myself.

'Bye, then.' She says.

'Yup. Guess so. Maybe...', but there aren't any words to come, and she knows it, and her face loses its softness and resumes its distance, its shield, habitually worn against all of the nonsense and bullshit she must have to endure in a job like that, dressed like that. I stare at the floor, cursing myself. The door closes gently. Like an enticing, verdant opening between some trees, glimpsed from a speeding car on a long trip, it flares briefly in your awareness, exerts a momentary pull, a longing to discover, to see if it was as nice as you thought it might have been, but you are already a long way away, and you know you aren't going to travel this road again.

I'm left to while away the rest of the evening, in uncomfortable solitude. The only certainty in life is the inevitability of having to throw myself upon the mercy of Mr. Watkins. To beg the state for the restoration of my benefits. The ultimate humiliation, of deeply unpredictable outcome. Then the resumption, maybe after further purgatory in Strangeways, of meetings, job applications, imprisonment at home with the human formerly known as Mum. A cycle of soul immolating futility. Watkins plus Warrington equals slow death.

My thoughts turn to Gary. My obsession with my own inadequacies distracts me from the scenario that threatens to engulf his life, with profound consequences. He may end up like me, in prison, but having lost his life's work. Conversely, I have nothing further to lose. It humbles me. I have knowingly brought the world down on my own sorry head. Gary has only worked hard, excelled, striven to be the best he can be, and now he'll be dashed on the rocks of circumstance. And what I can I offer him? Aren't *I* supposed to look after *him?* Useless big brother.

I do one last mental idiot check, to see that I have everything, and will leave no further trace tomorrow, to distract or annoy either Frankie or Gary. I just need to return his warehouse keys, when I see him. Mustn't forget. That would be typical Gene.

I stop dead. I am so stupid. I also feel properly scared now for Gary. Something clicks into place that justifies all my most lurid fears surrounding this whole debacle. Of course. Kavanagh plus Dmitri plus Lebid equals only one possible thing. Narcotics. I look at the keys in my hand. Right there, those little silver bits of metal, right there I have the means to get to the heart of the truth of this whole sorry farce. Maybe, if what my gut is telling me, I can give Gary ammunition that'll put his relationship with Lebid on a whole different footing.

The implications of what I'm processing are profound and terrifying. Seriously high risk. I have to make a decision, now, tonight. If I can get in there and find something…

~

Some three hours later, after riding discreetly to the warehouse, I am stood before the door. It was never going to be possible to just leave the fact of Kavanagh's involvement in this as inconsequential. I am duty bound to give Gary any possible advantage, to effect something positive in this life. The keys swing the inset door open, and the alarm starts its brief countdown. I clumsily punch in the alarm code from memory. Only as I punch the last digit does it occur to me; they may have changed the code. The horror of the thought mercifully has no time to gain traction, once I hear the triple beep of the code being accepted. I laugh grimly at my endless capacity to be a huge liability to myself.

The warehouse is in near darkness. The skylights and emergency lighting allow a dim glow to vaguely illuminate things, giving a slight relief to the shapes of furniture and packages on shelving and pallets. A mysterious IKEA in a ghost town, the shadow of people's lives and material yearnings, wrapped, coiled, ready to be unfurled and given life in their new dream golf box. Or probably not, now. In this light the one security camera won't even pick up a shape, never mind a face. I know that it's a pretty hopeless system, as I saw Dmitri cursing it on various occasions. I go to the work area and fumble around for a package knife, find one and think where to look. Where would you hide drugs in furniture? Come on think, I have professional expertise in this department, surely. If they were moving stuff, then it would need to be inside something that was leaving Spain. Or not leaving at all, and just being stored. All around me is the smell of cardboard and plastic, harsh, artificial and chemical. Surveying the serried rows of shelving, the endless anonymous piles of boxes, the ludicrous scale of the task walks up and smacks me full in the face. What a clown. The warehouse is full of bulky packages, where hundreds of kilos could be hidden if you wanted to. In the dark, with a small blade, I can't even hope to search effectively, never mind the fact the shelving is many yards high in much of the warehouse. And do I leave obvious signs of my search? Stupid. The inflated sense of my own abilities, of what I have convinced myself exists, now appears foolhardy at best, suicidal at worst. For a moment I walk aimlessly, trying to keep my composure, to think clearly and not get into a panic and do something that might, might what? Keep a grip on yourself Gene. I'm talking to myself, mantra like, trying to focus. I'm in the far corner, and I look back along a corridor between high shelf stacks. The smooth concrete dimly reflects the light from the roof, and I see an even run of square shapes in the floor. Electrical service duct covers, no doubt. I turn around. Behind me is a lonely pallet of random boxes. Precisely where another cover might be. My heart beat picks up. I search for a pallet truck and die inside at the noise it makes as I try to roll it as lightly as possible over to the pallet. Sure enough, the pallet is hiding another duct cover. There follows another nerve-racking search where I attempt to find a tool to prise off the heavy metal cover. I locate one of the many crowbars that are usually lying around the damn place, but not tonight. The cover lifts and I slide it back just enough to force an arm down inside and search around. Immediately I hit objects. I feel in the dark. Evenly ordered, regularly shaped packages, roughly the size of a kilo bag of flour. I attempt to scratch through the wrapping. I can't, so I pull out my keys and stab one through. Withdrawing it I hastily lick it. Bingo! My tongue is instantly numb. Cocaine. Pure. My pulse races even further, thumping at my temples. There follows an insane performance act as I try to balance the physical exertions of replacing all of this with the need for quiet. By the time I'm done, I'm sweating profusely and trembling violently. With enormous relief I exit through the door, and turn the keys. I pull my bike to me, ready to mount, gasping at my stupidity having left it there brazenly in the street for anyone to see. Then with a now familiar, sickening stomach lurch, I realise I haven't reset the alarm. The torture is too much for me, but I have to open up again and complete the task or who knows what may transpire. I am fumbling for my keys when I hear the distinctive sound of powerful engines, typical of the deep throbbing of souped-up Mercedes AMG's that are so common in Marbella. Or yellow American monster waggons. I hear them long before the lights are visible bouncing off warehouses at the corner of the street, about one hundred and fifty meters away. I frantically scan the street for cover. A bulky skip directly opposite, open topped, conveniently. Grabbing the bike, I race over to it and hurl it in, provoking a loud crashing on some kind of metallic waste, but I hastily follow praying to land on something more forgiving. I follow and land in between something like discarded duct pipes. Noisy but no sharp edges. I freeze myself and try and slow my breathing as I am deafening myself amid the silence of night. The lights of a vehicle now approaching play across the tops of the skip, and the powerful engine idles, as it pulls up close by. Two vehicles. I clench everything to keep as still as possible, as one twitch could send tinny scraping sounds into the night, so precarious is my perch on top of the unsympathetic waste.

Time freezes. I hear sounds of several people emerging from the vehicles. Keys open the door and listen to the subsequent silence. The silence of no alarm. My innards are doing somersaults and cold sweat is coursing under my clothes, but my mouth is dry as a bone. I maintain the freeze, eyes tight shut like a frightened child watching Doctor Who.

I wait.

'Bloody fuck you Darren.' The heavy Ukrainian accent and aggressive rasp, distinctively Dmitri. I can't hear the response completely, but can pick up the tone and rhythm of Darren's accent, protestations of something.

'I told you, stop smoking that stuff when you working.' Dmitri again.

'I'm positive I did, I fucking did.' His whining reaches me, and it would have been comic in another context.

'Shut the fuck up Darren.' A different voice. Similar accent. It's Kavanagh. The door of the warehouse slams. Rigidified, I consider my options. I attempt to raise my torso up, to peep over the rim of the skip, but a chorus of metallic scrapings erupts, amplified all the more horribly by the tubular nature of the waste. Climbing out would probably be heard inside the warehouse, with unimaginable consequences. The sweat starts to dry and chill me, I must relax into the metallic spaghetti. Wait is all I can do; bear out the agonising minutes of vulnerability, with no idea how long it will take.

The slap of something plastic drags my mind howling into consciousness, a searing panic resolves just as quickly into paralysis as I fully take in where I am again. I tense up, barely breathing, straining to collect aural data to orientate myself. Something has been dumped on top of me. I don't know at what point my reverie descended into blackness or for how long, but the panic surging over me is just about contained by gritting teeth and freezing my breath,

229

straining to achieve total quiet, invisibility. I hear voices again, but far less distinctly. Whatever has been dumped on me is big enough to dampen most sound. As I daren't even move I don't yet know if I'll be able to extricate myself from under it. It is heavier under here now. Then another thought comes along to scramble the overload of information. The rubbish trucks always do their rounds in the dead of night. But this is a skip. Maybe that's different. I want to laugh; it *is* funny in a way. I hang onto my freeze, aware yet again of the sweat chilling on me, aware I feel damp, cold, and am starting to shiver compulsively. Slight metallic scrapings emanate. I close my eyes, expecting this sound to give away my presence any second. I bury myself in my mind, trying to block out the present, searching for blackness, unseeingness, unfeelingness, only aware of my breathing, my shivering and the crazy lights dancing behind my eyelids as I scrunch them so tightly, I think they'll be swallowed up inside my head. I maintain this for what feels like an eternity, vaguely aware of engines, indistinct voices, fading.

First, I open my eyes. The vague glow of a nearby pale orange street light peeks through the layers of whatever was dumped on top of me. I listen, straining to perceive every sound. Only my breathing and the faint rattling and scraping of tin that accompanies my compulsive shivering. Every attempted move I make triggers a cacophony of metallic noise. I stop each time and listen. No signs of reaction, no voices. Just silence, a barking dog some way away, some mechanical hissing noises and refrigeration like buzzing nearby. Once I feel that the status quo is neutral, and I can stand the shivering no longer, I trigger the noisy process of clambering outwards, every scrape and bang sending lightning shocks of terror through me. I have been covered in detritus from the warehouse. My numbed senses nonetheless acknowledge the contents of the recent addition. Plastic sheeting, half used rolls of packing tape, cardboard and hardboard offcuts. I have a deflating sensation they have moved their stash. I extricate the bicycle amid what sounds like a deafening din, hurl it over the side of the skip where it crashes onto the pavement. I desperately try to lower myself down the side of the skip, but stiffness, cold and exhaustion result in me tumbling onto the floor in a painful heap. I pick myself up, every joint and limb screaming and straining, I am whimpering with sheer cold and self-pity, and a sort of desperate mumbling starts up in me. 'Please get me home, please get me home, come on Gene go home, go home now please' yet another mantra of fear to add to my growing repertoire. Light is breaking the sky, birds start up sporadically, and I somehow grapple myself onto the bike which mercifully still functions. Maintaining my mantra, I set off, snivelling in relief and desperation. The journey back to the flat is a slow torture, the cold burns me through as the dawn dampness doubles up the penetrating cruelty of it. I breath in painful slices, gasping and rasping to keep fuelling the crippled muscles, hanging on to consciousness until I am able to stagger into the block, and safety. I dive into the bed dragging everything I have onto me, duvets, extra sheets, a coat, a throw from the sofa, and wrap myself cocoon like and shiver myself back into unconsciousness, not even sure I will wake up out of it, so cold and nauseous do I feel. Not even sure I want to.

~

Consciousness returns again abruptly, jarring the still painful body, dragging my eyes open into stabbing shafts of light. Focussing onto a shape in front of me, I am about to scream with panic imagining I have been tracked back to my refuge, when I recognise Gary, and his voice registers on me…

'… the hell have you been? You're supposed to be on a flight in a couple of hours' but his anger fades momentarily as he takes in the sight before him. I am just starting to collect the same, and it's not pretty. I blink up at him. I am aware first of my odour, of dried sweat, of a rubbishy dusty metallic stench. The daylight reveals my filthy clothes, dishevelled and covered in plaster dust and sawdust. Blood

231

on my face and elsewhere one of my hands is cut messily, bloodily, but I have no recollection of the injury.

'What in God's name happened to you? You OK?' Gary looks genuinely shocked.

'I'm fine, yes, I'm Ok.' I pause, and Gary shrugs a 'what the hell is that supposed to mean' sort of shrug at me. 'I can explain. In the car. I'm packed, I just need a shower,' Gary is still looking in disbelief, 'seriously it's ok. Shower. Then we can go.' I drag myself up and stumble off toward the bathroom, aware Gary is staring at me with a mixture of fear, disbelief and disapproval. I'm in the shower before he has time to interrogate me further. Never has a shower felt so good. Some of the stiffness melts, the sticky, dusty crust washes through and I relish the smell of clean skin again, the stench of fear draining away down the plug hole. I will be on a plane and gone from this insane corner of the world in a matter of hours. The prospect of going home is a welcome relief. I'm out of the shower, into some clean clothes, abandoning the others where I left them, grabbing the tatty holdall with my worldly goods and bounding down the stairs without looking back. Gary is following, and still hasn't said anything further.

Once in the car, I turn to Gary to try to explain this new version of his world to him, but I'm stopped by his expression. He looks completely gutted, his face drained of colour, his facial muscles twitching, as though he is straining to contain something. And I hadn't even noticed, so preoccupied with my own fear have I been. He starts up the car.

'What's happened? Gary, you don't look good.'

He runs his tongue around his mouth, as much to stop his teeth grinding as anything else, the muscles continuing their dances around his skull. He is trying to compose himself to speak normally.

'Holme has screwed me.' Tears rim his eyes, he is completely close to breaking point. My own private hell is quietened and pushed back; what new visitation of chaos has arrived? 'He emptied the

232

accounts overnight; he moved all funds to Brazil. He didn't tell me he had special authority on all of the accounts still, I never thought to check, I trusted him. Lebid isn't getting his money. Everything gone. What a great reward for a lifetime's work.' He finishes and stares ahead, still driving.

'Oh no, Gaz, I'm so sorry.' I am stunned. All about me appears poisonous. The lush vegetation passing by, the white gleaming blocks, the blue canopy above, shimmering. It's a sick joke, a living, glossy real estate brochure, framing a vast stinking, vile swamp. It disgusts me, even as it laughs, rolling about in its voluptuous, seductive, self-satisfied hilarity.

'Gary, it doesn't surprise me. Lebid's a gangster, a drug dealer, and this whole thing is fucked up. But I've got a way out for you.'

'Shuttup Gene, you're out of your depth, you can't help with any of this. Just go home, and forget any of this is happening. I can deal with my own mess.'

'Jesus, you still don't get it do you? Yesterday I was cycling around the back of town, the golf courses, y'know? And who nearly runs me over in one of those great big Hummer things? Jimmy Kavanagh, Gary. *The* Jimmy Kavanagh! The acne faced psycho bastard himself, Gary. He is sitting in a yellow hummer with Dmitri, laughing at me, making jokes about how you can just go and open a chip shop in Marbella! Funny joke yeah? Kavanagh and Dmitri are mates, no, not mates, business partners, Gary. They have a business together, with Lebid, which is probably what is really funding your Holmeland.' I pause for breath, because I'm hyperventilating, with the sheer terrifying madness of the whole scenario.

'What the hell has got into you, Gene? And what was that ridiculous performance this morning?' Nonetheless he's trying to process it, do the equations, Kavanagh in the mix. 'Jimmy Kavanagh, with our Dmitri?'

233

'Yes, don't you get it, don't you see it all? Lebid. Three million in cash. In bags, from the back of a brothel in Madrid. Guys with guns. And then…' now I take out the keys from the flat, 'see these, the keys for the warehouse, right? After I saw Kavanagh and Dmitri, I figure this can only work one way. I went into that warehouse to find what I knew would be there. Kavanagh's a major league drug dealer, Gary.'

'How can you know that?' He sounds indignant, but appears increasingly anxious, as if he wasn't enough already.

'Because I was working for his organisation when I got nicked! I didn't know he was part of it until I bumped into him in a warehouse in Amsterdam one night five years ago. That was a pleasant surprise. I should have run then, but I didn't. And then look where I ended up. Gary this is all fucked, it's time for us all to run. That warehouse is full of coke. I went in there last night, with these keys, and I found their fucking stash of cocaine, kilos of it, and then they came and moved it while I was hiding in a skip outside the warehouse, and that's how you found me this morning. I spent the night in a skip thinking I was a dead man.' I could laugh, but I'm too tired. Drained.

Gary doesn't react, and I sit panting, wrought with anger and fear and confusion, but he stares ahead driving. And the penny drops. And sears me inside.

'You knew.' I am staring at his face looking fixedly ahead and he makes no attempt to contradict me. I can neither confirm nor deny that, sir, as they say. Nothing. 'Don't tell me you knew, please.'

I stare ahead as well. He knew. I am hollowed out. So tired. The world around me fades away slightly as I lose grip on the present, I want to fall back, to be weightless, to be transported out of the now, and to erase everything that has passed before me since I set foot in this ridiculous place. A moment of comfort, a fleeting glimpse of a place without madness, of dull simplicity. I am far away, the present

234

has receded completely, and only the sudden sound of Gary with his hand on the horn of the car jumps me back into the now.

'Jesus, get out of the…'

The words somehow evaporate and the world becomes only the view through the windscreen, futuroscope, technicolor, wide wide wide. The motorbike in front of us fills the frame, the rider and his passenger, faceless in their black helmets stare at us with their blank, oblong eye. The gun raises as if on cue. The muzzle flash is visible for a nanosecond before the cinema screen whites out and transforms into a cascade of tiny crystalline particles. The detonation fills my head with a roaring that maintains its pitch, and I am aware of further detonations, impact, something wet, a paroxysm of frenzied activity and a loss of equilibrium, I can't tell what is up or down, I am floating, flailing, formless in space. The sensation is maintained momentarily, or forever. I can't tell. Sense of time is completely incomplete. I taste stones, earth, my fingernails scratch uncontrollably at the surface, then wrench me forwards, onto my knees, feet, I crash into vegetation and I come to a stop, suspended, restrained by dense greenery. Momentary stasis. Confusion. I fling myself back into reverse, tumble onto my back, flip myself over onto hands and knees. I yank my head up to orientate, trying to get a fix on what is happening, where I am. I am staring through the open door of the passenger side of the car. Glass glints like Christmas sparkling decorations. Gunsmoke wafts, a chemical, burnt stink. Gary is motionless in his seat. I pull myself into the car, to help him, to say we'll sort things out, let's get to the airport. My hands are bleeding from the glass. I crawl up onto the passenger seat. I take Gary's head and I start shouting at him. I'm not sure what, as I am deafened. He ignores me. He stares out of the shattered windscreen. A simple, clean hole perforates his chest. His neck is gashed deeply. I beat him on the shoulder imploring him to get out because he is hurt. He needs to see a doctor, but he continues to ignore me. He is covered in blood. His neck wound is still seeping, which has covered his torso and is gathering in a pool in the floor pan of the car. My hands are completely covered, slippery and I cannot get hold of him to drag him out of the car. Everything is too slippery and sticky. I begin to lose my vision. I think I am crying. I think I am howling. I cannot do anything I need to do. Gary ignores me. Something, someone, pulls me out of the car again. I fight them off. I must help Gary. We need to get to the airport; we can run away from all of this. They prevent me from going back in. There are many people. They stand, eyes wide, mouths flapping open stupidly. I fight them all. They pin me down, and despite my best efforts I can do nothing. I vomit. Uncontrollably, and the people holding me back off. I stare at the mess of bile and the little yellow flowers that are tangled in it. What a pity, they were so pretty. Why has someone been sick on them? I sit up and look back into the innards of the Audi. The white leather upholstery is spattered in reddish browny bits. I cannot see Gary. Someone has put something over him. I cannot see my brother anymore, just a coat, in a car, on a road, under a clear blue sky on a sunny morning, in Marbella.

19

Ana sits across from me. Her face is a tortured, distorted mess of red skin, raw eyes, of straggled hair; her fingers rammed in her mouth, keeping her teeth busy, her chest occasionally heaving as she attempts to combat the enormous sobs that well up, choking them off by trying to push her fist inside of her mouth. An older Spanish woman, maybe her mother, is attempting to keep control of her. Some policemen stand near us. We are in a hospital waiting room. Gary is dead. I know that now. We are waiting for I don't know what. No-one has been able to explain anything to me. Ana is incapable of explaining anything. A woman appears who does not look medical, or police. She looks British. She is from the consulate. She has come to help, and to organise some things. I am to go with her, and she will sit with me while the police interview me. She says I need cleaning up. I nod dumbly, and follow, childlike. I look to Ana who sits rocking gently, held by the old woman. She does not acknowledge me, or anything. I leave with the woman.

An anonymous phlegm coloured room. I am dressed in some kind of hospital garb, greenish also. I have been examined, studied by anonymous doctors, stared at by anonymous officials and people in uniforms. I have been washed and changed, and I think someone may have given me an injection. I am calm, like I just got out of bed, so that can't be as a result of what just happened. Somewhere inside, muffled, lost, is a voice yelling for me to get away, to run and don't stop. But I only perceive it as far apart from me, it isn't me here now, it's the voice I left on the roadside. I have bandages on my hand, some kind of dressing on parts of my face. A man is in front of me, in a greenish uniform with a funny old-fashioned moustache. Why is everything a shade of green? He is talking, and someone is translating into English, the woman. He is writing things down, presumably what comes out of my mouth. I am aware of me making sounds, forming words, with much shaking of the head. I stare at the man and the woman, they repeat things, and look exasperated. They shake their heads. I don't care. I am left for a while in this anonymous room. This only serves as a canvass for abstract, dynamic explosions of glass and blood and white light and smoke and little yellow flowers and the faces of people, gawping in horror. Another greenish uniformed person sits in the corner, regarding me with concern. He gets up expressionlessly and goes out of the door, and momentarily another anonymous person comes in and says things and I follow them back to a part of the hospital with real people.

Ana and two older people take me, an arm around the shoulder and lead us both out to a little old car, that smells of dust and animals. Ana and I sit in the back, as these four people move away in the malodorous old jalopy, and the town slides by, the motorway runs for a while as the car strains and coughs to compete at such a modern speed, and then it gives way gradually to the pines of the mountains, and we climb up, and the road becomes dirt, and the car lurches and rattles and clanks. It is a car at home in the dust and rubble of the countryside. None of us talks.

When, eventually, we are divorced from the modern world, with barely a sign of civilisation except for poles and electricity wires, we stop. A slight, low house lurks behind a battered fence made partly of wire, partly of abandoned bedsteads and pallets, partly of ferocious looking cacti. A triumvirate of daft, mangy dogs leap and yelp as we approach. The old man calms them and pushes them brusquely and without any apparent affection into a wiry corral at one side of the building. They continue their yelping. The old lady heads for the house in a waddling gait that speaks of bad circulation and stiff arthritic joints, but also oblivious to them, so expressionless is her face. Ana beckons me to a low bench, with the wall of the house forming a back rest. We sit gingerly, and a stillness descends, gratefully free from anonymous people with their urgency and questions and ministrations.

Hills spattered with scrub, pines, evergreen trees and general wildness stretch away, to a sliver of sea visible at the end of it all. Occasionally, on nearby slopes, a vast white or terracotta villa erupts, framed by fortuitously planted palm trees, but other than that I am truly in the middle of nowhere. Silence. Not just from us, but all around, apart from the snuffling dogs and the occasional sound of chickens. A deep quiet, where the vague breeze that ripples around is afforded clarity and presence as though nothing else mattered or could be bothered to compete. I am aware of Ana's breathing. I am part of the world again, and a calm has settled.

'My grandparents' she offers without any other explanation. 'I'll introduce you in a minute. We are going to stay here right now.' She pauses. 'Until the police tell us it is safe. Safe for you. And me. I don't know...'

The silence resumes and deafens me. Every whisper of wind, the birds scuffling in the bushes, all the miasmic details of low-level background noise are writ strident and vivid, and turn my thoughts outward, and I see the world objectively again. The panic has subsided, and I utter my first comprehensible sentence for several hours.

'Thank you. I'm sorry. Everything that's happened, it's... I'm sorry it had to be you, I'm sorry...' and that's as much sense as I manage. Ana breathes slowly, rhythmically.

'Had to be me? I loved Gary, he was everything to me, what are you saying?' Accusation colours her voice, it stabs at me. I can't escape the feeling that what has happened was some kind of logical progression, of a causal chain, that he had become embroiled in. I am in some way being sucked into the same maelstrom; condemned by association, by my knowledge. Just what I have seen and what I now know sounds like a death sentence

'What do you mean 'had to be me'?!' she repeats, looking directly at me, the tone demanding I justify myself. I stare over the hills, finding no help, I scrabble in the overheated space of my head for a more sensitive and cogent way of saying what is eating me.

'Gary was... he was caught up in something that goes much further than selling golf condos. I mean that's what he was doing, that was his business, but I've seen other stuff, other people, that are involved in the bigger picture, and it's dirty. I think that's why they killed him. Someone took their revenge, or punished him, or, I don't know, maybe Gary knew stuff he shouldn't have known. I'm sorry it had to be you on the end of that, you don't deserve that.' I sound crass. I'm expecting to be shot down, to face her indignation, but instead her face tightens, the lips drawn thin over her teeth and her jaw clenches. She doesn't respond. 'How much do you know about the way Holmeland works. Really?'

She rocks back and forth, her hands tucked under her thighs, tears rolling down the coffee-coloured cheeks. She starts talking, barely audibly.

'I knew Holmeland was not completely clean. I know the image they project is just part of the brand. You can't find that kind of money, and break so much rules about planning and permits without being *enchufado*[18], you know, having contacts, the right contacts. And in Marbella the right contacts means money, you pay to get what you want. You pay everybody, the *concejales* in the town hall, the lawyers, the builders, the people in the Junta in Sevilla. Everybody wants their slice of the pie, I think you say. That's what my company lives off, making those problems of illegal plans go away, making it all appear legal. The right deeds, the right licences, the right permits, but all lies. And now it's all finished and someone killed him for it.'

---

[18] Connected

Then she breaks into sobs, and I cradle her until the sobbing subsides, after what feels an age. The sun is getting lower. On the dusty table with the cheap, plastic, chequered table cloth in front of us, has appeared a plate of cheese, and some salami, a dish of olives, a bottle of *Cruzcampo* beer and some juice of some sort. I have barely noticed the two old people, moving about us discreetly, not intruding on this continuing stream of grief. It seems incongruous in the circumstances, and then my hunger stabs through the other sensations. I suppose back home I'd have been offered a cup of tea, so this is the local equivalent I figure.

I am introduced eventually, formally, to the grandparents, Juan and Maria del Mar. They nod and attempt smiles, revealing fewer teeth than I thought was feasibly functional. They talk to Ana in heavily accented and indistinct Spanish, even with my limited knowledge I can't discern anything recognisable other than *'sí'*, which they pronounce without the actual 's' sound, half of the word, so it comes out as a sort of grunted 'he'. They know better than to try and talk to me as I plainly can't speak their own language, as I have no doubt Ana has explained. A chill descends as the sun is close to setting, and the air is still and the silence is now overwhelming. Ana leads me inside into another world, like passing through a door into another time. The house is one open space with a bedroom off to one side. A round wooden table with a cloth on it of faded floral kitschness occupies centre stage, complemented by an open range of a fireplace with a grate, a kind of barbecue and a pot hung from a chain. Smokey logs fizzle and crack into life. The gloom is interrupted by a gas lamp which creates a yellow halo, illuminating half of the space at least. A gas ring and bottle lies on a flat surface at one end, together with a sink, but no tap. I am offered a blanket which I accept as the chill is encroaching, and resign to the doggy smell of it. We sit around the round table as the two grandparents bow and retire into the dark meagre bedroom and close the door.

241

Ana stares at me for some time. She looks numb, but at least composed, not shattered and distraught anymore. Eventually she breaks the stillness, where to say anything is to risk reliving the trauma of how we came to be where we are.

'Welcome to Old Spain.' She says, without any irony or trace of disdain. 'My grandparents like it here, it reminds them of how it used to be. When things were, you know, less complicated.' Now she cracks an ironic smile. It's a relief, the first in the long day of ache.

'You mean they don't live here all the time?' I say naively, to which she shakes her head imperceptibly.

'This is how many people lived in the old Andalucía, under Franco. This is where we have come from, Gene. My grandparents brought me up from when I was fourteen. My mother died of breast cancer, she was only thirty-eight years old. My father was *traumatizado* by that, being left alone with a young daughter. My mother was the one who kept us, my father was a *chorizo*, you say a wheeler dealer. He thought he could be rich, with all the new money in Spain, but he was always making the wrong deals, always getting ripped off by the smarter more educated *chorizos*, the proper crooks. The kind of people in the town hall. They are just peasants who were smarter than the rest. So he went away, to Germany, and worked as a waiter and sent money to my grandparents who looked after me. Not here, in a small flat in San Pedro. They still live there, but this is our *casa de campo*. This is their place to escape back to their roots. With the dogs and the chickens and no electricity and water from the well. But it's good. No-one will find us here. And we don't know what will happen now, do we?' She fixes me straight in the eye, accusing, pleading, demanding the answer to the awful question squatted in front of us, filling the room, where all is silent except for the sputtering of logs on the range.

'What now, what now?' I repeat to myself. I didn't have a clue those few weeks ago when I arrived here, and now the absence of any vestigial meaning to my being here is inescapable. 'I have to go back to the UK. To see Mum. I need to explain what happened. I'm not sure when I can come back. *If* I can come back, even.'

'But you must. You need to.' She looks at me earnestly, imploringly. I must explain my humiliating circumstances and my stupidity to her.

'Well it's not that easy, you see-'

'I'm pregnant, Gene. I am carrying Gary's child.' I am still, and the room is moving around me, the ground even. 'We hadn't told anyone, it's still early. We were going to start a family, because it felt like the right time. But now, I do not know what life this child will have.'

This cuts, deeply. Just when I should be able to step up, to offer some kind of hope, support, I have to scuttle, beetle like, to my dung heap of a life in England. I explain to her the causal chain of idiocy. She is impassive. Silence settles on us both for some time.

'What are you going to do?' I ask, after failing to find anything within myself I can offer, practically. She ponders this for a minute.

'There will be a police investigation, obviously. They tell me we have to wait for an autopsy, as it is a crime, so I don't know when we can have the funeral. And I don't know what the investigation will bring up, and if it will make things worse. I don't know how I am going to survive right now. I don't know how to live without Gary.'

'I have a bit of money…' I stammer, but she puts her hand on mine, spares me further shame.

'It's not money. We have some where the investigators cannot touch it. Everything else will probably be frozen or embargoed, the government will have its revenge and take everything they can. Now I have no Gary, no job, no future. Everything is gone. What is the point anymore?'

I want to say some kind of platitude but none arrives, as I feel the same. My own limited world has been emptied out. My new knowledge of the true nature of the business, that was part-funding Gary's kingdom, burns the inside of my head and I don't know where

I can run to where it won't feel close. We chat for a while further, making vague plans about a funeral. Ana will try to sell their penthouse rapidly before it is possibly seized. She'll move back to her grandparents, or even stay up here. We both fear the unknown figures who took Gary's life, we both fear we may be inconvenient to them also. How can we know we aren't?

A beaten-up plastic sofa is my bed, a dog blanket is my duvet. Sleep comes swiftly, but insufficiently thoroughly. I float in a miasma of chills, of cold sweat, of breathing fractured by slight convulsions or sobs, I can't tell. Consciousness occasionally rears its distended, blackened head, into an unfamiliar world of silence, but complete darkness shrouds all, except for a vague frame of deep orange shadow where a window might be. I barely know if it's a waking or sleeping vision. The dancing fizziness of multi-coloured, ambient patterns behind my eyelids fill the lightless void. The smells run riot in this sensorial wasteland. Woodsmoke, dust, dog, pork fat, old clothes, plaster, even the damp cloth in the sink, the darkness and silence make them shriek. I roll vaguely through combinations and distortions of these basic sensations all night and only the light of dawn brings me to a consciousness that makes me realise that some of it was a sort of sleep.

Dawn brings further terror. The first day of this hideous new order. I move through it in a kind of trance. The old car transports me backwards in place and time. Four silent people. Smelling slightly of dog and fire. The limestone peaks and their shrouds of white painted concrete run in backwards motion as I retrace my route back to the airport. Everything unravels, the preposterous blue sky, picture postcard palm trees, too clean houses, oversaturated colours, the blinding, brilliant, crystalline light. A day so clear and pristine, it is at once a stupid over processed photo, a vast cauldron of delicious shimmering light and colour. The very air is solid, so vivid you want to bottle it, carve it with a knife, chop it into chunks and give it away as presents. The whole idiotic soap opera I have lived for nearly four weeks reverse winds, frame by frame.

As I stand at the gate to board the flight, I know I won't completely escape this place. There will be a funeral, Ana and I are bonded now, by fear and loss. Frankie will no doubt be devastated at the news, she obviously holds a deep affection for Gary still. I've no idea what'll happen to the remains of Holmeland. It's all irrelevant. The end of a silly TV series, which, once it ends, you wondered why you bothered watching. The light recedes as the plane immerses itself in the grey formless vapour hanging over northern Europe, and presently the dimly lit patchwork of brick, road, grass and trees and general sogginess appears, and becomes bigger as England comes upwards to the plane and sucks me toward it.

20

John Lennon Airport. Liverpool. Winding along corridors that are strangely hushed. Noise retreats quickly and softly everywhere. It's the carpet. The confined spaces. The complete absence of that brittle, clattering reverb that is the constant backdrop of any building in Spain, is quite unnerving. It's like something is being hidden, sounds are randomly selected out to die anonymously somewhere.

My grubby old holdall appears, noticeably different to all else by virtue of its age, obvious signs of inefficient repair with gaffer tape. Echoes of a more innocent, strangely uncomplex time. I don't know what I'm doing back here again, barely the lesser of two evils. My life has been boiled down to this infernal duopoly. There's nothing here I want. I don't want to go the house. I do not want to see my mother. I do not want to have to unpack this awful reality onto her kitchen table, lay it out next to the teapot and the bottles of tranquilisers. Much less do I want to grovel to Watkins. Any contact with the police will trigger instant arrest and confinement. The interminable bus ride only allows me further time to simmer in this evil stew of emotions.

I am stood outside the little semi. Trying to find the wherewithal to force myself in despite their being zero other options available to me. I open the door and a short, middle-aged woman stands, like a frightened owl, staring wide-eyed at me. And I at her.

'Hello, I'm Eugene. Is my mum at home?'

'Oh, of course, goodness, come in you poor love.' I enter, dropping the heavy pack in the hallway, stacks of local papers, unread, unopened mail, junk and god knows what else piled around make it difficult.

'Come in love, I'm Mrs Taylor, I'm from the charity, I've been filling in a bit 'cause Social Services can't get round as much as they used to. She's in here. I'm glad you've come, she's in a terrible state…'

I stop, to get a handle on things before meeting her again. 'She's heard? Who informed her?'

'It was the police, this morning, first thing. They came to see her, as they were notified from Spain apparently. She took it badly, so they called social services who got onto us. I've only seen your mum a few times, so I don't know her well, but I've been with her since this morning, wondering if there were any other family available. She hasn't said much about anything except poor Gary. Are you his brother then?'

'I was.' She looks askance at me, and I try to make an apologetic face. She turns away, appearing uneasy at this unexpected, unknowable presence I have introduced into the already disorientating experience she must be having.

Mother, Irene, is sat at the kitchen table exactly as I left her a few weeks earlier. I sit down opposite her, as Mrs Taylor cowers over by the cooker, uncertain of what may happen next. Inevitably she offers to make some tea. Inevitably I accept. My mother remains unaware of either of us. Time seems to have stopped in the house, with everything just as it was, even the clothes she's wearing, the formless colourless cheap over dress and a quilted thermal jacket, shiny with grease and ware and age. She looks like she's shrivelled at least two sizes within it. Her neck is scrawnier now, her head like a gargoyle's, the skin stretched more tightly around the jowls as the stoop seems much more exaggerated. Her skin is blotchy, which I don't remember. Her eyes have a slightly milky cast, she has a yellowy translucent pallor. The eyes are not looking at anything. Several pill bottles are on the table, biscuit crumbs, an empty cup. She is sixty-three going on ninety-five.

I stare at this living ghost in front of me. I look to Mrs Taylor, who returns my pleading gaze with an embarrassed squirming, and

247

turns to busy herself with the brew. Still no reaction from Mum. I decide to speak.

'Hi Mum. It's Gene...' her eyes waver, a flicker of something passes over her vacant but contorted face. The eyes slowly find me and try to focus. I take hold of her hands. They are shockingly cold, virtually lifeless, the skin dry and leathery, angular sharp bones, devoid of strength. 'I've come from Spain. I was with Gary, yesterday Mum. I was there when... it happened.'

It. The it. Two letters, one short word. It. Flesh blasted and scorched, glass spray, blood smears, light, noise, nausea, shock... my hands tremble, and I start shaking deep within me, a fat, slippery loose muscle spasm, slapping its flanks against my rib cage, like some grotesque hooked fish flailing on the floor of a boat rocking on a heavy swell. I look at the pill bottles and wonder if I should take one. I read the labels, trying to take my mind off the sensation within me. I am familiar with the names of the drugs. They are strong, potent barbiturate tranquilizers. Old school. Nasty and addictive. It is a relief to distract myself from what I am recounting. She is still staring at me, seeing me, I think. Tears rim her eyes. And that is all. For some five minutes I sit. Cups of tea are placed silently by us. Not a word passes between us.

Eventually I release her hand to drink my tea. Mum drinks also, slowly, barely lifting the mug, her head crooked over it, slurping. I motion to Mrs Taylor and we leave the room, enter the inadequate lounge which is chilly with non-use. The aged TV set, practically an antique, its green eye staring blankly at the featureless room, squats awkwardly. I drop onto a lumpy, antiquated vinyl sofa and Mrs Taylor perches on the arm of an armchair fidgeting.

'Thank you for being with her' I offer, platitudinous though it is. 'I was here up until a few weeks ago, and before that I hadn't seen her for a few years, because I was away. She's deteriorated a lot just in the time I've been in Spain.' Mrs Taylor looks pained.

'She's very weak' she says. 'She doesn't seem to have any appetite anymore. She gets meals on wheels a couple of times a week, but the care worker says she'll soon be too weak to look after herself, and they have more pressing cases to deal with. They're overstretched and they ration what they can do rather severely I'm afraid. We step in where we can to help, but Irene is getting to a point where she'll need twenty-four-hour care. She's not with it anymore, she's potentially a danger to herself.'

'So, they'll put her in a home?' I am out of my depth. The concept of people not being able to care for themselves has never impinged on my life-long litany of self-preoccupation. The thought of a helpless, ageing dependant is unnatural, it disgusts me slightly. Piss and smelly beds, lifting frail bodies, being attentive to someone barely on the edges of life sounds truly terrifying, and unexpected. It just has never occurred to me that one might arrive at this juncture.

'Well, only if they have room, and there's a lot of demand as you can imagine, what with the cuts...'

'So who's going to look after her?' Only once I've said it am I conscious of how callous this must sound. It is callous. I am experiencing an existential threat to my insular existence. Dependants are something I have studiously avoided always, hence no meaningful lengthy relationships with females. 'You're afraid of commitment' they would say, not ever realising that opposition to commitment is my default setting. I have a pathological need to not have anyone dependent on me, to have no thread of attachment lest it limit my capacity to please myself and inhabit exactly the mental and emotional space I consider my divine right. Afraid? No, commitment is just an aspect of human and social relationships I have expunged from my life highly effectively ever since the fire, as a necessary concomitant to survival, a basic modus operandi that guarantees my freedom. The freedom I torched the minute I broke my license. As I sit in the half-light of the semi-detached house, the freedom I imagine myself as always having evaporates before me in a muddle of bureaucracy, before a sneering Mr. Watkins. And the increasingly debilitated condition of my Mother makes the fact indisputable, a fait accompli. I am mortal, mere biology, forever chained to the sensations and truth of what happened only yesterday, of what happened twenty-four years ago. To the truth of my one remaining family member hanging in a haze of barbiturate half-life. To the truth of my status in the system. Criminal. These facts sum up all I am right now. What else is there? I see nothing.

'Well, there are plenty of private homes, or it falls to the family' answers Mrs Taylor, slightly pointedly, holding my gaze. The phrase surrounds and frames the dread within me, lifting it up, away from me, and placing it somewhere in the air, like a holographic embroidered picture, with the word 'family' in neat floral red letters. Family. I am of it, it is of me, but it is but a poisonous gas cloud, a ripe tomato wrapped with razor wire, floating uncertainly in the stale vapour of a house that has no life in it.

'Right, I see' is all I can reply.

'Well if it's alright by you, I better be off, you probably need to be alone with your mum.' Her face is tight, her eyes betray her extreme discomfort. This isn't what she signed up for probably.

'Thank you very much Mrs Taylor, you've been very kind.' It's an appropriate and truthful platitude at least. 'So, when do the social come again? Do they?'

Mrs Taylor is bustling to leave with scarcely disguised relief. 'Well, yes, they come two or three times a week, clean a bit, help Irene change and make sure she's taking her pills and eating something at least.'

'Ri-ight.'

And she's gone. The silence of the house closes in around me. I return to the kitchen and look at Mum. Her tea is half drunk. I make another cuppa for myself and sit opposite her. She stares at me. Searching my face. Then her gaze wanders away and loses itself somewhere beyond the walls of the room. The same expression as twenty-four years ago. She hasn't escaped for one single moment, not in all that time. I had escaped, but now I fear falling forever under the spell of death that has cast itself over us. The house is a black hole, pulling us into its void.

21

Three days. I crouch inside, trying to pluck up courage to take the next step. I don't know what the step is though. Stasis. Again. I don't even open the letters lying there from the probation service. I barely eat, my appetite is absent without leave. Mum doesn't want anything other than bourbon biscuits. When I get bored and buy a packet of custard creams to maybe inject some variety, she shows the most sign of life so far. Mumbling repeatedly about how she can't eat those, they're not proper biscuits. Only buying a pack of bourbons will calm her down. Three days making tea, gently explaining Gary isn't coming home. I am Eugene. Three days watching her in a deep fog. Her senses are so dulled, her physical strength so limited, she can barely achieve normal functioning consciousness. They aren't wrong when they say she'll need round the clock care before long. Three days where I live in a form of fluid suspension. The world is in slow motion, filled with a viscous yellowish liquid which I swim through, like an eel in a tank. My mind settles to numbness, my raging nausea and anxieties quieten, and a leaden tiredness accompanies every waking moment. Mum has yet to address me by name. Other than the simplest of requests or comments about something not being what it should be, like the milk or the biscuits, no conversation attests to any sign of intellectual function. I don't know what her dosage is supposed to be, it's not clear from the bottles, she self-medicates as though on autopilot. I have known people purposely inject these medicines intravenously when they wanted a particularly dramatic rush, after too many days on amphetamines, and here my mother's tolerance appears to be that of a seriously hardened addict. I attempt to hide the bottles at one point to see if I can slow down the consumption, but the reaction is one of low level but alarmingly intense anxiety that looks potentially lethal, so I shelve any plans of trying to affect her consumption. Stupid of me, I should know better.

On the fourth day, the Wednesday, the carer from social services turns up, surprised to see me, and a little put out no-one has informed them. They are strung out for resources and they wouldn't have come had they known a family member was available. I think I am being judged, and the carer sets about some domestic chores accompanied by some sarcastic references to them not having been done despite my presence. I decide to venture out into my old neighbourhood for a change of air, leaving wordlessly, guilt wracked, inadequate and resentful. I head for the town centre, some twenty minutes' walk from our estate. The sky is a leaden, rolling grey curtain, fresh with the smell of rain. Being April the temperature is not chilly, but it feels like a house without the heating on all the same. Like it should be warmer.

The streets are slick with moisture, car fumes mingle with spring grass smells. Tired daffodils and croci wink from straggly, muddy lawns. The sky is enormous and overbearing, because everything is absolutely flat. After a month of living in a place where mountains dominate the skyline constantly, and previous to that, a prison cell, this unlimited expanse of sky is chaotic and overwhelming. Or maybe it's just me.

I find a bank that is prepared to change money eventually, and ponder how much of my secret stash of Madrid brothel cash I should change. I must get back to Spain to report to the investigating police in a few days. Or maybe weeks. The thought raises the residual anxiety again. There also has to be a funeral. I have to contact Ana at some point, another onerous connection with reality almost too painful to consider. And all of that is contingent on my being free. I am effectively now on the run, and I haven't dared confront this, or articulate any plan of action.

I change one Bin Laden, the pretty purple five hundred euro note. The name comes from the fact that, like the man himself, most of the five hundred notes in Spain have mysteriously disappeared. This bill elicits some curious glances and even questions as to its origins, which I didn't expect. I mumble something about working in Spain.

I stand outside the bank, unwilling to return to the house, relishing for a minute the business of a world passing me by without noticing me. I want to relax and be normal for a while, to be anonymous. I walk. It's an identikit British high street. Red brick, pedestrianised in part, the faux rustic wrought iron street furniture; the same council grown potted plants; the same chain store names with the same plastic signage and frontages; the same Victorian era church standing forlornly, trying to lend some air of significance to the humdrum homogeneity all around. A pub. I don't recognise it, or the name, as the pub I do remember in that spot has undergone a renovation into something altogether unfamiliar. It has the same air of faux rusticity as the street furniture; painted signs in florid script, nicely upholstered patterned banquette seating and carefully glowing lighting. It's a kneejerk reaction to how I remember pubs being: dirty, scruffy, unpretentious, functional and often intimidating. This new establishment screams 'family'! Nice food! A brave new world with all hints of social sub-cultures and economic disadvantage erased by the tasteful, historical framed prints on the wall and the pseudo Mediterranean pub food. It even says 'tapas' on the menu, though nothing familiar except patatas bravas reveals itself. I ask for a pint of bitter and the barman gestures to the long line of craft ales. I randomly point at one with a name that reminds me of some old war story I read as a child.

I sit in a corner where I can survey the entire establishment. People eat at proper tables with napkins and wine. Business types. Yummy mummies, or maybe nannies, trying to be relaxed and sophisticated with a bottle of sparkling something, while attempting to manhandle small children and a car crash of prams and shopping bags. The toddlers are decidedly unenthused by the environment, making the whole social interaction way more stressful than it was intended to be.

I neutrally observe all of this life go on. People coming and going, normal, happy, or at least behaving as such. It's a Wednesday lunchtime after all. I am drinking my third pint. Being a real ale, the military sounding drink is rich and potent and I'm decidedly woozy, but warm and possibly more relaxed than I have felt in many days. I have retraced every step of the last few weeks in my mind's eye. Even the shooting. I have replayed it several times, as if by seeing it over and over I can desensitise myself to at least the horror of the moment. What I cannot articulate or expel is the underlying fear of the invisible and inchoate forces that produced this trauma. Who exactly is behind it? What would Lebid stand to gain by doing this? Was I the target maybe? What did Gary really know? My mind races, but in a more proactive way, without the anxiety and gut-wrenching fear that has accompanied me for more days than I can actually believe. This is no way to live I tell myself. The fourth pint confirms this. A plate of patatas bravas that tastes not remotely like what I had in Marbella stops me becoming too dizzy. I am lecturing myself somewhat pompously now, pleased with my line of thinking. I'm not going back ever. Ok just for the funeral, in and out in forty-eight hours no more. Edges soften, muscles release, sounds blur.

I jolt awake to hearing my name. 'Alright Gene mate, long time!' I fix on the face, it's not someone I know well, I can't even remember his name. Another stands behind, unknown to me. 'You'd nodded off there, mate. I'm not disturbing you am I, only…'

I stare blankly back. They invite themselves to sit down as I come to.

'Oh, sorry about that, yeah, I must have. Things have been a bit…' and I stop myself. I'm looking at them and I'm thinking, this isn't an innocent social encounter. 'Sorry what was your name?' I ask, to fix this person in the frame of things.

'Andy, Andy Fairclough, I was at Bridgewater with Gary, you remember? This is my colleague, Howard.'

'Hi, nice to meet you,' says Howard giving me an over strong, unnecessarily sincere handshake.

'I'm so sorry about Gary. I'm gutted, awful news, you must be shattered.'

I stare for a moment. I've not had to talk about this to anyone yet. Four days have gone by and I have not articulated any opinion, emotion or reaction to anyone about the shooting. Mum just heard the bare bones, which she wasn't able to compute anyway, despite how many times and ways I tried to put it. Now I'm supposed to find a civil, sentient response to someone I hardly know, and I am decidedly drunk. I just shake my head, mumble 'sorry don't really want to talk about it' and start to drain my pint. I make to get up and head for another, but Andy jumps up.

'No allow me, please, what are you on?'

Now the other one sits beside me, Howard. He's silent for a moment, and I stare ahead of me. Having to interact with other humans is a genuine shock to the system and brings into clear relief how the beer has compromised my hold on my thoughts and motor functions. Conversely the sensation is not at all unpleasurable.

'Shocking business really. My condolences. To you and your family' says Howard with what might be genuine sincerity, but that isn't the point that hits me. I let out a contemptuous snort.

'I am the fucking family. This fine specimen you see before you is the last fully functioning member of the once illustrious…' and I tail off. I'm giggling.

Howard isn't fazed. He continues. 'That must be hard I'm sure, to be almost alone, just you to carry on forwards. I didn't know Gary, but he sounded like he achieved a lot, he had everything to live for.'

I look at the man properly for the first time. He's unduly expectant of what I'm going to say.

'What the fuck is it to you, anyway?' is how it comes out, though I'm not sure I wanted to phrase it that strongly, but hey. I notice Andy is still at the bar, although the pints have been bought, he's hanging back. I feel I'm being worked. My stomach takes an involuntary flip.

'I'm sorry' Howard resumes. 'It's a shocking crime, and people here have been genuinely upset by it. Many people knew him here, there's a lot of interest.'

'What the fuck are you telling me this for?' I'm half offended and half fearful.

'I'm from the South Warrington News. Andy knew your brother well, and when he saw you in here, he gave me a call, because it would be really interesting to get your side of the story. Let people know, it'd be a tribute to Gary, that people locally would appreciate.'

Andy sits and places the pints down. 'I thought you wouldn't mind, it's caused a bit of a stir locally, and Howard here can deal with it exclusively, tastefully, so you're in safe hands. Gary was a good mate of mine. I'm only interested in honouring his memory.'

I pick up my fifth pint and start to drink it steadily. It's tangy and cool, and slides nicely down, as my thoughts remain unclear. I feel a great deal of indignation, I feel invaded, in fact all sorts of things I haven't yet had to feel in this ongoing process of living after the fact. I can remember the smells, sounds and sights of the chip shop fire. Two disasters vividly tussle in my mind right now. I lay the images out in my head. I've seen it all. I am still here. I am staring into space, not hearing the one called Howard. I take stock of what has been visited on me, and I accept it as the way things are. It is my burden and I carry it. He stops. I look at him, wondering why he has stopped, wondering what he was even saying.

'People really want to know about Ana, his partner, about his job' he continues. A violent jolt of disgust. I try and collect myself. This is enough, this isn't going to go on, I need to remove myself from this situation. I am talking to myself in a paternal, tolerant

257

manner. I have everything under control, I shall sip some more of this fine ale.

'Why don't you fuck off and mind your own business?' Said clearly and calmly. Again, I don't think that was what I wanted to say, I mean it was, but not quite that way.

Howard shows no sign of offence, Andy twitches nervously and is about to make an intercession, by his body language, a conciliatory one, when Howard says directly 'Who do you think killed your brother?'

There's a pressure in my head, like someone sitting on it and I'm struggling to get out, or maybe it's the room that is spinning. The floor tips 45 degrees. I drink more from the glass, searching for the cool calmness of the tasty fluid. With one last gulp I turn to face my persecutor and spray him with the mouthful of beer. I slap him hard on his right ear, and he moves to avoid me as I lurch toward him, but actually I am just falling over plain and simple. The table flips as my elbow and body weight crash into it, glasses break and pandemonium reigns. I am sat on my bottom looking out at the pub interior, Andy and Howard are standing some way back. Andy is attempting to wipe Howard down with a napkin and the barman is moving towards me with an unamused expression. I feel vindicated. I have acquitted myself appropriately and disciplined these disrespectful vultures. I feel no remorse, just rather pleased with myself. The barman is saying something about the police, that I shouldn't move or he'll do I don't know what but it doesn't sound friendly. Howard is talking again.

'You're a fucking idiot Eugene! We could have done this the nice way, but now I have to use this, this is what it'll be, you fucking prick, and you ruined my suit. You just got out of jail, you don't need this kind of trouble, but if that's what you want...' and I'm up quickly because he's pissed me off now, because he's right and I'm going to slap him properly and how, but the thought is overtaken by an impact to my midriff which takes my breath away and I see stars and the world goes dark for a moment.

From my prone position on the floor the barman leans toward my face, 'I told you, enough!'.

22

The grinding of the lock as the key turns and opens the heavy door, hurts. I have a pounding pain just behind my forehead, and the light in the corridor makes me wince and squint. I am led to a room with a table and two chairs. The police officer stands against the wall, and the door opens and an older man sits down and faces me. He has a uniform on, and his demeanour funnily enough appears sympathetic and indulgent. He looks at me, then at the documents on the desk. Then at me again. His face does seem familiar from some time long ago.

'Hello Eugene. I am very sorry to have to see you like this, given the circumstances, but then given the circumstances maybe it's not so surprising. It must have been a terrible shock. We were all very shocked. It's not many people get hit by a double whammy like that in one lifetime.'

'Erm, yeah, it's... not been a good few days. Years.' I am drained. I have nothing to add.

'Superintendent Collins. I knew your dad, matter of fact we used to play cards together. He liked a bit of poker. He was good an' all. Took me to the cleaners on more than one occasion.'

'Oh right, I see' and I find myself smiling. Some pre-fire flash of memory, of warmth, of humour, sneaks in under the defences.

He continues, a bit more seriously. 'I've had a word with the gentleman concerned and he won't be pressing charges. A bit out of order doorstepping you like that. But it's just as well though, isn't it?' I know what he's going to say. 'You're on license. You've gone AWOL, and now this offence, you could see yourself having to finish the full sentence. Is that what you want?'

'He was being disrespectful.'

'Be that as it may. It didn't help you'd had a skinful though did it? And you'd barely eaten. You look a bit gaunt, you need to eat a bit, get some rest. Get healthy, you've got a tough job ahead of you dealing with this. You need to grieve, sort things out for yourself.' He taps the side of his head.

'Grieve. Hmmphh, I'm not sure that got me anywhere the first time around.'

'Well I can get someone to see you, things have changed a bit since then, we have people who are very good at helping people with these kinds of issues now.' His tone is genuine and I'm confused by what he means. 'You know, get some counselling. You're probably suffering a certain degree of post-traumatic stress.'

'I think I can say I have been feeling stressed' is all I can think to respond with. The thought of having to work through any of this with a concerned stranger is not something that fills me with the remotest enthusiasm.

'Look, there's not going to be any charges, so you've got lucky. Here's what I'm going to do. Given the circumstances, of this, of your father, I can recommend that the probation supervisor not take further action. I will make this go away, Gene. But you have got to watch it, one more slip-up and you're back inside, go straight, do not pass go, do not collect two hundred pounds.' He looks me in the eye. His concern is genuine. I want to hug him. I want him to hold me and stroke my hair, and give me a playful punch in the chest and tell me it's all going to be okay. My eyes rim with tears.

'You'll need to see Watkins as soon as possible. I would change your supervisor if I could, but that power I do not have. You have to deal with what you've got. I'm sticking my neck out as it is. And I will make sure you are able to attend your brother's funeral. Come on, let's get you home.'

~

Home. Good grief. Home is where the heart is. I awake with a raging thirst, a still pounding head. My old bedroom is now spartan,

261

largely full of boxes of god knows what and a lumpy, over soft bed, so I feel I've been trodden on every time I wake up. I wander dazedly over, flick the heater on in order to have a bath in the old tub. The house is chill. It's not a home. It's a shell with a broken soul inside it, counting the days unknowingly, until mercy relieves it of its burden.

In the kitchen, my mother moves at a snail's pace, and achieves a cup of tea and a plate of bourbon biscuits. It takes her an age, and she barely acknowledges my presence the whole time. I still haven't had anything approaching a meaningful conversation with her. I fry myself some bacon, and put some of the square white flaccid bread into an ancient toaster. There is something timelessly English about the smell of bacon on flaccid white bread, with cheap margarine. Bacon is eaten all over the world. I have eaten it all over Europe, but this version is unique to us. I sit down to eat opposite my mother.

'I got in a bit of trouble yesterday' I say. 'Got in a fight. Well, I didn't, no, what I did was.I attacked a journalist. He was being nosey.' No reaction. I change tack. 'Mum, Ana is pregnant apparently. She is having Gary's child. You are going to be a grandmother.'

The minutes tick by. Still no reaction. I finish my bacon butty and I lean my head on the table. I despair. I go up to the bedroom and lumpy bed and I fall onto it and let out loud sobs. They overcome me like a river in spate. I drown in them, it drains out of me, wrenching the breath from me, the hot saltiness purging my eyes and my nasal passages. I hug myself as the waves of grief and release roll through me. At some point I fall into unconsciousness. I don't know how much time passes. I awake and take that bath. I come down again, feeling somehow different. Mum is where I left her. The TV is on in the other room, so she got as far as doing that, but she is back at the table, staring out of the window. I sit again.

'So this journalist had the cheek to ask who killed Gary. I hit him and I was arrested and taken to the police station. That's why I was late. The superintendent, he let me off basically. I won't be going back to jail, Mum. He knew Dad. Superintendent Collins! They played poker together, apparently Dad used to win lots of money off him.' I laugh out loud. This change of volume, of tone, produces a flicker, for a moment her eyes find mine, then resume the milky stare. I am clearing away the things, wondering what to do. What to do now. Later. Tomorrow. Whenever. I should phone Ana. This changes everything, but I don't know how, or what I should do.

'It was always the money.' Just like that. It was Mum's voice.

'What? What did you say? Mum, what did you say?!' I sit again. I am frantic. 'What was the money? Please Mum!'

Nothing. A slight tremor in the eyes, movement *behind* the eyes, a faint burning ember. Minutes pass. Then barely audibly, without looking at me...

'Gary's never coming back, is he?'

'No Mum. He's dead.' That's all there is to say. Another minute passes. The stillness is extreme. Only my breathing is audible, and the muffled rattle of daytime television in the other room. Still expressionlessly, she gets up, takes her bottle of medication and slowly, painfully slowly, heads toward the succour of the TV. I remain seated. Time stands decidedly still. This house is the static locus around which all else of consequence and inconsequence moves. Here all is frozen. Embalmed. Fixed. Permanent. Immutable. Canned laughter and tinny tunes of some god-awful quiz on the TV permeate the house. I pick up my coat and walk out. Into the world. Again.

It is just past lunchtime and I am peckish. I walk through the endless circular residential streets, with the boxy semis crouching one by one. They are all of a colour, dull reddish brown of brick or grey of pebble dash. The only colour is pinpricks of yellow and purple in garden beds still mushy with leaves from last autumn. Damp sticks to everything, and clouds broil overhead, ever visible and kings of the vast sky above the flat land. Aimless at first, I start to develop a pattern, covering whole blocks methodically street by street. I suck in all the clues to the lives within the little brick boxes. Some are clad in faux stone or some other finish. Some have different window frames. Each box represents a slice of life, a set of relationships, a mini-culture, a microcosm of humanoid ecology even. Visual cues abound, from the cars, to the state of the gardens, whether a burglar alarm is installed sentinel like on the front of the house. Curtains, blinds, nets, variations of window design and glass style. The houses are by and large of similar origin, age and design, yet multifariously modified and individualised. I compare them to the house my mother inhabits. A garden run with weeds, dirty net curtains, grime of weather and traffic deep on the windows, it speaks of a life withered and evaporated, barely a residue within. Occasionally, other houses display such signs of dysfunction, but I am surprised nothing matches what I have to call, for want of anything else, home. I am the alien, touring this planet, studying the lives of the inhabitants, musing over their peculiarities and eccentricities. I smile grimly at the oddities of people's urges to differentiate themselves; the religious iconography, which is surprisingly frequent, the ostentatious claddings and garden furniture, fake weather cocks, garden gnomes, plaster cats creeping over roofs.

I start to enter the city centre and stop at a Greggs to grab a pasty. It was the default food on my wanderings of past years, which shocks me, as it isn't nice. When did I ever think it was? Peppery and stodge filled, an approximation of something meaty, with a squelchy pastry crust that mushes up like cement filler. People troop in and out carrying pastry constructions of all types with fillings of varied anonymity, salty or sweet and not much in between. I long for the sound of a roaring *cafetero* and a *cafe-con-leche*. I'd never even been a coffee drinker until last month. Now I'm an addict. I come upon a Starbucks which I believe is synonymous with coffee. I stand at the counter surveying a tediously long list of coffees with names dominated by Italian words, none of which makes any sense to me.

Why didn't I learn about coffee before I left for Spain? The girl behind the counter looks Mediterranean. I chance my luck.

'Can I get a *cafe-con-leche*?' She breaks into a broad grin.

'*Claro que si, hombre!*'[19] and then in accented English 'well I can give you the nearest thing, I'm sorry we are not in Spain. One medium latte.'

'*Gracias*'. I'm showing off.

'*De nada*'.

The coffee is not a patch on what I had gotten used to. Bland and too milky, no bite. The Starbucks is weirdly quiet, sounds are muted, the staff too slow and gentle to create the din of my local cafeteria in Marbella. It simply doesn't *sound* like a place you'd get a proper coffee. At least the muffins are good and the sweet fruity stodge makes me feel sated, approaching normal. The notion of a good cup of coffee is the one thing I am attached to in this moment. A sort of grounding. This town I grew up in presents a face I don't recognise, one that is over made-up, barely disguising the lines of age and stress, the greasy pallor, pock-marked, tired. The dominant aromas are traffic, frying and cigarette smoke.

I wander on, scanning, searching for something to connect to, to hang an element of my psyche on to. I come across a chip shop. I stop. Deep breath. The fumes reach me, but they are different and do not trigger that lethal scent memory that can be so punishingly vivid sometimes. The oils in modern frying have changed dramatically, I assure myself, 'fings ain't what they used to be.' I peer through the window. The workers are Asian. A wide range of comestibles from mushy peas to tandoori wraps, pizza to southern fried chicken jostle for my attention. Choice. Lots of choice. Everywhere I look around are shops, stalls and eateries, all full of choice. Just so much of everything. Each business is crammed with options of whatever, many of them barely differentiated from the options around them.

---

[19] Of course, man!

How many brands of baked beans? How many different cuts of jeans? How many versions of a mobile phone, that all do fundamentally the same thing? What should I choose? Why should I choose? I stand amidst the din of the town centre and I try to connect myself to a part of what is on offer so that I might make a *choice*. Even if only theoretically. Pretend. Window shopping. I seek to connect but I cannot. I stand in front of a home decor shop staring at a display of a multitude of expertly made plastic flowers, curtain fabrics and table lamps. They refuse to meet my gaze. They do not reveal their essences to me.

Darkness grows. Many of the premises are shutting. The time is gone five o'clock, and I wonder where the day went, is still going. Everything around me is bent to one end. Buy and consume. All around me are brand names, signs, adverts, an endless array of options, an invitation to choose and BECOME. Become what? Why become? Can I not just be? Be what? I stand stock still, asking myself these repeated, fatuous, rhetorical questions, a dull sensation of panic playing at the edges of my consciousness. Why? I am stood in front of waste paper bin on a busy high street, doing nothing. Musing at the sheer volume of discarded, branded food wrapping, beer cans and cigarette packets. I become aware of the glances that people shoot at me as they walk by. Alarm, fear, distaste. All discreet and subtle but definitely there. Why is he stood there? Who is he? What does he want to do? He doesn't look normal. He's not right in the head. He's a fucking weirdo…

'Are you alright there sir?' I am jolted out of this funk. A policeman beside me. He wears a bright hi-viz jacket, it gleams in the passing car headlights in strange ways. He is deformed and bulky through all of the equipment he carries about him. He fixes me with a stare, both friendly and suspicious. I stare blankly back at him.

'Um…' I don't know what to say. Am I alright there? Am I at all?

266

'Is anything the matter?' He steps toward me, hands neutrally joined behind his back, but his head cocked at an inquisitive/aggressive angle.

'Er, what d-d-do you mean?' I stammer. I am sounding guilty. I sound like I have something to hide. I haven't got anything to hide. I stand, wishing I had something I could hide.

'Is everything alright sir?' he now says, more emphatically.

'No everything is shit actually'. I meet his stare. I am offended he should feel he even has a right to ask me. No of course it's not fucking alright. Nothing is. Everything is fucked. It was before I went away, it was when I came out, and now it's triply fucked. Monumentally fucked. My breathing has become deeper and more rapid. My chin and jaw are clenching.

'Well I'm sorry to hear that sir, shall we just move along then?'

'What?' What? I am here in this moment, faced with all of *this,* all of this stuff around me, all of this world and all that has happened, and will happen, and I am trying to process it, and he wants me to *move along?*

'Let's just move along, shall we?'

'I'm thinking'.

'Well, I think you might be more comfortable doing your thinking somewhere else.'

'Like where?'

'Now then sir, let's not make a scene.'

'A scene? What, like in a play?' Passers-by are glancing uncomfortably. The fact I am merely stood, on a street, with a policeman talking to me, appears to mark me out as something. The orientation of myself and the policeman toward each other manifests a simple tension that says, look, trouble. Something's going off.

'Now let's not get lippy, son, I'd just like you to move along, please.' The politeness is so at odds with the effrontery of what he's asking me, I start to laugh. Unfortunately, the laughter probably sounds a bit hysterical. He steps closer. His arms are now in front of him and he is gesturing down the street in that passive-aggressive hand gesture that policemen always use. I calm myself and stop laughing, but remain still. He is still stood there, his gesture the same, his eyes holding mine. I hold his. I do not want to 'move along', for I have no good reason to move along for.

'Do you have any ID sir; can I see some ID?'

'No, I haven't got any on me.' Matter of fact. The mutual staring goes on. He reaches up for the radio on his chest.

'What's your name and address, please?' The radio sputters into life, its crackle and squawk draw more attention. Some adolescents stop and hang nearby, expectant and amused. He repeats my reply into the apparatus. 'Do you have anything in your pockets sir?'

'I beg your pardon?'

'What's in your pockets?' The formality has gone now. 'Let me see. Do you have anything on you you shouldn't have? Have you taken anything? Are you on something? Ay?'

I find myself turning out my pockets, fumbling, showing coins, random receipts for things I have bought during the day, and a lone Yale key. It looks decidedly pitiful.

'No wallet?'

'No'.

'No ID, no wallet. Just wait here. Don't move.' He walks a short way away from me and starts to consult his radio, his eye constantly on me the whole time. I am trying to find some indignation, or even anger. I search within and all I can find is a headiness, a disconnectedness, as though I am spectating this whole scene. I have read the script. For I know who I am. I am the ex-con. I am a public menace. A hardened criminal who has peddled death to teenager. That's one version of it. But I don't know the end of the scene. I can choose my lines, but not his.

268

A police car draws up beside me on the road, and the copper asks me to get in. This brings whoops and hollers from the youths. The scene is going according to their expectations at least. They don't drive off. I am asked what am I doing, why am I here, where am I going, and all manner of things. I am back in the scene of four years ago, justifying and accounting for my very being with all the pathetic details of a life that felt insignificant and inconsequential in every possible way and utterly criminal. The only difference is that this time I have nothing to hide. I relay to them all of the events of the recent days, in chronological order. I luxuriate in the detail, I take on the role of narrator and refer to myself in the third person, using rhetorical questions to frame and move the narrative on.

'And thus, does Eugene find himself sat in a police patrol car in his home town on a Thursday evening at 6.17 pm.' I conclude with a sense of satisfaction. I have a sense this narrators' voice is perceived as disrespectful and a bit of a liberty, but it's not untruthful or illegal so they bite their tongues as I reel off my sorry tale. The original policeman gets out, beckons me to do so as well. He comes over to me as I am back on the pavement. The youths are expectant and attentive still.

'Alright Eugene, you've had a bit of a rough time, but you've got to wise up. Show a bit of respect, don't stick your neck out, don't invite trouble. Watch your lip. With your record, people, not just us, are going to assume the worst. So go on, get along now. Good luck. My advice, move somewhere new. Too many ghosts for you around here if you ask me.'

They pull off in the car, leaving me standing staring, again, vacantly along the street. I am aware of jeering and cries of 'wanker' from the youths. I wait until the patrol car has gone. The youths are hanging back in a recess of the wall of some superstore, smoking, giggling in their huddle. I walk over to them, and their attitude changes. I walk straight up to who I perceive to be the ring leader. To within barely six inches of his face. I stare into his eyes. He tries to

269

not bottle out, to hold my gaze, but the longer I maintain the dead-eyed neutral stare, the more nervous he gets. The others have fallen completely silent. I'm not sure what I'm going to do. I only know I want to hurt him. I want him to feel pain, to leave him squirming in agony on the floor. Right now, it would make me feel good. He shoves past me, and the four of them sprint away, their bravado extinguished and put to flight by the weirdo in the street.

I walk on. Something pokes through, a smell, an atmosphere, something different, less artificial than commerce. The river. I am stood on the wide Kingsway bridge over the river Mersey. It's familiar now, a strange environmental battle between the fumes of the city, and the adjacent countryside and dark muddy water. Nettles, damp rotting vegetation and random flowers sneak beneath the overall traffic fug and foggy aura. The whiff of the brown water, all manner of detritus lurking within, is a slightly rancid, rotten background tone on which all else is overlaid. Being near the river a palpable mist produces bizarre halo effects around the street lights. I remember the bridge well. The combination of place and smell opens one of those forgotten trap doors in the back brain, and vivid distant memories tumble out.

~

Standing on the wide stone balustrade of the bridge, pissing into the water, drunk on Diamond White, aged fifteen. Ignoring the horns of the affronted motorists passing by. Watching Doug, our resident nutter, so pissed he decides to jump into the welcoming darkness. The screams of the accompanying teenage girls, horrified and also terrified. They'd come along for the craic, attracted by our generosity with the cider and braggadocio. Now they are palpably terrified of these maniacs they have hitched up with, but are too far to walk home on their own in the recently descended darkness. Doug is hooting with laughter, his howling, echoing up metallically from under the bridge as the current pulls him under the arch, his frantic splashing sounding like he is in trouble. I stand on the bridge, still

270

pissing, admiring the stream glint in the lighting as it arcs into the muddy, smelly darkness. I climb down, and collapse against the wall of the bridge, helpless with laughter. The girls, three of them are leaning over on the other side, yelling crazily, presumably at Doug. After a time, I wander over, weaving through the cars that honk hysterically, voices yelling in exasperation at the young hoodlum trying to get himself killed, you should be ashamed, what do you think you are playing at. From the other side of the bridge a figure trudges forlornly toward me. It is Doug. His breath is rasping, his clothes cling, sodden, to his gangly frame. He is starting to shiver. He isn't laughing.

'Where were you ya twat? I nearly fucking drowned!' and he grabs my lapels, and shakes me in anger, 'you daft bastard I coulda drowned' he slurs.

'You daft bastard, I didn't fuckin' tell ya to jump in the fucking Mersey!' and I am again helpless with laughter. Doug stands. He gets the joke, but he's too wet and cold to find the laughter he knows he deserves. The girls plead for us to take them home. We turn away from them and head in the direction of Doug's house. He has to move or he'll freeze and someone has probably called the pigs by now. We leave the girls to their fates, too ignoble, young, stupid and embarrassed to know what to do with them. Doug vomits periodically, wracked by shivers, and we weave our way home as quickly as our debilitated systems allow us.

We must have made it home safely, as we are both still alive today. Or at least I think Doug is. I don't know. What happened to all of them? I lost touch. With everyone. With myself I suppose, until Strangeways flung myself into my own lap and I sat there with my lost self, staring up at me with a sort of 'what the fuck' expression on my face.

'And I turned myself to face me, for I had never caught a glimpse, of how the others must see the fakir'. Ziggy Stardust jumps unbidden into my head. Layers of dead rave music have decayed

271

enough to let those first illicit wondrous listenings re-emerge. Huddled in the sitting room playing Dad's old vinyl of this analogue android androgyne, his high-pitched plaintive voice loaded with strained sexuality and longing. The psychedelic poetry of the lyrics haunted me when I was eleven, transported me out of the oppressive fug of my parents' mutual dance of abhorrence of each other. The tales of warped sexual identities, barely disguised paeans to confused gender and tawdry sexual practices I suspected but could not identify fully, lacking the lexicon of New York or the gay underground of 1970's Soho. I was alternatively addicted to the seductive elitism and highly stylised posturing of Brian Ferry and Roxy Music, the decadence and decay and disillusion drew me in and sustained me within the fractured emotional ecosystem of the home. When did that start? The deafening echoes of their silent disdain, pinched faces twitching, were drowned out by the deep, lustrous, forbidden, velveteen soundscape that caressed me, and drew me deep into its bosom. A hard rock balm of endless healing, a sensuous and fantastical nether world that held me completely apart from the bitter psychic smog of their steadily dissolving marriage.

Those albums were destroyed by the smoke damage of the fire. Why did my father have these albums? I am struck by the profound dissonance between his character as I experienced it and the sensuality and romanticism it must have taken to be into that music in his twenties. I never thought about it then. Never wondered why he kept them but never played them. It makes no sense now, just leaves yet another shivering, effervescent question mark dancing among the ruins of the emotional memory bank of my (non)relationship with my father. Before I was old enough to understand what made him tick, why he seemed so fractured and beaten by his marriage, he was gone. Immolated by a random gas explosion, and all those fabulous vinyl jewels went with him. They were the only things I missed in that house. Well, that and my fishing tackle. Such was the loss and trauma, all things associated with the event were erased from my life and mindscape. Especially those.

Crack baby crack, show me you're real. Smack baby smack, is that all that you feel?

~

The brown, slightly malodorous water slides slickly underneath in a steady, unbroken, Zen-like motion. Faint ripples and swells undulate, catching the colour of the ever-present street lighting, a dark unctuousness flecked with slivers of sodium orange. I stare for a long time, laughing internally at the memory of Doug's flailing and wailing in the filthy water.

'Hey, mate! Are you alright?'

The sound of the unknown voice is shattering, the awareness of now had receded so far, it surprises me how far I have to wrench my focus back to the world. I am disorientated.

'Don't do anything daft now. It's not worth it', says the uninvited voice. I turn around and fix upon a man, standing about ten feet away. His face is silhouetted by a hood, and the overhead lighting. A dog skulks, literally, around his legs, trying to make his mind up whether to growl or whimper, and it comes out as both. My presence appears to disturb him. I make a non-committal shrug.

'You sounded like you were crying, I thought you were going to jump or something. You wouldn't be the first off here, you know. Are you okay? Do you need anything?'

Ahh, a concerned member of the public, how noble. The concern at once humbles me and irritates me.

'I was not going to kill myself' I say neutrally. 'It wouldn't make much difference.' This really stumps the man. But not as much as the next thing he says stumps me.

'Eugene?'

'Yeah. Who wants to know? Do *I* know you?'

He takes his hood down. The dog remains suspicious. I recognise the face as one I have known, but have no idea who he is, anymore. A hand is outstretched, to shake.

'Nigel Sharp. I'm a mate of Gary's. We were at school, remember? Well, I was a mate. So terribly sorry about the news. I couldn't believe it, I…'

I hold up a hand to stop him, before he babbles his embarrassment and shock out into a pile on the floor.

'Nigel. Yeah, I remember. Sorry, I'm a bit…' I shake his hand leaving the sentence to fall into the river. It has no useful ending.

'*Are* you okay? You did sound like you were, sort of whimpering and you looked like you might do something… I'm not surprised with what you've been through. I still can't believe it…'

'Thanks. But I'm okay. Well, as much as one… well, you know…' and we stand facing each other in the orange haze, faint miniscule droplets swirling around in the musty breeze. I don't want this conversation. This intrusion. Of no use. But it would be rude to walk away, to ignore the man's sincerity. The dog plainly searches for a distraction, longs to be gone from this lonely bridge.

'What are you doing out here, Eugene, tonight, I mean…'

I stand in silence on the edge of an eternal dark sea. Part of me wants to wade out, be sucked into the depths, rendered inexistent. Part of me wants to turn away to the light, humanity, communication. A minute passes. An uncomfortably awkward minute. For Nigel, at least I suppose.

'Look, I live just nearby. Come and have a drink. Take the weight off your…'

And another string of human words dies on the cross of immortal uselessness.

'Yeah, sure' I say eventually. The opportunity to experience human warmth releases me from the shores of the evil smelling lake enough to at least back a few steps away from it. And follow Nigel.

We walk in silence toward some recently built apartment blocks, pleasantly detailed in faux Victorian gables and window frames. Like oversized yellow brick Hansel and Gretel multi-story houses. We enter a portal, leaving the damp air for the mechanically scented environment of a hallway. Nigel leads me into an interior that is at once imposing in its simple message; the warm, neutrally scented flat is expansive, generously appointed with carefully chosen lamps, recessed lighting. All furniture and accessories perform a carefully coordinated dance of colour, pattern, texture; every element carefully measuring its effect relative to its housemates. Prints decorate the wall, iconic reproductions, hinting at hipness and culture, but anyone can hang a Warhol. It speaks confidently of a material affluence, accomplished and unashamed, and yet amongst the magazine-like comfort I search for a sign of character, of who these people are. There's no mess, no sign of children or some ill contained hobby's detritus, or much sign of anything other than an ability to buy stuff and put it together to a certain effect. The dog sits obediently before the fire of fluttering blue flames, appearing miraculously out of a spotless brushed steel and glass box.

A well turned out, and stylishly dressed woman is staring at me in shock. I wonder why she'd be so dressed up just for hanging around the house. She isn't expecting visitors evidently.

'Stacey, you'd never believe who I bumped into...' offers Nigel by way of explanation.

'Oh, well, hi, how do you do', she offers a demur hand which I accept, uncomfortably aware that such is the sterility and perfection of the environment, my hand even smells grubby and my whole body has a skein of grunge and staleness, it reaches out from me, penetrating this virgin and vulnerable ambiance. I think I detect a disguised wrinkle of the nose, and intake of breath as the Stacey sizes up this unexpected, unquantifiable element arrived in her lounge on a Thursday night. She turns the soap on the telly off, flashes a look at Nigel that clearly reads 'WTF, who is this?' and turns to me.

275

'So you must be…?'

'Stacey, this is Eugene, Gary's older brother. I bumped into him while walking the dog, he was… out for a walk.'

'Hi' I say limply.

Stacey moves around plumping cushions, pointlessly moving the few objects on various surfaces, to some unknown effect.

'I'm sorry, I wasn't anticipating guests.' Another momentary eye flash at Nigel.

'Sit down Gene, what would you like to drink? Do you drink wine?'

'Sure whatever, thanks.'

I sink into the white leather of a long comfortable sofa. They both disappear into the kitchen to organise the hurried, unbidden hospitality. I make out the outlined tones of strained conversation, snatch words, of Nigel being grilled, and I distinctly catch the word 'prison'. I endure a short stretch of silence but for the clinking of glasses, of plates and cupboards. They both sweep in and a bottle of wine, plates of some kind of oriental designer snacks, and napkins appear. They arrange themselves on the two over-sized leather armchairs opposite me.

Now we're here Nigel doesn't know what he wants to talk about. Stacey says nothing, just looks sideways, encouraging him to take the lead and occupy the silence. Nigel goes through the ritual of pouring wine into proper glasses, clinking glasses, offering condolences. I've never drunk wine in glasses like this in a house in England. Wine is something people in Europe do in restaurants, I can't help finding this odd in a sitting room in the north-west of England. It must be normal. It's just a measure of how far I am removed from the reality, the normality of what is life for people, the rest of the world. I am an imposter, the director is going to yell 'cut!', and scream at an assistant to find him another extra, I'm not right for the scene.

I field polite enquiries as to what Gary had been up to, acknowledge the evidently sincere shock and regret, that such a traumatic event could visit one of their own kind. I report it neutrally, with no reference to my being there. Nigel is also in real estate. He had followed Gary's career with interest, admiration even, though they hadn't spoken since Gary left for Spain. Stacey is perched on her seat, unable to relax, eyes darting nervously toward her husband. She has trouble making eye contact with me, though is able to scan my appearance, measuring it. I have a pair of battered trainers on, baggy jeans slung low with a conspicuously colourful belt. My hoody carries a logo of some Amsterdam rave club I can't recall, beer stains fleck its front from recent days and my hair is a fairly unkempt mop. I am dressed like someone twenty years my junior, a lost skate dude approaching middle age and not yet realising. They are both immaculate, although just sitting watching TV on a Thursday night.

Conversation slows, having exhausted polite trivia about Gary, condolences and the fact I don't exhibit any curiosity whatsoever about their lives doesn't exactly feed them any opportunity to maintain the chimera of sociability. Stacey is starting to visibly squirm. I am gulping the wine, rather than sipping it and appreciating it, as Nigel ostentatiously does. Maybe he was hoping to use this as a hook to some manageable conversation, but that doesn't really work, as I ask to help myself to more. It steadies me, in this oddly alien environment that is oh so comfortable. The inevitable question. What have I been doing all these years?

'I heard you had a spot of bother' says Nigel, as if by downplaying the fact it will be easier to broach it, lay it out. Stacey's eyes almost pop out of her head. The wine is rich, fruity and lubricates my still swirling state of mind. I release a bit into the expensive sofa.

'A bothersome three years in Strangeways for trafficking of class A drugs, released early on license for good behaviour. Not as serious a sentence as I might have had as I was duly repentant and cooperative. Although I didn't grass anyone up, otherwise I wouldn't be sitting here before you now.'

Poor Stacey is rigid.

'Bloody hell, how did you get into that mess?' says Nigel. I actually appreciate it as one of the first genuine things said all night.

I outline briefly a trajectory from gig promotion to packing and driving vans loaded with Dutch ecstasy. Stacey looks mortified. As if she'll catch some sort of social pestilence from merely hearing about it. After this brief narrative comes to an end, she leaps in to steer the conversation away to somewhere manageable.

'It's such a shame what happened, and in of all places, in Marbella. We were thinking of holidaying in Marbella, weren't we Nigel, but after this I'm not so sure. I mean, if it can happen there...'

'Yes, it's quite shocking isn't it, don't you think? You move to a fabulous place like that, to get ahead, and then that goes and happens' adds Nigel.

There's a silence, as I can't think of any further platitudes to respond with, and what would be the point. My brother's murder reduced to the measure of the value of a city in Spain as a prospective holiday destination. I reach to finish the bottle. Their uncomfortable, subtle shifting of weight tells me they are now slightly lost and wondering how to get out of the blind avenue they have driven themselves into, by inviting my baggage into their carefully constructed domestic paradise.

'Marbella killed Gary' I say, expressionlessly. Their discomfort increases. 'Well you read all about it in the papers, didn't you?' I'm assuming all the salacious details have been spread across the tabloids for several days, but I don't actually know, having avoided any contact with the mediated versions of what I lived through barely a week ago.

'Well, actually, I only read the report in the Telegraph, which didn't give much background, but I'm sure the police there have everything in hand.'

I burst out laughing. I can't help myself. The great edifice of turpitude and venality, the shameless greed, the hubris, and the flipside of simple, pure, murderous intent, shrieks in my head, and these two poor souls struggle to compartmentalise and wall off all of its implications and truths, without even getting close to contemplating the reality. The neat journalistic phrases of the Telegraph report serve to frame the event for them. Well, that is as much as anyone would want. Oh, for such simple vistas. Oh, for a mere picture, a grainy news photo, mere hints of horror. TV reports featuring police tape, cutaways of shattered glass, people standing in a Marbella street, detectives working studiously, portrait shots of the handsome successful man in his prime. Eyewitnesses tutting and fretting to the camera, shakings of the head. Here of all places. Here in Marbella. Carefully mediated, edited horror, packaged, reduced to the bearable, standardised into anonymity. Just another shocking crime in a fucked-up world. And here's Gillian with the weather...

'Well, after I'd wiped Gary's brains off my face, checked I was still alive, and then tried to explain what had happened to his partner, the police were happy to wait until sometime next week to talk to me properly'. I'm not sure where this sudden facetiousness has come from. Fatigue?

Stacey has gone white. Nigel looks like he's been punched in the face.

'Marbella isn't all it's cracked up to be, frankly' I add, and drain the glass of wine. Stacey jumps up and runs through a door, it slams shut, barely hiding the sound of vomiting. Nigel goes after her, but the door is locked, and only a desperate 'go away' arrives between coughs and quiet sobs.

Nigel returns, furious.

'Look, that really wasn't necessary. I mean, bloody hell Eugene...'

'Sorry.' Expressionlessly. I mean it, but it seems pointless to add expression to it. It's irrelevant, all things considered.

279

'Oh my god, I didn't realise you were there. Jesus Christ, what you must have been through…'

He sits. It's bizarre to be here, so far away and watch someone I barely know so bewildered and affected. They should have been left with the detached shock via a newspaper, the tut-tut of disapproval and head-shaking empathy.

'You'd better go. I think Stacey is quite upset; she doesn't have a strong stomach. I mean… Oh god, I'm so sorry…'

'Yeah, I'm gonna go. Look, I'm not really with it, I'm still trying to deal with all of this. Apologise to Stacey. Take care of yourselves, I'll see myself out.'

And I go. I could have added, 'you have lovely lives, and I'm sorry I exploded a shit-bomb in your nice living room, but I don't know where to explode all the shit-bombs I have inside and this seemed as good a place as any'. Poor buggers, they didn't deserve that. Ha-ha, maybe that policeman was right. I need counselling, I have been traumatised, I need to be helped to grieve.

We lob a few further sincere platitudes at each other and I hustle myself out, into the north Cheshire air. I'm heading home, as my interactions with human-kind all end up in difficult situations. The empty darkness vibrates, the miniscule moisture droplets waft and swirl about me, giving the black air palpable form. And I want it to disappear, to be pulled into that liquid black hole, want the light, the dark, the street and the whole sorry excuse for a life to be sucked away into the unknowable, leaving a pure, simple, clean vacuum.

As I walk, I draw myself in deeply, hoping to have the least possible awareness and contact with the outside world. I keep my head down and after forty-five minutes I am again standing outside the sorry semi-detached house. I stand for some time, staring at it, and trying to find a reason to enter, and trying to find an alternative. None present themselves, so I go in anyway. The stale, acrid air of shrivelled life, the fatty pawl that fills the house envelopes me and sticks to me, entering osmotically and percolating into every corner

280

of my body and brain. Mum is sat in the lounge, a tray of biscuits and several half empty tea mugs at her feet. She is staring blankly at the television, fingering a pack of her medication.

I sit wordlessly. I change a channel to something more bearable than yet another stodgy drama with the same old luvvies going through the motions in an identikit plot. No visible reaction from Mum.

'Good evening' I say eventually. 'I went for a bit of a walk, took in the old town, you know, a bit of a walk down memory lane.' Purely rhetorical, what a son *might* say to his mum if he'd been away from home awhile. 'I even bumped into one of Gary's old school friends. He'd heard, he was quite shocked. I assured him the police were doing all they could. It was nice to catch up.' Now I'm being theatrical. I wonder how long I could go on in this vein, how long I could fill the void, for the void to resume milliseconds after I stop speaking. So I stop speaking and let the void resume. I watch telly. Some panel show. Mostly men I don't recognise with slightly overdone hair-styles and clothing, projecting an image of queasy confidence, early middle-aged, white and middle class. They laugh and cajole and make fun of each other, they beam, or smile sardonically, and the audience laughter rolls around them, floats them along on a sea of reverence for their evident celebrity. It's a quiz or something similar with the subjects evidently related to more people like themselves and other shows off the telly. It's just one almighty, narcissistic, TV celebrity wank fest.

I turn it off and look at Mum. No reaction, just the stare into the distance between her and the telly.

'Come on Mum, shall we get you to bed?'

She looks directly and deliberately at me. Expressionlessly. She continues to fiddle with the pill jar very slowly. Her stare becomes more intense now, a slow pressure behind her eyes she doesn't know how to let out.

'Mum, are you alright? Can I get you something?'

281

The stare stays fixed on me and grows. I get up and take her arm to raise her up and lead her out. She responds, and the eyes peer up at me as she lets me lead her up to the room. Her arm is fragile like a breadstick, her body has no elasticity or dynamism. A bundle of twigs held together by dry stretched skin, propelled by a wheezing couple of sacks somewhere inside her.

She makes no effort to undress, just draws the ugly, worn, nylon duvet around herself, then reaches for her pill bottle. She shovels out a good number, and stares at them for a long time.

'Mum, that's too many' I say. She doesn't respond. I take her hands gently, and shuffle most of them back into the brown plastic jar with its little white lid. She takes four, drinks shakily from a plastic bottle of water, and floats back onto her cushions expressionlessly. Her breathing slows, and she closes her eyes, her face shows a vague rictus of sorrow. I am just about to get up to leave, and her hand finds my arm, and for a moment squeezes it. She holds on, but that is all. After maybe a minute, it releases and she slips into unconsciousness.

I make my way back to the lounge and sit. I stare at the grey oblong. See the dancing clowns prancing behind it. Although the TV is off, I know they are there, each tiny filament filled with some kind of distraction, of idealised personas, of fictitious inconsequence, of modulated and mediated pointless neo-realities. Layer upon layer, so tightly packed I can see all of them. Hundreds of layers, thousands of people, all kinds of not-real life metaphysically fizzing away just behind. I sit staring into the screen until their presence fades. I will them to withdraw, to suffocate them in the greyness of the glass, in the pale formless light of the room. Until the utter quiet of the house stifles the multi-layered circus. Stillness. As though just one last movement from me might push a button and all this space, the walls, the furniture, the air itself would vanish into a tiny blip on a screen, then fade forever.

I don't know how long I sit in the silence. I am aware only of something being drained out of me. A slight suction, subtly bleeding my senses gradually toward nothing. The screen of the TV is infinite, bottomless, the repository of souls, of meaning. My father is deep in there along with the fractured and frenetic memories of division and confusion, of desperation and flight, of cries of longing for absolution, for release. Gary is in there, he dissolves before my eyes into the greyness, the crystalline chunks of blood-spattered glass, wheel and spray ever outwards, replacing his form with a distantly diminishing cloud of fragments and of flesh that struggles against the suffocating void. Now it reaches out, wrapping its faded edges around my ears, embracing my neck, writhing around my wrists, trying to pull me in, filling the room, clouding the edges of my vision. I am weightless, and immensely heavy. I try to pull myself up, but my stomach won't follow, it pulls at my throat until with an anguished grunt I tense my neck enough to create some kind of rigidity in my body that enables me to stand upright. I walk up the stairs. The familiar creaks and squeaks of the wood laugh at me, forever the same, refusing to change or modulate. I go to Mum's room. Standing over her, only the light from the landing revealing the outline form, comatose. The breathing is barely audible. The shadows pulse grey, reaching out.

I cradle mother's head in my hand and with the other lift her pillow out. It has a slippery synthetic cover, with orange and purple flowers, a decorative bad joke, a screaming anomaly. I place the flowery pillow over her face and apply some gentle pressure. I sense the respiratory motion of her chest slowing steadily, shuddering barely perceptibly, and I hang the tension of the pillow just enough to maintain the ever-decreasing strength of her breath. The shadow embraces me, wrapping around my torso, uplifting under my arms, aiding the not inconsiderable muscular tension required to control this action over the endless unknown minutes that pass. A twitch. A momentary shudder of the body on the bed. I remove the cushion and look into the barely visible face, floating in the shadow. Nothing, no breathing. I place my ear on her chest. I wince at the acid, unfamiliar,

283

alien odour of her body and clothing. I struggle to place and summon one more comforting from when I was little; my face buried in her apron, soaking up my salty tears, her familiar workaday smell of wool and chip fat soothing whatever minor cataclysm had become me in the rough and tumble street of my childhood. It remains an idea, a concept, divorced and distant, like a specimen in a bottle on a laboratory shelf. Tears run from my eyes and dampen her cardigan, but no sobs emerge. I am held in the motionless, denuded atmosphere, as the heat leeches out of my mother's body. Eventually, the lifeless temperature of it impacts on my consciousness. I pull away. I am light headed. I pick up the bottle of pills from the side of her bed and walk downstairs. The pill bottle is comfortable in my hand. I resume my stare at the oblong of the television as the greyness once again reaches out to surround me. I feel it advance and greet it, giving myself to it…

23

A noise. Pallid daylight. Stiffness. Eyes blink. I drop something. A still full bottle of pills. The TV is in front of me, the oblong appears impotent and old, fragile, a remnant of an already bygone age. A woman walks into the room. I stare, blinking uncomprehendingly.

'Oh hello, you're still here.' I'm not sure if this is a statement or an accusation. I *am* still here, and it confounds me. 'Fall asleep in the chair, did you? Bit of a late one? Where's your mum, not up yet?'

My sluggish body struggles to work as my brain demands '*Why* are you still here?!' The scene is not one I rehearsed for. Only one option. Act normal.

'Erm, no I guess not. Christ what time is it? I don't even remember nodding off.'

'Don't suppose you would' says the woman huffily and leaves the room, headed upstairs to do her job of caring for my mother. I rouse myself enough to place the bottle of pills on the sideboard among the tatty papers and detritus of other medicine bottles and tea cups. It stares back at me, in disbelief. I turn away from its accusatory gaze. Sit back down and wait. Everything is normal. Just another day I tell myself. Into the kitchen. Make a cup of tea. The woman enters the room behind me. I turn around.

'Do you want a cuppa?' I ask.

She is looking at me. I wonder what she will say next. She steps forward. Places a hand on my shoulder. She squeezes it slightly.

'Your mother. She's passed away. I'm sorry. She must have died in the night. I'll call the doctor.' I don't know how I should react. I hadn't anticipated having to confront any of this, of even being aware of the consequences of my own actions. 'Don't do anything, leave her there. The doctor will deal with everything.' She looks at me. There is kindness and empathy in her face, concern. 'I'm very sorry for your loss' she says.

I wander into the sitting room and sit where I was, staring at the blank TV screen again.

'Do you want me to call someone for you?' says the woman. I think for a while.

'No. It's alright. There's no-one left to call.' I turn on the TV and let the people forms and sound forms of some form of life in the old box wash over me, and I stare, pulled like a dog on a lead through the hours that come.

Occasionally I am interrupted by a professional person. A doctor. Ambulance men. I respond with whatever is necessary. No, she didn't complain of anything. I was out most of the day, but she seemed normal when she went to bed. If you know what I mean. No, I don't know an undertaker. Thank you for the recommendation. Yes, I will start to inform relatives. There aren't many. A lawyer? A will? Okay, whatever you suggest…

I am guided, prodded, aided and advised throughout the day, by people who only show me kindness and concern. I have a string of appointments I must attend and book, arrangements I am responsible for, communication, certificates, things to sign, a life to tidy up, a former existence that requires all kinds of mundane formalities and procedures so that it can be properly erased. Her body is whisked discreetly away, I barely notice it go.

This process goes on for several days. Everywhere I am treated with kindness, sympathy. I meet professional people of various walks of life. An undertaker, a lawyer, a doctor who was responsible for the death certificate. He is brief, minimalist. He appears to have more pressing and stressful duties elsewhere. Natural causes, hardly surprising all things considered.

Watkins, when I eventually secure an appointment, is all empathy and forgiveness. He cuts me a considerable amount of slack. I am able to travel to attend Gary's funeral at least. My license is maintained, essentially unaltered. I have dodged a bullet. This time, metaphorically. No mention of Superintendent Collins. All is presented as the largesse and beneficence of Watkins, and I am to be grateful solely to him. That much is clear.

I meet an estate agent. The house will be sold. I meet a person who will pay me a sum of money to remove everything from the house. I spend a lot of time on the telephone trying to track down the few relatives my mother had. People I haven't seen since the fire. People who for some reason distanced themselves from this trauma, as though the stench of it would intoxicate them. All express the usual sentiments, and I respond with the usual platitudes. I mimic people's tones and expressions, respond in similar ways, keep the small talk going, accept condolences and ask after people's wellbeing. I am an actor in a play I have created. I haven't yet asked myself why I am even in the play, truly. But I am here, performing my lines, and as I lacked the courage to take on my other role when the moment presented itself, the least I should do is perform this one properly. These motions fill the days, and I find myself enjoying the stage. I understand the role, and the lines come naturally if I stick to the script that everyone appears to be using. But another scene is coming up I am trying not to think about, as I have no idea what the lines will be. Ana's script, not mine. I need to call her. I was supposed to call her days ago. Ten days since Gary's death, and I have no idea how to face that. This play is easy here, everyone makes it so, but the Marbella act is unknown and I can't find the lines anywhere to learn them.

I call her in the evening after a busy day dealing with all the various scenes, all of which went well.

'Hola Ana, it's Gene. How have you been? I'm sorry I didn't call sooner, something has happened…'

'Where have you been, Gene?' she cuts me off. An indignant silence bellows from the phone, with hints of snuffling. She tries to put sentences together but can't. I don't know how to draw her out, or how to add further grief into the already full cauldron. The telephone receiver burns my ear and sends hot fluid through my body.

'Look', I decide to be direct, 'my mother died six days ago. Natural causes. There's a funeral tomorrow. I've been very busy…' but I'm cut off by an animal wailing that terrifies me.

'My god, I'm so sorry about your mother why did she die now, she had something to live for. Gene, you need to come back to Spain as soon as possible.'

'I am allowed to attend the funeral, but only that. If I don't come back home, they will put me back in jail. For three more years.'

'But Gene! There are things, Gene, things Gary knew. I'm afraid Gene. Very afraid. I need to tell you lots, but I can't tell you over the phone. You must come back to Spain. For me, for Gary, for the baby. I can't do this alone. Come soon.' And she hangs up.

I am still for some time, then eventually release the receiver from my ear, placing it quietly on the phone. Separating the voices in my head is causing me difficulty. Some of them are laughing hysterically, some shouting angrily. I recognise them all as mine, fortunately. I turn on the TV and allow its output to create a backdrop of normality, and I head into the kitchen to make a cup of tea. I have learnt over these days that these rituals are marvellous at filling time and controlling the interior noise, they allow you a place to park up your mental traffic. You can follow what is on the screen as though it's real and important and give yourself to it, align yourself with the people on the telly and follow their world. I'll deal with the various voices at some point. They all have a legitimate point of view I decide, but we are where we are, and what's done can't be undone. Tomorrow is a particularly complex and challenging part of this production I am in charge of. The house breathes a little. The light spreads a modicum further. Already so much has been cleared away. A skeleton of a place, soon to be packed into a truck and sold to who knows who, to become part of their story, to witness a new non-drama elsewhere. I watch telly all evening, flicking aimlessly between different stories and personalities, strolling through various universes, having a rest, saving my energy for the big day ahead.

24

The day of the funeral is bright, with a stiff breeze. I arrive at the crematorium in a taxi. It's out of town, in the leafy, wealthy suburbs. All is calm, each house in the area is surrounded by sizeable lawns and manicured greenery. A comfortable affluence and orderliness pervade the entire environment. The chapel itself I have never seen, but it conforms to this general air and mood. We weren't a Christian family, and apart from my father's funeral, I've never been to a church before or since. Not even a wedding. Memories of my father's service are hazy. It was a terse and speechless affair mostly. The awful circumstances of his death made the entire event something people wanted to forget. It was quite some time after the fire, due to inquests and investigations. Leaving time for the rumours of the affair to take hold, to poison and pollute the minds of people; to allow judgemental, holier than thou prejudice to reign. Few people spoke, or hung around. Relatives tutted and talked in quiet groups. I remember Mum just clung to us both, trembling, not making eye contact with anyone. Seeing his coffin lowered into the ground closed some kind of door in my mind. I'm still not sure what that door was, or where I'd find it, and I'm not looking to today.

We left the graveside without further contact with anyone there, retreating to the digs we had been granted by the council, until we were able to find somewhere more suitable to a fractured family of two boys and grieving, traumatised mother; the house which is my current prison and haven.

I am planning to go ahead with the same performance I have been maintaining thus far this week. The events in Spain shall not affect the script. I will close off this chapter completely, with the minimum of deviation. I am secretly rather pleased with myself, at how I have handled what was an altogether unexpected and unplanned sequence of events, with potentially catastrophic ramifications should certain truths been known. Gary's funeral will be an altogether more demanding and unpredictable scene.

I stand alone, in front of the chapel, surrounded by the daffodils and wet grass, the first buds on the trees peeping out. Spring-ish. I'm still alive, and the fact mocks me. After killing my mother, it was a simple step, the logical, grand gesture of my own suicide, completing the disastrous path of destiny my life had followed for so long. The delicious irony, that I would use the supplies of her medication to complete the circle, softened the barely hidden terror of what the actual act entailed. It was easy, to slip into unconsciousness and eternity in front of that grey oblong with all its hidden profanities and inanities. It was to be the final *coup de teatre*, presented to myself in my life's darkest and most deranged moment. As I stand before this chapel, about to witness the cremation of the poor woman's mortal remains, my own pitiful cowardice accompanies me. As I sat in that house, I worshipped the idea, the symbol of the act, and yet I didn't get even as far as taking the lid off the pill jar. I fell asleep in the chair and was caught in the morning with my mother dead in her bed. Such was her sorry degraded state, no-one even suspects her death was anything other than natural. A broken woman, ravaged by deep, paralysing depression, and the final straw of the murder of her son were too much for her. Poor Mrs. Phillips. She deserved better. The last few days have been a performance, a facade. The fates howl with laughter at me. My purgatory is to face these mourners, and the rest of my life.

The sound of voices. A small phalanx of people is heading towards me. Distant relatives some, mostly not. None of whom I recognise apart from a couple of the carers who have passed through the house. Then a portly, ugly, elderly man in an expensive suit appears. He still has the swagger I recognise from eons ago, from his son even. Old man Kavanagh, the ex-lover, and Jimmy's wretched progenitor.

As the posse of mourners approach, I feel my whole life has been leading to this moment, but I don't know why. For some reason a calmness settles within me. In the remaining minute it will take for these people to arrive, I must choose what road to take. I can end this now. Give myself up, give them the truth, have them put me away, end the need to struggle against all of this. A living suicide in jail for life, the least I deserve. An abdication of everything. Or go on.

Frank Kavanagh sees me, holds my gaze, with the familiar contempt. Twice in two weeks, in Marbella, and in Warrington, I have had to endure it. Would I give *this* man *that* satisfaction?

'Thank you all for coming.' I resume the role. It is impossible to do anything other than carry on this tragi-farce. I field all the usual sincere condolences, the rituals and clichés, I bat them back and forth like a seasoned tennis player of social etiquette. Little matter that none of these people have shown the slightest interest in my mother in at least a decade. Little matter that the concern they show me is of the same shallow hypocritical smarminess. It is the scene we all must play out.

'She was a fine woman, your mother' intones Kavanagh, pompously. 'I've missed her. You wouldn't understand, you were young. It was another time, a particular situation.' His self-satisfied paunchy face is cocked to one side, and he regards me with a withering condescension. 'She was a special lady.'

I hold his gaze. Eventually I simply say 'Bullshit.' I turn and lead the mourners inside.

The vicar moves through the routines and says things about Mum that are entirely theoretical and rhetorical. People nod meaningfully, and now it is my place to say something. I stare at these few pinched faces, who look back at me with barely disguised disdain. While I don't know any of them personally, only by name and old family tales, I know they will have carried along with them their preformed neatly packaged judgements, and I know where I stand in their eyes.

'My mother's death is a sudden and shocking event; the culmination of a series of accidents and tragedies that robbed her of the will to live.' Frowns break out, looks are shared. 'She was robbed, for most of her life. Of her time, of her happiness, and finally of her sanity. Destiny failed her. The system failed her. I failed her.' Shifting of weight, ostentatious fidgeting and embarrassed coughing.

'You all failed her as well. If you are family and friend enough to be here now, why were you not family and friend enough to have been there for her through these last twenty-four years of decline and decay? What is family for? What are friends for?' Two people turn sharply and exit, mumbling their fury. With my mother we bury the very idea that this is a family. It disintegrated long ago. We gave up on it. Me. Gary, and all of you who knew her. We killed her slowly with our neglect, and fear, and cowardice...'

The muttering is rising, and everyone is now making to leave. The vicar looks stunned but doesn't know what to say.

'And we come today to do what? Make ourselves feel better? Pay the respects we withheld during her life?'

'Shame!' someone shouts as they retreat from the chapel.

'We are here to witness failure. A failure of love, of compassion and of humanity. I plead guilty, as much as any of you.' The last person shoots me a filthy scowl as they leave through the door. Only old man Kavanagh is left. He claps, slowly, sardonically. I turn and shake the vicar's hand briskly, whose mouth is flapping comically, with no sound coming out. I make to leave and Kavanagh steps out and blocks my passage. He leans in, macro focus on burst blood vessels in his nose and his eyeballs, the flabby folds of tired skin all around his eyes and jowls.

'You disrespectful little fuck,' he spits the words hard in my face, 'I ought to give you a good hiding.'

'Well that would be more than you've done for these past twenty years, ay?'

His face spasms with fury, but he collects himself, and a smile creeps onto his now crimson visage.

'You've got more balls than your dad ever had, I'll give you that.' He appraises me further then turns abruptly and stalks out, leaving only the echo of his laughter and disdain behind him. The great bulk recedes into the daylight outside.

'Well, that was quite the most disgraceful spectacle I have had the misfortune to witness!' The vicar has found his tongue.

'Really? I thought it was entirely fitting actually. Yes, I think, all things considered, that rather hit the nail on the head. I still have my brother to bury, and that should prove to be a wholly more complex affair. I won't require you for that one. Cheerio.' I walk down the aisle and into the air.

I decide to walk along the road before taking a taxi. I am aware of a car slowing behind me along the kerb. I sigh and stop, wondering if Kavanagh or some distant family member wants to make a further scene. As I turn round, the window of a fairly sleek black saloon lowers. Superintendent Collins leans out. I am surprised and for a millisecond panic flickers, but withers as quickly. I follow his beckoning to climb in, and as I slip into the comfortable upholstery I feel the whole embrace of the criminal justice system, receiving me back into its bosom. A kind of relief settles. No unknowns to fear. It's a repeat episode and I accept my fate. I stare him straight in the eye, but say nothing, awaiting, and curious that he should come himself, with apparently no back-up other than the driver. The car moves off.

'I am very sorry indeed for your loss, Eugene. I knew your mother well and it has been terribly painful to see her these years.' I am confused, I am in a different scene all of a sudden. 'I haven't been able to visit her as regularly as I'd have liked, but I've always had an eye out for her. I kept her updated on your progress in Strangeways, and tried to make that easier for her to deal with.'

'Thank you, I didn't realise...' I trail off.

'I've seen some things in my time in the force, but I've rarely seen someone have to suffer the triple whammy that life has inflicted on you, Eugene. What happened to your father was a terrible injustice, and your brother, that is just cruel and from what I understand he was caught up in forces he couldn't control. The cost to your mother has been terrible, and she's paid the ultimate price. I always thought the grief would do for her in the end.'

Something is banging at the inside of my head. Rewind.

'You said *injustice*.'

He's quiet for some time, but fixes me with his eye. The houses slide past the window.

'Eugene, you deserve to know the truth about your father's death.'

'Truth' I repeat. Without expression. I am formless. I have turned to air in anticipation.

'What I am going to tell you is *off the record*. I hope what I am about to say will help you come to terms with what's happened and help you rebuild your life. Only you can do that, and you should never attempt to act on any of this information. If it were known I was the source, I would lose my job, and my pension. So what I am telling you isn't told lightly. Do you understand the implications of what I am saying? Do I have your assurance this information stays between us?'

His eyes fix me and penetrate. The uniform, his status, the car, the circumstances, all make me solid and heavy again, pinned into the seat. At the mercy of history.

'Yes. Okay. None of this is official or from you, I get it. But what about...' and I gesture toward the driver with my eyes. Collins lowers his voice.

'Not to worry, he's a close personal friend, not police. Okay?' He looks ahead and settles in. I think the car is driving aimlessly, as we are wandering through suburban streets, Newton le Willows probably. 'Your father liked a card game. This much you know. We

295

played poker. He was pretty good and when his luck was in, he would clean up. He got ambitious. I think he thought he could escape the chip shop with a few more winnings, change up your lives. Your mother was I think somewhat embarrassed by the business, she thought it was beneath her. It was a source of friction between them, this I know. From your father. Over the cards, a few whiskeys. We were friends, up to a point.

'He wanted to get a bigger game, higher stakes, bigger winnings potentially. He asked to get on a table with some men whose business interests weren't innocent, shall we say. Much bigger money. I begged him not to, I knew these men, as we were constantly monitoring and investigating them. Once he decided to rub shoulders with them at their poker table, I had to distance myself from him. I couldn't be seen to be playing poker with people with criminal associates. It saddened me. I lost a friend.' He pauses reflectively for a moment. 'One of the men at that particular table was at the funeral today.'

The seat is bottomless and I may slip through it onto the road. 'Kavanagh.'

'Yes, I'm afraid so. Your father had a good run, made some money out of them. He was naive and trusting, and also blinded by his own unrealistic sense of his abilities. They let him win. Got his confidence up, then set up the typical sting. Higher stakes table. Your father put everything you had into one game. They were ready for him. Whether they had a marked pack, or whether they just worked together to bring him down, it doesn't really matter. He was a lamb to the slaughter. They took him for everything he had, and more. He was now owned by them. The profits from your chip shop were owed, with interest, to the mob.'

'The mob. Italian mob?' I'm confused.

'Might as well have been. You know Frank Kavanagh's accent. He's an Orangemen. In the seventies and eighties, paramilitary organisations needed funds for their war in Northern

Ireland. Kavanagh was a bag man for the protestant paramilitaries, the UVF, and worse. Your chip shop was used to launder funds from criminal sources and funnel it through to the brigades in Belfast. It meant you had a thriving business, but also that your father was owned by the Belfast protestant loyalist mobsters. Behind the politics of the troubles, most of them were just that. Gangsters. And a war needs money.'

Flashes of memories wink out from the mists, disconnected fragments, vignettes of oddness and incongruity. Men with Belfast accents. Briefcases. Sudden trips to Belfast Dad never talked about, it was just 'business', 'looking at possible premises for another shop…'

'You probably never knew you had a chip shop in Belfast, did you?'

I shake my head dumbly.

'Well it was yours in name only, part of the conduit for funds. Your father had little to do with it other than signing cheques and leases. Maybe in time he could have paid them back and they'd have left you all alone. But Frank Kavanagh as you know is an arrogant bugger, who likes to get what he wants. And he wanted your mother. Once he was in your family's orbit, he was smitten with her. Showered her with gifts, flattery, you name it. He was cock of the town, and she fell for it all. Thought she deserved better than being the wife of a chip shop owner. Once she'd fallen for him, they had a barely disguised affair for years.'

'Of that, I don't need reminding.' Bingo. All those evenings. A familiar pang of disgust adds itself to the stew of emotions brewing within me.

'Gradually your mother understood the nature of the business arrangement, but she went along with all of it. It was just part of a life she wanted. I can only begin to imagine the humiliation your father felt.'

I am aware of hot tears coursing over my face. The driver passes a Kleenex back. I am a lost child. And I know much more, worse, is to come.

'We were aware something was going on that wasn't healthy for your family, or very legal, but these guys were good. It was difficult to prove anything, and there was, I am ashamed to say, a certain institutional unwillingness to delve into the details of the affairs of businessmen with Loyalist connections. If Kavanagh had been a Republican, this story would have had a somewhat different ending, albeit not a happy one either.

'So eventually this torture became too much for your father. He took a step that unfortunately sealed his fate. He decided his only way out was to turn informant and bring the whole thing down. He would lose everything, but he'd be free. And he assumed he'd be protected for his pains.'

'A supergrass.' It sounds comical, ludicrous, the sort of things that don't happen to ordinary working folk in the North-West of England.

'Pretty much. He made a deal with elements within Lancashire CID and Special Branch. Now you see why this is off the record. Your father's story involves people at the very heart of the legal system during a particularly sensitive and volatile political epoch. You wouldn't have sensed it back then, at your age, but the entire British state was bent and distorted by the war in the six counties.'

'I remember some slanging matches and fights around, among some of us at school. It was always involving Kavanagh junior and some of the Irish, the Catholic families. One of my close friends, his folks were Belfast Catholics, he got a rough ride from Jimmy. He explained it to me. The civil rights movement.'

'The McCaffreys? Yes, they had a tale to tell.'

'I can remember United and Liverpool fans shouting Celtic and Rangers at each other, between themselves. You heard it on the

298

Match of the Day. It was background noise. We weren't religious so it was never aimed at us.'

'Your father had put himself in a situation of great danger. He demanded protection in return for his information. He was impatient as he was naturally terrified, and wanted them all to be arrested and you all given new identities. He worked and lived with all of this inside him throughout 1982. You can imagine what that must have been like. The investigation had its own agenda as well. They were always wary of doing anything that might tip the balance of power in the favour of the provisional IRA. It was way more complex than your father imagined. The details of your father's information informed a wider investigation of the people much higher up the chain of command. We are talking about the real bad guys now. The men, both Republican and Loyalist who lead the death squads, who made the bombs. They were much more important targets than Kavanagh, and his chip shop funds. What your father gave them allowed them to work people higher up. They were able to force some of those people to turn super grass for good plea deals. Protection, just like your father wanted. Basically, Special Branch, partly through your father's help, were able to turn some Loyalists to the Crown's evidence. But it's a slow, delicate, dangerous process. Witness protection takes time to create and implement. He told your mother, because he hoped she would come with you, that she would choose the family over Kavanagh. He assumed Kavanagh and his ilk would end up behind bars. It was a gamble, and he was naive. Kavanagh was never going to go away, he knew too much, was too well connected, and he wasn't who they were really after. Special Branch didn't act as swiftly as they might have. So while he was still here, he was a sitting duck.'

'They found out. That's why they killed him' I say. I didn't know I could entertain any further horror in my mind. One question had to be asked. 'Who told them, how did they know? Was it Mum?'

The answer to this threatens to cleave me in two. He regards me with deep sympathy. None of this is easy for him.

'I have never heard anything that suggests your mother betrayed your father, any more than she had already done, if you'll excuse the expression. And she broke it off with Kavanagh. They expected you would all be whisked off into witness protection. I think she was probably relieved at the prospect of a completely new start.'

'So what happened?' I am breathless. New, shocking pieces of an old jigsaw. I could have had a different life. I was poised at the edge of a field of milk and honey, where all would have been new, and free of the stench of the corrosive life of our house.

'Witness protection was being organised, but not fast enough. Kavanagh found out. Through one of his own, who had a relationship with a particularly compromised undercover Special Branch operative. Kavanagh acted swiftly. And ruthlessly. A loyalist bombmaker, contracted by Kavanagh, basically staged the explosion on your chip shop. Your father was murdered by one of the very men who had traded information for protection. Your father's killer still lives, here in England, under a new name and identity. At the time of your father's murder, he was a protected asset of the British state. Kavanagh's action was revenge for your father's treachery and for the loss of his love. Nothing more. But such was the currency of these men, death, blood, bombs and bullets, it was just business as usual, and that's how they settled scores. The whole story of a gas explosion was the official cover up of what was in fact an assassination. It is not something I have found easy to live with all these years.'

I notice the driver glance up in the rear-view mirror at Collins. His expression tells me their relationship is other than a professional one. We are still driving. The questions queueing in my mind nudge me to give them voice.

'If you know this, how did they get away with it?'

'The CID officer who investigated the explosion was absolutely thorough. He had enough contacts within Special Branch to know everything around Kavanagh was rotten, and the chip shop was not what it appeared to be. No-one in Special Branch expected Kavanagh to pull a stunt like that, and when he did, they wanted it very much brushed under the carpet. The bomber was in their protection when he did it. That's embarrassing. A trial of that man may have undermined more important prosecutions; discredited a major plank of Home Office secret policy. Kavanagh's organisation was still moving money to the Loyalists. No-one wanted to give any possible advantage to the Provos. That was not something that people wanted to disrupt at the time. It's a complex web. The whole of the troubles is immensely political, but most of the people involved, from my experience, are opportunist thugs, criminals and psychopaths. Detective Inspector Geoffrey Treece found considerable evidence to suggest criminality in the case of the explosion. However, such was the political capital invested in the main investigation and its results, there was no way the truth about your father's murder would ever see the light of day. It would have opened a large, politically embarrassing can of worms. The inquest was a whitewash. It broke Geoffrey's career completely. They slapped him down and shut him up. He was initially transferred to CID in Wales, but he was so disgusted he went back to uniform. He took early retirement. It was a disgrace what they did to him, a superb officer. And a good friend. He lives somewhere on the Costa del Sol, as do many retired officers.'

'So the guy who murdered my father, on behalf of Frank Kavanagh, is still free?'

'I am afraid to say he has been protected by the British Government ever since. As has Kavanagh, but only indirectly, as his affairs were neatly expunged from the official records.'

'But how is that possible?'

'Politics Eugene. Politics is bigger, more powerful and rottener than any of what you or I will ever be involved in.'

Well Marbella had taught me as much in no time. I am exhausted. My mind has been seared by successive electric shocks.

'Why are you telling me this?' I am conscious this is a highly irregular chat. Collins is risking everything.

'The truth can set one free Gene. You deserve to know the truth. It's my burden, one I'll have to carry to my grave, as will Geoffrey.'

'So, what now? Superintendent?'

'Live, Eugene. Make your peace with history. Serve out your license properly. This knowledge I have given you could be immensely troublesome for me. However, it is almost certainly a death sentence for you, if you were ever to act on it or reveal it to anyone. Close the book on all of this Eugene. Move to a place where nobody knows you. Where English villains and retired policemen don't live, where people you know don't sell drugs for a living. I could put in a word to that effect with Watkins.'

'And where's that?'

'Well it's not the Costa del Sol. Frank Kavanagh still holds a candle for your mother. He was here today. Unbelievable. It's all still very much unfinished business Eugene. You need to get as far away from all of it as possible.'

'I need my own witness protection programme.' He actually laughs at that. I realise we are outside my house.

'Good luck Eugene.' He gives me his card. 'If you ever need me, you can call. But you should walk away now. Don't turn back. If I never hear of you or from you again, that will mean you took my advice. I hope that's the case. Take care.'

The driver has opened my door. He's not an actual uniformed policeman. I don't know who he is. We get out. The Inspector looks at me, still with kindness in his eyes, but also regret, even shame. He gets into the front seat with the 'driver' and the car pulls away, and I am stood in the milky light in front of the shabby, grubby house again. It is, to coin the cliché, the first day of the rest of my life.

25

The plane descends towards Malaga. That strange topography, so rugged, so dry, spattered with white Lego brick houses, slides by revealing the ribbons of condos on the coast. They sprawl and unfurl along the flanks of the mountains. It feels more familiar than the first time only some six weeks back. The irony of Collins' words are not lost on me. But I am after all, obliged to return to the Costa, to enable the police to understand more of the murder of my brother. The notion that evidence, information, the truth, can be quite so deadly has become a central preoccupation of my waking hours. These compromises, I now understand, have formed and warped my life for more years than I can guess at.

I have to be questioned by the Spanish judiciary in some form. Gary's assassins will be still on someone's payroll. The sensation of relentless exhaustion and mental shock treatment has subsided. Since Collins' revelations, I have managed to put so many things into place in my head. A whole landscape of confusion and bitterness, of self-flagellating grief and depression has become clearly delineated and deconstructed. Everything makes sense. All of the smouldering misery of my parents' marriage is but a clear symptom of the facts I am now in possession of. These facts have saved me. The truth has shone a light into the jagged, dark crevices of my self-esteem and rinsed the well of despair clean. The endless, formless grey cloud that lay at the back of all my thoughts, that shrouded my soul for so long, has evaporated. The light is blinding. It purges guilt, self-pity, the nihilism and illuminates all around me. I am unfettered, released, renewed. But I have no idea what I am going to do. I know what I should do, take Collins' advice. An idea that feels strangely unsatisfying.

Watkins has granted me a window of ten days, to encompass the police interview and the funeral. I am keenly aware of the potential cost of reneging on this deal. I have hired a car. I have means now after all, at least some. I arrive at the apartment in Sueño del Mar and let myself into the complex. Ironically, Gary's murder precluded me returning his keys to him. I am also cautiously excited by the prospect of seeing Frankie, all but briefly. I've no idea what may or may not be possible, but the company will be welcome at the very least. I have to start somewhere. I have wondered if I should be hiding, and who from? I now know if someone wants me dead, then there will be no escaping that fate.

I open the door to the apartment and the first thing I notice is the smell. Flashback, memory jolt. Stale beer, cheap cigarettes and hashish. I walk in and drop my holdall on the floor with a slap which catches the attention of two young men sprawled on the sofa. No sign of Frankie.

One of them, looking up from rolling a joint, stares for a second, then simply returns to rolling. The second one eyes me ferociously and asks, with an ill-disguised show of impatience,

'Can I help you, mate? You looking for someone?'

I stare at the scene, one not altogether unfamiliar. Crushed beer cans, empty vodka bottles, full ashtrays, take-away and pizza boxes piled on a sideboard, and the detritus of twenty-four seven joint rolling all over the coffee table. I don't say anything, just hold the insolent one's gaze.

'I'm talkin' to you, dickhead.' His accent is southern, Essex probably. His mate finishes the joint and sparks it up and takes a long slow drag. He offers it to me.

'Wanna bang on this mate?' The accent is northern, similar to mine, but stronger. Somewhere near Manchester.

I ignore the offer. I am still observing them silently, and they start to shift and exchange glances.

'Where is Frankie?' This question is not answered, but greeted with giggles. 'Where... is… Frankie?' They stop giggling.

'She's not 'ere,' says the Northerner.

'Thank you, that's fairly self-evident. Where is she? Does she still live here?'

'Pardon me mate, but what's it got to do with you? And who let you in? How d'you get in 'ere?' The Essex geezer stands up as he talks. He's tall but looks out of shape, like he lives on beer and joints. Been there, done that.

'I have a key' I say brightly, waving it at him. 'Because this is my apartment.'

Essex geezer appears slightly confused, processing the implications. He eventually draws a conclusion though.

'I don't fink so mate. You see we got this off Frankie, bought the lease off her, didn't we, y'see. Paid six months up front, right. So you can take yer bag and fuck off out of my gaff.' His colleague is transfixed, stoned, unable to handle the sudden air of menace in the room.

I have to laugh now, shaking my head in disbelief.

'And I presume Frankie took your money and pissed off back to Essex, correct?'

'Maybe, but like I said what's it got to do with you?' His shoulders involuntarily start to spread backwards, the habit of years of confrontations no doubt.

'Frankie has turned you over I'm afraid, boys. It was never her flat. It belongs to Gary Phillips.'

'Erm, sorry to disappoint you mate, but he's dead.'

I am juggling a range of emotions now, but rather like a vision mixer in a TV studio. The main me is sitting in a seat at the back of my head, behind other lesser versions of me going through different reactions. A me of quiet rage, another of contempt, and another flailing uncontrollably and cursing their insensitivity, full of righteous indignation. A last one is feeling murderous. I am observing various parts of me play act these emotions, sincerely, but only in my head. Externally I am completely calm and still.

'I know he's dead, I was in the car with him when he was shot.'

His face changes dramatically, a wave of realisation, embarrassment, anger, and then fear washes over it. He thumps his mate's shoulder,

'Fuck me, it's 'im.'

No response, Northerner draws a long toke, trying to distance himself from the scene. His face is a mess of slow-motion confusion.

'You're Gary's brother, incha.' He continues.

'Yes, and as his brother, I am his next of kin, and as his next of kin, this apartment is mine.'

'Next of what?' says the stoned Northerner.

One of my angry characters comes to the fore.

'Gary's dead. I'm his brother. So everything that was his is mine. So you are in my apartment. So you are going to have to leave. Get your stuff together and get the fuck out of my apartment.' It may or may not be legally accurate. Essex boy doesn't want to accept this version.

'Sorry mate, a deal is a deal. And anyway, you could be anyone.'

'But I'm not.'

'Whatever, finders keepers, we've paid up, so that's that.'

'Is it?'

'Yes it is.'

Stalemate. Nobody moves.

'Are you going to let that burn out?' I say to Northerner.

'Uh?'

'You're wasting a good joint there.'

'Uhhh, yeah. Want some?'

'Don't mind if I do.' I reach to take it from his hand, but instead I take hold of a half-finished bottle of spirits and in one swift move smash it down through the coffee table. Glass and vodka spray everywhere. Turning swiftly I palm the Essex boy's face, slamming him into the wall, and instantly have the jagged end of the bottle placed pointedly under his chin by his ear. With my free hand I grab his testicles as hard as I can and squeeze. My face is pressed hard into his. For some reason I am enjoying the sensation. Very much. Recent insights have given my mind a clarity of vision and purpose that enable me to channel hitherto troublesome emotions refreshingly effectively. The rush of adrenaline and a terrific feeling of self-righteousness is intensely pleasurable, exciting.

'Two weeks ago I was wiping my brother's brains off my face, and you think you can just walk in here and take over his fucking property, and you think I'm going to be alright about that?! Is that what you think?' I bring my knee hard into his balls and he hits the deck like a sack of spuds, almost vomiting with the pain. Northerner is trying to push himself backwards through the sofa.

'Not very polite your mate, is he. No manners.'

I squat down to his level. He looks over at the other, to me, waiting for some kind of decision or possibility to present itself to his stoned mind.

'Uhhhh...' is all that comes out. I slap him hard. The sharp shock makes him start to whimper but I suspect it's more from humiliation than pain, and maybe fear.

Essex boy gets up gingerly, a slight fleck of blood under his ear. He wipes it off, sees his hand, looks at me. I am still brandishing the broken bottle.

'So, what's it going to be boys?' I look from one to the other.

'Alright, we'll go. But we want the rent back.'

I laugh back at his face. The cheek!

'Well I think you'll need to talk to Frankie about that, won't you. Get your shit together and get out, now.' There's a moment of silence, looks dart between the two of them, a conversation of the eyes, that arrives at the same conclusion between both of them. They

307

aren't going to fight it out. Disconsolately they proceed to gather up their sad possessions. A considerable amount of smoking paraphernalia, some skanky clothes in old holdalls, iPods, mobile phones and tired, filthy sneakers.

Essex boy opens a drawer and tries to place a brown paper package discreetly into his bag.

'Whoah there, wait up!' I wave the bottle in his direction. 'What's in the package?'

No reply, just more looks between them.

'It's coke' says Northerner.

'Fuck' says Essex boy, glaring at his partner in crime.

'Oh, sweet. And whose is that?'

'It's not ours, we're holding it for someone. I wouldn't get involved in that. You don't want to go there.' He is obviously scared of whoever he's talking about. And no, I don't want to go there. Anywhere near.

'Well take your filthy shit with you then, I have no need for it.'

In a few more minutes they are about to leave the door. Their body language is sheepish and pathetic. Essex boy bristles and points at me.

'Jimmy's gonna hear about this, then we'll see what's what, you cunt.'

I walk right up to him, holding his gaze.

'Jimmy? Jimmy who?' I think I already know.

'Jimmy Kavanagh. That's his fucking coke, he ain't going to be 'appy.'

'And why would Jimmy trust a couple of stoned out losers like you with a bag of charlie?' There's another conversation of eyes, but nothing is said. This sounds like a bluff, or exaggeration, or wishful thinking. 'Well tell Jimmy I'd be happy to discuss the issue personally with him. And I shall advise him frankly not to entrust you with his business.'

308

His distorted face struggles to conceal a range of emotions, and before he lets anything further escape he struggles out the door, not looking back. The Northerner follows sheepishly, then at the top of the stairs he turns to me.

'Sorry about your brother mate, that's fucked up that is.' And he leaves.

'Yeah, thanks' I say to the retreating figure. And I mean it.

I turn back into the flat, surveying the wreckage. The silence is oppressive. I wish so much Frankie was here. But she's just one rat from the sinking ship, and at least she took those two fools to the cleaners. Cheeky of her, but she figured that was the end of the road with all the Phillips boys. Reasonable assumption, all things considered. With a half-smile, I start to clean up. I am processing the detritus of a lifestyle remarkably similar to my own, prior to Strangeways. The food consumed almost solely from cheap take-aways. The sheen of tobacco, grass and hashish crud covering the main table surface. Bins overflow with cans and bottles, full ashtrays lurk on surfaces, ignored and stale. A mixture of clothing would have been draped willy nilly on any spare upright, be it chair, lamp, or whatever. Sundry CDs, tapes, vinyl, cables, recorders and other musical paraphernalia would have formed mini piles in various corners, and a variety of hi-fi equipment, some working, some not, would have formed a ring along the remaining surfaces of the room. These guys appear to have relied on only the TV for entertainment, and their taste in take-ways was alarmingly limited. I'm probably fortunate in this respect. I still wonder which vultures helped themselves to my things when I was on remand. I suppose I could buy some new clothing. That still feels like a step too far. I manage after a couple of hours to return the flat to something tolerable, even homely. I search for something to eat or drink, anything. Nothing presents itself and I am too exhausted and frazzled to venture out. My mind is still and hard as a stone now. The din of things needing to be attended to, the packs of 'what ifs', 'who dids' and 'where ares' howling as they roam my thoughts, is such that I drain an unfinished bottle of cheap whiskey and slump into the clean bed that had been miraculously left alone by my erstwhile flatmates. Thank heavens for small mercies. I give myself to the blackness.

~

The blackness doesn't last long. For days my sleeping mind has been a frozen wasteland, few dreams, just a fug of random memories, snatches of life gone by, so brief, jumbled, no coherence. This night I am dropped into Technicolor drama. Warrington and Marbella morph together. I serve fish and chips in a noisy Spanish style cafeteria in Warrington. Palm trees line the streets and the sky is blue, while the squat houses remain browny grey and ugly. Gary and I argue about visiting Mother. We blame each other for all manner of forgotten slights and grievances. We go home and sit in silence with her. Frank Kavanagh is watching TV in the lounge, ignoring us. Mum is a ghostlike presence, saying nothing but her eyes scold us, sear our souls. Gary says he must go to work, and I run helplessly after him, to escape the prison of the house and its decay. We are driving, somewhere, for how long I don't know, and then the shots. I have a vivid sensation of the warm liquid parts of Gary that spatter my face. I scream and writhe under them, but no-one hears me. Not even me. Gary is not there. I am standing over my mother. I wipe my face and stare at her. The pillow I am holding over her face is stained with Gary's blood. This evidence will give the game away, I must wash the pillow, wash the blood... I try to leave the room, to find the bathroom, but the house dissolves into formlessness, the bathroom is so far. I am alone somewhere indistinct, panicking that I have left the pillow. They will find it, they will know, they will come for me. Wake up I tell myself. Wake up, it's only a dream. If you wake up, they won't find you. Gradually the ambient vapours become the room around me, and I grab for the pillow to find it is there. It is my pillow. I am in the now again. Exhausted. Relieved. I remain awake, fighting off scraps of dream that attempt to cross into consciousness, people, cars, shards of windscreen.

At some point I wake up. I must have stemmed the leakage and fallen back to less tortuous blackness. The day is already blasting brilliant sunlight everywhere. It is around ten o´clock, but I feel the heat. The floor to ceiling windows of the apartment act like a greenhouse. Now I understand what the impenetrable plastic curtains are for, keeping the sun out. I throw open the sliding door and delicious waves of warm air, rich with the smells of unfamiliar flowers and shrubs rise up and penetrate every corner of the place, chasing out the staleness, sweat and nihilism of its recent tenants. I am mesmerised for a while. Until the sensation stops. I sit down and try to order my thoughts, a giant litter bin of IOU's, 'to do' notes, hate mail, and random sheets of arbitrary rants against injustices wrought upon me and my family. I grab at the obvious bits of paper: visit Ana as soon as, arrange to give a further statement to the police. And then? Fragments of writing leap from the mess of papers: run away, go home, score some weed and get wiped out, find Holme, find who killed Gary. I laugh. And do what, precisely? Tell the police. Leave the police to sort it out. Run away. Go home. Kill myself. Ha-ha. I figuratively set fire to that note, I know I'm not capable. Even I learn from experience sometimes. Look after Ana. Meet my niece/nephew one day. Get a job and be normal. Do what Mr. Watkins wants. Stop taking drugs of any kind. Take lots of drugs. I rummage some more. Take off to Asia and travel aimlessly on the proceeds of the sale of the house in Warrington. Open a chip shop in Warrington. Shut up. Run away. Go and get a coffee in the cafe and have a nice Spanish breakfast. Cramming all the papers and notes gleefully into my mental pockets I dress in some of the anodyne recently bought clothes, they are more comfortable in this climate. I'm out of the flat and bounding down the stairs to my hire car. Relieved to be in the day. Dreading the visitations of the next night.

Once in the familiar cafeteria, I attempt to order in Spanish, a *cafe con leche*, and a bread bap which consists of a pork filet, *and* serrano ham, with a fried green pepper and mayonnaise. A *mollete serranito.* Quite possibly the most superlative sandwich ever invented. I am centred now, allowing the ludicrous decibel level of screaming coffee machine, clanking glasses, yelling waiters to wash over me. It's not as loud as I remember it though. I feel safe momentarily. The cafe is markedly less populated than it should be at 10.30 on a Tuesday. I eavesdrop English voices from the next table for a while. Difficult not to when one hears the name Holme pop up. The conversation is a shared lament of some real estate agents, between what sounds like a Brit, a couple of Dutch and a Russian, in English naturally for the Brit's sake, I assume.

Doom. Gloom. Desperation. Cut and run. Wages and commissions unpaid. Clients scared away. Shootings… Sounds like the birds have come home to roost and the goose of golden eggs has been well and truly cooked. I don't feel any specific sympathy. You live by the great property bubble sword; you must be prepared to die by it. Literally, it seems. This chokes me for a second and I have to refocus and get a grip.

'Excuse me.' It's me. Butting in. Surprising myself. And them. 'I heard you mention the Holme shooting. Has that affected things? How's business?' Might as well be direct.

Fucking wanker!

It's the end of Marbella.

It's just Spain, bound to happen.

All bubbles burst.

Bollocks!

They were too greedy.

Fuck this place.

I'm done.

Bulgaria is where it's happening.

Fuck off, get into Morocco, dirt cheap land.

This place is finished.

You're right there.

I'm back to Holland, at least we have a decent social security system.

Nothing for me in Russia, I go to Bulgaria.

The kids will miss their friends.

My wife is looking forward to getting out of here.

Who are you, you seem familiar.

'Erm, naaah, I just came over, looking for work, like. Any suggestions?'

'Are you kidding?' says the English one, 'Over fifty building projects totally paralysed, most of the town hall still in jail, sales have dried up like that-' clicks fingers '-suppliers are going broke, no-one's paying invoices, the entire cash flow of the whole coast is screwed, and it's all because of that arsehole Holme.'

'No, I blame his side-kick, the poor fucker who got shot.'

'Holme set him up and did a bunk, it's obvious.'

'Where is he now?' I ask, for what it's worth.

'Brazil' says the Russian.

'Naaah, he's in the US' contradicts a Dutchman.

'*Niet*, my friend, this I know. From people. But he won't be able to stay, they will find him.'

'Who will find him?' My eagerness is like a bad fart gone off all of a sudden. All pause and eye me more closely, with suspicion and distaste. They exchange glances. The Englishmen gets up, placing a twenty on the tray.

'Well this one's on me guys, one for the road. All the best, good luck.'

Hands shaken, commiserations, as they disperse. The Russian is last to leave, but before he does, he leans in to me.

'I wouldn't waste your time here.'

'So not much work then?' I'm still playing the game.

313

'I know your face. This is no place for you, and no-one is going to employ you, especially you. I am sorry for your loss. Go home. It is all over here.' He's gone, and I am leaden in my seat. He's right. I am doubly damaged goods, with no safety net, with an aura of death and chaos around me.

I negotiate the little car gingerly around under the palms, trying to get used to the wrong side of the road again. Holland is a long time ago now. I eventually locate the parking under Gary's penthouse block, and head up. The visit to the cafe was a slap in the face, a wake up, a reminder of my naivety and how small a place Marbella is. I'm radioactive. I'm potentially a marked man. I can feel the scrappy note in my pocket, the one that says 'run away' in red capital letters. Ten days. Is it enough to put everything to bed? What's even involved? I'm grateful Ana is a Spanish lawyer. She will know exactly what needs doing.

Ana opens the door. Her eyes search may face, tracing the similarities to Gary, feeling the shock of body memory provoked by our inevitable similarities. Dressed simply, ungroomed, no make-up, she seems so girlish. So diminutive, vulnerable and lost. She beckons me in and goes about distracting herself making tea. Little is said. Pleasantries are pointless. My brother's death colours the very air around us, inescapable, all enveloping. She sits, coiled up, hugging herself, sipping English tea on the designer sofa.

'I'm so sorry about your mother. So much to bear…'

We are silent for a long time. The girl in front of me flushes, and from somewhere she finds energy.

'You need to get down to the *Comisaría*[20], make the formal statement and answer all of their questions. Which won't be hard because you don't know anything they could be interested in. You're lucky.' Her face tightens now and she sucks her lips in. 'The police did an autopsy, as a formality, and released the body today. I'm glad

---

[20] Main police station

314

you are here. We can have the burial as soon as possible. I will organise it for Thursday. It will be private, just me and you, maybe Rafaela. Things here are strange, and everyone is blaming each other, it's horrible. I don't want anyone to know, no press, no friends.' She snorts derisively. 'Friends… It is something like this tells you who your friends are. Thank you for coming back.'

I'm silently crying. Tears rolling down my cheeks. So different from the ludicrous bitter spectacle in Warrington, I shall have to observe Gary's funeral intimately, with his one true companion, with none of the absurdities and ritualised hypocrisy of Mum's funeral, all the more absurd as I was the author of it all. Even weirder still in the light of new knowledge. I have come to see her mental collapse through a wholly new prism.

Eventually I ask her 'What are you going to do? What happens now?'

'I will fight to get everything I can from this for our child to have a good life. I must keep this apartment, to sell. I must preserve my good name, so I can work once more, once Marbella starts to function again. I want to find Holme and make him pay for what he did to Gary. The truth about Holmeland must be exposed, and all the people involved must face the consequences. It is my work to make this happen, so that what happened to Gary is not the only punishment for this terrible system we have created that is consuming our country.'

Her face is resolute. This beautiful thing on the sofa has a shining light of determination pulsing within her. It surprises me.

'Aren't you sick of all of this? The people who murdered Gary aren't afraid of you, or probably anyone. You can't go up against them, how can you?'

Her face doesn't change.

'I am a lawyer. I have spent years shuffling papers and hiding lies and politicians' crimes, all in the name of business, to sell houses, to sell the Marbella dream. And look what it has brought me. I can fight them, because I know how they work, and I know the law. The government is out to get them, and I know where the evidence is.'

'Ana, this is dangerous, we are talking about international criminal organisations. You think I don't know anything? I saw things going on here Gary wouldn't even talk to me about. He knew way more than he was ever telling me. His business associates are dodgy as hell. I know them because they are the same people I was working with indirectly when I went to jail for three years.' I am sounding panicky, because I am. 'And I carried a bag of illegal funds to every politician's friend, that Sorzano guy. We were stopped by the police, and they let us go, because someone at the top is on the inside of all this. Everyone is in on this. The government, the police, the East European mobsters, fucking hell, even the Warrington mafia are involved, people I grew up with! They are running around here murdering the people who get in their way! And you think you can fight them?'

The foes ranged against us are terrifying and virtually untouchable. I for one do not want to pick a fight with them. Then it occurs to me, I already have done. The previous evening. Fuck.

'I know, Gene. You are right. But if we do nothing, they win.'

'But what can you do? You're going to have a baby in a few months!'

'And when the baby is an adult, and it asks what happened to the people that murdered their father, I want to be able to tell them that I fought them. That I helped to bring justice, that I made a difference. That I did not just run away and carry on with all of these liars and thieves, like nothing ever happened. How can I? While they turn our country into their stupid playground with their drugs and *putas*[21] and cars and crazy houses, when the normal people in Marbella have nothing!'

'You want to take on the whole system.'

---

[21] Whores

'Maybe.'

'How will you do it?'

She goes quiet. Her face twitches with anger and indignation, her eyes flicker from side to side, searching for something to focus on, to still the turmoil within. This passion disturbs me. Such determination, such a sense of righteousness, a clear cause to fight for; this is completely alien to me. The opposite of my life-long self-satisfied, self-destructive, hedonistic nihilism.

'I know how they turned this town into their gold mine. If you are a lawyer here in Marbella it is difficult not to be touched, to be corrupted, because this is how it all works, ever since Gil decided to make Marbella his personal kingdom, and all the people like him.'

'Who is Gil? Does he have something to do with Holme?'

'I'm sorry Gene, this is nothing to do with you, you wouldn't understand. This is not your *tierra*[22], your *pueblo*[23].'

'Maybe I want to understand.' I say, and it sounds decidedly inadequate even to me.

Ana cracks a half smile, which penetrates the weariness edging her whole being.

'How to explain to you how Marbella is like this, *dios mío*[24], that is a job.' She pauses to collect her thoughts, put the memories in order. 'When I was studying law in Malaga in 1991, a new mayor came to Marbella, Jesus Gil. He was elected because he was a fat, rich property developer who promised to make everybody else rich. He gave away lots of presents and made a big noise. Once he became the mayor, he was running the town like his personal private club. He made every department of the municipality into a private company. So it is all just a business. And his friends run the businesses and fill their pockets. Even the socialist politicians couldn't find out what was happening. It is a private club, for the *enchufados*. As I told you, this

---

[22] Country
[23] People
[24] My God

317

is how Marbella works. Well, it did up until two weeks ago. When I graduated, I came back to work here in my *pueblo*[25], and I was lucky to get a job in a *bufete de abogados,* you know, a lawyer's offices. I was a junior, but because I was pretty and hardworking, they brought me into the better projects straight away. I did a lot of work with all of the developers, and because my bosses spent more of their time having lunch and parties with Gil and his amigos, I ended up doing much of their work too. So, I have seen how all things really work in Marbella. And if you wanted to work, that was the work there was. I did think maybe to leave Marbella, but it was exciting. I hate to say it, but I enjoyed it, up until…'

'Two weeks ago', I fill in.

'Gil was so corrupt, but he made the money flow and paid off everybody, and everybody made money, so he got away with it, almost. But he became too stupid, and when he sent Marbella town's money to his football club in Madrid, he was caught and he did get sentenced, four years ago, so he was not mayor anymore. But he left his boys behind to carry on his work. Gil died of a stroke and heart about two years ago, but Marbella stayed the same. I was not sad, he was an arrogant pig, and completely corrupt. But it all just felt normal after so much time. All my adult life and career has been this.' She gestures dismissively at the town beyond the walls of the apartment.

'Aren't you in danger of being charged, will they come for you?'

She breathes in, considering. It is obviously at the front of her mind.

'My bosses have been arrested, but they have been released for the moment. Maybe they will eventually be in trouble. So much dirt, it will be so hard to make everybody be punished. I never signed anything, nothing of any of this is in my name. In the end it is the politicians who have been taking all the money to let the Holmes do

---

[25] Town

their business. The business is legal, in everything except the permission to build in the first place. We give the people who buy the houses proper deeds and documents, they pay proper taxes, but really the house they buy is illegal under the law of Spain. But who is the criminal? The builder or the mayor? Or the lawyer who makes the deeds, even though even I know it is deeds for a house that can never be legal?'

'Gary knew this, he told me as much.'

Now she really laughs, but she's laughing at my naivety.

'Yes, everybody knows this. Maybe not the foreigners who buy the houses, but all the politicians, all the builders, all the police, all of us lawyers who make it happen. When Gil came to town, he tore up the rules and said Marbella is open for business. Even when they sent him to jail, it was not for this. Nobody has ever been prosecuted for building in Marbella. But maybe it was so big the government had to stop it. So now, everything has changed for ever. This time it is not going to be business as usual. The government in Madrid have taken over Marbella. The town hall is closed. Many people are in prison, but some still find the money for bail. Now there will be investigations and trials and this might take five, maybe ten years. The Marbella I know is dead. It is what killed Gary, so I am not sad.'

We are silent for a while. I admire her composure. Explaining all of this, and having clarity, knowing in two days she will be at Gary's funeral, and her whole life has gone up in smoke.

'What I don't understand Gene, is who killed Gary and why? And I don't know that the police will be as interested in a murdered *guiri,* probably murdered by other *guiris,* as they should be.'

'Seriously?'

'Some of the police have many things to hide, it is all part of the same thing.'

'But they want to speak to me still.'

'Yes, they will do all the right things, but it depends who is behind it, and what their relation, if any, is to the authorities.'

'How can that happen in this day and age, here, in Europe?'

She laughs with that faint condescension at my naivety again.

'And your country is so different? You wouldn't say that if you were Irish.'

I am about to say something but the words die stillborn. My recent insight into British crime and punishment thanks to the Superintendent smacks me in the face again. Nothing you could make up ever seems as weird as what is actually happening behind the tenuous mask of civilisation we cling to, without ever realising how fragile and porous it is. Why have I been gifted such insight by such unlikely circumstance? I feel so drained. Useless. And dirty. Able to put my mother out of her misery, and then resign responsibility for it all. To shrink away from the horrendous truths screaming in my face, to skulk listlessly behind my habitual posture of fecklessness, when so much needs to be faced, to be redressed, to be avenged. Shit, vengeance. The first time I have properly thought of the word. The elephant in the room, it stands before me. It reeks with animal funk, primordial, blood, sweat and anger, adrenalin and fear.

'Gene? Are you okay, what is it?'

I zone back into the room, and find I am clenching the squelchy arms of the white leather, my nails have marked the otherwise pristine finish, and I am sweating. She sees she has my attention again.

'There is something you need to know,' she continues, and I have sense of dread this new knowledge will dovetail nicely into the apocalyptic soup simmering around me.

'Our lawyer contacted me today, personally. He is understandably rather stressed with all of this now, but this is not the main thing he is afraid of. You need to know. It is too much for me on my own.'

'Jesus, what now?'

'Gary has made a dossier of many things, papers, contracts, emails, files of sound recordings, telephones, many things.' Her breathing is quickening and she is fidgeting visibly. 'Don Alfredo, our lawyer, he has this parcel of documents in a safe deposit box in a bank. He wants to give me the key, and he wants me to destroy it. He is afraid of what it might contain. So far, I have not taken the key, but he is begging me to deal with it. He wants to have nothing more to do with me. We are toxic, you see. There are no friends when the world is made this way, with these people.'

'So, that was maybe some kind of insurance policy, for when, if, things went pear shaped. It's funny, he did seem worried, like things were spooking him and he couldn't put his finger on it.'

'Yes, I know, and he wouldn't even open up to me. Now we see it was obviously justified, he wasn't being paranoid, as I said to him. I am afraid now to find out what he might have known. I don't know what is underneath all of the usual theatre we make with contracts and papers and *notarios*[26] for Holme. But this may be the ammunition I need to bring them all to justice. Will you help me, Gene?'

She looks me dead in the eye, unflinching, her almond shapes with their rich hazel green shows her pupils dilated. It would be seductive if she wasn't so obviously terrified. And I am stumped for words, and resentful she is demanding this of me. Then I feel ashamed of my resentment. I grind my teeth; I can't dodge this. No exit from the storyline presents itself, and unlike back in Warrington, I am most decidedly not writing this script. Marbella becomes more concrete in my mind; it slips properly under my skin. I cannot view it from a distance anymore, through a veneer of bemused contempt and supercilious incomprehension. It has now put a needle into my arm and all of its poison is now dripping, saline-like, down the plastic tube

---

[26] Legal notary

into my circulation. Moments pass. I try and collect my thoughts. What would Gary have done?

'Does *anyone* else know of the existence of this package?'

She mulls this over.

'I don't think so. Don Alfredo is worried enough about its contents that he would not reveal its existence, I think. But if, or when, he is questioned, he may try to protect himself in some way.'

'Has he got things to hide?'

'Not because of us, he handled our personal affairs, but I don't know what other clients and projects he may be compromised by.'

'Maybe you should neutralise him by getting hold of it and telling him you destroyed it. I think he'd believe you.' I'm being optimistic. Ana frowns.

'Maybe. Maybe he would want proof. He is pressuring me to get rid of it.'

'That's not a good sign, that your own lawyer wants you to destroy potential evidence, so why not hand it over to the police.' I think I am being practical, safe.

'Maybe to the *fiscal anti-corupción* but who knows what is in it? If there is a leak, a *chivato*?[27] The source will be obvious and that is something I don't know how to deal with. Who can we trust?'

The use of the first-person plural confirms my helpless inclusion.

'Well…' I say, and have nothing to add. I stare dumbly back at her. 'I don't know. This is a bit beyond anything…' I stop as it's plainly useless what I am saying. 'We could run away, leave Spain…' This thought dies a similar inevitable and forgotten death.

'You must go to see the police, this we know. Don't tell them anything they don't ask you. Stick to the ordinary details you know, nothing Gary might have said.'

---

[27] A snitch

She doesn't even know of my night in the warehouse, let alone the steaming piles of current and historical manure I have left standing in England.

'Well, I can probably do that okay, act dumb, a lifetime of practice. I have to be back in ten days. If I break my license again, I will serve the remaining three years of my sentence. I'm not a free man. It's just borrowed time.'

'Everything has changed now, Gene.'

Everything. Has. Changed. My freedom hangs by a thread, and the facts increasingly demand that I engage, that I take on the forces lurking behind the headlines. I am utterly unqualified to meet these demands, I tell myself, my hands are tied by the British criminal justice system. My time-honoured instincts are to evade such responsibilities, to blot out the inconvenient or uncomfortable with chemicals. The imploring look on Ana's face tell me the habits of a lifetime are past their sell by date. No matter what Watkins says.

'I will get back to you as soon as I have made that statement. Then you need to know what's in that dossier, and you need to know how to keep it safe. We need to know.'

'Yes, we do.'

A pact is silently made. And a bond. Even though I have no idea how I can honour it without compromising myself catastrophically. We sit silently for a while, subtly embarrassed by this bizarrely induced intimacy.

'Okay, I am going to get off,' I say as I get up. 'I need to go and buy some new clothes.' It is a form of forward motion. I do need them.

'There's plenty here…' Ana offers almost unconsciously, a habitual kindness and consideration detonated by the reflex realisation of what it means. Dead man's clothes. Neither of us say anything else, just a short embrace, and I leave.

A tortuous two hours later, I have bought some attire more adjusted to the local climate. It isn't inspiring. It's a struggle to think about tomorrow, never mind what I'm supposed to look like. So I have suitable, anonymous, functional garb. I can throw away the awful, battered remnants of my bygone days, stop clinging to the dreary old familiarities, in all their distended, faded, stained and torn shabbiness. I am trying to believe I'm not that person anymore.

I swing into the gate of the underground garage to the block of flats. I notice with a lurch inside, the daft shiny yellow bulk of a Hummer, parked outside the main portal. There could be lots of those in Marbella I say to myself unconvincingly. The consequences of last night's enjoyable bravado may be imminent. Dry mouth, heart bouncing against my ribs. I shall try on my new clothes, it's not him.

I turn the key in the lock with trepidation, stare into the flat. Silence, there's nobody, and I let a long sigh out which turns into a sharp intake of breath as a violent thump in the back propels me forward through the door and onto the floor of the hall, neatly folded new clothes flying everywhere. Before I can even register what or who, a force around my collar lifts me up and I fly into the lounge and am pushed onto the sofa, where I turn around to discover my persecutor. Jimmy Kavanagh naturally. What knocks me sideways is Darren, standing behind him. An armful of clothes land on me, and I pick myself out of them and start to fold them neatly, completely ignoring them. Something comes over me, a heaviness, a smog of resentment and anger and despair and indignation, it hollows me out so that where fear should be, only indifference dwells. To them, to my own fate, my own being. Kavanagh is just the personification of the endless dance of death that follows the Phillips family, a smirking voodoo doll, a pockmarked stocky persecutor, a poisonous drip drip drip.

''Bout time you bought some new clothes Eugene, you look like a fucking tramp,' he says, all sarcy and pleased with himself.

'You don't look so hot yourself, if you don't mind my saying' I respond, which earns me a hard slap across the side of my head. My ear rings and stars dance in my vision, but the pain is curiously satisfying, like a relief, like a promise fulfilled.

'Don't get lippy sunshine,' he growls.

The absurdity gets too much for me, and I burst out in a fit of hysterical giggles, while they both stare at me, genuinely nonplussed, and I say between the riffs of laughter 'Or what? What are you going to do? Kill me? Well, why ruin the habit of a lifetime?' I stop laughing and find myself seized by an anger that makes me dizzy, the pressure behind my eyes forces tears out, but I don't sob, I yell, with all the accumulated and righteous fury I can muster.

'Go on then! Get on with it, finish it off! If it makes you feel better, don't leave the fucking job half done, you evil, inbred, fucking Irish cunt! Wouldn't look good would it, you got your reputation to think of ain't ya! Your fucking mongrel family fucked my mother, you fucked my dad, you fucked my brother so you might as well fuck me, go on get on with it! See if I care, see how good it feels, be my fucking guest.' Compulsively I lurch forward and grab him, but he finds my wrists fast enough and holds me off, easily. I continue to rage at him, as I say who knows what more, the blood is rushing, I'm slobbering and panting and howling at him and it feels right, rewarding, natural. But I'm aware the energy is about to expire, his grip won't be broken by me and then what am I going to do? Further reflection is precluded as some mighty impact occurs, a light flashes behind my eyes, then instantaneous blackness.

A sensation of stiffness and pinpoint pain located above my ear is the first evidence of regaining consciousness. An image fades in of two figures on the sofa facing me. I recognise them and the pieces immediately preceding the now fall into place again, and I am fully back in the room, as they say. They are both sipping beers. Darren looks at me like he's seen a ghost, something has spooked him, out of his usual frame of reference. Kavanagh, predictably has that same sardonic sneer on his ugly acne-scarred mug. I glance around.

325

'Where's my clothes?'

'Darren chucked them in your bedroom' answers Kavanagh.

'I hope you didn't ruin them, cost me one of those nice purple bits of paper that lot did.' Darren peers in confusion at Kavanagh for a response. My behaviour has quite clearly wrongfooted him. Not so Kavanagh, naturally.

'Yes, you should show a bit more gratitude to Darren here' he adds.

'What?' and after a short reflection that doesn't solve this conundrum, 'Why?'

'Because he did you the favour of getting your flat nicely rented out to two fine young gentlemen, and getting rid of that useless tart who was taking the piss.'

'You took advantage of my brother's death to install squatters in his property. I can't blame Frankie for making a profit off your cynical lack of respect for anyone. Sounds like she took those two clowns well and truly to the cleaners, good on her an' all.'

'Yes well, be that as it may, your actions last night seriously jeopardised an important investment that young Darren had just embarked upon. And we are here to seek redress.'

'Jesus what happened to you Jimmy, did you swallow a dictionary or something?' I brace myself for some kind of violent rejoinder but none comes. Instead he cracks the top and hands me a beer. I accept. It steadies me, the rant and the blow have left me rather spent, and I'm aware I haven't eaten for some time, and my stomach is like a washing machine on maximum spin.

'For what it's worth, Eugene' which he says with exaggerated poshness 'I studied an Open University Degree in English literature.' Darren stares now in stark disbelief and distaste, at Kavanagh. Kavanagh regards Darren with an expression that makes him stare at the floor and visibly shrivel. He turns to me again.

'Seriously?' I say.

'Course not, you fucking muppet. I just happen to like reading historical fiction, about great wankers from the past. You can learn a lot about people and power from reading y'know.'

'Speaking as a nearly failed anthropology student, I would concur dear Jimmy. So, what's the problem Darren. My apartment, for it is mine-' if you can't beat them, join them '-as the next of kin of my dearly departed brother, was illegally let without my due consent, and therefore I took it upon myself to evict the callow fiends who had abused my rights of ownership.'

Darren shifts uncomfortably. 'Will you stop talking like that, it's not fucking normal'. Kavanagh lets out a belly laugh.

'Darren, what *is* normal in these troubled times?' I patronise back.

'Listen you daft ponce, you fucked up a new scheme I was getting going and caused me a lot of embarrassment' Darren responds. He doesn't do assertive aggressivity nearly as well as Kavanagh.

'And I give a shit? You cunts murdered my brother, so you can all fucking rot in hell for all I care. Now get out of my house.' I fully expect some further brutal assault but Kavanagh remains surprisingly calm. He slurps his beer pensively.

'I can understand your outburst Eugene, but things are not what they seem.'

'Yeah right, you're Mother Teresa in disguise.'

'Show a bit of respect, and hear me out. It might be in your interest.'

'Seriously?' I am also a bit confused, certain logical expectations are not being fulfilled.

'You assume I am in business with Mr. Lebid and am responsible for your brother's murder.'

'Well someone killed him, and it seems pretty evident it's your organisation, why else would he be dead. I guess Holme slipped your net so you thought you'd exact your revenge on him.'

He doesn't respond initially.

'I personally had nothing to do with your brother's death. I didn't know it was going to happen, and I don't think it was a sensible thing to do. It has jeopardised what was set to be an exceedingly profitable operation.'

I'm scrutinising his face to get some kind of clue as to this man's sincerity, even surprised that I am doing so. None of this is playing out as I instinctively felt it would. 'Seriously I had nothing to do with it.'

'So who did then?'

'For fucks sake Gene, I'm not going to tell you that. It doesn't matter. This is much bigger than you, and even me, and it will eat you up and spit you out like an orange pip, so what the fuck are you doing here in Spain? What on earth have you come back for, there's nothing here for you, only trouble.'

'Or the unborn child of my dead brother.'

'Really? She's up the tub? Whoops. Anyways whatever, very noble of you an' all that, but you can't help her. It's all gone legal now, you've got the entire Spanish state coming down on the heads of all those thieving little cunts in Marbella, and good, decent honest to God drug dealers like ourselves can't even make a proper living anymore because the whole system is fucked. It's between them now, so everything that Holme and your brother worked so hard for has gone to shit. Nothing is going to happen here, your brother was collateral damage and they ain't going to be too interested in who did him in, 'cause they've got a lot of dirty laundry of their own to wash.'

'Collateral damage?' This phrase penetrates my skin. It stings and runs deep.

'Look Gene, I'm not a social worker, I'm not an estate agent, I'm a certain kind of businessman and I do my business as I see fit and I'm good at it. You were too, once, remember? You did your time, you didn't snitch, and I respect you for it. If you had, you'd be dead already, you know that. You were in the business, you're just like us, and if I hear any more of that bogus moral superiority bullshit, I'll kick it out of you till you bleed, do you hear me?'

I'm incredibly tired. I want the sofa to swallow me in its squidgy, bland softness. I am powerless and drained and sick to my bones of these people. Of Marbella. Of my whole stupid life, because he's right, I was one of them. I have no morally superior position; I've shared the same gutter as these two in front of me. I have even killed my own kin.

'Whatever, what do you want?'

'First, keep your mouth shut. You tell the police nothing, about anything, it's not your business. It won't do you any good anyway.'

'Ha, and my brother?'

'Nothing to do with me, I told you. Some people were obviously interested in having him out of the way, for reasons I am not party too. But he was in it up to his neck along with Holme. You can't get to the people who did your brother, so forget it. Go home, Eugene.'

I hold his stare for some time. He's right, I should go home. But because it's Kavanagh telling me to, that in itself raises my ire. How much longer must we run from these people, be bullied and belittled, and ultimately killed? He and his kin, as much as I can tell, are the true, original architects of my family's trauma. Something inside me demands, screams, that there shall be no further capitulation. No, not anymore.

'No. I've got nothing to go home to. Remember?'

'So, you gonna stay here, and do what? Avenge your brother? You want revenge? Then find Holme. He set your brother up to take the fall. Collateral damage Gene, it's all much bigger than you and me.'

'Holme?' My thoughts revolve and churn, the dossier, unknown information, secrets and lies, more rancid corrupt Marbella shit no doubt. Holme. Disturbingly, I find Kavanagh is being sincere.

If not completely truthful. It doesn't lessen the depth of my hatred for them. But what to do? Finding Holme would bring a sort of wholesome reckoning, close the circle, almost. For Ana. And Mum? Dad?

Stalemate. Kavanagh inscrutable. Just his form in front of me is latent with strength and menace. Darren is the opposite, skittish, nervy. A silence ensues with me holding Kavanagh's gaze for an extended time. Only the sound of our breathing is audible. A mobile phone pipes up and Darren nearly jumps out of his skin. Kavanagh cuts the call off without even glancing at the apparatus and holds my gaze still.

'So,' I say.

'So,' responds Kavanagh. It's chess time. My life cannot be just this reactive, chaotic ping ponging around, battered by the strange forces fate has marshalled. I must choose a road, make a plan, set a path towards some kind of light, some form of resolution. The thought inspires me, it comforts me. I accept all that has happened, all that is around me, I psychically let all of these reeking vaporous elements infuse my being and lift me up.

'So,' I continue 'I am going to bury my baby brother. I am going to live here, in this apartment. This will become my home, that is my right. I will lend whatever support I can to my brother's widow and to my future nephew or niece. I am not interested in you, or your business. I am only interested in seeking justice for Gary. I have only one responsibility in life now, to my brother's legacy and his child.'

This is one of the versions of the plan that ran through my head, the one selected for public consumption. Darren looks incredulous, but can only gape at Kavanagh, waiting for his boss' reaction. Jimmy Kavanagh finishes his beer, then looks at me and starts to laugh. He laughs for some time, his head shifting to appraise me from different angles.

'Really?' he says. 'Poor little bastard, Uncle Eugene. I gave you the chance to walk away just now, from your indiscretion. You declined, didn't he Darren?' Darren nods dumbly. Kavanagh gets up, picks up and brings over a duffel bag. Out of it he produces the pack of cocaine I had sent off with my squatters the previous evening. 'Darren here was using those two scallies you evicted last night to fence out this stuff. They weren't the brightest buttons in the box, and obviously had no balls...' he stops and glares at Darren, who is protesting with his eyes and a pained grimace. He is utterly dominated by Kavanagh, a lap dog, a simpering compliant poodle. 'What?' No response from Darren, as the tone of the 'what' brooks no reply. 'Exactly. I warned you.' Darren shrivels into the sofa. He returns his attention to me.

'Darren was using the two ex-residents of your brothers flat to steadily shift and package a good amount of snow, and was set to make back his investment fairly quickly. Why don't you explain, Darren for fuck's sake, sitting there like spare part. This is your mess, you take it in hand.'

'Yeah, right sure' and Darren struggles to rumble up some kind of air of competence and authority.

'So, right, I took on this package, which weren't cheap as I'm sure you appreciate, and I trained up my two fellas and that was going nicely and I was on target to meet the payment and make a tidy piece right? Then you fucking show up and blow the whole equation to pieces without so much as a... As a...' His indignation has got his vocabulary locked up.

'A by your leave?' I offer.

'A what? Whatever! Listen you have right royally fucked up my operation, so you are going to sort this shit out. And if you don't, I will fuck you up, or I will have you fucked up proper, right?' He sits, panting.

'So, what are you saying, Darren?'

'I'm saying sell that shit as soon as you can, or you're gonna face the music.'

331

Kavanagh is nodding his agreement. 'Fair's fair Eugene' he adds.

'Ahhh right, so Jimmy provides Darren with a new business, and needs to protect his investment, and Darren needs uncle Jimmy to back him up to lean on me to protect his investment and debt to Jimmy, and then everything will be okay. And once again it's the same routine of a Kavanagh shitting on a Phillips to make their own filthy way in the world.'

Kavanagh visibly tenses in front of me but somehow regains his composure. He leans forward and this time his voice is straight, neutral and emotionless. The threat is as clear as it ever needs to be.

'You need to clean up your mess after you Gene. You know we always protect our own. If you insist on being here, you are a problem. A liability. You know what lengths I will go to, to manage problems and minimize risks. You're back in the game Gene, and don't fuck up. There's no more room for fuck ups where you are concerned.'

He stands up and holds out his hand for me to shake, with a fat, stupid, insincere grin on his face. I give him my hand and he draws my body to him, enveloping me in an iron embrace. The hard mounds of muscle are extraordinary, it's a warm chunk of smooth brick that has me caught, and he presses his mouth into my ear and whispers.

'You should know Genie boy, you can check out anytime you like, but you can never leave. I'll be in touch. Darren...'

He turns away and exits directly. Darren looks dumbly at me. He picks up the duffel bag and pulls out a compact electronic weight scale and other drug paraphernalia. He tries to appear authoritative and in control, but it doesn't become him somehow.

'Three hundred and forty grams in total. You can charge at least sixty euros a gram to the right clients. Twenty grand, more or less. Right, so, micro scales, bags and wraps, all you need. I suggest just go for five and ten gram wraps, no point in fannying around with small fry. It's all ready cut. Don't cut it with anything else, or we will know and the consequences…'

He tails off, not able to spell out the threat in words.

'The consequences, Darren? What might they be, spit it out.'

'Oh fuck off Eugene, you know. You just put yourself up to your neck in it, and you didn't even have to be here. You know how it goes, like the man said, just sort it out, because I sure as fuck am not carrying the can for this if it fucks up. I'll be right happy to watch you take the shit. You think yer clever, 'an that, but you ain't no different to anyone else when it really gets down to it, ay? I'll check in with you every few days to pick up cash. Welcome back. Dickhead.'

He turns for the door and I watch the chippy, bouncy little figure trying to act with a measure of casualness and status.

'Darren?'

He turns back to me, feigning exasperation but he can't hide the discomfort of this evening still dragging on.

'What now? You're wasting valuable dealing time y'know, haha. Ay.'

'Darren, I know, I *know* the cost, it was three years of my life. And three more still to come by the look of it. I knew the cost when I saw Gary's brains on the inside of his windshield. The question is, is do you know? You're not made for this shit. Neither am I. Kavanagh, he is. Are you him? Can you go to those places, do those things he does? Is that you?'

Darren 's breath quickens, his composure hanging on by a thread.

'Just fucking sell the stuff, ya middle class wanker.'

I can't help but smile.

'That's a new one, but beside the point now isn't it. We are in this together, we are just little people Darren, because you ain't one of them, and you will be the next collateral damage, just as likely as I will. I'm still new here, who snorts the most round these parts.'

'Jesus, do you really have to ask?'

'Yup'.

'Well your brother's employees did a good job, but they're history. Party people. And film production crews.'

'Eh?'

'Yeah, remember the guys on the Madrid exhibition job? Those guys. Jonno. Talk to them.' And he turns on his heel and practically scampers out the door.

I wander out onto the balcony unsteadily and slump into a chair. The waving palms and distant sea sooth my senses. I try to take stock of the new facts of life that have accumulated so rapidly since my return. It's noisy in my head for a moment. The angels of goodness flutter fitfully inside, legions of paranoias about prisons, and guns and drug gangs yelling their chorus, beseeching me to eschew the mistakes and habits of a lifetime. I bat them aside, and allow the space in my head to clear now. I focus on the glow of the horizon, of the setting sun, this still alien panorama of sub-tropical deception, this chimera of civilisation and modernity. The cocaine package on the coffee table behind me trembles, beaming its corruption towards me. Its white lines spray out like a lattice work through the sky, linking up into a great canopy of crystalline euphoria around me, a canopy that envelops all, everyone, this coast, this system, this cancerous reality they all run around selling so frantically. It links it all. I am on the inside again, no longer the ex-con, innocent Joe, figuring out how to piece together normality. I am on the inside, pissing out. In Marbella. My enemies are so close, I smell their deodorant, their stress sweat. Keep your friends close, but your enemies closer goes the saying. I have virtually no friends, but being so close to my enemies puts me where no intentional effort could have got me. My and my family's persecutors are within my grasp, the web of relationships is dusted in white powder and radiates out from me as I sit and watch the sunset.

26

Daytime. Again. The package is still on the coffee table where I left it. Three hundred and forty grams worth of trouble, of stress, of putting up with idiots and crazies, of probably returning to prison for ever. The night before I quickly fell asleep on the sofa on the terrace and stumbled into bed at some uncertain hour. Now, for the first time, without thugs breathing down my neck I can trace the sticky fibres of the mesh gathered around me. Tomorrow we bury Gary. The following day I have to visit the *Policia Nacional* to make a statement. Today I have to prepare for my future, or at least the first few steps, and hope I am not prematurely drowned in circumstance. To leave Ana alone, with her dossier, her baby, whatever tediously endless legal proceedings may haunt her every step for years to come, is my instinctive default position. I *should* run back to Watkins' embrace and pay my dues, free of this decadent dung-heap of moral turpitude. But it spits in the face of my dead brother, and father, by extrapolation. It negates the responsibility I have to my one, soon to be living, family member. Some twisted logic, some contorted happenstance has given my life a purpose.

I start to package the cocaine. I sense its power, its potential, its ability to transform all it touches. Ultimately, negatively. Like it or not this stuff is the holy grail of hedonism, for which humanity will commit all manner of compromise. A substance so worshipped it can deform the economies of entire continents, mould entire legal systems to its warped caprice. Oh, the irony. I try a small line, just to know what it is I'm selling. Chop chop snurf… okay. Decent hit. It's not heavily cut and the cutting substance is innocuous. Quality stuff. But I'm not fooled, part of me is deep enough buried to be suspicious of the wellbeing infusing me, to recognise its superficiality. I must maintain this hidden core, this ice cave of realism, keep it safe behind the locked gates of my loneliness, the last refuge, while I set forth on this road to sun-soaked oblivion. And I do see only oblivion. Anything else, any kind of normality or freedom from the chains of criminal bondage, feels absurdly naive, definitively unattainable, simply too dull and pointless because of its inherent impossibility.

In several hours, the coke is bagged and packed. There it sits. Correct to a hundredth of a gram. The contents of the table in front of me translates to a serious sentence. This action is unequivocal. My fate is coalescing. You see, Watkins? I am bending my will to impact on the forces around me to shape my own destiny. I, not you, not the system, I, Eugene Phillips. This is perhaps the only forward motion I have experienced in years, an equanimity, and it's not the coke. I accept whatever my fate shall be.

I raid the memory of called numbers on my mobile. It still belongs to Gary's company, and functions, at least for the moment. After a few mishits and odd conversations in several languages I don't speak, I locate who I'm looking for.

'Hey, Jonno, it's Gene, from the Holme job, Madrid, remember?'

'Who? Holme… sorry mate…'

'The exhibition build you did, in the San Pedro warehouse. I saw you in town, a couple of weeks ago, with the girl…'

'Okay right, how's it goin'?'

'Well it's not really is it, that's why I'm calling.'

'Sheeeeeeyit, yeah that's right, so sorry, that was your brother, ohmigod, that's bad.'

'Yeah, putting it mildly.'

'So what you up to?'

'Well, I'm looking for work, like on a shoot…'

Jonno sighs, and the previous friendliness evaporates. 'Sorry mate, but that's not my call, each department puts its own crew together. I can't really help.'

'Yeah understood, but can you put me in touch with someone who might be able to help. I kinda need a break, you know what I mean…'

'Yeah, I'm sure you do, okay. Let me see what I can do, can I get you on this number?'

'Yep anytime.'

'Ok leave it with me, bye.'

Inconclusive. But maybe something. I contemplate the problem, how to shift coke in a town you don't know. This is new for me. I was the Trip Master General. From Liverpool to Hamburg people knew me for pills of all flavours, good times and purity guaranteed. But pills are so not Marbella. Virgin territory to be sure and I don't even know who the competition is and whose patch is which and what trouble I may be walking into. Because this place is like everywhere else. The bottom line is you get shot when things fuck up. Tomorrow is Gary's funeral, as if I needed reminding. I will meet Ana at ten, then will be taken somewhere, with people I haven't met. No Phillips or other family in attendance, I have pretty much made sure of that over the last two weeks. It does not trouble me. I am curious to know who will be there. Whereabouts on the scale of sincerity/hypocrisy they will be located. I decide to scout out my market. I pull out something fairly bland but smart and head out. I decide not to bring any product with me. I need to understand the lie of the land. And generate welcome distraction from tomorrow's colossal demands on my equilibrium.

I head down to the port in my little car. Puerto Banus must be a good place to start. Despite my history I am quite the ingenue. It's a pleasant night. I think it's a Wednesday, and with a sting of shame I realise I don't know what day it is. All I know is tomorrow is the funeral and the rest is shrouded in mists of the unknown. I walk along the portside. The boats are moored to jetties in rows. The names reveal the various vanities and peccadillos of the owners, none so much as the boat named 'Muff Diver'. Opposite the boats the cars line up as though rehearsing for a Monte Carlo rally. Lamborghinis,

337

Aston Martins, Porsche, Ferrari, Bentley, Maserati; the calling cards of the inordinately wealthy. At the corner of the port closest to the biggest boats, I am accosted by a beautiful but overly plasticized young woman. She is in a dress that leaves nothing to the imagination, her tight, pert bum vibrating alluringly with each clip clop of her inevitably high, bright red, platform-cum-stiletto heels, set off with obligatory boob surgery. She looks fifteen going on twenty-eight, her long loose hair is flicked frequently to and fro around a face that is plain, but has been so superbly sculpted by colour and shade and eyelash additions that she is like a magnet for your eyes. Everything about a female's more obviously physical attractions has been so well directed, squeezed and pointed to maximum effect, I can only marvel. Why didn't girls look like this when I was younger, I reflect, when it might have mattered? I correct myself, remembering how the more ostentatiously attractive girls back in the day used to terrify me. It would only have made life more confusing than it was. It would take a much plainer, less demanding girl, with a penchant for my easily available class A stimulants, to draw my interest. The relationships I had were rarely more than passing co-habitations of drug use and partying, and I fear me getting laid was as much to do with my access to such, rather than any personal qualities I was in possession of at the time. She appears to be part of a flock of these creatures, tottering on their heels, strapped and stroked, holding leaflets and vouchers of some kind.

'Alright my love, looking for a table reservation, top place, port views?' She has a Frankie kind of accent, decidedly not Spanish.

'Erm, what?'

'Are you in a group?'

'Nope, I'm on my todd. Is that a problem?'

'Well it's a minimum spend of six fifty per table, bottles start at one sixty for non-premium vodka or whiskey.'

'And where is this fabulous bargain to be had?'

'Terra Firma sky bar, down the end, y'see the terrace at the top, great views, really good DJ, he usually does Ibiza but he's here in Port.' She waits for a response from me but realises I am not the target audience, and she clumps back toward the other primped flamingos, and I overhear 'Nahhh, forget it, he's a loner, nothing goin' on with him.' The flock moves toward a gang of not-so-young men but dressed as though they are, polo t-shirts, slacks, smallish beer bellies. Probably golfers as I have seen the same attire on people carrying the clubs all over the place on this coast. I decide to head for the aforementioned sky bar.

I find a flight of stairs at the end of the port jetty, rising up to where the noise is coming from. I pass by two enormous doormen; the pumped bulk of the steroid soaked muscles requires me to manoeuvre between them.

'Can I see your reservation slip, please' says the girl in the ticket booth, heavily accented English, probably Latin American judging by her jet-black hair and face reminiscent of Mayan paintings.

'I don't have one, I just wanted to go in on my own, have a beer, y'know, I'm new in town.'

Not a flicker of recognition of the details just, 'Sorry table reservations only, minimum spend…'

I cut her off and decide to bullshit.

'Listen, I'm working with a film company, we are going to make a show here and I'm looking for possible places, can I just have a look around?'

The noisy gang of golfers has arrived behind me, and she glances at the sea of already drunken faces.

'Yeah okay, sure, go on up' and she gets on with her proper clientele.

I stroll on through, emerging onto a wide terrace that snakes around the main core of the building. I take in the excellent views of the mega yachts moored below, and of the harbour entrance. A full moon casts a silver rippling pathway across the Med towards me. It is undeniably beautiful. A veritable poorer man's Monte Carlo. The terrace is already crowded with groups gathered around tables, either all male or all female, interspersed occasionally with smaller groups of mixed but older people. Hubbly bubbly pipes are being chugged on and shared around. Each table has a great pile of mixer drinks, a bucket of ice with gargantuan spirits bottles lit by some kind of light in its base. The group stand or sit around this altar of alcohol, slurping on their vodka and tonics and moving listlessly to the beats. I'm seeing predominantly provincial British people, with a few obvious other nationalities. I recognise instantly at one table a group of Dutch guys, simply because of their height and the dress style which is simpler, more knowing and individual, familiar from my days over there. The British tend to dress with a pack mentality. A pair of voluptuous Latin girls walk past and stand around scanning the tables. They aren't in a group. Ah, of course. They are hookers, expensive ones probably, given the personal jewellery they sport and the superior quality of cosmetic surgery than that exhibited by some of the British girls on their hen nights.

A corny fanfare blares out and a couple of waiters emerge carrying ice buckets high above their heads containing champagne, with short miniature fireworks attached to their necks. People gawk and holler, and a photographer appears and follows it to the table where he shoots shots of the moment, no doubt to be flogged on later at exorbitant prices.

A group of girls emerge through the door looking considerably more elegant, richer, it's obvious. They are a mix, Spanish, Scandinavian looking maybe, or Russian. One of them is familiar and I cringe inwardly. My last night out, barely three weeks ago, the great party. It's poor Britta, whose evening I so conspicuously ruined. Just as I make my mind up to make a run for it, she sees me. I make a run for it anyway. Once out on the portside again I resolve to leave my market research for another night.

'I think you owe me an apology.' Ah. Britta, obviously, and I turn to face my accuser. She is standing, arms folded, head askance looking at me with a thunderously indignant expression. Then she softens. 'But I am so sorry about what happened. It must be awful, really. You have my deepest condolences.' Of all the people who have said this to me of late, this one sounds sincere at least.

'Ha, you could say that. And then my mum died a week later, of… shock, probably.' Strange to be a petty liar about such a momentous thing. So easy. A monstrous crime of mercy dismissed with a fib.

'Oh wow, that is really bad. Come on, let's go get a drink', and she hooks her arm in mine and leads me off in the same way as that night, though I doubt this night will lead to a scene in a toilet.

We are sat in one of the less noisy bars along the port front, in a booth, discreet, away from the humdrum of face painting hedonism. Apart from ordering drinks, neither of us has said anything.

'So', she says.

'Mmmmm. So. I do owe you an apology. I do have, umm, some issues maybe, and he touched a nerve. I had to get something out of my system, and it's just unfortunate he pulled my trigger.'

'Well, yes, I certainly didn't think that behaviour was habitual.'

'No, it's not'. Well, not habitual, but currently constantly latent within me.

'It was mortally embarrassing, but you did do me a huge favour. He was so ashamed he packed up and went back home to Dubai. He'll probably show up again when everyone here has forgotten and moved on. Once the next pathetic social scandal has blown up.'

'Glad I could be of service.' She giggles endearingly.

'Well, I was having a really good time up until then, you were a very silly boy to go and ruin it all.' I can't figure out whether she is being flirtatious or not. 'You didn't ruin anything, what happened to your brother ruined everything. It made me feel sick. Marbella is tainted. It's poisoned. It's one thing drug dealers murdering each other, that's just inevitable, but Gary was like one of us. He was one of us!' Her anguish is genuine, even if a tad egocentric. 'Is it true you were in the car when it happened?' Her face is a death mask of horror. Being so close to the bloody reality of the deed disturbs her but probably, typically, also fascinates her.

She mulls over the whys and wherefores offering much sympathy, trying to understand what forces were involved. It's as though only understanding the full facts will make her able to cope with being here, being part of that scene she so loves. The beautiful Marbella people. It wears my patience a bit.

'Britta, you need to understand that there's nothing exceptional about this. I haven't been here long, but I have gained an insight into how this place works, what really drives things behind the glitz and the parties. It's not pretty. It stinks. It is, in fact, rotten to the core, and all of this scandal with the town hall and so on is just the tip of the much deeper iceberg, which only gets dirtier the further below the waterline you go. I have to face the fact that the people who did this walk among us, and if I stay here, then that danger is just part of where we are.'

She shudders, and looks tearful.

'But how can people live that way?' I cut her off with my laughter, and she flashes me an indignant grimace. 'How can you be so flippant?'

I grab the waiter's attention and order more drinks. I'm enjoying the company, no matter how painful the subject of conversation is. It feels better to be airing this, of being able to talk about it, even as I psyche myself up for his funeral tomorrow.

'Look Britta, I don't mean to patronise you, but think about it. We went and did coke together in a bathroom near here. Where did you get that coke? Who sold it to you? Where did he or she get it from? What route or gang brought it to us here in Marbella? How do they do business, and what do they do to protect their interests?'

'But Gary wasn't involved with drugs,' she says indignantly, pleadingly.

'No, that I truly believe, he wasn't. But everything is a network. The whole town hall thing, the bribes, the backhanders. Where do criminal gangs wash their drug profits? Every time you buy a gram of coke, you are buying into a system; a system that has tentacles everywhere, that often, ultimately, reaches the extreme of people getting shot, who otherwise have nothing to do with that whatsoever.'

Britta is visibly struggling to process this, that her hedonism is part of a bigger, deeper package of evil. It's something I have always been surprised by, the inability of drug takers to see they bear some responsibility for the whole mess. Maybe not as much as people like me, though.

'But you took it quite happily!' She throws back thinking that it's a simple blame game, that she's no worse than anyone else.

'Britta, I've taken more drugs than you can shake a shitty stick at. But mostly anything but cocaine.'

'Oh, Christ you're not…'

My empathy, or attraction, for this poor naive soul is in danger of causing indiscretion. First rule, don't advertise your business unless you know the buyers are in on the secret. No, don't get high on your own supply. Second rule, then.

'Of course not.' Big fibs. What else can I say. That I've just done three years for that particular crime? No, better put this conversation to bed. 'But think about it, where do you get your coke, where do people do that around here?' I continue. Fishing.

'Don't you know?'

I shake my head simply.

'Waiters. In most high-end clubs one of the waiters is the contact. He has the cooperation of the doormen, and so the clients don't have to travel with the stuff. They can get it where they want to party. Plenty of waiters around have a side-line in that. And other things.'

'And who do you suppose supplies them?' She doesn't answer, she just curls her bottom lip. The penny is dropping. 'Do you take much coke?'

'No!' the indignation is comical. 'It's just for fun, parties, going out, y'know.'

'Yes, I know'.

Silence falls.

'I better go join my friends,' she says, readying to leave.

'Yes, they'll be wanting you to pay your share of the table minimum no doubt.'

She laughs at that, and it's my turn to feel patronised. 'I don't pay for that. The one guy who was with us? He's stupidly rich. He pays. It's his price for being seen with us gorgeous things around him. We get free drinks and he gets to show off to his friends. This is Marbella, I *never* pay for drinks.' She gives me a peck on the cheek and is gone, and indeed, I am paying for the drinks. Which, this being port, are shockingly expensive. So at least I learnt something tonight. Makes a change from it being the doormen.

I decide to repair to another club in the vicinity. I think about where Gary's party was, as it appears to be the main club around, but then think better of that idea. They won't want to see my face again, for a whole host of reasons. As I pay my exorbitant bar bill, I strike up a conversation with the waitress, who, naturally speaks English. I enquire where I can find a really exclusive private club, with style, I don't like the port, too downmarket, y'know. She mentions a name which I recognise as Gary's place, then she corrects herself, as that has shut down temporarily, because, well you know what happened. I didn't know that had happened. No wonder Frankie disappeared so promptly. Then she says another name. I decide to head there.

The directions I am given prove accurate. I thought she was joking when she said do a U-turn by the mosque. Sure enough, there's a vast opulent mosque nuzzling next to a much vaster, more opulent Arab palace. Yet another flavour to the insanely cosmopolitan layer cake that is Marbella. Judging by this, they appear to be the icing on it or thereabouts. Not far past this, I am lost in green trees until a splendid, equally Moorish looking building emerges out of the gloom. This must be the place judging by the inevitable collection of fancy sports cars. I drive up and a wordless flunky gestures for my keys, hands me a token, and disappears with the crummy hire car, with barely a glance. Maybe the car already said to him there was no tip coming on this one. Is that what I am supposed to do? More wordless flunkies beckon me through the Moorish style arch into a grand open-air interior which is indeed doing its best to emulate visions of a Thousand and One Nights. Palms abound, and it's like a mini Alhambra Palace, with groups of sofas around low tables, resplendent with massively ornate hookah pipes. Waiting staff drift miraculously, their flowing dervish gowns making them appear to float on air. Each one is of such a striking demeanour it's fully evident that you have to look a certain way to work here. And then the inevitable question, 'Do you have a table reservation, sir?'

'Umm, no I don't, I was just going to sit at the bar if that's okay?'

'Certainly sir, but there'll be an entrance fee of thirty-five euros without the reservation.'

'Do I get a drink with that?'

'No sir, I'm afraid not.'

I drop another of the Bin Laden's on the cashier and she barely flinches. I notice in the deep till drawer and veritable bundle of the elusive little beasts. Birds of a feather flock together, evidently, in Marbella.

I wander in towards the long bar. Everything is back lit and low light, from dozens of small lamps and recessed lights, all in exotic styles, warm and cosy, hiding, no doubt, yet further exorbitant prices. I sit on a stool and order a beer from the young man with Omar Sharif model looks.

'That'll be eighteen euros please… *Gracias.*'

Oh well, I am now expecting to be left breathless by the pricing in all of these places. Subtle ethno-fusion lounge sounds warble through invisible speakers. A considerable relief from the awful low-rent techno house in the sky bar. I sit and take in the panorama, sipping slowly, nibbling on the generous bowl of fried somethings that detonate noisily in my mouth with every crunch. It's dead. A desultory two groups are sat close by, with the customary ice bucket, grandiose bottles and mixers and the hookah pipe. They are dressed in a similar style to the elderly Spanish bourgeoisie I encountered that first night in the restaurant. Blazers, passé shirts, cravats… but the women not so. They are all much younger than the men, elegant, and ostentatiously sexy. Trophy girlfriends.

'Is it always this quiet?' I say to the barman, to relieve the boredom.

'Well yes, it is early. And it is April, we only open this week for the season.'

'Aha, early you say. What time does it warm up?'

'Usually around two to three.'

'Okay. Thanks.'

I'm seriously doubting the usefulness of this strategy. It could cost me a week's wages in beer, hanging around here, whatever a week's wages are for normal people. Even a weekly wage is something not familiar to me. Tax, social security, wage packets, not something that has ever featured in my line of work. I have left little trace of anything within the system as such. I couldn't even hazard a guess at how much I have earned over the years. It came in irregular wedges of cash, which felt like a lot in the moment, but the weeks of eking it out until the unpredictable arrival of the next one, were punishing some times. For all I know I was ripped off and badly paid.

346

It's shocking now to consider, I *don't* know. And here I am paying eighteen euros for a beer, which is effectively half a pint! I chuckle. Out loud I realise, as this engenders a response from someone who has drawn up beside me at the bar.

'What's so funny? Let us know the joke.' The slightly clumsy English and the sort of Scandinavian accent are instantly noticeable, but this is forgotten when I behold the person addressing me. Nothing I have seen in my life has prepared me for the vision in front of me. Despite everything I have seen in terms of how far people here will go to stretch their appearance toward some weird kind of culturally ordained extreme, I still stop. My first reaction is I want to run, laughing, choking on disbelief, out of here. Before me is a female, I think. She has evident iconic features of the female of the species. Breasts. Stupidly big ones, comically inflated to near basketball dimensions, supported by a thin, but tautly muscular frame, revealed by the skimpy top and hot pants and sheer stockings. The curves of the bones have taken on a sort of extreme support roll, for the ripped sinuous muscles, so devoid of fat or body liquid the veins are pronounced on the surface. She has not so much a six pack as a cheese grater stomach. Gloriously silly pseudo-erotic tattoos spiral about the straggly limbs, dragons and campy Frank Frazzetta maidens, demons with huge penises, and quaint slogans in bad English. 'Love is to be the best.' Profound. It's taking a while to process the welter of information such is the strangeness and distance from a normal human form this woman has managed to achieve, so much so that when I look at her face, it takes further time to register. I struggle to hold onto my composure, lest I offend the girl. I am staring at what once was the normal, natural face of a young girl that has taken a journey into a David Lynchian parallel universe. I wonder if there is LSD in my beer. Are those actually her lips? To my distaste I find I recall those awful images of grotesque racist caricatures in Tintin comics of Africans where the lips are exaggerated beyond all reason, but this girl has done a similar thing, quite intentionally. Her lips are bulbous distended bananas about four times out of proportion to the rest of her features, painted violently pink and heavily glossed. Coupled with the fact her eyes naturally aren't large, but rather ordinary dull, piggy affairs, the effect is to leave the whole face languishing in the shadow of these monstrous distensions. Then I notice the cheeks. Ah yes, they've been pumped full of something, un-naturally pointed cheek profiles, but dwarfed by the scale of the lip job. Her eyebrows appear to have been tattooed into place. The hair is cut into a shapely black bob, framing the face perfectly, prohibiting any way to hide the full crimes of surgery. And she's looking at me, expectantly, to answer her rejoinder. I am still processing all of this, and am plucking up courage to reply when I halt, literally breathless. The words die on my tongue. A second woman comes up from behind her and stands with her friend. Her sister, it is apparent for they are, indeed, completely identical. Identical in form, comedy boobs, in muscularity, in tattoos of similar theme, in distended lips, but this girl is blonde.

'Oh my god you're twins!' Is what I blurt out.

'Yeah, you can tell can't you. Are you alone? You're cute, maybe you have a baby brother for my sister. Buy us a drink?'

The effect of this is strange. My face wants to twist itself off the bones of my skull, leaving my teeth to grind in frantic futile circles, as I try to exhale through the base of my spine.

'Are you okay?'

I'm not sure what the exterior signs of these symptoms are, but I pull myself together, trying to push the troublesome part of me into the back of my head, so it can observe the ostensibly normal part of me functioning out front.

'Yes, sure, fine, what would you like?'

'Long Island Iced tea.'

'Me too' pipes up blondie.

'Barman, please, three long island ice teas, *gracias.*' Internally I laugh to myself as to what they will cost.

348

'So. You're twins… and, er… you've had the same beauty treatment… I see.' Jesus, what do I say to these two? As much as they have willingly entered into some kind of pact with a hoard of demonic cosmetic surgeons, I feel intense pity, then guilt for that, as who am I to judge. I have always tried to forgive people their weirdness. Few people in my adult life have been 'normal', and I soon learnt to not get hung up about other people and their often monumentally irritating idiosyncrasies. Life would have been too stressful to take umbrage at every deviant lifestyle factor, or case of flakiness and downright craziness. None of them were worth the effort anyhow.

'Where you from,' asks dark bob one.

'England'.

'Yes, I can tell.'

'And you?'

'We are from Sweden.'

'Right. And you live here? Or on holiday?'

'No, we live in Marbella now. I'm Agneta' says blondie.

'And I'm Freda. You know, like Abba?'

'Wow, seriously?'

'Yes, seriously, we changed our names. We do everything together.'

'We are identical twins, and we want to create ourselves as unique, doubly unique.'

'We eat same food exactly, same work-out, every day.'

Our drinks arrive and I simply place a yellow two hundred euro note on the bar. The two girls clock this straight away. My change is less than a hundred euros. Oh well.

'Our bodies are our work. It is a project we start when we are eighteen.' Affirms Agneta.

'We save a lot for our first implants, and we weren't happy, so we make another one when we are twenty…'

'And this was better, and gave us some work for magazines…'

349

'And now we are here in Marbella to look for sponsors for our next stage.' Says Frida in complete sincerity.

'Sponsors?' I still think there was LSD in the beer. 'So, you want to try and get someone to pay for your surgery?' Both nod enthusiastically, again in such a way it's clear they see nothing unusual about these life choices.

'With the right sponsor and the right manager, we can become famous and unique. I think it's important to have a goal in life.'

'Our goal is twin perfection.' They both beam with satisfaction. 'Your name?'

I pause for a moment wondering if I should take on a pseudonym, just bullshit, as you never know, Marbella is very much a goldfish bowl, but I can't think of a sensible enough name, and so Gene stumbles out.

'OK Gene, what do you do?' Again, I'm floundering for some kind of credible story that won't lead back to the hell of recent weeks, as I hadn't considered how I would explain myself and everything to anyone henceforth. I fall back on historical bullshitting.

'I'm a DJ.'

'Oh cool' says Agneta. It might indeed appear so to her, and maybe standing behind some decks by the beach in Marbella, or in some reincarnation of the hanging gardens of Babylon style nightclub, really is cooler than a warehouse in northern Europe. As I blather away a pile of invented nonsense about the swinging nights in Amsterdam, Liverpool and Manchester, dropping as many names as I can recall, I am able to reach that disconnectedness again. I am sat back deep behind my eyeballs, hearing my own voice remotely, watching the performance with amusement and a shade of embarrassment. It's all pitiable bragging, ticking off a list of cool points, the DJ's, the drugs, the late nights, the cars, narrow escapes with various police forces. I glamorise, embellish and completely invent past events so that their aura assumes something that at the time I would have been utterly contemptuous of, the idea it was somehow the apogee of hipness and social success to lead such a lifestyle. I knew then it was only ever an evasion, a subterfuge, a construction of an approximation of life that filled the time, a Valium pill that softened the putrid patina of reality. As much as I enjoy the idiotic, rambling hyperbole of my imagined life, aided by the longest of island iced teas, I retreat further into my disdain of this version, until I am so in awe of my own mythology, I am disorientated by uncertainty. Maybe that's what I thought my life was? Maybe I was so out of it I've forgotten what myths I told myself, and others.

'Still don't know what I was waiting for, my time was running wild, a million dead end streets and all the time I thought I'd got it made, it seemed the taste was not so sweet. So I turned myself to face me, as I had never caught a glimpse, of how the others must see the fakir…'

I am aware of the two girls staring at me, laughing slightly in embarrassment and disbelief. Others are looking over from tables, witheringly, pityingly.

'You're a singer as well?' Says Frida.

'What?' I'm befuddled by this.

'Stick to DJ-ing' adds Agneta.

I look from one to the other. What I thought was an unbidden dredging up of yet another of Dad's Bowie albums in my backseat sanctuary has translated into me singing aloud.

'Erm, how much of that did I just sing to you?'

'How much of what, I've never heard this song…'

'I was singing right?'

'Well, yes… are you okay?' The pair of them seem uncomfortable, the supposedly entertaining bloke with the cool history maybe a bit weird.

'Naaaah, only fooling, course I was singing. I do it all the time, just burst into tunes. It's my Dad's fault, playing me all these records when I was young, he'd get me to learn the words and … y'know…'

They are nodding, but their glances are drifting off, seeking a distraction, an excuse maybe. And one duly presents itself. A group of middle-aged men come in, long leather coats, accompanied by bigger men who are evidently not *with* them, but looking after them. Body guards. And not particularly discreet about it either. Both the girls' faces light up, and without a backward glance they slide off their stools and sashay over to the men, who greet them old fashioned style, formal cheek kissing three times. The group moves towards me, the girls with their arms hooked inside the elbows of the richest looking man. He glides past, ringed by his heavies and shoots me one inscrutable, expressionless but penetrating glance.

'Thanks for the drinks…' says Agneta, with a self-satisfied smirk and they move over to the biggest group of sofas and tables, where an enormous array of beverages is laid out waiting. It's far more than the group could consume in a week, let alone a night. Conspicuous consumption at its finest and most decadent.

I think I was just the baby-sitter. The girls must have been waiting for him, or any other of the types that would be willing to have these two freaks hanging off their elbows. And I admit I have to include myself in that happy club.

I am distracted by the barman, as he passes a receipt over to me. I hadn't paid for any further drinks, nor am I aware of how many more we may have had. I am, it now dawns on me, rather drunk. The amount on the ticket just induces a dull, sicky feeling of disappointment and pity. This fascinating evening has left me with little change from five hundred euros. I stare woozily around me. To my relief I appear to be inhabiting my mind in a more unified form, and the club buzzes on with its low, opulent drone, without me. I sit alone, out of place, out of mind, I am from another planet to these people. How on earth did I imagine I could sell them coke? How on earth am I going to shift any of this wretched stuff? Why am I doing this? The phrases start to revolve in my mind. A mist of self-pity descends, multiple what ifs and whys and wherefores charge around

352

inside me. I order yet another iced tea. It comforts me and turns the harsh noise of my mind to something more soupy and tolerable.

'So simple minded, he can't drive his module, bites on the neon and he sleeps in his capsule, loves to be loved.'

Dum, dum, dum, da-da da-dum, dum, dum, da-da da-dum, dum, dum, goes the guitar riff in my head. It is pleasingly Neanderthal, completely perfect in its simplicity, so satisfyingly guttural and erotic. The Jean Genie lives on his back. Empty glass tapping on the bar, the stomping simple beat has total, forward, unstoppable motion.

'Jean Genie lives on his back, Jean Genie loves chimney stacks, he's outrageous, screams and he bawls, Jean Genie let yourself gooo-ohohhhhh…'

'Sir, please!' The vexed face of the barman comes into focus. 'You are disturbing the clients, I am afraid I have to ask you to leave, please'.

'But I'm the Gene Genie, Eugenie Genie, dah dah dah dahhhh.'

Okay so if they don't want me, I'll go. I'll take my money elsewhere. They're all looking at me now, oh yes, they notice me now.

'Fucking wankers.' Did I say that aloud or think that? Oh, it must have been aloud because the barman is behind me now. I'll go. Yes, I'll go. Dum dum dum dah dahhhhh da dum dum dum to the car.

I have keys. No I don't, where's my keys, oh shiiiiit… oh. Piece of plastic, give it to the nice man. He gets my car, for I am the Gene Genie.

'Sir, do you think you should be driving, there is a control nearby, you…'

'I am in control! Yes'

I know how to work this thing. Great, let's go home. Relief descends, if I can only drive this shit box on wheels, god it's such a jerky car. It revs too much. But I'm okay to drive, just take it nice and easy. Don't do anything stupid, no-one will notice. Windows down, motion, cool breeze, relief. Brrrrmmmmmm off we go home again home again jiggedy-jig.

Up ahead, blue lights and men in uniform. A waving yellow ice-cream cone pointing at me, beckoning me. A man is holding a machine gun. A machine gun? A fucking machine gun!? He is stood in front of my car. Someone wants to talk.

'Yes?' He talks in Spanish then something I understand…

'Control. Please, breathe here'.

It's that machine again.

'Señor, leave the car.' What does he mean?

'*Has sobre pasado el límite permitido de alcolémia, no se puede continuar*[28], get out of the car *Señor*'.

I'm aware of sweat chilling and trickling down the small of my back. I appear be in a bit of a situation. What is all this, blockades, machine guns, it's like fucking Belfast or something, I, erm. What. Should. I do.

'*Pasaporte.*'

'Haven't got it.'

He is holding a torch into my face which is deeply intimidating and uncomfortable as I can't see anything, just the glare of the light. Only a group of shadows looms around me.

'*Identidad.*' The man with the machine gun has joined the group. I should be scared but it's verging on comic farce, a machine gun for me, the Gene Genie. They've got the wrong guy.

'*Identidad, por favor*', this time rather emphatically.

'*Señor*, you must come with me.'

This I do not like. I would prefer not to. Gary tomorrow, sad day, Ana, I have to be nice, not going to be easy. Gary, Holme, faces, events, guns, I need to go home. Wait. Grapple my mobile out. Madrid, night, other policemen, yes! Phone number, phone them up.

---

[28] You have passed the permitted limit of alcohol, you cannot continue

354

I locate the number from those weeks ago, there are barely any others. It rings. Man with machine gun has raised it, and officer is shouting at me. Voice comes on line.

'Listen Señor, I am a colleague of Holme, Vladimir Lebid. I made the delivery to Sorzano. Of the money. I know what the money is for. Now please tell the policeman to let me go. This is your problem not mine.'

Some babbling in Spanish but I stick the phone firmly into the gesticulating hand of the officer. He pauses and listens. Quickly he turns and walks away, out of my sight. I am not moving for a machine gun points at me. Nobody moves. Nobody says anything. My breathing deafens me. I taste the corrosive chemical sensation of the acetone in my breath, my body and lungs grappling and expelling the copious levels of alcohol in my blood. Voices still, inaudible.

The officer reappears, hands me the phone. The others back off and mercifully the machine gun points back towards the ground.

'*Adelante señor*. You go. This time, but Señor, Marbella is change, *entiendes*? Next time, *habra problemas, me entiendes? Problemas*[29]. Go.'

The pointy yellow electric ice cream cone beckons me back onto the highway. My hands are shaking, and I feel more aware. My coordination is foggy, and things are blurry ahead of me. Only by sobering up slightly do I perceive I am truly shitfaced. Driving home is a terrifying ordeal. The concentration on coordination has me sweating buckets. Finally, home. Keys, fumble, door, and delicious swirling, nauseous, blackness.

---

[29] ...there'll be trouble, understand? Trouble.

27

Inchoate sounds. Half formed thoughts. Something niggling. I am aware of a great sadness. An urge to weep. A dread weight pressing on me. I flail, but in slow motion, the sticky blackness around me makes everything strangely weightless yet immensely heavy. A face swirls into view. Ana. Red rimmed eyes. She is in a room which is dilapidated and dirty. A table with a heavy table cloth, and curiously, a large plate of *jamon*. I try to mouth something to her, but I am aware I am only wearing my underpants. Again. I curse myself for having forgotten to dress properly, what can I do now, I gesture helplessly. Her expression doesn't change, just a shadow of contempt passes over and washes through me. Daylight enters into the room. Day enters into my head. I am in my bed, in the apartment. Seconds pass as I compute how I came to be in that situation, and where I am now and what is supposed to happen next. The dread and weight, and sticky slow-motion helplessness is still with me. The funeral. This is why I am here now, this is what must be done. Various pieces of the narrative that led me here start falling into my mind, tumbling out of the fog, the thumping, head splitting pain I am experiencing. Mouth dry. Breath stench. Sweaty clothes, sheets disordered. Nausea still. Fatigue. I want the blackness to reclaim me. For a day. Skip this episode. Jump to tomorrow. It never happened. I don't need to see this one.

Shower. Dress. Strange new clothes, sterile, lack of personal scent, unfamiliar, stiff, smelling of chemicals and air-freshener. I don't fully recognise myself in the mirror. Who is he that looks at me? A sense of utter uselessness descends, suffocating me further. I want to close my eyes, rid myself of the nausea, the hangover, the physical discomfort of being conscious, and give myself to sleep, a sleep that doesn't have to end. I don't need to wake up. I can just sleep. Sleep. My innards twist, and the moment on the verge of the welcoming void vanishes like smoke from an extinguished match. I am propelled back to the lavatory and vomit violently. For a while I slump over the bowl staring at the bile, sobs rack and grip my frame. Salty tears flow abundantly, mucus fills my nose and passages. For how long I don't know. When I stand up eventually I am purged. I am steadier, can focus. I need to change my shirt. Pathetic. Look at you.

Wash, change, freshen. Drive car. Park at favourite cafeteria near the warehouse and down two strong *cafe con leches*, a *mollete serranito*. Familiar noise, quieter than usual. I grow into myself again. Thoughts line up in a discernible, cogent order. I marvel in horror at my behaviour last night. I am laughing at my outrageous bravado with the police. I cackle at the absurd Swedish surgery twins. What a remarkably, brilliantly, fabulously twisted and deranged world, inhabited by such beings, swimming uselessly in the cesspool of their own futile self-importance. I emerge into the blinding sunlight, and ironically salute the great gleaming blue canopy hanging over me. I admire the heavy palm fronds and their rubbery rustling and smile to myself further. For some strange, quite frightening reason, it feels like home.

~

Everyone is peculiarly polite and composed. Ana looks calm, and striking, in a simple black dress. Rafaela is with us, and someone I hadn't met who turns out to be the lawyer, Don Alfredo.

That is the funeral party. One can taste the appalling grief, swimming invisibly in the air between us. We shall not acknowledge it, we shall not give it the stage it so thirstily seeks. The sheer incomprehensibility of actually attending the funeral of one's own brother, so brutally cut down, renders the entire event a touch of the surreal. The enormity is so huge, I fail to connect with the grief I know must reside somewhere. I float outside it, watching the show with a numb bemusement.

A ride up into the hills, driven in a large Mercedes by the lawyer. All manner of disconnected thoughts and images of a life lived and lost float through. It's like being properly stoned but without the pleasurable sensations, an untethering of the mind, allowing it to unlock the serried filing cabinets of memory and dump the contents straight into your lap. Multiple images of Gary, back in Warrington. Family life. The dark times. Random interludes. The smell of fish and chips. Mum, healthy and happy, looking foxy as she struts out to 'bingo'. An entire life compressed into specks of glitter broiling in the heavy paperweight's water. All that life, sensation, hope, potential, experience... We survey the simple grey-silver metal coffin on the dais. The graveyard is indeed a yard, walled, a patio within a square of graves stacked up one on top the other. A simple plaque, and a coffin slid into a slot behind it. A priest mumbling in Spanish, looking sympathetic but reserved, going through the arcane motions, none of which can stand in the blinding light of the facts. Like so much here, due to its stark difference to an English life, it has a movie-like quality. We should be cowboys. Repair to the saloon to toast our fallen gringo companion. The spaghetti western graveyard, compact, with its bodies stacked, smack bang in the middle of the painted white village on the mountain gives it a theatrical, rhetorical feeling. Death as a grand gesture, a cinematic flourish, an event immortalised. I like it. In a weird way, it is what Gary would have wanted. A very Spanish end.

A couple of startled tourists do a double take. As though the cutesy rustic graveyard was for their amusement, part of the heritage, the cliché Andalus. Yes, the walls indeed hold dead people. Didn't you realise? Behind them, as they drop their cameras in shame and embarrassment, mortified to have entered at the moment the true nature of the place has been slapped in their faces, moves an elderly man, obviously a Brit, standing alone, watching us. He is taking part. In his way. His eyes meet mine. Something connects and I am disturbed to wonder why. But he stays in his zone. Keeps his confidence.

~

Back in Marbella. Ana and Rafaela embrace. Rafaela appears to have aged ten years, her shape has changed, she stoops slightly, as though winded, her expression one of faint, indignant surprise and bewilderment. The dream is up in flames, and its noxious stench is all around us. We breath it in, and it laughs as it tickles our throats and nostrils. Ana and I are to sit with Don Alfredo and hear Gary's last will and testament, as they say. Rafaela says her goodbyes. I have occasionally seen people who, vividly, have been broken by life. It pains me to see one so young and beautiful smashed in such a way. It makes Ana's demeanour all the more impressive.

We ensconce ourselves in an office, high up in a block on Marbella's main street. This central commercial thoroughfare is schizophrenic. Office buildings jostle with designer shops, touristy boutiques and a variety of everyday businesses. It's part European working street and part tourist resort.

The room is dominated by a clumsily pretentious and oversized mahogany desk. Photos of diplomas and citations, old alumnae, pompous group shots of what I assume are local big wigs cover the walls. I spot Sorzano in amongst them, stood next to a larger than life portly chap in a loud shiny suit, with a giant bulbous nose and a sense of importance that breaks the frame of the picture. A mafioso Cyrano de Bergerac. Ana clocks my gaze.

'Jesus Gil, the chief architect of all you see…'

'Oh right.' He resembles the legend I'd been building a picture of. The cliché, with his shiny suit, hilarious belly, cigar, surrounded by flunkies and a woman dressed as though she were trying to outdo Joan Collins in Dynasty-esque outrageousness. Don Alfredo is audible babbling at his underlings in the hall, he sounds tense, tetchy. He sits before us with a bundle of papers ostentatiously wrapped in ribbons with antiquated wax seals. He shakes my hand briskly, but noticeably barely makes eye contact. Likewise, with Ana, which really unsettles me. Isn't this the man they entrusted with their personal affairs? Clearly, the poison cloud of the great Marbella crash is souring every filament of the town's relationships.

He launches into Spanish at break-neck speed, his tone at once officious but also dismissive. Although I don't understand anything, the mood, the sense of what he is saying is unmistakable. I study Ana's face for signs, but she remains focussed on the lawyer, her face calm and neutral. I detect a tension in her neck, as she holds this shield against the increasingly testy tone of the old man. At the peak of his diatribe, he ceremoniously takes out an antique looking key, places it into a simple envelope and slides it slightly aggressively over the table to her. She calmly places it into the tote bag on her lap. He takes one document out from the fat file, then hands the bundle directly to Ana who places it expressionlessly on the floor. He opens the remaining papers and then turns to me, and switches to perfectly fluent English with only the slightest of accents.

'In accordance with Spanish law, Mr. Phillips, in the absence of any other heirs or closer living relatives to your brother's estate, you are the sole inheritor of his remaining assets. I understand your mother is recently deceased, so the assets that were left to her pass to you by default. All the details of the assets are contained in the paperwork held by Miss Garcia '

'Yes, but I don't want, I mean I don't need… I mean what about Ana, she's going to have Gary's baby…'

'Mr Phillips, Miss Garcia was not married to your brother, and the law does not recognise their relationship, in this case, as a de facto partnership due to the fact your brother was not a Spanish national, and he has not been resident for ten years in Spain, nor in a relationship with Miss Garcia for ten or more years. I am sorry for your loss. Miss Garcia will explain everything to you, she has all the relevant documents. I wish you good day.'

To my amazement, he picks up his pen, puts it ceremonially in his inside pocket and stalks out of the room. Ana simply beckons me with a glance to follow her.

We find ourselves back in the street, scooters rasping, taxis honking, and the general hubbub of a big city enveloping us in its anonymity. This part of Marbella, as small a town as it is, feels much bigger and grander than you might expect. But only for two blocks.

Ana's bottom lip trembles imperceptibly, tears rim her eyes, and she breathes deeply to contain herself. Time passes, and I stand, clueless, in the street wondering what just happened. Ana is a lawyer after all, but I think I just witnessed her being walked all over. Eventually I need to say something, but it's not maybe the tone required, but I can't put it any other way.

'What the fuck was that all about?'

Ana snorts derisively.

'Come, quickly, let's get out of the street. Follow me.'

She stalks off down the road and I have to quicken my pace to keep up with the diminutive young woman. She turns into a building, presses a green buzzer, there's a click, and we enter what I now realise is a banking hall. The air is chill with aircon, and quiet like a library. Various heads tilt upwards to clock the new arrivals, a subtle but instant reaction. Brows furrow, people nudge or signal with their eyes to colleagues, and a palpable unease fills the air. Ana turns to me.

'You are witnessing just how toxic one can become in a town full of liars and petty thieves.'

An unctuous middle-aged man in an ill-fitting suit approaches us, barely able to prevent himself from wringing his hands. He starts to explain something in Spanish, when suddenly Ana explodes, and with a power that defies her size, starts tearing verbal strips off the man, but not only him. She gestures generally to the bank's employees. A customer leaves a desk with his business unfinished, and with a knowing glance at Ana, walks out. Every eye is upon us. My throat dries, I am utterly confused as to what is or isn't happening.

361

When Ana has finished, the bank manager beckons us to follow him and we are ushered behind the counter and into a small private room. Ana sits wordlessly and I do so also. The man reappears with a metal deposit box, and puts it down, and withdraws, also wordlessly. The silence is killing me. What is this game everyone is playing? Ana takes out the envelope with the key and opens the box, pulls out plastic wallets containing all manner of documents, CD's, cassette tapes, and various computer disks. There appears to be a welter of material.

Ana stares at the contents of the box, uncertain as to what to do. I am beside myself but must try not to get excitable, given the circumstances.

'Ana, I know this might not be the best time, but please explain to me, as simply as possible, what is going on.' She can hear the barely contained anxiety in me. It's funny how physical violence is relatively comprehensible as a force. It hurts, and it's demands and consequences are unequivocal. Conversely the everyday business and legal systems of the town itself conceal multiple threats, enemies and compromises.

'Yes, now is probably the best time, really. We are safe in here. Once we leave with these documents, we won't be safe anywhere until this is all over, whatever that means.'

Her expression is not one I've seen on her before, she appears to look through me, through the walls of the soulless bank itself, to who knows what perceived hell of insecurity and uncertainty.

'What happened with Mr. Alfredo?'

She pauses. Her stare returns to the space we are in.

'Don Alfredo was our personal lawyer. While we were wealthy, and Gary was rising up in this world, nothing was too good for us. Like I say, you know who your real friends are when things like this happen. Gary managed to transfer the penthouse to me, but he had to put a lot of pressure on Don Alfredo to do it. He didn't even have time to change the will he made before we met. The penthouse and our joint funds are all I receive. And they killed him the day after, and I have been fighting with Don Alfredo to make sure that it was completed. It has not been easy to do this with all of... you know.' I nod, I can't imagine having to think about dry legal scuffles burdened with the horror we have in us. 'Because of the way Spanish law classifies the common law partnership, regarding a foreign resident, I was unable to be recognised as his common-law partner as you know it in Britain. I only found out after the shooting what Gary had done with the apartment. He was afraid something was going to happen, for sure, and that was the only way he could leave me some kind of assets, as I was already a joint owner, and he dissolved his share in my favour. Don Alfredo didn't even confess it; I had a tip off from someone in his office. He has completed Gary's wishes but he is furious I caught him out, that his treachery has been discovered.'

'But what would he do with it?'

'I'm sorry Gene, this may hurt you what I am going to say. Gary's original will, made maybe four years ago, left everything to your mother. Don Alfredo knew this, and was also aware that your mother was incapable of managing her own affairs. Gary wanted to provide for her, and once Alfredo had power of attorney, I think he was planning to fill his pockets. In Spanish law, two-thirds of your wealth must go to relatives closest to you. Gary would know that if something happened to him, I would be in trouble. At the last moment he managed to save something for me. But now, you are Gary's only heir. Everything that was his is yours now.'

'Well, like the flat, for example.'

'Yes. Yours. His car, but...' and she shudders, and pauses, collecting herself, minute muscle inflexions playing over her. 'There will be some money, cash in some private accounts, the share in the club, also all of his shares in Holmeland, and some other business holdings.'

'Er, isn't Holmeland worthless?'

'It's complicated, but yes, potentially you would inherit a huge debt liability. If you choose to be the heir of Gary's estate, you will be taking on all his problems. Is that what you want?'

My head hurts. For someone with a history of living cash in hand to mouth, evading even the most basic credit cards and bank accounts, this prospect is nothing short of mind warping.

'Well, no. If I renounce this, then I renounce the apartment, right?'

'Basically, yes. But I wouldn't worry about it right now. I have to deal with all of this. Don Alfredo wants nothing further to do with this, he has his own fires to fight. We are on our own. Things move slowly here, especially now when everything is taken to Madrid. It's out of our hands. Stay in the flat until someone throws you out.'

'And how long will that be? Days, weeks?' I imagine having to find a place to live will be a nightmare given who I am and my uncertain resources, and even more uncertain legal status.

'Years.'

'Good grief.' Sclerotic bureaucracies have their advantages. 'Is Don Alfredo an enemy now?'

She ponders this one a while.

'I don't think so, but he will inevitably have problematic connections and projects he was involved in. And as Holmeland was the fat rotten tomato of the whole bunch, he wants one less problem to be associated with. He also knows these documents could potentially be very dangerous to some dangerous people, after what happened to Gary. I think he's just frightened. It's not often your best client gets shot by the Ukrainian Mafia.'

I haven't dared to talk about the whys and wherefores of the murder with Ana. But she obviously has thoughts on it.

'Is that what you think this is?'

'The contents of this box will probably tell us the answer to that. I am shocked Gary was keeping this kind of information so comprehensively. He never confided in me on this. Or anyone.'

She starts to lay out some of the material. Apart from the typical masses of photocopied documents, we find a considerable number of CD's, and even some VHS tapes and mini-cassettes, Dictaphone style I assume. Three undeveloped 35mm film cassettes, a compact camera, and a couple of packs of prints. Finally, a box of vintage floppy discs and some other digital drives complete the hoard.

'Where do we start? I'm not much use on computers. Shouldn't you hand this over to the police?'

Ana looks at me quizzically.

'Gene, the important things will be in Spanish, and you won't understand most of the content anyway. It will take me weeks to work through this. Before I do anything with it, I need to understand everything. I could give it to the *fiscal anticorrupción,* but then it becomes evidence and I will never see any of it again. Evidence I may need to protect myself with. *Algo es cierto,* I am not safe with it here. Stories will leak out. From this bank, from Alfredo's office. Maybe someone at Holmeland knew Gary had all this.'

We are interrupted once more by the bank manager. He coldly lays a briefcase on the table and places a bank slip before Ana. She signs it wordlessly. He leaves with a toneless *'Gracias, que pases un buen día'[30].* Ana ignores him, and opens the briefcase. Which is rammed with clean bundles of cash. Pretty yellow 200's, green 100's and even some Bin Ladens.

'Jesus H Fucking Christ… oh, sorry, I didn't mean to…' and I run out of steam. Added to the radioactive trove of documentation here is yet another pile of cash of who knows what provenance, and I am stuck in my seat, the air pressing upon me. It all adds up to trouble I don't understand. Ana is checking the bundles, counting,

---

[30] Thank you, have a nice day

jotting down the amounts, until she's satisfied. She takes a bundle of 200's and slides it across to me.

'What?' is all I manage.

'I have taken everything of Gary's and my cash, and I am getting it out of the way. The courts may try to seize everything. I have to live…' and she places her hand on her as yet invisible baby bump. 'You are Gary's heir now, so quite a bit of this is yours. But if you accept it, you accept the liabilities as well.'

My mouth is flapping open and shut, but no sound comes out. Twisted, contradictory emotions and thoughts produce a system crash in my mind. None of this computes. Ana's hand seeks out my cheek, her eyes meet mine. Her calmness and composure have a stabilising effect on me.

'Gene you need to live too. Take it, why not? We won't do anything legally about your inheritance. The system moves very, very slowly and we have far more important things to deal with.' She glances at the document trove. 'I'm leaving. A friend will pick me up now. I need to hide, and to work through what Gary has been concealing from the world all this time. I will be okay.'

We leave the bank, with little further said, the eyeballs of the employees throwing darts against our backs. Outside a car is waiting, driven by a young woman of similar age to Ana.

'My old best friend,' she says to me, 'a real friend, the only ones you need.'

She hands me a bunch of keys and an envelope.

'This is for our apartment. Just keep an eye on it if you are in town ever. See what mail arrives. But otherwise, stay at the flat. Once I make sense of all this, I will be in touch.'

She climbs into the car and is gone. I feel leaden and deeply alone. The wedge of money burning a hole in my pocket. And with a spasm deep inside, I remember the cocaine stash waiting for me, its lethal energy sneering at me, pulling me toward it. I stand paralysed on the busy pavement for a moment, accepting the fact I will have to drive back to the apartment, and resume the task of disposing of the coke. Or what? Maybe run for it. Just as a shabby indistinct plan of jumping on an aeroplane to somewhere different, where no-one has ever heard of me tries to gain leverage in my head, a voice interrupts the frantic chain of thought.

'You look like you could use a coffee.'

The man from the cemetery, distinctive, I recognise him instantly. Ex CID Inspector Geoffrey Treece turns out to be charming and not nearly as brittle or pompous as some ex-policemen I've met. Tall, still fairly fit, with swept back white hair, he appears to be the image of the affluent retired expat, except that his Spanish is near fluent. We sit in a cafeteria on the main road. After explaining himself and apologising, going through the correct condolences, and ordering some rather delicious cakes, he leans into me confidentially.

'Eugene, you and I have similar problems.'

'How so?' I hope I'm not in for some kind of self-justifying sob story. I've been trying to escape my own for two decades.

'We have both been the victims of deep injustices that have dominated our lives. I have been fortunate to move on and make a different and by and large, happy life for myself here,' and he pauses and takes in the scene, the scent of Jasmin floating in the air, the picture postcard Andaluz charm, 'but I and especially you, have been denied justice for the wrongs that were done to us.'

'Agreed' I shrug.

'I hadn't let this bother me too much in recent years. I followed the rise of your brother's fortunes here from a distance. It was gratifying to see that one of you at least had escaped the cloud of the travesty of your father's killing. So when I saw the news of his murder, it awoke some strong emotions. Indignation. Regret. Fury even. It has disturbed what was, to be honest, something of an idyllic life, or so I thought. Which maybe I could have contained, I could have perhaps shoved the old demons back in the box I left them in in Lancashire.'

This distracts me momentarily as I curse the fact that my own demons like to buy plane tickets to wherever I am.

'However, I had been having a couple of episodes recently' he gestures parenthesis at this word, 'and I saw the doctors. Very good health service here by the way. It so happens I have incipient Parkinson's disease. In a few months, I shall be a shadow of the man you see before you now, Eugene.'

Strange emotions creep over me. The intimacy of his revelation is uncomfortable, our fates are tumbling downwards together helplessly to who knows what denouement. This man I do not know, with whom I share a peculiar bond, our stories entwined like creeping weeds in a garden. I am wondering if Collins prompted him to make this contact, but that would contradict Collins' own warning. No, Treece is sincere and acting independently.

'I am really sorry to hear that.' Facile platitude, but what else would one say?

'The Americans have an expression they use frequently, like most of their distortions of the mother tongue, I find them reprehensible, but there is one that now seems to be rather apposite. I feel I need closure. Before I'm incapable of closing a door even. Do you know what I mean?'

I let out a deep sigh, of recognition. The only sense of closure for myself is some form of oblivion, self-inflicted or otherwise. Do I need the burden of someone else's need for the same? He takes my silence for some kind of comprehension.

He takes me back to the early eighties, and offers me the selected glimpses of the world I grew up in, and what his struggle with it entailed. I am humbled. I never imagined anyone would have suffered so much for defending our interests. And we knew nothing of this man. He daily fought to bring the Kavanaghs and their kin to justice, involved as they were in extortion, gun running, money laundering (thanks to our family business) and drug dealing. He ran informants, stings, undercover operations, worked closely with

Special Branch in England and the Six Counties over the water. His perspicacity, however, deeply rattled the fine frame of quid pro quos that flowed like a river between the British Government and the Loyalist paramilitaries. Just as Collins explained it. He sought justice, especially for my father, but came up against a political expediency that, with hindsight, may have appeared justifiable, at least historically speaking. But he is adamant the concomitant sacrifices and omissions, the cynical compromises, enabled murderers to evade trial, and an organised criminal network to flourish as it was deemed expedient to the greater goal of peace in Northern Ireland. The lack of justice for my father was but collateral damage, in a ruthlessly dirty political war, whose compromises were so ugly, they remain buried as official secrets for the foreseeable future.

I see just a network of duplicitous mercenary ideologues, sitting on top of the same sort of gangs of self-enriching thugs I see here in Marbella. Indeed, some of them are one and the same. But what shocks me is how the elements of the system sought to isolate themselves from the brilliant police work of a superb detective. The unofficial briefings questioning his honesty and competence. The buying off and neutralisation of witnesses to shield the entire supergrass program from scrutiny. The destruction and suppression of evidence. All of this reflected on his professionalism and integrity. The *coup de grace* was my father's case. Magically buried by mysterious court orders, uncontested. A whitewash of an inquest. Case files simply gathered up and locked away under restrictions of national security. Treece himself ostracised by huge sections of the profession, demoted, sent out to the Stix to mop up burglaries in some forgotten rural enclave. Resigning that position to go back to the beat and police with simple dignity, taking an unusually generous and early retirement package, signing a draconian non-disclosure agreement enforced at the level of official secrets legislation. Becoming a benign and respected member of the expat Costa del Sol lot. Golf, bowls, English Sunday roast for only nine euros at the Rose and Crown, Manilva, a sleepy beach-side town at the edge of the tourist belt. The collateral damage of an entire career. Which brings us to the present day.

'When I started my own digging after the shooting, some alarmingly familiar names started to pop up. There's a network of retired police here, and through them and connections in the UK with Serious Crime Squad, Europol and so on, it's amazing what you can find out. I'm aware that your nemesis Jimmy Kavanagh is active on our doorstep. I know he is in the mix somehow of all this. Did you know?'

I look him in the face, and being a copper, he can probably read all that plays across it. The confusion, fear, desperation and helplessness. He must have sat across tables in interview rooms with countless faces like mine.

'Jimmy Kavanagh is alive and well indeed, Inspector. And too close to home.'

'I see. Please don't call me Inspector, Eugene.'

'Sounds to me like you are coming out of retirement.'

He can only smile at this. Like someone who's just rediscovered what they used to be good at before something else got in the way.

'Maybe we should go and talk somewhere less public' he responds.

Driving toward the apartment, Treece following in his car. I turn into the top of the street, and the bright yellow of the Hummer is visible outside my block. I turn off onto a side street, and decide to head for Ana's flat. Once through the rigmarole of finding entry codes to parkings and doors and lifts from the envelope, we arrive in the calm, minimalist sanctum of my late brother's home.

The inspector sits and I hand him a tonic water from the gargantuan fridge.

'What was all that about Eugene?' He doesn't miss a trick, this one.

'Kavanagh. Waiting for me.'

'I see. Are you mixed up in something Eugene?'

'Keep your friends close.'

'And your enemies closer.' He fills in neatly. 'High risk strategy, no?'.

'Somewhat.'

'Do you want to tell me?'

The offer opens like an enormous sliding window. A great space into which I can unload everything. I figure, why not? The burden of so many variables, so much history, bad blood and ever-present danger makes the offer the most relieving thing to happen to me in weeks. To confide, to put it all out there. This man I have never met, a retired CID inspector. A man in possession of the darkest truths of my life, his own unresolved burden. I recount the story of my adult life, bit by bit, blow by blow, evasion by evasion. He asks pointed, penetrating questions, expertly piecing together the grim tapestry. At an opportune moment, we avail ourselves of Gary's supply of outstanding single malts. I suppose it's mine now. A good ex-copper likes a decent whiskey. The montage of my life lacks some details. I principally leave out the mercy killing of my mother. A mercy to her, and to me, as shocking as it is to acknowledge it.

Feeling overly loquacious we arrive at the present day. Today. My license and current status. My inadvertent entry back into the world of trafficking class A substances. I also acquaint him with the existence of the trove of documentation, inwardly pleading forgiveness from Ana, but justifying myself with the idea that I need allies, and that the Inspector's secrets are far more burdensome than mine, so we have a solid pact of confidentiality. Mutually assured self-destruction. USSR and USA.

'I think Ana could be a useful ally for you. Nearest thing you have to family now. I hope we can meet. I may be able to help. You see there is a long continuum between what I dealt with all those years ago, and what has just happened.'

The whiskey has us buried deep in the designer armchairs. It's late. Hours have flowed by; time has stood still as these two stories danced around the maypole of the common event. And one of the main protagonists moves around freely in this very neighbourhood. And I am still beholden to him.

After a silence of some time, as we both mull over the labyrinthine compromises and failings of the system and our lives, I offer to make coffee. A clumsy and over long search for invisible cupboards and utensils results in a cafetiere of pleasingly aromatic brown stuff, mostly under the Inspectors guidance.

'I have to thank you for being so frank with me, Geoffrey. It's helped me clarify a lot of things. And here I am, the only Phillips left standing, and nothing's changed. They are all getting away with it. I remember when I was young and we'd watch the news, or some detective series and it was just that, it was a thing divorced from you, it happened on the news, on the telly, it wasn't real life, our real life. There's that cliché that says in London you are never more than about ten foot away from a rat. You just can't see them. That's life isn't it? It all appears civilised and seems to work, but you are never more than a few feet away from that rat. Whether it's a Kavanagh, or a dodgy real estate salesman, or just a corrupt police officer or politician. As though all of this place, our world, is just built on top of a bloody great cesspool, and if we jump up and down too hard, the surface will crack and we'll fall in and drown.'

He ponders this for a while, sips his coffee. 'Seems to me Eugene that, through accident and design, you've fallen through the cracks. You're swimming in it. What are you going to do about it?'

I snort in frustration.

'What can I do? Run around killing people? That just perpetuates the cycle, and anyway I'm not capable.' A momentary chill reminds me that actually, I am

'You have an ally. With evidence.'

'True. But only she has the knowledge to use it effectively.'

372

'Yes, but I meant me, Eugene.'

He's looking me straight in the eye. There's a supplication somewhere in his expression.

'I don't see how you can help. I have to deal with the Kavanagh situation, it's my own stupid burden, then I'll wait and see what Ana comes up with. Or maybe just cut and run.'

'You can't keep running Eugene. I ran, for my own sanity. And it's been good, I've had a nice life for a few years. But deep down, I'm still angry. My partner passed away last year, I'm beholden to no-one anymore. Never had kids. No real friends, just acquaintances. Parkinson's is a miserable, debilitating, slow death sentence. Conversely, with the benefit that, in the not too distant future, I shall be incapable of standing trial or giving evidence.'

This sounds morbid but shockingly realistic. I wince at the thought of the clarity he has of that particular death sentence.

'Trial for what' I ask, already half fearing the answer.

'For breaking the conditions of my non-disclosure. The Official Secrets act can be savage in its powers.'

'And what would you disclose?' Whatever it is, it won't bring anyone back.

'Maybe everything. Maybe, with your own mountain of evidence, there would be enough to bring the entire nexus of corruption to book, going right back.'

'But that's just your word, who will believe you twenty odd years later?'

'No Eugene, I also have my treasure trove of documents. I have evidence, damning evidence, which in the right hands could cause a huge amount of damage, to all sorts of people. I kept all I could from the case once I detected which way the wind was blowing. The rest is from freedom of information requests, Irish sources, even Republican sources. They would only be too happy to highlight the government's duplicity and hypocrisy.' Official secrets, Loyalist assassins, the entire British state, who does he think is? I'm scared

I've confided in a deluded, bitter old man. 'You see Eugene, I have nothing to lose, and I want closure, as I said. You must be my avenging angel. God knows you deserve the privilege and opportunity.'

'But how the hell can I do that!?' He's certainly deluded if he thinks I could ever be that. I immediately feel ashamed, throwing his last hopes for justice back in his face. 'Why don't you just take it to the press?'

'On its own, it probably isn't enough for a newspaper to risk a fight with the courts and the Official Secrets Act. The public interest defence has to be overwhelming. As part of a nexus of international crime that incorporates everything you have described, that could be in the public interest, of more than one nation even. And that way, you can take them all down, not just some Loyalist bomb maker. You get his bosses as well. You get the Kavanaghs, the Lebids, the Holmes of this world.'

'Oh sweet Jesus.' I have no words. It is an insanely huge burden and a vast mountain to climb, legally, personally, practically. Could Ana cope with having this added to the existing struggle? What right have I to drag historical vendettas into her personal tragedy? Expose her to even further threat?

'Eugene, I can make all of this information available to Ana. If you think she is capable of taking it on. Your job, now, is to protect her. Protect the information.'

Having fallen through the cracks into the cesspool, the only thing any of this will do is to weigh me down and finally drown me. We bid each other good night. I can't wait to leave the apartment, the echoes of Gary's life, sundry ghosts too ghoulish and numerous for my state of mind.

Approaching my apartment, there is no sign of Hummer. Only a note under the door.

'Nine thirty sharp. Police. Will pick you up be ready (sic)'.

374

Great. An enormous heaviness accompanies me as I, slow motion style, put myself to bed. My brain has ground to a halt under the sheer weight of input. Incipient panic is suppressed by fatigue and the cacophony of information, jostling to file itself away inside the whiskey addled cranium.

'Fuck it. What does it even matter?' I say to no-one in particular. Amazingly there are still vodka bottles lying around in the flat, and so one more full glass of quality booze goes down and I slump into sleep thoroughly intoxicated yet again.

The night passes in sweats, waking or half-waking moments, filled with blackness and paranoia of hidden assassins, grinning thugs, lines of coke and women with outlandish breasts and lips. A tawdry Technicolor trip, where everything smells of strong alcohol and perfume, and I am merely a spectator, staring at it. Everyone ignores me, because once again, I am standing in my underpants, and have become invisible.

28

I stare ahead of me, as we slide under palms, the sun roof of the idiotic Hummer revealing my favourite Hollywood echo. Palms, the tree of the desert, here in serried rows, trained and ordered into endless phalanxes to frame and decorate the concrete blocks that march on and on. Given what I have seen of the countryside, palms don't grow amid the oaks, olives and eucalyptus. This is pure ostentation. And it works. Kavanagh is saying something but I'm not listening.

'Earth to Eugene Fuckwit, come in please!' Accompanied by a hard slap on my temple. He has my attention again. 'So you know how this goes. Schtum, minimum necessary. And you tell me everything afterwards.'

'Whatever you say.' Neutral. I'm wrapping myself tight, trying to insulate myself from the reality, making a witness statement of the murder of my brother.

Yet another dull office. Men in the blue uniforms of the national police. So many different policemen in this country. A duty solicitor and translator. Questions come and I answer them. They are all discursive, filler details, bare facts, time stamps on a video of horror, but nothing about the horror. A piece of paper is placed in front of me, the lawyer nods for me to sign. And that's it. Information of no consequence, nothing that might lead to suspicions cast, lines of investigations opened, motives suspected and analysed. The word whitewash comes to mind, in Inspector Treece's voice. The same as happened to my father. A violent, horrible, illegal death has just been tidied up, normalised and filed away. Again. Another Phillips. Three down, one to go. I recite all of what I can recall in a monotone.

Kavanagh grimly smiles, nodding ironically. We pull up at the block.

'Same shit, different country, ay Eugene?' No response is required. I shrug. 'Give that guy a call again, the carpenter, film job.'

'Why?'

'There's a big shoot on, and all those poncey twats in their black jackets snort like it's going out of fashion. Go and shift some product. Justify your useless fucking life already.'

He shoves me out of the vehicle, which being so high off the ground, I can't judge the height, get my legs tangled and fall idiotically, humiliatingly, into a pile on the tarmac. It's painful, but no damage done. The Hummer accelerates away with a guttural roar, leaving a cloud of noxious exhaust gas around me. It is a metaphor for everything.

Inside I stare at the packaged-up coke. The tone of the questions from the police simply confirmed my worst suspicions. Gary's death will not overly trouble the authorities, yet more collateral damage to just another foreigner on the make. They will clean up their backyard, put their house in order, make the right poses for the evening news, and Holmeland will all be just a footnote in the history of yet another boom-and-bust cycle. Nothing to see here, move along.

Fuck it, let's just do this. I call the carpenter, Jonno. He initially offers disinterest and inability to help. Until I mention the coke.

'So, you can get some snow?'

'As much as you like, quality stuff, barely cut. I believe your clients might appreciate a little quality, am I right?'

'Look, we use a bit, y'know, to cope with the workload, but them tossers from London man, they fuckin' love the stuff. I'll take some for my crew, and I'll just put you in touch with the production manager, cos he's in touch with all the people that count. Be down at reception in the Hotel Arcadia soon as you can. Ask for Sergio.'

'Sergio who?'

'Doesn't matter, just Sergio.'

'Okay cheers bud'.

And so, for better or worse I embark fully on career number two trafficking class A narcotics.

~

It's not hard to spot the production crew once I'm in the lobby of the hotel. There's a meeting room that is buzzing with activity. People stare at laptops intently; others babble incessantly on mobile phones. Others shuffle papers, stapling up packages of some kind of information. I slip discreetly into the maelstrom. At the far end are different people. They stand out because they are very much older than the youngsters racing around, and so obviously English, prime WASPS from home counties public schools. You can't miss them. The bright rugby shirt with turned up collar, the pearl earrings, the designer sandals and work bags. The expensively casual clothing, smart black jacket with smartly wrecked jeans. I'd get the same lot sitting in VIP areas in clubs back home, whingeing about the quality of the vodka as they guzzled pills, somehow managing to be polite and ruthlessly condescending at the same time.

They sit aloof from the hubbub, being tended to by various people. One person in particular holds their attention. He is short and podgy, with an overly boyish face, made to appear older by his double chin and prematurely thinning hair. He is slightly hyperactive, but his posture is one of authority and high status simply by the exaggerated slouch. He occasionally barks orders at underlings who run away with pained expressions. Is this Sergio? He doesn't look Spanish, but yet another of the WASPS, albeit a hipper, more bohemian one.

Someone notices me, as I am patently not busy or engaged in any of what is around me.

'Excuse me, you can't be in here. You need to go.' Slightly accented English.

'I'm looking for Sergio.' I offer.

'What about? Does he know you?'

378

I have to think on my feet. 'We have met, but he may have forgotten, it was a hell of a party.' I'm taking a chance on him being part of the Marbella scene at least. 'He said to look him up as soon as I was in town again. He said he had something for me?'

'Wait here.' The young woman moves off looking flustered, as to why she has to deal with something so irrelevant to the immediate task to hand. I wait. The anthill thrums on around me. People constantly enter and leave, collecting not inconsiderable amounts of cash. Everyone has an officious but highly focussed air. The cabal at the end of the room have now received an enormous delivery of sushi and cold beers and the relaxed, indulgent demeanour contrasts heavily with the frenetic activity in the rest of the room. She makes her way over to them and gets the attention of one of them. Two of them now get up and make their way over to me, and then continue outside past me, and with a slight head gesture the Spanish looking one of them beckons me to follow. We enter one of the hotel's lifts.

'Sergio.' He shakes my hand.

'Paul,' says the other, who I had already clocked. He is very much English, with that sort of region less accent a certain class of Brits have, neither obviously posh nor specific to a place or age group, a strangely anonymous way of talking.

'Gene, pleasure to do business with you.'

'Ah yes, the business. I like directness. We like it don't we Sergio? Cut to the chase, why not.'

My hand goes to my bag, but he snorts slightly derisively.

'Slow down, Genie boy, let's get to the room first then inspect the merchandise.'

'Yeah, of course, I thought...'

'Ooo, did you hear that Sergio, we've got a thinker.' He has been wearing a slightly sardonic smirk since I met him, which only gets bigger now. We enter a room, an ample suite with spectacular views over the curve of Marbella's shoreline. Contrasting with this

379

opulence is a scruffy holdall open on a bed and various casual, branded clothing items are strewn around, mixed up with a range of computer gadgetry, cameras of varying sizes and types, cables, chargers, leftover room service detritus, glasses and a couple of fancy brandy bottles. Like a spoiled overgrown teenager's bedroom.

Sergio says nothing, maintaining a dutiful, neutral attentiveness, studying me all the same.

'Word has it you are the man with magic powder, so let's have a look' says Paul. The smirk is still there but he is noticeably twitchier. I hand him a one-gram wrap. Trial size. He takes it, chops a line on the coffee table and snorts it using what appears to be a gold straw he pulls from his black designer jeans. He returns his gaze to me, the smirk broadening.

'Hmmm. Yes… that's nice… mmmmm, that's very nice. How much?'

'Well, I think you know what you have there is quality, which is why I have only five-grams wraps at four hundred per wrap.' I figure go in hard, and brassy, these people won't respect a street dealer mindset.

'Okaaaaay, eighty a gram. Really?'

'I could go to seventy but I'd have to include some baking powder type impurities, and it would be a shame to spoil such a fine product.'

He spills out, chops and snorts another line, and holds my gaze again. The smirk is transforming into something else. If I was a woman, I think he'd want to fuck me right now. Maybe he does anyway.

'I'll throw in the gram there as a gesture, an offering, to a good business relationship. I can see you appreciate quality.' He wipes the residue from the table onto his finger, rubbing it into his gums.

'Sergio, we'll take ten for Jed, and I'll take ten. That should get us through this fucking circus without too much anguish, don't you think? Sixteen hundred. Can you make that work? Lose it in the art department or something, yeah?'

'Paul, Jonno is not happy, maybe we need to give him what he needs, you said we have to really mind the budget on this one, I don't know how we can.' He has the air of someone who has to deal with a slightly troublesome youth, wearing kid gloves, able to keep his boss in line without overstepping his limits. Paul gives him a withering look. Sergio visibly gives in with an air of habitual defeatism.

'Good chap. Pay young Gene here would you. Fancy a drink Gene? Or a line?'

'I'll have a drink, I'm partial to brandy.' I confess I'm partial to anything violently alcoholic these days.

'So you don't get high on your own supply Gene? Like to keep things business like, good man. I respect that.'

Sergio has fixed us both a brandy, and places sixteen hundred euros under the glass, still eyeing me in that non-committal way.

'So, Gene, tell me about yourself, where did you pop up from. Last powder I bought in Marbs was cut to shit, disgusting stuff. What's the story? This is seriously good blow. Is there something I need to know, who are you in bed with, you're not a street dealer? You sound educated.'

Before I get a chance to reply Sergio leans over and whispers something. The way Paul regards me now says he has been appraised of the eventfulness of my recent life.

'Seems you have a bit of a story. Sorry if I'm intruding, who the hell am I? You probably want to get on…'

'No, it's cool.' I'm not missing a chance to cultivate a client with this scale of appetite for the wretched stuff I am saddled with. I take a long slug of the drink which worms its way down, easing away some of the awkwardness from this first deal. 'It's not been an easy few weeks. I only came down here a couple of months back, and then this happened. I was working with my brother, he set me up with a good little job, life seemed to be sorting itself nicely. Then… boom.' He winces visibly at the thought. 'And as everything has suddenly turned to shit in Marbella, I had few options open to me, not knowing the language, and being the brother of the recently assassinated property mogul leaves me rather tarnished. Damaged goods. But it being Marbella I found an opening, you might say. Friends of friends.'

'Indeed, a rather tasty one I must say.' Paul studies me still. His aura of the over entitled pudgy brat isn't helped by the puffiness of his face, the victim of too many irregular expense account meals and too much vodka overriding his coke habit's ability to lose him weight. It occurs to me his lifestyle isn't sustainable long term. Sergio cuts in, he's been fidgeting the whole while. Paul is radiating bonhomie and tolerance all of a sudden, and another withering glance admonishes Sergio's urge to get back to work.

'Look I have to get back downstairs, keep this show on the road. Do you need work? Proper work, not… you know?' he says, laying a hand on my shoulder, giving it that gentle squeeze.

'Well, yeah, I'm really on my uppers, so I'm willing and able. What do you need, I'm not exactly *au fait* with what you're running here.'

'We need plenty of goffers on a job like this. Can you drive?'

'Oh yes, I've driven all manner and sizes of vehicles in the course of my, ahem, career, know what I mean.'

He smiles conspiratorially.

'Come with me, I'll put you with the agency, they need a driver who can look after their specialist needs. Jed is someone who must be looked after. Welcome to the circus, the great putrid whore that is advertising. *Vamos.*'

I am back downstairs in the long room full of the busy ants. I am waiting, for who knows what. I waste an hour of staring listlessly, drifting off in the babble of Spanish and English, all talking about things I don't understand. So much activity and all of it strange. Then

382

a face I recognise. It's my contact from the construction crew, Jonno. He sees me, nods acknowledgement, but he's distracted and preoccupied. He's with two others, also who worked on our ill-fated trade fair build in Madrid. Eventually they get the attention of Sergio. The discussion that ensues is animated, and mostly in Spanish. Sergio is trying to defend some kind of immovable position, with a range of shrugs, blocking gestures, dismissive waves. The more adamant the constructors become the more Sergio becomes defensive, dismissive. Jonno breaks away and squats down by my chair.

'Hi mate, I see you got in the door then?'

'Yeah, thanks, I owe you one.'

'Okay, see me in the bogs in a minute and you can slip me a gram. This is turning into a shitshow and we are looking at working through the night, so any help appreciated.'

We rendezvous minutes later in the toilets in the lobby of the hotel. I give him a one gram wrap, and wave away his token offer of cash, which he fully expects me to; I can tell by his swiftness in pocketing the cash again.

'Just out of interest, did you manage to sell them any blow.'

'Sure, twenty fucking grams. They're monsters these guys.'

'And did you hear mention of how they were paying for it?' He looks at me knowingly.

'Well, would you Adam and Eve it, but I do believe finding the money in the art department was mentioned.'

'I asked yesterday', he continues, barely concealing his anger 'for four lads for two days to get this built on time, and I was told the usual bullshit of we're over budget, you got to suck it up. Sixteen hundred euros on blow? That would have paid me three lads, and now we have to work all night so they can put more up their noses. Bastards, it's always the fucking same.' He tries to control his breathing. 'When it all goes to shit, I'm not cleaning up the mess, I tell you. I've never walked off a job but I think this one could be the one.'

'Why, what's the problem?'

'Nothing you wanna know about. Don't get involved. Sit in your minibus, play dumb, and just make sure they fucking pay you at the end of it. See ya.' And he's gone in a fume of testosterone and bile, sweat and exasperation.

I skulk discreetly back into the production office, and an arm grabs me.

'Right, there you are.' The same young woman from earlier.

'Here's the keys. Van's downstairs. Take them to Da Brunos on the Paseo, wait in the van, and then make sure they're not too late back to the hotel. Here's your call sheet.'

'Where's Da Brunos?' Stuff is happening too fast.

She regards me with a withering exasperation. 'You're the agency driver, right?'

'Yeah, I spose so…'

'Well you should know then. Find out. And fast.'

She's gone, blathering into a walkie talkie, exuding stress and fatigue. I examine the document in my hand. It's a smallish spiral bound booklet with a cover lifted from some Warholian ironic image, featuring a stunning girl and floating telephones in faux xeroxed psychedelic floatiness. As I marvel at this artwork, I fail to notice a gaggle of black clad media types staring at me with an air of polite impatience. It's the strong whiff of several expensive brands of cologne that brings me back to the now.

'So you're our driver?' says the lead male, his unkempt hair and beard contrastingly markedly with the sheer cut of his immaculate black blazer and jeans.

'Jed?' I hazard a guess.

'The very same. You are our driver then?'

'Er, yes, erm, this way.' I stride off as purposefully as I can, down to the garage to search for the minibus. I wander in between rows of cars, while behind me my ravenlike charges mutter and sigh.

'Why don't you click the keys, and you'll probably find the van by its giveaway orange flashing lights?' Says another beardy black blazer man. The condescension is all the more penetrating due to the casualness with which he says it. I squeeze a blob on the bulky car key, and sure enough a van about twenty meters away emits flashes and bleeps.

'Right, there we go.' I offer them a sheepish smile and receive not much in return but a strained neutrality in all their faces. I manage to gather some instructions off the bloke in the ticket booth about where the restaurant is, mercifully it's close by and even a numpty like me can navigate along the seafront of Marbella. As we drive, a studied lack of small talk hovers in the van. A couple of questions between them regarding details of arrangements, but apart from that it's a weirdly guarded silence. I decant them in front of what appears to be a fancy but cheesy Italian place, right on the water. As if from nowhere, my nemesis, that young female production assistant Maria del misery, appears and ushers them in, talking to the staff. Once done, she returns to me.

'Stay here in the van and wait. Once they're finished take them straight back to the hotel, do not take them to any other place, even if they ask, we've got a five thirty call tomorrow.'

'What, in the morning?' I'm genuinely shocked as I can't imagine what you'd do at that time in the morning in any business.

'*Joder, de donde han sacado a este jillipolla?*[31]' Her tone makes me decide to not ask what this means, though '*joder*' appears to be the all-round expletive to Spanish as fuck is to English. 'It's all in your call sheet. Sit here and read it and don't mess up tomorrow.'

'Do I get to eat' I ask, now tormented by the pizzery aromas drifting over.

'You are working. You get to eat when you've nothing else to do. *Coño!*' Another familiar sounding expletive.

---

[31] Fuck, where did they find this dickhead?

Two hours pass where I have nothing better to do than read the booklet, which I thought was some kind of artsy left-field manifesto. It is in fact an intimidatingly detailed list and itinerary of everything that is going on. Apart from the nearly seventy plus names, all of whom come with a title of their position or occupation, endless lists of equipment, most of it incomprehensible to me fill the pages. A bazooka? A ubangi? Fuller's earth? A 'cartoni dutch head' sounds like some pleasuring one might find from an Italian whore in a backstreet in Amsterdam for all I know. My reading of this litany is periodically interrupted by Jed, the first dishevelled beardy black blazer man and a female side-kick, grey shapeless tube dress bob cut mean-faced bitch queen. They appear at least three times to do a line together and mutter to each other, purposefully inaudibly, but the tone makes it clear they are involved in a certain level of business-related stress with their pasta and prosciutto. Once they have all strolled back, I head to the hotel with them. The conversation this time is more animated. Lubricated by various intoxicants no doubt. It consists mostly of sneering hilarity at the quality of the food and the wine list, and how outmoded it was, lacking in any sense of where modern Spanish cuisine had gone in the last few years, how no self-respecting Italian in London would be seen dead… and blah blah. I'm tempted to ask them what do they bleeding expect on the sea front of a holiday town on the Costa. As it is, I get lost and spend ten minutes longer finding the hotel by which time the coke is wearing off and they troop out wordlessly into the hotel without a backwards glance.

I am about to pull away with huge sighs of relief belching like the diesel smoke out of the minibus, and I nearly run over Beardy Black Blazer man, who has darted back out from somewhere.

'Hey, you're the contact for the erm, blow, right?'

Glance around. No-one close or watching.

'I am.'

'Okay, you got another five?'

'I have'. I hand him the little package. 'That's four hundred, please.'

'Good man, sort it with Paul, okay. Cheers.' And he's gone. Just plain strode back into the hotel like he was God on earth. This guy is going to be so wired tomorrow, and I have to babysit them for the entire time. It says so in the call sheet thingy. Note to self, make sure I find Paul tomorrow.

~

I'm playing it by the book. I have digested the timings, information, maps and more. It's military in its size and precision. A convoy of some fifteen vehicles of various sizes, winding its way up into the mountains in the chill pre-dawn air. I have been given a walkie talkie which occasionally crackles with instructions and verifications, mostly in Spanish, so I don't know what I'm missing on the whole. I just follow the lights in front to wherever the hell this amount of people and equipment could find a place to work in the open countryside. We turn onto a dirt track and the van lurches and rolls for some time on the uneven surface. Occasionally a sickening thud or scrape provokes worried yelps from the metropolitan boys and girls in the van. You don't get roads like this in Soho. And I'm not used to driving on them, so I am as intimidated as they are. The beam of the lights flares off the road into the dark void. I have a sneaking suspicion there's a long way down off the side of this track, but I can't see shit so I'm gripping the wheel white knuckled, lest the blackness swallows me up. We emerge round a hillside onto a flat esplanade illuminated by enormous working lights. A large encampment of trucks is already here, and mercifully a full scale, open air canteen with a sizzling grill sending luscious aromas of eggs and bacon into the damp, brittle air. We are in the middle of absolutely nowhere in a temporary metropolis of bustling madness. My charges kick back and slurp mugs of hot stuff while all around people busy themselves. Maria del Misery finds me again.

'Well you got here, no fuck ups. Good. We are on channel four.' She fires off without looking at me. She's studying the activity around her.

'What? Channels?'

'On your walkie! *Joder.*' The black hand radio has a selector and I gingerly switch it to the four. 'You stick with the agency all day, make sure they have plenty of drink, snacks, whatever they want. You don't talk about anything you hear in the crew, any production details, just speak when you are spoken to and take care of them. Can you do that?'

'*Si señorita, sin problema.*'

She flashes me a contemptuous look, but can hardly complain I'm trying to speak the language.

The light starts to come up. It's bloody freezing and I'm shivering fit to die as I hadn't considered the climate inland might not be so balmy as on the coast. No-one notices, or doesn't bother to, I can't tell which. Thank god for on set catering. Three bacon sandwiches and four coffees in, I think I can make it through. All of this as the light reaches across great sprawling, rolling hills covered in waving green wheat and pock marked olive groves. Occasionally ragged swathes of rock pop up, and the whole landscape is framed at its distant edges by an enormous series of ridges and forests. Only a handful of scattered white farm buildings, and a splash of white and terracotta are visible in the far distance, some lost pig sticking village. It is awe inspiring in its wild purity and scale, and takes my mind off the shivering. As the sun breaks, its impact is instantly warming, and the blood tingles and life returns to my extremities. We march off away with the agency types from the base camp and along a rutted track into a long bowl of a field.

A smaller encampment of pop-up tents, plus trolleys of equipment, are placed a short distance from an extraordinary scaffolding dais with a giant mobile phone on it. Some kind of bizarre mechanical armed machine, like a transformers toy for real, squats next on it, in a field in the middle of nowhere. Quite the most unexpected collection of lunacy you could invent around here, I'm sure. The agency ensconce themselves under a black sided pop-up tent full of video monitors. I am to stand sentinel, and waiter, at the door and do my job.

Someone somewhere shouts 'action!', and their heads all concentrate on the monitors. My walkie continually crackles with Spanish, I move away and can get a glimpse of the shooting further down the field. Models dressed as nymphs swirl around on the dais, which has fake wheat all over it. The phone is somehow spinning, and the giant mechanical arm is moving around in repeated patterns. This is all that appears to be happening. During the pauses people move things around, attend to the girls, but most people are standing around, like me. The agency in their tent stare with bored expressions at the monitors or pore over the playbacks of what just happened. Which seems very little. There's mumbling and pointing and sighing, and messages fed back to a guy who walks back and forth between them and the camera team the whole time. All is a bizarre combination of tension, stress and enforced idleness on most people's part. Once attenuated to the splendour of the landscape, I am bored stiff.

Jonno ambles up the hill toward me. His eyes are red rimmed and he's pretty haggard, accompanied by two more guys in similar condition.

'Hello mate. I see you lucked out. Video village duty. Nice work if you can get it.'

'Jesus, you look done in.' I try to console, ignoring the jibe.

'All-nighter, wasn't it, cos they wouldn't pay for three more riggers. Fuckwits. I told them the arm is probably too heavy, it won't be steady. If it ain't steady then it's all a waste of fucking time. They should have put it on the ground at least.' He shakes his head in disgust.

'You've lost me Jonno.'

389

With an enormous effort he summons enough energy and civility to calmly explain the scene before me. 'Robotic arm with a camera, repeats exact same movement every time, so you can overlay images one on top of another and create all kinds of wonderful visual tricks. Except if there's any movement on the arm, it doesn't work, you can't use it, so all of this busting our balls is a waste of time. You wait, by lunchtime they'll have twigged, it's not gonna match, and the whole caboodle will be fucked. They never listen to us; all think they know better. Wankers.'

He plods on without looking back, his contempt drifting behind him like a bad fart. A cloud through which I see Sergio running, after Jonno.

'Jonathan, where are you going?'

Jonno and the two others keep walking, backs to their interlocutor.

'To bed, where do you think.'

'There's a vibration. You need to fix it.'

This time Jonno stops, and they converse more quietly so I can't make it out, but the discussion is terse. After a crescendo of intense gestures, Jonno blows a gasket such that everyone within reasonable distance can hear.

'We've worked twenty-six hours straight, and I told you what the risks were. You made the decisions, now you have to suck it up. I've never walked out on a job before, but believe me Sergio, there is a first time for everything, and I am not prepared to be responsible when people go against our advice. You lot made this problem so you lot can fucking well deal with it. I'm going to bed.'

Sergio yells at him but it's bouncing off Jonno's retreating back. I turn around, the exchange attracted a bit of an audience. Beardy blazer man is frowning after the retreating figures, and Paul, in a complete nervous state, runs up the hill. He's dabbing his nose with his forefinger, and the sweaty sheen on his skin says it hasn't been an easy, or a sober morning for him. Sergio and he join the posse in the video village tent, pull down all the sides. I'm standing there wondering what will happen next when Maria del Misery, who appears to be next in command under Paul and Sergio yells at me. Like she's been wanting to for a while but now has an excuse to do so properly.

'Jane, get away from there, go sit in catering with the others, *coño, eres un idiota.*'

She can't even say my name correctly.

'It's Gene actually. Rhymes with machine.'

But she's gone, babbling angrily into the walkie. People start disconsolately walking up from the dais below. Models wrapped in blankets, hiding their svelte chiffon clad legginess. I decide to wander over to the monstrous transformer arm to see what all the fuss is about.

In the middle of the field is an extensive and heavily built scaffolding platform next to the giant mobile phone model that stands on a green painted metal post. The robotic arm indeed resembles a science fiction toy, but it has a camera mounted on its end, rather than a laser gun or some such. Two guys sit listlessly sipping teas in Styrofoam cups, dangling their legs off the platform.

'Alright?' one of them says. They're English it would appear.

'Yup, just wondering what all the fuss is about. Everyone's in a bit of a funk up there. Something to do with this thing is it? I mean what the hell is this?' I am genuinely perplexed as to why a piece of technology like this would be stuck in a muddy field in the south of Spain.

'Ha, yes, Movi Tron is misbehaving today.' Adds the other guy.

The machine has a huge rotund base with wheels that rest it on a short rail, mounted on the platform which is about four feet off the ground. It has a long thick telescopic arm supported by huge pneumatic pistons, and on the end is a sort of cage housing the biggest camera I have ever seen. The whole thing must weigh several tons.

Scattered around are several chunky metal ingots which have been taken out of the interior sections of the machine.

'So don't tell me. Movi Tron is vibrating. And that's not good.' I hope they don't take offence. They both laugh wearily.

'This beauty is normally capable of shooting perfectly identical repeatable movement patterns, enabling any number of complex overlaid composite effects to be achieved.'

I'm none the wiser. 'Like what, I'm not really up on this kinda thing.'

His evident fatigue and disinterest are no match for my desperate curiosity.

'Well, you seen that Kylie Minogue video, where she walks around the square and it's one long shot and by the end there are four Kylie Minogues in the picture? You seen that? Well that was shot with this machine.'

That looks to be as good an explanation as I am going to get, and I wouldn't know a Kylie Minogue video if I ever saw one. No idea. I haven't even owned a television in recent memory. This is rather sad now I reflect on it.

'What's all the metal lumps?' These have piqued my attention, something nagging at me.

'Ballast. To work, the machine has to be super steady. Steady means heavy. Trouble is, heavy in a field doesn't make steady, especially on a frigging scaff platform. I said it was a stupid idea, but the fucking producer and the client think they know better. It wobbles, only a bit, but it only takes a bit to fuck it all up. We are trying to make it lighter, but it ain't gonna work.'

'Hence the crisis meeting in video village?'

They both laugh at this.

'Yeah, they're trying to talk their way out of this mess. But this has to travel back to the UK tonight, it's booked for another job in three days, can't cancel it. Do you know what these cost a day to hire?'

This sounds excitingly dramatic.

'No idea, how much?' My eagerness must sound childish.

'Mind your own business' says the other guy.

'Sorry, just thought… So you are taking it back to the UK, how long does that take?'

'Forty-eight hours, with two drivers.'

'OK, thanks guys, good luck with it, yeah?'

I leave them to their sulk and commiserations. Memories are niggling at the back of my mind, faces and places and certain activities. Would it be possible? I turn around and walk back to them.

'Sorry, I'm just curious, I used to drive a lot of equipment around Europe, sound equipment, you know. Do you get much ball-ache from customs with something like that? I used to have a terrible time. They fucking hate rock'n'rollers.'

'That's cos they're all dickheads' responds the grumpier one. His mate is less bolshy.

'Naaah, it's cinema equipment, we never get any problems. This moves about Europe so much it's just waved through. We are always on a tight time deadline; they know we'd be screwed if they started playing silly buggers. They don't give us a hard time. Why would they?'

'Yeah of course, it's kinda specialist isn't it. Thanks, it's been fascinating.' My mind's gears are now fully churning, but to what end I haven't dared think of yet. I stroll back up the hill to see if I am needed yet. I never imagined this filming malarkey would be so boring. I suppose if you aren't acting in it, it's endless amounts of hanging around smoking fags and drinking tea. At least it appears that's what most people are doing.

My walkie pipes up. 'Rocio for Jane, Rocio for Jane'. I fumble it and find the button I'm supposed to squeeze.

'Yes, how can I help.' I hear nothing, then realise I am still squeezing the button, so I release it and it sputters back at me.

'…and Paul back to the hotel now. Where are you?'

I walk around the tent to see her.

'I'm here and it's Gene. That's my name.'

'Go. They're waiting for you by the van.'

I depart wordlessly. I am already convinced after a mere three hours I'm not the right material for this business. But it may lead to something. Already has.

I find Paul and Jed waiting, and visibly agitated. Their snivelling says it is partly chemically induced. A potent cocktail, stress and coke. Life shortening, ultimately.

'Where to, gentlemen?' I already know but I like being ostentatiously polite to all these people whose manners have been washed away by VSOP cognac and expense accounts.

'Hotel, and hurry.'

Fair enough.

'What about the others?' I have abandoned most of my charges on set.

'Just fucking drive,' snaps Paul.

They sit on the bench right behind me, and such is their agitation I can clearly hear the conversation. Due to the decisions made about the sighting of the mad machine they can't deliver the shots they need. Re-siting it is a huge job so the whole project is derailed and the beast has to drive back to the UK before the end of the day. It sounds like there's a blame game going on between them. And the stakes are high.

'That was your call Jed, I only deliver what you ask for, you know that' presses Paul.

'Bollocks Paul, you said there wasn't enough money for the extra riggers, and it's not my fault if the client insists on the sizing against everyone's opinion.'

'Exactly, so you have to push this back on them, they have to see that surely?'

'I can't go back to them for a whole day's more budget, are you crazy?' Jed, his shock of unkempt hair seemingly turning grey by the minute is gesticulating, flashes of his flailing visible in the rear-view mirror. 'They've already said, they see this as the production's responsibility, which means me and you Paul. And they even threatened to lawyer up, they're playing hard ball on this.'

'What about an insurance claim, it's a legitimate circumstance. Equipment failure, act of god, whatever the fuck, claim it on the shoot contingency insurance, we've done it before.' Jed doesn't respond but his panicked breathing is audible over the engine even. 'Jed... tell me you've got shoot insurance. Tell me.' Paul now sounds scared. Jed's silence continues. I wish I could see his face. It's probably not the moment to bring up the four hundred euros worth of blow I'm owed for. 'What the fuck is going on, Jed?'

'I'm going under!' Jed is nearly screaming now. 'My back's against the wall. I'm fucked!' He bangs the side of the van which makes me jump and swerve slightly.

'Driver, what the fuck?' says Paul. I don't answer. Silence for a moment, as Jed appears to calm down a little.

'The bank won't extend anymore credit, I had to cut some corners,' he continues. 'I took a calculated risk; the premium was like seventy-five K for full coverage on this. I just don't have the solvency. The bank is at my throat.' He is practically whimpering.

'Jed, I'm seriously exposed on this. You've only given me a 25% advance, and I never do that. But we go back. I'm trusting you, I've gone out on a major limb here, you gotta come through for me. I have to pay all these people still.'

'I know man, I'm sorry. But you should have said there was an issue.'

'Don't you put this back on me, I told you exactly what my construction chief said, I didn't take a position on it. The buck stops with you on this.' Paul's indignation has him practically spitting the words, indeed I can feel the spray from his lips on the back of my neck.

'You should have given him what he wanted' throws back Jed.

'Oh yeah, right, after you demanded I take the 1600€ for the blow from his budget because *you* thought we had some slack in there. The only slack around here is you Jed, because now we are all standing here pissing into the wind.'

The pitch of near hysteria continues. I don't follow the next few exchanges, because I am processing an idea, numbers, probabilities and some straight forward gut reactions. A dirt road leads off right up ahead and I swing down, without warning, throwing the two men around.

'Hey for fuck's sake, driver!' I ignore them and force the van along the dirt road such that its rolling and bouncing makes it difficult to even talk. I pull violently to a halt and turn round to them. Their faces are masks of bewilderment by this point.

'Right, let's put aside the fact you two still owe me four hundred euros for the wrap Jed took to bed last night, as I assume your current financial predicament means I am unlikely to be paid. And that I'm not the only one facing this scenario, correct?'

'Who do you th-'

'Am I correct!?' The sudden forcefulness of my voice and my demeanour stops Jed in his tracks. His face is glistening with sweat, he's breathing unevenly. I can tell he badly needs a line to stave off this stress assault on his body. Paul looks from me to him, plainly worried he has no control of anything anymore. That things are perhaps decidedly out of control all round. He wipes his face.

'Correct, I... guess... yes.' He forces it out.

'I may have a solution for your immediate financial troubles' I say. I have their attention but their faces are pictures of exhaustion and befuddlement. 'It's not a conventional solution, but it could be a quick one. I will need your full discretion, cooperation, and that of the men with your fancy robot arm machine.' No response. I continue.

'I propose to seal three kilogramme packages of uncut cocaine into the ballast ingots of said robot arm, and transport them back to the UK. If you can get me two trips in that truck, you can make enough to solve your current cash flow crisis.' I pause to let this sink in. I have somehow amassed a bunch of hunches and impulses and come up with a conclusion. That Kavanagh and his associates, maybe even Lebid, are stuck sitting on the coke from the warehouse. Because of the shit hitting the fan in Marbella some kind of disruption or fall out has happened. Why else would someone like fucking Darren be going anywhere near shifting keys of blow, with the actual blessing of Kavanagh. It's a hunch, but I'm convinced I can raise the whole game and get right inside, with leverage, by shipping what I think they can't move.

'Are you proposing what I think you're proposing, erm, what's your name?'

'Gene. I'm proposing to shift enough cocaine to the UK to put maybe a hundred grand in your pocket. I need two weeks, that machine, and bingo, done. How you split it is up to you, but I want access to that machine in that truck. Two trips. Two weeks. That's all.'

They both blink at me, trying to process the idea. Paul is the first to respond.

'You jumped up little hoodlum, who the fuck do you think you're playing with here. You're just a sorry little street dealer, down on his luck, washed up because baby brother got himself offed by the Marbella mob. How dare you try and screw us, this is real business, we have a serious problem and we don't need advice from some loser I condescend to give a job to, you little-'

'Paul! Shut the fuck up!' Jed cuts him dead so forcibly even I'm stunned into silence momentarily. 'You, what's your name, Gene' he continues 'who are you and who are your associates?' Paul is mortified, he's slipping into something that is way too outside his comfort zone.

'The cocaine as you know is of high quality. I have three hundred grams sitting at home right now. This isn't small time stuff despite what you might think, Paul. I have contacts here who have been moving significant quantities of class A drugs through Europe for over ten years. Things have been, as you so insensitively mentioned, somewhat troublesome round here lately, and we are looking for a good and reliable route for a shipment or two.'

Paul is dumb. Jed now confirms his worst fears.

'Okay, Paul, I think the gentleman has a proposal worth considering.'

'Are you-' but Jed literally sticks a pudgy, sweaty finger hard into Paul's lips and holds it there.

'Paul, my dick is hanging out on this. I am totally overextended at the bank. I have no insurance cover to pull this one out of the bag. If I can't reshoot this and deliver, we are all fucked, we all take the hit. Everyone. You, me, the crew, the suppliers, even the agency. We're all *fucked*, man. The bank is this far from calling in the exposure to me. If that happens, and it will happen if *we* don't deliver, I lose my house, my company, everything. I'm history. And what's your exposure to me?' Paul processes this for a second as Jed releases his lips.

'A hundred and seventy thousand.' Paul says sheepishly.

'So that's a hundred and seventy thousand good reasons why we are going to do this, clear?'

Paul buries his head in his hands, and through the fingers comes back a muffled 'clear'.

'Thank you, gentleman, I shall take you back to the hotel and go and visit my associates.'

29

The speed of Kavanagh's reaction is a glorious vindication. He practically bit my hand off, metaphorically speaking, though I'm sure he could literally do it as well, with a little provocation. I have arranged to introduce him to Paul and Jed, to cement the relationship. The kinds of quantities involved are not something I am comfortable with being middle-man for. My end will be five grand per key delivered, and I'm responsible for coordination and monitoring. Jed will receive his end of the deal in Essex. We are adjourned in Paul's suite. Their faces changed abruptly when Kavanagh walked in, as the full nature of what they'd embarked coalesced around the bulk, the barely concealed menace, the tattooed, pock-marked, muscled up bulldog nightmare of a man that is Kavanagh. It immediately intimidated them. We agree to two shipments. One for the reshoot, which Jed feels confident enough to have rescheduled on the basis of the new business environment, and a further bogus shoot a week later, for which they need the magic arm of course. Then one of the men I talked to earlier enters and is introduced. His face says he has already been appraised of the use of his truck and machine, and presumably is in the same position of having too much to lose to back out. Then Kavanagh springs a surprise on us all. There's a knock at the door, and on opening, Dmitri walks in. He takes out two bindles of coke, heavily bound in tape. Kavanagh glares directly at them and smiles an unfunny smile.

'These two keys are going in that truck tonight.' Glances are exchanged, people twitch nervously.

'But there isn't time to seal them in the ingots' says the owner of the Movi Tron.

'Doesn't matter. If this idea is as fool proof as we think, it won't be a problem will it. Wedge it in with the ingots and get it delivered. My contact will be at your warehouse waiting. Trial run. Just so we all know what we are dealing with.'

'But…' starts in Paul, but is shut up by Kavanagh's wide hand gripping his chin and cheeks. He freezes with terror.

'You. Talk. Too. Much.' He looks around at all of us. 'If it doesn't get done, deals off, and I think you all understand the implications of that for your respective businesses.' No-one disagrees. Jed studies the floor.

'Good evening gentlemen, we will see you all soon.' He gestures to me to leave.

I am sitting in the back of Kavanagh's idiotic Hummer. My head has relocated back to its position on my neck after having swum around loosely in my body for the last hour or so. I am swooning at the speed of events, at how I have somehow slipped onto the inside track. Where I think I want to be, but without daring to articulate exactly what I might do with my new found position. First things first, though.

'The remaining coke in my flat. I'm not dealing it, it goes in the shipment, agreed?' I state plainly, business like.

'Agreed' says Kavanagh from his driver's seat. Dmitri flashes him a glance. Darren, sat next to me, stares at me with unbridled awe and probably even jealousy.

'Initiative. Imagination. Maybe we'll make a proper drug dealer of you yet, Eugene' he adds.

'Before we go any further, James, can we drop the Eugene malarkey. It's Gene. Okay?'

Kavanagh's shape in the seat in front chuckles.

'You're a cheeky middle-class cunt… Gene.' And nothing else is said as we proceed to finish the initial mission. We transfer to less conspicuous vehicles. Dmitri and Darren head out on scooters to scout for police road-blocks. Such is the geography of the coast, pretty much all traffic is forced onto the long coastal highway to go anywhere at all, even to the corner shop, and occasionally a road

400

escapes up over the mountains into the interior. The forces of law and disorder only have to set up road-blocks on key intersections and they are able to intercept much of the flow of vehicles in any one area. However, being creatures of habit, they use a series of fairly predictable positions which can be surveyed effectively, allowing for routes to be planned to circumnavigate potential searches. Kavanagh is briefing me as to the modus operandi of moving coke along the coast. Inside track. To where?

I meet the Movi Tron truck in some lorry park I don't recognise the location of, near Estepona, I think they said. We wedge the bindles of coke deep inside the innards of the Movi Tron. Kavanagh is to rendezvous in two days with them in Essex. I stand to make ten grand, just out of this one shipment. We mostly work in silence, the palpable tension in all concerned means we have little beyond the necessary to say. The two drivers of the truck are palpably terrified, and trapped in a horrible helter-skelter not of their own making. They visibly shake, but whether with fear or sheer, furious indignation, it's hard to say. Probably both. They scramble into the truck and draw off wordlessly, only shooting me a glance that is a mixture of pure hatred and desperation.

I am inside my comfort zone. Deja vu. Loading trucks in the night with barely anyone talking, focussed on the job, fears reigned in to keep everything running smoothly, keep tempers even, and be discreet. I pity them, pawns in a game spun out of control. It shouldn't have to be this way. If they are pulled, they'll carry the can for Jed's turpitude. And my cunning. It never ceases to amaze me how all the people I know that take drugs, be it coke, pills, smoke, whatever, are utterly oblivious to the real machinations that brings the drug to their sweaty grasp. Unseeing of the violence, menace, and multiple corruptions inherent in the process; unaware of how it corrodes the souls of those engaged in it, draws them all into a noxious swamp of compromise and amorality, so that they live often materially affluent lives, but lives permeated by the corrosive vapours of fear and brutality, contempt and ruthlessness. As addicted and incapable of escaping its clutches as any heroin addict is. And I know I'm back. Like some awful TV drama cliché, the recidivist loser kid from Warrington is at it again. Couldn't make it in the straight world, fucked up his only job, broke his parole, and he's back to the only way he knows how. Full circle. Death wish. Putting a match to the remaining shreds of his nearly regained normality, to torch it once and for all. Kilos of coke. This is big time. High stakes. If it goes wrong, it's either a beating and a bullet, or a life in the slammer. I go through the familiar motions of stashing narcotics with this realisation swirling around me and have to accept it, as though I am not capable of, or deserving of, anything better. This is rock bottom. But that's okay. Because I have nothing to lose. Unlike before, where I was living the life I thought I wanted, the one that protected me from personal relationships, emotion, responsibility, the one that kept me stoned enough to believe my own sad publicity, the knowledge I carry with me now sustains me. It frames all of this around me. The lines of causation, the blood and vengeance, the bizarre fates born of so much human frailty that have brought me here to this moment, fortify me. These fates, this world, this cauldron of corruption is what I shall use to drown them all. I just don't know how. I haven't figured it out yet. But only by diving deep into the filth and the sludge can you find the pearls that will set you free.

A painful slap suddenly brings me out of this reverie.

'I'm talking to you Gene, you daft cunt.' It's Kavanagh. I am in the innocuous looking Skoda, heading back to Marbella.

'Sorry, what?'

'Something on your mind? Something you wanna share with me?' A threat is implicit in his tone. Always. I smile. 'What the fuck is so funny, *Eu*gene?'.

'It's just like old times. I was just remembering, all those nights, ferries to Holland, Herman the German...'

402

'Bollocks to that, Gene. This is the proper stuff. This is Marbella. A man can really live here. Nice houses, pool, gorgeous birds by the ton. Sun, sea, sangria and lots of sex.' He sounds genuinely chipper, for once.

'Sex and drugs and rock'n'roll, all my brain and body need.'

'What?'

'It's a song, from when we were nippers.'

'Sounds about right. Never heard of it though.' I doubt much of nearly forty years of popular culture ever made much impression on Kavanagh. His life has been a singular pursuit of domination. Whether back home back in the day, where he ruled our neighbourhood by fear and intimidation, seemingly immune from police justice for his sundry acts of meaningless violence and theft, or on his current trajectory, nothing hints to anything vaguely cultured apart from his fascination with crime novels and history. He is mostly id. A simple brutal ego, serving an id that thrives on power and violence.

'I ain't got the rock'n'roll but the rest is easy peasy. Time for a celebration, Gene.'

'No thanks, I'm done. I'm going home to crash.' Another slap, which says succinctly I'm not going home.

'Can you stop slapping me?'

Kavanagh guffaws with laughter. 'Not until you stop being a poncey little cunt!' And another slap. There's something endearingly juvenile about it, except it hurts considerably and he should have grown out of it by now. It amuses him, plainly. I resolve to suffer an evening of unpredictable hedonism in the company of people I pity and loathe. And fear, which is why I shall cooperate. I truly have made a pact with the devil.

We are back at Kavanagh's villa. The Skoda is stashed round the back of an enormous three car garage, containing the Hummer, an excessive Harley Davidson with American Indian paraphernalia, and a sleek Audi sports car, nothing like Gary's.

403

'Ultimate escape module, the brand-new Audi R8, four hundred and twenty-eight horse power, nought to sixty in four and a half seconds. It can just about outrun a police helicopter. And the birds love it.' His grin is a mile wide.

I'm already realising that Kavanagh, underneath the narco exterior is still a teenage, testerone infused, thick as shit, old-school macho northerner, impressed by fast cars and big tits. So Marbella suits him down to the ground. Why wouldn't you swap Warrington and Rotterdam for this?

The interior I am invited into is the exact opposite of Gary's apartment. I have to bite my lip to stop myself from laughing out loud at the ridiculousness around me. The walls are a shiny purple. Huge ornate baroque style standard lamps abound. On the floor is what appears to be a real tiger skin rug.

'Don't step on the rug, it's real. Don't want your mucky boots on my little tigger.' My heart sinks as this is duly confirmed. It sits in front of the over the top fireplace. Chrome and smoke glass coffee tables abound, skirted by long white, leather chesterfield sofas. A vast, chromed drinks trolley positively groans with bottles of the now familiar premium vodka brands and single malts. Not a bottle of wine or bubbly in sight. At the opposite end of the vast room to the fireplace is a semi-circular sofa facing the largest television I have ever seen.

'The sixty-five-inch plasma ten-eighty hi-def telly. Sit down, take yer shoes off and relax. The boys will be back in a minute.'

I can't wait. I do as I am told. He flicks on the telly which blasts vibrant, crystal clear colour images at me, and the sound booms out of a surround sound system. He pops it onto MTV and I am immersed in bubble-gum pop in surround sound and colour. It's impressive as well as ridiculous.

'What's your poison?' he asks.

'Ay?'

'Drink, ya muppet!' He feints to slap me again, but he's smiling, and this time it's playful. It's surreal. I'm trying to process all of this, Jimmy K being chummy and relaxed in this palace of excess.

'Vodka and lemon, please Jimmy.'

He roars with laughter. I'm nonplussed.

'Please!? You was properly brought up weren't you Genie boy. Wish some of these pricks around here had your manners.' He's mixing the drinks by the giant trolley as he talks. 'Take Darren for example. He can grunt, and sometimes he puts more than five words together in a sentence, but mostly he grunts.'

He sits at the other end of the semi-circular sofa, drops the sound a bit on the cinema set up and considers me over his enormous vodka and tonic. I am wondering how far I'll get drinking nearly pint-sized glasses of vodka.

'Darren, y'see, he's useful, and he's willing. I mean what the fuck else is he going to do? But he's only ever going to be a runner, a lackey. Bless him. Thieving little fucker he is, which can be useful. But you…' Oh my god, what is this now, a heart to heart with my nemesis? 'You have pleasantly surprised me Gene. And impressed me. The way you spotted that opportunity, the way you sussed out those two fancy-arsed media muppets does you great credit. And it will fill your pockets. Initiative. Creativity. I like that, not enough of it about. It also makes you a dangerous little sod as well. I shall keep my eye on you even more than I would normally. That's the trouble with being intrinsically bright, like your brother. Icarus, innit. He flew too high, and his wings melted.'

There he goes again. Hints of wider intelligence than the public persona he ably demonstrates to most people. No tact though, as ever.

'Well, we are going to celebrate to seal our newly established mutual interest,' he continues. 'I want you to feel part of the family. I want you to feel that you're one of us now Genie boy. Let bygones be bygones.' He's wearing that sardonic smirk again, slippery, shape-shifting, bullshitting bastard that he is. He could be genuine, but it's still menacing, disturbing. 'It's important in this game, as you know, that we can trust each other.' Then he drops the sardonics and is fixing me with a penetrating glare. My sphincter tries to fold in on itself. 'You were a useless little shit when you was a nipper, and you got what you deserved. I saw what you did in Holland. You did your time and you didn't grass. That went down well. And now here we are…' and he lets his words hang, waiting for I don't know what. Well, I've put myself here, in this sofa, intentionally, consciously, so I have to step up.

'Who'd have thunk it, ay?' He throws his head back and laughs at this, then just as quickly fixes me with the glare again.

'Waddya mean, Gene?'

I have to think about this next answer, can't joke around it. How do I put this?

'Well, let's say our relationship thus far has been… complex? Fraught? Unnecessarily antagonistic?'

He laughs yet again, taking time for the chuckle to die away.

'Gene, it's been entirely and necessarily antagonistic. I'd have thought you'd have understood that by now.' I choose silence on this one, merely raise my glass and take a long slug. 'But you have a point. We have miraculously come to a new understanding, so I think it's a good thing to clear the air a bit. Set some things straight, make sure we all understand each other, that there's no lingering… resentments, like?'

I could say some things that would probably get me killed right now, that would make me feel a whole lot better regardless, but this isn't even about me anymore, former me that is. Stoner glum Gene.

'I think that is long overdue. The bygones are indeed bygones, this is the Brave New World is it not? The phoenix rising from the ashes of the monumental Holme cluster fuck. Fuck all that

406

aspirational golf bollocks! Let's give the people what they want, and make shit loads of money doing it! Here's to class A drugs!' I stand up and raise my glass. 'Let's give all those image obsessed narcissists, those useless, shallow, preening party ponces exactly what they deserve! Fuck the lot of them and show me the moneeeeeeeey!!!' I am screaming with glee, and I'm not sure why, but it feels good, and it satisfies my contempt for the craven pursuit of drug fuelled hedonism, which is mostly due to my weakness for it, rather than some morally elevated insight.

'Fucking AAAAAA!' yells Kavanagh and crashes his glass against mine, ice cubes and liquid splashing onto the plush sofa. No sooner does this happen than a diminutive middle-aged Philippine looking lady in a classic French maid's outfit appears and fastidiously mops the slops.

'Thank you, Concha!' She shoots him a look and retreats. 'She hates it when I say that.'

'Uhhh, why?'

''Cause she's not called fucking Concha, hahaha!'

'What's she fucking called then?!' I am warming to the frenzied stupidity and wonder briefly if there was something else in the vodka.

'I dunno, Esperanzo or something unpronounceable. Whatever. Anyway, calm down Gene.'

'What?' He has turned serious, not sardonic, and my instincts have barely started to palpitate when a figure appears at the other end of the lounge.

'There's someone that needs to meet you.'

He sits and is quiet. A man enters the room. It is Lebid, approaching me. Lebid himself, unaccompanied by goons. He's dressed in an extremely well-cut cream suit, with a pink shirt, open at the collar. His hair is slicked back, he's tanned, dripping in gold jewellery, and looks every inch the middle-aged matinee cinema idol.

He takes my hand, and embraces it with his other, and looks me straight in the eye.

'Hello Gene, it's a pleasure to meet you finally.' I am speechless. 'Please, sit down.'

His English is excellent. I'm gawping at him, trying to process what is happening, trying to separate my stored up baggage, my actual conceptions of the man and my presumptions about his involvement in Gary's murder, trying to push them away from thumping the back of my eyeballs, so I can compose myself and carry on the new performance in this hastily and recently written script.

'Well, erm, what a surprise. It's erm, good to meet you too.'

His gaze doesn't flicker. It's also the first time I've ever seen Kavanagh switch off his alpha male persona, his need to be the dominant being in any particular space or situation. He is all deference and humility. I am trying to concentrate and block out the myriad screaming voices inside my head.

'Jimmy has told me how your initiative is helping us. I am very pleased, and a little surprised. I know things have been somewhat turbulent recently, and the tragic loss of your brother must have affected you terribly. And yet here you are. It's impressive, and interesting. To what do we owe this daring improvisation?'

Noises be still. Crush the thundering cacophony. Focus damnit.

'Mr Lebid…' I see it now, it's just an endless roiling motion, all of it, everything that has passed is just random stuff that washes over us endlessly. We either sink in it, swim with it, and maybe just surf its wave for a while. I just need to swim….'I've had a pretty rough ride these past few years. Well, for many years. Gary was my brother, who was lost to me, and then I got him back. And then he was taken from me, just when I realised what I had again. So yes, I am trying to readjust, to get a foothold on life again. There's only me left in my family, I've lost both my parents as well, but I also feel responsible toward Ana. She will bear his child, who will by my kin.

That's something worth striving for, staying alive for. And despite my university education, my only skill set still relates to this activity, maybe because it's the only thing I have allowed myself to learn to do.' It's a humiliating admission, but par for my course. 'So, when shit really hits the fan, you have to dig deep, find a way back up. I've been around here long enough to get a feel for the place, and certain things fell into place this time, so I would be a fool not to seize such an opportunity. Opportunism. Experience, I dunno, just a hunch, a feeling for it. I think it will work. I have no idea about anything after this deal. I haven't had time to consider that yet. I've barely buried my brother.'

This last phrase hangs heavy in the air. No-one speaks. The sofa squeaks reluctantly as Kavanagh's considerable bulk twists involuntarily. Lebid is inscrutable. A considerable achievement, a great talent in certain worlds, to be able to appear civil, composed, friendly even, yet be utterly and completely inscrutable; to show no weakness, let slip no cues or hints as to the workings behind the slick hair and expensive cologne.

'Your brother was a remarkable man, Gene. He laboured in the shadow of and service of a greater ego, a mentor yes, but also his gaoler. Your brother had the talent to do great things, to be a serious asset to Marbella. It is nothing short of tragic what happened.'

Is he really saying this? I could fall over, roll on the floor, if I let my composure slip for a second, laughing in disbelief, exasperation. Confusion. The scene before me fades, I am floating several feet behind myself, listening intently.

'Did you have my brother killed, Mr Lebid?' I zoom back into the scene. I detect a faint hint of human under the cologne, as though Lebid's body releases a miniscule puff of adrenalin. Or is it Kavanagh, whose snort and flinch presage some habitual violent rejoinder, but a simple show of a flat hand of Lebid's stays his impulse. Lebid doesn't take his eyes off me, and he still reveals nothing. Not even a flicker of something, no matter how tenuously related to a thought or emotion.

'Gene, I will not begrudge you the temptation, for someone in your position, to entertain that consideration.' Kavanagh lets out a long breath and his cobra's strike appears to be stood down. The sofa echoes his relaxing frame. 'Holme was an ambitious man, a high achiever, but nowhere near as intelligent or talented as your brother. Holme overreached himself, and your brother tried bravely to avert the destruction caused by his decisions. For this perceived treachery, Holme had your brother murdered. I feel very let down by him, but I cannot waste further time and effort on this ultimately disappointing affair.'

Still the desire to laugh hysterically threatens to drown my equilibrium.

'So you wouldn't be available to testify on his behalf, bring Holme to justice. I think Gary deserves it.' It seems reasonable to ask, but given who he is, and the context, it's ludicrous, satisfyingly so. It's also signing my own death warrant. I am spectating an expert player in his element, giving the faultless, totally controlled performance of lying, that only highly ruthless, accomplished, truly powerful men can deliver. Except that he corpses ever so slightly. A slight flinch of the neck muscles and reflexive swallow ever so slightly ripples the calm surface of his composure.

'Be careful what you wish for, Gene.'

Oh, you silken smooth whore, you voluptuary, you temptress with your calm and politesse, your guilt reeks such that I can smell it over the Hermes scent, the Armani cut, the careful tan.

'I'm sorry, Mr. Lebid, excuse me, I am being naive. Forget I said it.' Nothing further to be gained by this line. I'm just planting a flag with my own jaded colours on his consciousness. We are jousting, feeling each other's skills and moves. We are in a dance, and I have probably stepped into my brother's shoes.

410

'It's been difficult, I understand. I am confident we can settle things with Mr Holme over time' he replies. 'I must say goodbye, and entrust you to Mr. Kavanagh's organisation. My time here in Spain is over. I have been badly let down, and will not waste further time or money under such circumstances. Good luck, Gene.'

The faintest of smiles that accompanies this chills me, as he shakes my hand and leaves. As he disappears through the front door, he leaves instructions. 'Take him through the M.O. Jimmy'. The use of the standard police terminology doesn't make me feel any better.

Jimmy has stood up and has turned to face me. He scans my face, pulls his fist back, but before releasing the crunching blow he laughs, drops his fist, and moves toward me. He envelopes me in a bear hug that steadily becomes tighter, the hardened torso crushing the air from my chest. His mouth is next to my ear, and he speaks in a similarly polite, vapourless tone to Lebid.

'I don't know whether you are bloody stupid, very brave, or just a cheeky little cunt, Gene. But the worst thing about it is I think I am actually beginning to like you.' As he steps back, he delivers his customary side swiping slap, which given his taut, vindictive force, knocks me off my feet. He is now laughing uproariously. 'Jesus Christ we really are going to have to toughen you up Genie boy. What are you made out of? Cheese spread? Fuck me. Here, have another drink. Conchaaaa!'

Concha is dispatched, and expressionlessly fixes us more gargantuan vodkas. I'll die of alcohol poisoning long before Lebid has me offed. Kavanagh starts to take me through my responsibilities and how it all will work. It turns out the lucrative commission per kilo isn't so lucrative after all, as the costs of prepping the merchandise for transport are mine. I am a separate business. I won't have anything further to do with anyone except Darren, unless specifically necessary. Darren is the courier who will ensure the packages arrive to be prepared for sealing in ingots. The metallurgy involved in this process is also my responsibility. I never thought I'd need the services of Herman the German again. Where do I find his equivalent on the Costa? Jonathan. Of course. Maybe he's up for it. I need premises, equipment, discretion, plausible deniability. I've got a week to ready it for when the Movi Tron truck makes its first trip back. All communication with Paul and Jed is handled by Kavanagh. I'm mercifully out of that loop. A neat bindle of ten grand is placed on the table, reward for the two keys already en route as we speak. It will enable me to set up everything else. Christ, I am really going to have to work for this money. As we go over this, people are arriving at the house. Darren and Dmitri I know. Others not. Concha is kept busy dishing out vodkas. The sound system has been turned up and I struggle to hear Kavanagh over the din of ugly techno music and drug dealer ribaldry.

'So that's the set up.' Kavanagh is winding up my initiation. 'No phone calls. Text messages will be used with simple code phrases, written on this piece of paper. This paper doesn't leave this house. Learn before you leave tonight.'

'What, after all the vodka you've poured down me?'

'Step up Genie!' Slap. Again. Just the bruising from his endless thumps will give me an extra layer of protective scar tissue at this rate. 'Stay as long as you need, just be out of here before morning.'

'Morning?'

'Yes, because for now, we party. Come on, come down to the dungeon.' He gets up with his vodka, and everyone else is deferentially waiting for him to lead the way. Familiar churnings inside commence as we head down some stairs toward a basement. Am I to receive some brutal initiation, what wonders of sadism or moronic bravado are about to be visited on me?

We emerge into a cavernous underground space, the warmth and humidity wrap themselves around me instantly. It is an underground spa. A round pool is equipped with bubbling water jets and spouts. To the left, on a platform is a vast jacuzzi. To the right are the inevitable white sofas, a bar, and a full sound system and DJ set up. It's a microcosm of Marbella itself.

'Darren, put Frankie on' orders Kavanagh.

'Right boss.'

In a moment Frankie Goes to Hollywood's 'Welcome to the Pleasure Dome' is booming through the speakers. Meanwhile I survey the decor. Gone is the faux baroque. Instead it's white and plain, with inset lighting, forming a backdrop, a gallery wall, for the *piéce de la resistance* of this particular pleasure dome. A dozen or so huge full colour photographs, printed onto enormous glass sheets decorate the interior. The quality is spectacular, rendering the impact of the subject matter all the more overwhelming. On the walls are twelve ludicrously endowed women in poses of pornographic intensity, a veritable masterclass in sexual gynaecology. The eye cannot escape for a moment the photographically enlarged thighs, buttocks, breasts and vulvas. It is queasy making, especially after all the vodka.

Kavanagh gestures, arms aloft, like the high priest. Bizarrely, he reminds me of Holme. The music goes off, and everyone pays attention.

'Right listen up. Most of you know who this is.' He gestures to me, provoking a few sniggers and sighs. 'Well you might think he's a wanker, but...' and he has to pause over the hoots of derision and agreement, '...but his initiative has put us back in business.' The noise settles to a curious attention and scepticism. 'He was a wanker when he was little, agreed.' Cackles, snorts of derision again. 'But now he's working with us, and he has a little operation coming up. It's his show. So it's his to fuck up.' He smiles leeringly at me, but everyone is now paying serious attention. 'Usual protocols apply. Do your jobs. Instructions will be issued later this week. Keep an eye on the usual channels. New codes for text messages will be given, so nobody go off the radar. So, and I never thought I'd say this, show Gene here some respect. Now, let's party.'

Bizarrely people make their way over, pat my back, shake hands, deliver the odd Kavanagh slap, but not nearly as painfully. Then, Dmitri approaches. He takes my hand and the shake turns to a furious grip so I have to use all my strength to not yell in pain. He leans into my ear.

'I see you, Eugene. Like your brother, you not one of us, you just on for the ride. I *know* who you are. I watch you, don't worry.' He winks and releases my hand. His sullen contempt for me has never changed, it's consistent and pure, cutting straight through, like the purest cocaine. It's enough to bring all of this madness into brutal relief. I stand alone now as the drinking starts. Watching. I am not of this, as Dmitri says. I am a passenger, disposable, a convenient tool, a hapless mark, a useful idiot. But I am finally on the inside, in the belly of the beast. I need to see the Inspector as soon as possible. From here I must be able to start the endgame. Just being a part of any of this makes me as good as dead sooner or later. I'd happily trade a few more years behind bars to take a few of the bastards with me.

Despite the heat and humidity, I shiver, nausea and fear rising above the vodka. My knees are jelly, the task before me swims around my head. Darren walks up to me.

''Kinell, relax why don't you, look like yer at a funeral or something' he says, unhelpfully.

'I was just a couple of days ago if you recall.'

'Shit, yeah, sorry mate.' He pauses reflectively, and hands me the joint in his hand. I draw on it gratefully, a smooth aromatic weed, just what the doctor ordered under the circumstances. The sloshing inside slows and the nerves tingle and liquify up my back and neck. 'Funny old world innit.' I look at him, the spindly frame, the sticky out ears, the half naïve, half worldly-wise face, and start to giggle. He joins in and we smoke the spliff, chuckling, watching Concha run around to the bellowed demands of various Neanderthal acolytes of Kavanagh's. He gestures to Darren, who jumps to attention.

'Hey up, it's the main event. Wait till you see this…' and he heads back to his DJ decks.

I'm on my own, as welcome as explosive diarrhoea in a sauna, still considered the wanker as no-one takes a blind bit of notice of me now.

Darren cranks up the sound, Prince is singing 'you sexy mother fucker', and then a raucous cheer goes up. Through a door at one corner of the room enters a parade of girls. Not just any girls. Young girls, long legged and blond mostly, clad in the inevitable tight-fitting provocative paraphernalia of pole dancers. Indeed, two of them launch themselves onto the pole I hadn't noticed in front of the banks of white sofas. Another couple kick off the heels and slide into the Jacuzzi, followed by a couple of guys, peeling t-shirts off as they go, revealing the evidently standard muscled torsos with tattoos and numerous dubious looking scars. There's at least ten of them, and while maybe not your actual super models, the combination of clothing, heels, bare flesh, hair, make-up and the overacted eroticism of their movements is effective enough at bypassing any embarrassment or ideological qualms that may have attempted to impose themselves on my perception. Well, that and the vodka-marijuana cocktail have me goggle-eyed. But naturally, they are all ignoring me. Until Kavanagh pulls a shortish Asian girl to him, who behaves considerably more shyly than the others, most of whom are already grinding themselves against someone. He says something, points over at me, a gesture some others pick up on, and a gallery of faces watches, leering with amusement as the girl snakily walks over to me. As she arrives in front of me, she places her hands on my shoulders and leaps up, seizing my midriff with her surprisingly powerful thighs, nearly causing me to topple over and I lurch a couple of steps to regain balance. The hoots of laughter and derision are audible even over the volume of the music.

'Hi, my name Sally.'

'Gene.'

She presses her lips to mine and her tongue darts in and rapidly explores, as her lips pucker and press. Then she heads off down my neck, sucking hard, licking little crevices I had forgotten existed, setting off chills and spasms in various corners of my ears, chin and mouth again. Electric currents spark up from there to my loins, animated by the marijuana into a surging sizzling all over my skin.

'You want to go to bedroom?'

'Oh yes please' I respond without a shred of self-examination. She leads me like a naughty child across the space and back towards the door, as people laugh and hoot at me, a couple of wanking hand gestures are offered my way, but everyone is too caught up in their own lust to worry about our need for privacy. Except Dmitri. I catch his eye just before we disappear through the door. Sat motionless, nursing a can of Coca-Cola, alone, fixing me with a stare, inscrutable, expressionless, like an uglier version of Lebid. He's singularly not behaving like everybody else. It dawns on me he must be the enforcer, the one sane, sober psychopath who keeps an eye out for the chiefs, keeps everyone in line and knows all their secrets. Yes, that would make complete sense. Never lets the guard own, loses control, always maintains vigilance and readiness.

We disappear into a small room evidently kitted out for intercourse; I'm relieved to be out of Dmitri's glare. I imagine him as Sauron, up in his citadel, beaming malevolence over the world, while the Orcs cavort and fuck under his one watchful Eye. I am so taken up with this nutty fantasy metaphor, wishing I had a ring to make myself invisible, chuckling as I imagine Darren as Gollum, that I take some time to realise I am semi-naked and a small Asian girl with skin smooth as alabaster is writhing about me, as I am her, and I am sinking gratefully into a swirling pit of carnal sensuality. She stops momentarily, causing a yell of anguish from me, but places a finger to my lips and produces another spliff from her clothing. We smoke it together, communicating in giggles and licking of body areas. Then I give myself to it all, the smell of her skin, sweetly spiced, the dense black hair, full lips, gyrating hips, it envelopes me, dimensions crumble and time warps in a massive haze of smoke and sex, and I'm gone.

Consciousness drifts in. Of my own sweat. I am damp. Limbs are intertwined, a body is stuck to me, sticky, dark hair glistening in the low light. Hours must have passed. I don't know. I study the face in front of me. The transportive qualities of powerful weed and numbing effects of vodka have considerably diminished. I am aware a person is here with me, not some erotic abstraction. I pull my head back, and meet her eyes. She is barely a woman, I think, I can't judge. Remorse starts to creep like a cockroach across a kitchen floor. She stares into my eyes. She has a shadow around one of them, I go to touch it but she flinches. A recent bruise. The cockroach kicks up. She draws away from me and gathers the one sheet around herself, rocking herself slightly. The kitchen floor is alive with cockroaches. She moves to get up, but I reach out and gently pull her back to me, easing her resistance back, until I pull her into a spoon position, and nuzzle my face in her hair. I stay here for some time while I try and fathom how I feel about this, what just happened.

'Sally?' She tenses perceptibly, but I wait. 'Sally. That's not your real name is it.' The tension releases and she turns over to face me. Tears rim her eyes, which only makes the dance of the roaches even more frenzied. 'Where are you from?'

'Laos.'

'Really?' I immediately feel stupid, what did I expect, why does it matter to me? Am I trying to humanise her in my eyes. Dance roaches dance. 'When did you come to Spain?' Jesus, what am I trying to do.

'Mr K say we not to talk to the clients.' The fear shadows across her face.

'Don't worry, Mr K is a good friend of mine.' Bile rises within me. No matter how I try, I can't figure a way I could have a sincere conversation with this girl. My role as exploiter and she as exploited is hewn in granite, solid. I want to smash my head against a wall, then curdle at such a self-indulgent melodramatic gesture. Face it Gene. Look where you are. See who you are. I am drained. I pull her to me and hug her close and, against my expectations she responds, and sniffles quietly for a while. I turn her over to face me. 'One day I will try and come back for you. Take you away from here. I promise.' I think I believe myself but a giant cockroach stares at me, face to face, his tentacles twitching in hilarity at my moral posturing. Fortunately, this surreal reverie is shattered by an enormous thump on the door. It opens as we ludicrously scrabble for the sheets to appear decent. It's Dmitri who opens the door, observes our postures, and snorts derisively.

'Party over. Time for you to go to work. Come, I take you back to your place. Move.'

And the door slams. I look at 'Sally'. The life has retreated back from her eyes, a veil has fallen over the pretty face, as its spirit withdraws itself back into the frail sanctuary at the core of her being. I am all of a sudden completely invisible to her. She gets up, dresses wordlessly and leaves the room without a backward glance.

I am in a car with Dmitri. It is an uncertain time of the morning after the night before, before dawn, mercifully. I am being drilled in the code words and phrases, an apparently banal and barely credible set of euphemisms for drug moving activities, that we must use for the texts. Any detective could see through them, but it's more about plausible deniability. It makes the evidence trail that bit more shaky. Indistinct. Debatable. The drive is interminable, and Dmitri's pressure relentless and malevolent. He pulls up outside my block and turns to me.

'So. Eu-gene. U for useless. If you fuck this up, or try to fuck us, I will put bullet in you myself. *Da*?'.

I meet his glare.

'Whatever. I had a nice night. She was cute. You ever tried her?' I figure the female of the species is the only chink in his armour.

418

The look on Dmitri's face is satisfying. Without my current status he would have killed me then and there. 'Night, thanks for the lift.'

'You dead man. Maybe not tomorrow, but one day, Useless Gene.'

The car accelerates away so violently the door is flung shut and nearly chops me in half, but I pull back with merely bangs and bruises. Shaking now, I run to the flat, I plunge my hands under both running taps, splashing myself over and over with water, I grab a toothbrush and scrub a scrub till the bowl swirls with blood and spittle, and rinse and splash until the bathroom is awash. I stare intently in the mirror at the head of a giant cockroach.

30

Thank the Gods for Jonno. I am able to get him on the phone the next morning. He meets me in my flat and I explain the gig to him. He also has his arse hanging out, financially speaking, thanks to Jed and Paul's incompetence, so he's revelling in helping the machinery they are both now embroiled in, and I am also paying him a fat lot of money to be the smelter and engineer of our little project. Further still, he has dragged me up a hill outside Estepona to a shabby villa belonging to a contact. I survey the premises. Behind some tall fences overgrown with dense vegetation covered in multiple colours of flowers, sits what in England would be called a big bungalow, but because it's Spain it's a villa. No matter how grotty. It is a C-shaped building, with terracotta walls, roman tiles, and a stone forecourt with a couple of straggly lemon trees. Adjoining the left side of the building is a large, high garage big enough for a truck to park in. It has ugly unpainted metal doors front and back. On the opposite, back side of the villa is a decent size pool filled with green, turgid water. Olive and lemon trees have been planted here and there, pruned in an attempt to produce natural shade, but run to seed. French windows run along the back facades, opening most of the villa onto the garden and pool. In another time and different circumstances, it would be a nice place to live. But the grass is uncut, the trees suffer from die back and any amount of rubbish and abandoned equipment collects dust, paintwork and panelling cracking and warping away in the relentless Spanish sun.

We adjourn inside, where the owner plops three cans of Cruzcampo onto a filthy kitchen table.

'Bloody hell Derek, it's only half eleven,' cajoles Jonno.

'Well don't fuckin drink it then' huffs Derek, 'no skin off my nose, is it.' Derek is maybe sixty, or a messed up fifty, crew cut, rotund, round faced and surly. Ancient acne scars pockmark his face, reminding me of Kavanagh. His cockney accent is as broad as his girth, his teeth yellow from tobacco and the whole place reeks of stale cooking fat, accumulated grunge and cheap cigarettes. I leave the can untouched. I don't know where to put myself as I fear contracting something if I touch a surface. It's disgusting, even by my former standards.

My body recoils at the thought of anymore drinking. I have mused, these few mornings past, as I stare into the unshaven, pale and haggard face in the mirror, with its newly forming bags under the eyes, what this is all doing to my long-term health, never mind my sanity. Depressingly the distance from me to Derek isn't as far as I'd like to think. The conversation continues.

'So, two months up front, sixteen hundred a month, for a minimum of a year. The market's just gone to shit, and I can't afford to tart the place up, I'm kind of stuck with it.'

'You're out of the game then?' enquires Jonathan.

'Yeah. My knees are gone, the younger guys are undercutting us all the time, and they're mostly muppets. The production lot from London these days… 'ave you seen 'em? Barely out of nappies, jumped up over-entitled public school knobheads who got a job from Daddy's best mate. Not a clue. They haven't had to work up the system, don't know their arse from their elbow most of 'em,' grumbles Derek, pulling on his third cigarette already.

'What is it you do? Did?' I ask.

'Key grip. Thirty years and proud.'

I look at Jonno blankly.

'Grips are the guys on a film crew who handle all the equipment that supports the actual camera. Tripods, dollies, cranes. They put it up, push it, pull it. Heavy work, hard.' I nod my comprehension.

'Young man's job,' says Derek in between a calamitous coughing fit, 'younger than me anyway. The missus fucked off on me, with Pedro from the restaurant down the way. Can you believe it? So there's not much left for me 'ere. Pity. But it's not the same no more. It's all golf, and sunbeds and poncey clubs. I'm off back to Dagenham. Mi bruvver's got a garage there, I can help out, get a proper pint when I want one.'

I wonder inwardly why Derek ever bothered coming here.

'Sorry to 'ear that' Jonathan commiserates.

'You're doin' me a great favour. You get on with it, and I'll load up the truck and I'll be out your hair in three days and it's all yours. So what you doin' then, what makes you wanna shack up in this old shithole?' and he descends into a mixture of laughter and further coughing.

'Well, I've just moved down here, and I'm looking for a place to do up maybe, while I, er…'

Derek exchanges a look with Jonno, holds up a hand, as if by apology.

'Don't worry son, none of my business, just get on with it, good luck to you.' I have the impression he knows exactly what's going to go down in his former dream home.

It turns out old Derek has some rather useful equipment in his garage, none of which is of much value to anyone else. There's a lathe, and other machine tools, a winch running on a trellis across the ceiling of the workspace. In short, it's perfect for our purposes. And cheap as chips, discreetly hidden, up a dead-end dirt track where no-one ever goes except Derek and two old Spanish guys and their mouldy dogs, tending their barren allotments from their shacks. I almost feel competent myself. Herman the German would have loved this place.

We waste no time putting together our workshop. First, we blag an amount of scrap zinc and lead from local scrap metal yards, which abound here. Jonno's near perfect Andaluz opens doors I never could. Getting the two huge butane gas tanks takes a good deal more effort, a signed contract, a paper trail of sorts, but needs must. They have to be delivered by a crane truck, so hopefully we won't be too delayed as we are now on a tight deadline. Builders sand will have to do for moulds. Jonno fortunately has his own arc welding kit. With a smelting bucket, we are ready to go. This turns out to be a considerably expensive champagne bucket for jeroboams, made from solid stainless steel. If the Corte Ingles ever knew why the scruffy *guiri* wanted such a thing. I certainly got peculiar looks from the assistants, parting happily with three hundred euros. They probably don't sell so many.

No-one will think it strange how much pizza we are eating, I hope. Darren appears twice a day on his pizza delivery scooter, carrying two kilos a time. The same methods of scouts and look-outs clear the way for the coke to find its way along the coast to us. Here we are able to steer the Movi Tron truck into the truck sized garage, stack the ingots in the beast and send it on its way. Derek sees much of this activity as he readies himself, loading his own truck with personal items, obsolete bits of film equipment, stands, rails, tripods and other peculiarities. The worst of which is his pool table, which nearly kills the three of us. He says nothing, just nods knowingly and chuckles to himself, between wrenching coughs that shake his whole frame, and threaten to put his fag out, spluttering as he does. I am counting the hours till I can empty the house of its gruesome filthy furniture, and take a gallon of bleach and detergent to the place. It's unsanitary.

Occasionally I receive texts. The scarcely veiled impatience and fury is comical in its euphemisms.

'When can we pick up the fucking shopping, we're starving'

'Sorry, still haven't defrosted it, and we couldn't find any eggs. Ask me tomorrow'

'I need to borrow the car and it isn't available the day after tomorrow. Pull your finger out.' And so on.

Eventually, eight days after my night in Kavanagh's villa, a GB plated truck rolls quietly into the villa garden and just squeezes into the garage. Jonno is just welding up the last ingot halves. The delays have been from the amount of space we have for moulds, and how long the ingots take to cool, but especially how fast you can melt down scrap using three paella burners stacked one on top of another with the big champagne bucket perched precariously on top. Actually, Herman would have pissed his sides at our performance. The whole process has been three days of sourcing equipment and set-up, plus a further four and half days of smelting and sealing. Some ingots are still hot to the touch as they are loaded into the base of the Movi Tron. We have barely slept. As the truck lurches away along the dirt track, anonymously, as close as we are to sprawling industrial estates and farm buildings, scruffy yards and building suppliers, Jonno and I high five and crack open beers, slumping on one of the filthy sofas in the tatty old lounge, still reeking of stale tobacco.

'There you go, Jonno. Five grand. I couldn't have done it without you, not a hope in hell.'

'I'll do two more loads, then I'm out of here. This place is so burned. Eighteen years, slinging my arse around this madhouse, it's been a bit of a roller coaster. Thanks. It has probably got me out of the hole Paul left me in, and he may yet even pay me, thanks to your little scheme. Hope springs eternal.'

'What film was that a line from? Or was it a book?' I ask.

'Buggered if I know. Gene... you know, this business is not one you can walk away from. I can, I'm going to put a lot of miles between you, me and this, but you are in it up to your neck with whoever these people are. How do you figure staying ahead of the game?'

Of course, I haven't thought of how. The hazy end game I have in mind is not one I could share, as I can't articulate it, depending so much as it does on Treece's abilities to draw in the forces of law and order, to marshal the information we all share and make it work against them all. Ahead of the game? No, detonate the game entirely if possible. Achieve closure.

424

'Well, I figure I'll diversify. Maybe just grow hash under lamps in this nice big garage. Should keep me nicely for a while.'

He shakes his head and chuckles.

'Mad fucker. Where did you come from? This coast. It really throws up all sorts. I shall miss it, but Jesus, it's going to get messy here.'

'Pretty messy already mate. Trust me.' Nightly visions of Gary's brains on the windscreen testify to that. Jonno makes to leave.

'Get some rest Gene, you look like shit. Take care, okay?'

'No worries, thanks, see ya next week. I'll text.'

Yes. Worries.

I'm left alone. I send the confirmation text. Silly codes.

'Shopping delivered, let me know when you can pick up some more groceries.'

'Great, get me two dozen eggs please. Need them for a week on Tuesday.'

Banal texts laden with implications. Jesus, this is going to be relentless. Twenty-four kilos is a lot of smelting and welding. If I have to order more butane tanks, I'm worried I'll trigger suspicions. Hopefully we won't need it, as I'd need to somehow disguise what we're up to to any delivery driver. It's bound to arouse curiosity. It's a Saturday night in April, the breeze blows in warm and perfumed from the terrace windows. The dusk sky glows a collection of purple, orange, pink and pale green hues behind the Sierra Bermeja, twenty clicks down the N340. It's beautiful. But I can't see it. I'm dead with fatigue, my lungs scorched from metallic vapours, and gas fumes. Darren wasn't too amused when I insisted he bring real pizzas, we had so little time to pause and eat. He received an ear bending off Kavanagh that set him straight. I have thirty-six hours before I have to crank up the whole operation again. It's a deadly treadmill, and not one I can simply step off. The drugs trade has a horrible basic logic to it. If you can successfully move product a certain way, you move as much as you can while you can, and if it gets burnt, you isolate yourself from the minions doing the dirty work, and set up elsewhere. I know I'm just going to be collateral damage somewhere down the line. I'm not part of the inner circle. I'm totally dispensable once this route dries up. And that could be in two weeks, three at the outside.

I'm meeting Treece, I need him to find an endgame for me. I need to see Ana as well, see if she has any clarity on what Gary knew, what really went on behind the hype. I feel ill at ease in my own skin. A separate layer has been inserted underneath, just over my muscle tissue. It envelopes me in a sort of putrid body stocking, it niggles and itches, it allows me no true rest, the ability to disconnect or relax. It fuels the sweaty nightmares and visions of the shooting that plague my nights more vividly than ever. There isn't enough vodka in the world to knock it out, so I've stopped drinking so much. I have resigned to live, squirming amongst these sensations, of dread, fear, the low decibel hum of quiet panic. Jonno didn't notice much, just thought I had the shits, due to my frequent visits to the toilet to vomit. The taste of bile is permanently resident in my mouth. My breath must stink, but I'm past caring.

I meet Treece in a quiet cafeteria on the edge of Estepona. He's taken aback.

'What happened to you? Are you okay? You don't look well.'

'Ha-ha, really, it's just the pressure of being an international commodities trader.'

'Remind me not try it.' As if he needs reminding.

'Come on,' I leave a couple of coins on the table to cover my coffee, 'I've got a lot to take you through.'

As we drive out of town through blocks of residential apartments, I fill him in on the breakneck narrative of events. Barely two weeks from snagging a dumb job on a shoot to having despatched over twenty kilos of uncut Columbian to the UK. Treece's eyes are wide, and he listens in silence. He appears daunted, and frankly, scared.

We arrive at the villa and I take him straight to the garage. 'Come Monday, Jonno and I will be taking delivery of maybe four kilos per day, couriered here on a moped. We'll melt down this scrap, create two halves of each ingot in these moulds here, weld them up, and they are loaded onto the truck, which stays here barely an hour. Next shipment is twenty-four kilos. Most likely ten days later there'll be another one. That's our window of opportunity to nail this down.'

'And how are you going to do that?' he asks blinking, overawed by the actuality of the scene.

'Well, you tell me, you're the policeman, how *do* you take down a smuggling ring?' I'm confused and indignant. Wondering why I've put myself here if not to bring it all down on our heads. 'Stake outs, raid this place, catch us in the act, raid Kavanagh's place. I'll give evidence, witness protection, bingo, job done.' I'm twitching, practically hyperventilating. It all sounds clear to me at least. Or am I living in my own crime movie, did I miss something somewhere?

'But Gene, this is all so sudden. This is serious stuff, high stakes, and I haven't even got off the ground yet. We're in Spain, I can't simply pick up a phone to CID or drug squad.'

'But… you said…' I slump onto the ground. My legs won't support my weight. I keel over onto my side, and I close my eyes. Sleep is coming. I'm so tired. I want to sleep. I must have fallen asleep, as I am now awoken by Treece slapping me.

'Gene. Stop this! Come on, let's get you up. Is there a bathroom here?' I gesture to the end of the lounge. 'Right come on, you need a shower. You stink, you need to get a grip if we are going to sort out this mess.' I rail against him, pulling away, stumbling.

'Fuck off, who are you, my Dad? If you don't want to sort this, I'll do it myself,' and I flail at him and babble some more, I'm not sure what even. Next thing I know he's got me an arm lock and has frog marched me to the shower. Old copper's tricks.

'Gene, listen to me, you're in shock. You are most likely suffering PTSD; it would be perfectly normal. You're losing your

427

grip, you're fatigued, you probably haven't eaten properly in days, and you've been taking god knows what by the sound and look of it.' He pretty much pulls my clothes off me. And now, yes I do catch the animal funk of my fetid body. The cold shower blasts lights through my head, my metabolism takes an adrenalin kick. My howling can probably be heard down the hill. Towelled down, dressed again, villa locked up and out into the car. Treece is driving. I am calmer, clearer, the interior body stocking has loosened its grip of dread enough for me to feel hungry properly.

'I'm taking you down to Manilva, we'll get you a good meal, and you can sleep over. We can talk over how to do this. I don't know if I can get through to the right people in time, make things happen. I don't know if people will take me seriously, I left under a pretty big cloud twenty odd years ago. I'm history. But, hope springs eternal.'

'What? Who *said* that?'

'I've no idea, some film or something, I think. Come on. Let's go and eat.'

It's only a fifteen-minute drive down the coast to Manilva, but I am fast asleep the whole way. We dine largely in silence, partly out of discretion, and partly from the fact I am filling my face without pause. The classic Andalusian bone broth of *sopa de picadillo* is amazingly restorative. It sets up my appetite perfectly and I am able to put away another favourite from my short stay here, the *Plato de la Montaña*, an outrageous mountain of pork fillet, sausage, chorizo, black pudding, two fried eggs and a mountain of sliced oven baked potato mingled with green peppers. I feel human again, and certainly smell closer to one than a stray dog.

Once cocooned in the Inspector's sofa with a nice hot cup of PG Tips, I am able to explain the narrative more fully, the wider nexus of Lebid funding the Holmeland development, his cover business of furniture for drugs, whores and who knows what else. And also the fact that he now has divested himself of these assets and has possibly left it all in the lap of Kavanagh. I debate with him the possible

428

identity of Gary's assassins. We decide we need to involve Ana as soon as possible to see what her document trove might reveal, to shed light on who knew what, when, what kind of leverage and liabilities really existed amongst this cabal of corrupt players. Its tentacles are so far reaching, it is daunting. His face is stern, and I notice tremors that are subtle, but involuntary. He catches on, reading my thoughts.

'Yes Gene, time is not on my side. All the more reason I suppose to move heaven and earth. I really don't have much to lose anymore.' He grips my hand and his eyes cloud for a moment, but he resumes his composure just as quickly. Old school.

'So,' I pick up on our thread again 'there's multiple fronts on which a police operation could work. The villa, time it to meet the truck, Kavanagh's place and all the girls, that's a flock of potentially powerful evidence and witnesses. Wherever they store the coke, as tracking Darren can reveal that. The hardest thing is still connecting it to Lebid. I'm sure he's very well ring fenced from any direct connection to any of this now, other than by association with Holmeland. And even then, I don't know if there is a paper trail that leads to him. He may have already left the country. Ana would know.'

'Your analysis is right Gene, I hope Ana is willing to engage. I can understand she may fight shy of revealing her hand right now, breaking her cover so to speak.'

'I can try and impress upon her how we need her to come through with whatever she can. I'll call her tonight so you can hopefully meet as soon as. She also may have contacts in the police, I've no idea. At my interview about the shooting, they were perfunctory. I mean, they were ticking boxes, confirming preconceptions, as far as I could see. They weren't digging for much for sure.'

'Extraordinary' says Treece, shaking his head. 'My concern is how watertight is this police force. As with all criminal organisations, there will have been some penetration of the police system by Lebid.

My line of attack is going to be at the highest level I can access, through the UK.'

'Oh?'

'Yes, I have at least some friends back there, so do you.'

'Superintendent Collins. Yes, I think I can say he is a friend.' Maybe the only real one I have left. Certainly, the only person on earth who might actually look out for me. Into this select club I can now add Geoffrey Treece I suppose.

'He can give us credibility, open the door to Europol, because only through them can we get the Spanish Police to act on any information. He won't be happy to have this land on his doorstep, his eyes are firmly on retirement, and I just don't know how quickly any of this moves these days. Technology has changed, but humans still appear to be the same imperfect species, regardless.'

'Were you two close?'

'You might say that.' Treece's expression is subtle, but I think I am meant to perceive their bond went beyond the professional. I marvel at the layers to all of this... history, for want of a better word.

This forms the plan as it exists, in all its shakiness and implausibility. I will resume my drug packaging enterprise, even try to slow the whole thing down, extend the available time for surveillance and reaction as much as possible. Maybe Kavanagh will play into our hands and seek to send ever more shipments. Who knows?

I turn my attention to the past. Closure for both of us. What possibilities exist from the evidence that Treece still holds, to effect some kind of retrospective action on the real authors of our own tragedies.

'Geoffrey, your document stash, how safe is it? Do you have a copy? If something happens, if things go... wrong,' just saying it is enough to bring a weight down on us both, the stakes are so high, the risks so unknown, 'you want that information to be in the right hands. Collins?'

'No! That would compromise him horribly, potentially destroy his career. I wouldn't wish that on anyone else.'

'Right, yes of course' I concur. Silence. 'Ana?' Saying it gives me a violent stab of remorse. But she has unfortunately been woven into the fabric of this poisonous tapestry. She has possibly the ability and motivation to make information count, to seek 'closure' herself. It's all linked, all written in the same font, embroidered deep into our psyches now.

'Well, it's an idea. She's probably one of the few people we can trust. Who would know what to do with it all in the event of…'? We both fall silent again. 'You better call Ana.'

It's not an easy conversation to have. Ana is still traumatised and struggles to maintain composure, understandably resistant to engage with anything outside of the sphere of immediate necessity. Eventually she consents to meet the Inspector, who is burdened with the task of explaining the bigger picture to her, getting her to somehow accept the game plan we are starting to execute. It won't be easy for her. However, she has spent time combing through the package Gary left. Initially she's reluctant to reveal anything, she oscillates between feelings of impotence and despair and a vengeful indignation. I have one question that takes an awful lot to get around to.

'Ana, have you found anything to suggest that Gary had information he may have used to put pressure on Holme, to threaten him even. To, maybe, leverage Lebid against him.' There's silence. I continue. 'I met Lebid. I spoke to him, in person.' Silence still, but I pick up the increase in her breathing, the tension. 'I asked him directly who was responsible for Gary's murder. He pointed the finger at Holme, which may seem obvious. But maybe Gary pushed Holme, both of them even, and that…'. It's not a sentence I can finish. Eventually Ana replies. Her voice is slow, composed now, and I recognise that ability in her to quickly focus and contain the maelstrom, and think straight.

431

'I was not going to tell you this,' she begins 'but I found recordings of many phone conversations. Gary was increasingly, in the last days, gathering more information, recording everything, downloading and archiving thousands of documents, emails, and recording most of his phone conversations.' She struggles with the picture she has built of what Gary might have known, of what he didn't reveal even to her. 'He was certainly preparing to protect himself, but I have not found anything so far that points to Gary having direct knowledge of criminal things. You know, like drugs, or other activities. Apart from the usual.'

'The usual?' What is usual in this cauldron of filth I wonder.

'Yes, the bribes. Cash. Presents. Expenses from people who had no right to claim expenses.'

'Like?'

'Dios mío! Everything! Restaurants, holidays, renting Ferrari, Rolex watches. *Es increíble*. But what is incredible is he recorded it all. I have a spreadsheet which is a parallel accounting system, with names, details, places, dates. For me, having this is very dangerous, because it gives the *Fiscal* everything they need, but will they give me protection? Many people will try to stop me if they know I have this information.'

'But nothing you have seen or heard that would suggest Gary tried to threaten either Lebid or Holme, to protect himself, or who knows what?'

There is a tone of vindication in her next phrase. 'The last thing Gary said to Holme was 'They will be coming for us, for all of this. I have everything I need to take you down with me, Mike, no matter how long it takes.' She leaves this hanging in the air, as the floor shifts underneath me. She goes on. 'I think Holme communicated this to Lebid, because he was unwilling, or unable to pay Lebid back so he made Gary into the bad guy. How do you say, the fall guy?'

432

'The fall guy, indeed.' It's all so credible, so gut wrenchingly unfair, cynical.

'Gene, do what you have to do, I will help in any way I can, just don't ask me to reveal my information yet. I need to still hide all I have, until the time.'

'Thanks Ana. I won't let you down.' I can't recall ever saying that to someone, let alone meaning it.

'*Un beso*[32], I will talk to you very soon.'

Treece is looking at me, nodding. He's heard most of the conversation.

'One way or another' he starts, 'the truth will come out. Whether the forces of law and order are up to the task of doing their duty on this remains to be seen. My experience doesn't make me wholly confident. We must, Ana, you and I, whatever happens, make sure all this information sees the light of day, and what will be, will be.'

'It's the least we can do.'

We look at each other. A complete unspoken understanding of what we are about to try and all of its implications bind us. A form of strength is returning to my mind and body, like I finally have a backbone, and whatever comes our way now, is just fate. We must face it.

'One thing,' something has been praying on me, and I'm not sure if it's the right course of action, but I have to ask, 'where do you think I could get a gun.'

Treece initially explodes with laughter, but gradually sees I am serious.

'Gene, how do you think that will help you? Help us? The Costa del Sol may still be a bit Wild West, but we are not cowboys. Especially you.'

---

[32] Big kiss

'True. But it might, in the worst of circumstances, make a difference. I have survived one shooting this month. It would make me feel, I don't know, like the odds were slightly better?'

He shakes his head, chuckling. I'm glad he finds it funny.

'Actually, I have a hunting rifle. Bought it a few years ago, when I was friends with some ex-Spanish police chief. I was trying to fit in, do the landed gentry bit, but they're not my types, hunters. I never got around to selling it. We can take a look at it in the morning. Sleep on it, ay?'

'Sure.'

I do sleep. Mercifully, dreamlessly for once. Exhaustion is my nurse.

31

Geoffrey takes me through the workings of a hunting rifle. It does feel decidedly Wild West. While I want to giggle, the seriousness of the implication, of my willingness to contemplate the possibility of it being used, is enough to drown the giggles. More sobering are the limitations of the gun itself. It's not Rambo, more De Niro. It's a deer hunting rifle. Bolt action. A .203 calibre. One bullet at a time. I decide to take it with me regardless. It's totemic. The sensation of it in my hands gives me some bizarre sense of empowerment, though I know it is pure illusion.

I stash the weapon in the boot of my car, and will only unpack it at the villa. I'm heading home first to pack clothes and supplies so I can live a fairly sanitary life at the villa this time around. Proper food, get the hot water on for showers. Wouldn't want to drive Jonno away now. No sign of Kavanagh's crew or cars on my travels. Just a solitary text message on Monday morning, 'Omelette is on the menu, it's our best seller. Expect demand for eggs to continue.'

Jonno arrives and stops to regard me. 'Blimey, you look a whole lot better. I wondered if you'd even be here, thought you might have collapsed, done a runner, you were pretty messed up. Hahahaaa, you smell better as well!'

'Just as well, looks like there's as much of this as you want, for the moment.'

'Really? Might need more of an incentive to cope with the work and the inherent risks, know what I mean?'

'How much incentive?'

'Eight grand a shipment?' He's tentative, but serious. If only he knew. He's going to be sacrificed on the altar of my vengeance. And like I care how much money is involved in this anyway, I'm not realistically going to see any of it if the plan works, and if it doesn't, I'm just a walking dead man. But I need to keep up the pretence.

'Eight! Shit, Jonno. Seven.' He eyes me.

'Seven and a half. For the next three and then it goes to ten.'

'If we shift that much, I'll make it twelve. No problem. Deal?'

He breaks into a lascivious smile. 'Ay ay captain. Let's smelt.'

And so we smelt. It's dirty monotonous work, hot vapours, fumes and inherent danger. The gantry winch above allows us a certain security and efficiency, we don't have to handle the champagne bucket. Frankly without this place, none of this would have come together in the same way. We'd be working at half the speed and taking much bigger physical risks. I doubt my business colleagues appreciate that.

Darren appears periodically, looking humbled. He's running a twice daily gauntlet, with enough coke to put him inside for a long time, unless he sang like a bird. Difficult choice. No doubt he reports back in detail. We don't discuss anything; everything is very much need to know only.

For three days I hear nothing. I sleep at the villa after twelve-hour stints at the champagne bucket. Then on Thursday night a vehicle comes up the hill in the dark. This sets in train a domino sequence of paranoias, the adrenalin rush is debilitating, so sudden is it. I pull out the rifle and crouch peering out the front bedroom window. I don't recognise the car. It halts outside the tall, locked gates. I am taught, poised, and terrified. I can vaguely make out two figures climbing out, through the dense vegetation, silhouetted as they are by the light of the town below. Then a voice.

'Gene?' It's Treece. I collapse on the floor. Laughing out of relief and the incongruity of it all. I unlock the gates and he introduces me to a short Spanish man, in his forties I estimate.

'Gene, sorry to creep up on you. Let's go inside.'

'Christ, Geoffrey, I might have shot you.'

He stops and regards me, then sighs.

'Ahh yes, I'd forgotten that. What a delicious irony.' We share a look, unwilling to say anymore on this memory lapse. 'This gentleman, you don't need to know his name, for reasons you can understand, needs to acquaint himself with the lay-out of the whole place.'

'*Hola señor, encantado, mucho gusto*[33].' He shakes my hand firmly, then takes a camera out of a case he is carrying.

'In the dark?' I ask, slightly bemused.

'Absolutely. You may yourself be under surveillance.'

'And you just drove up to my gate.'

'In your neighbour's car. We borrowed it for a small fee. Only other car that is ever seen on this track. Plausible deniability Gene.' He smiles.

'Right. And who's he?' Treece doesn't answer. 'Ahh, yes. Need to know only. Fine'.

'He needs to see everything.' Treece pulls me away from the man. 'It's been bloody ridiculous getting someone in the system here to respond, even Spanish Europol are pulling their hair out at the local attitude. And trying to keep it in among a tight circle is proving hard. Our friend here is getting photographic evidence to convince a person who needs to be convinced. Show him the ingots, the smelter, the actual coke. It's an infra-red camera, no need for lights. He's doing this off his own bat, frankly. Gone out on a limb. He's proper Spanish drug squad, comes highly recommended.'

'By who?'

'This has been cleared by Europol. But they still need to work through local forces. Seems they don't have enough men on the ground to do it all themselves.'

'Blimey, well done Geoffrey. I would love to have seen Collins' face.'

---

[33] Hello sir, pleasure to meet you

'Oh yes, that was a conversation I shall treasure and dine out on one day. Well…'

He meets my eye. I see the face of a man facing his own mortal end. It cuts. I move out to help our mysterious guest. He goes about his business in silence, occasionally letting out a low whistle of appreciation, especially when I reveal the twelve kilos of the next consignment already received.

'*Impressionante. Ok, Jefferay, vamos. Todo bien.*[34]'

'You're going?'

'Looks like it,' responds Treece.

'Why no calls?' The Spanish drug squad officer must understand some English. He makes the finger to lip gesture, then points to his ear.

'*Quieto, hombre. Mas Seguro.*[35]'

'Were you able to see Ana?' I address Treece again.

'Yes. It was difficult. I admire her strength, to bear all of this. She has copies now of everything of mine. I hope to see her again very soon, to organise what amongst that information would be useful if this all goes to plan.'

'And if it doesn't go to plan?' He doesn't answer, initially.

'Well, maybe Ana might be able to effect some kind of… well, she'll have all the evidence, whatever happens. I must go.' He shakes my hand. So formal, English. And ever more bizarre under the circumstances. Before he passes through the gate he says simply, 'Sit tight Gene, carry on. It'll all come out in the wash as they say.'

I'm left in the dark, in my filthy villa, with my one bullet rifle, with hundreds of thousands of pounds worth of cocaine. Wondering how all this will end. If it will ever end. If I won't spend the rest of my life around people I loathe and who disgust me. Doing things that appal me, and cause who knows what harm to who knows how many others. I've been fixated for some time on an amorphous idea of

---

[34] Impressive. Okay Geoffrey, let's go, it's all good
[35] Quietly, man. It's safer

vengeance, but maybe what I simply need is redemption. Just run far away from it all. Join a Buddhist monastery. I slump onto the stained old sofa again and start to laugh.

32

'I've got a bite!' says Doug. I look at his float. The cute little piece of cork with its pink, fluorescent, bulbous body lies motionless in the still greenish pool. I look back at my own, a taller, slim, orange tipped porcupine quill. Nothing. I resume channelling the maggots, allowing them to squirm along the intricate maze I have carved for them in the mud at the edge of the pond. We are sat at the rim of a perfectly round pool, in the shadow of the pit head wheels of the nearby colliery. Slag heaps border the field, and the lush green contrasts with the brooding greyness of the mound that stretches a half mile into the distance. Only years later will I understand the abundance of such round ponds, often occurring in series across areas of countryside, all of similar size, all over the north west. There's a weird irony to the fact that the leftover craters from German bombing gave generations of kids the opportunity to go tiddler bashing in the fresh air, gave frogs places to breed, water birds a home. In short, a whole ecological niche was created.

'There!' I look over again at Dougie's float. A slight bob, sending two ripples outwards across the mirror sheen. The anticipation is delicious. The unseen beast, cold and slimy, hidden in the utterly opaque water, circling, using its senses to ascertain the comestible nature of the maggot it can barely see. If the poor drowned larvae aren't totally insensate already, its wriggles may just prove tempting enough and the fish will dart at it. Such a move will be reflected on the surface by the sliding downwards of the float, the trigger for all kinds of drama, variable outcomes of frustratingly unpredictable odds. The cold blooded, fairly basic animal can have no idea of the reaction about to take place above its watery haven. Two nine-year-old boys are about to be riven with an excitement, an

440

ecstasy of expectation, a potential catharsis out of all proportion to either the skill or reward of the catch. Another bob, a series of bobs, as the float starts to track away from us, but it doesn't progress much. Doug is clutching his rod like it was the rail of a boat he's fallen off, while the sea tries to pull him to certain death. Every ounce of our being is focussed on that tiny movement.

'Wait till it goes under' I counsel in hushed tones.

'Come on take it, ya bastard!'

Bob, bob, slide. Then it stops. We are in suspended animation. Anti-climax. Gruelling.

'Left it. Shit' sighs Doug. 'I could swear that was a good one.'

'Leave it, it might just be messin' with it. It'll come back.'

We wait. The still green surface refuses to reveal its secrets, mocking us. Disconsolately Doug reels in, hoists up the tackle, swinging it in deftly and catching the hooked maggot directly with his hand. He looks close and then reveals the shocking truth to me.

'Bastard sucked it!'

I look, and indeed the evidence is undeniable, for there hangs the maggot still attached by its behind to the hook, but it is merely a skin. The head has been squeezed by the fish's delicate but strong lips, and its fluids have been sucked out, without the fish ever coming close to taking the hook, or dragging the float in any definite way that could trigger the all-important strike. The maggot hangs pathetically, denuded of fluid, life. The fish race has outsmarted us once again, have mocked us. How can creatures so small, so limited in higher brain power, such limbless wiggling little sprats, exert such a hold over us, tease us so completely?

Suddenly an enormous splash rends the calm of the pond, and both of us momentarily fantasize that some gigantic carp has expressed his hunger and gameness. But the way the ripples pulse outward in perfect round layers, and the distinctive plopping sound, reveals the horrible truth. It was a brick. So absorbed were we in the drama of the maggot sucking fish, we had failed to notice a small posse of boys had approached the pond edge opposite. They are hooting with laughter. They are mounted on bikes like our own, but they have been customised. Mudguards stripped off, white walls painted on knobbly tyres, ape hanger or cowhorn bars added, giving them an outlaw, transgressive image. Immediately we sense we have a problem. Somehow, a type of boy always shows up who simply needs to inflict humiliation and intimidation on all those around them. It's not that they are bullies, they're much more. They gather acolytes around them. They strut. They hurl abuse and scorn. The one before us now has been preceded by his reputation. The new lad. We'd heard as you do, in the playground, about the new family on the estate, the Paddy. He was a bit of a gangster, people whispered. This kid was a piece of work. Proved himself cock of his new school on his first day, picking up someone's flask and hitting them around the head with it. He was due to be expelled but a visit from the father to the school's head mysteriously averted this course of action. Nothing happened about the incident, and the kid became de facto cock of the school, creating a local legend overnight. We'd all heard the story, but had yet to see this mythical creature. We knew how to recognize him. He had a pizza face apparently. Appalling, repellent, personality deforming acne. Across the pond, mounted on a yellow painted bike sporting chequered racing tape and cowhorn bars with tassels draped from the hand grips, was the kid known as Jimmy Kavanagh. Pizza face himself.

'What the fuck is that round your neck, you shithouse?'

Doug clutches the Manchester United scarf he always wears. It isn't unknown for one's football allegiance to attract aggro from other club's fans. It's an occupational hazard of being young in the north of England. I have no affiliation, but am evidently guilty by association. The three start peddling menacingly towards us.

'Fuckinell, pack up,' says Doug and we frantically start to reel in. This is like chum thrown to sharks. They accelerate towards us; the Kavanagh kid leaps off his bike and pulls the rod from Doug's

grasp. It doesn't occur to us to fight back. We don't know what it is to fight, it's not part of our make-up, being as we are, fortunate enough to have grown up in a housing estate relatively free of social issues and delinquency. Not that we know that. But more because there is something utterly terrifying and paralysing about the direct, brute aggression, so meaningless and unprovoked, so dynamic and rapid. And this lad Jimmy is maybe two or three years older, thick set, with a barrel chest, a short, broad, ugly skull, and fat wide hands with pudgy fingers. He probably weighs as much as Doug and I together, as we are pissy little bean poles in comparison.

Kavanagh tears the scarf from around Doug's neck and drops it into the mud at the edge of the pool. He grabs the collar of his Parka coat, forcing Doug toward the water.

'Stamp it down. Drown yer fuckin' orrible scarf, ya Manc twat.'

The accent has a Liverpool twang to it. He's obviously moved east recently from some new town hell hole like Huyton or Kirby, places we daren't go. Probably a Liverpool fan then. Or just plain vindictive. Doug, shaking, ashen faced, squelches his beloved scarf into the muck, the water and slime rising up over the sides of his trainers. He grimaces as his shoes fill with cold, stinking water and sludge. The other two kids merely watch and yell obscenities and guffaw, high on the power and cruelty of their leader. Then it's my turn.

'What you lookin at, ya twat?'

I am transfixed by the eruptions on his face. I've never seen a particularly bad case of acne close up. Random small shadows of purple and red, blotches and blemishes. Some are faded, others raw, even dressed with yellow pinpoints of puss, occasionally weeping. Early, hormonally dysfunctional juvenile stubble is visible in a little tuft on the end of his flat chin.

'What you lookin' at!!!?'

443

He screams so forcefully, his bulk lowering over me, and in my blind panic I blurt out 'Your pizza face!'.

The time between the realisation of my error and the slap of the thick hand to the side of my head is a nano-second. It is quickly followed by a violent shove that sends me off my feet and into the shockingly cold water of the pond. I struggle to my feet, the water reaching my waist. The two kids above are falling over laughing, gesturing, applauding Kavanagh. He isn't laughing. I have inadvertently hit his sore point, the one vulnerable chink in his armour, that he no doubt compensates for with doubled ferocity. I stay where I am, I realise he isn't going to wade out to attack me further. Doug twigs this as well, and wades a couple of yards out to join me. This elicits a fairly contemptuous laugh from Kavanagh, but I can feel it's put on. He's piqued now, unable to execute the coup de grace of whatever form is customary to an eleven-year-old proto-thug. He calmly picks up the tackle box and couple of camping chairs and hurls them at us. The floats scatter, daintily decorating the surface of the pond with our shattered illusions. The two kids pick up the script, dismount and go over to our two bikes. Doctor Martined heels pound into spokes, wheels buckle, paint chips. Kavanagh climbs up the bank of the pond, seizes each bike and hurls it into the centre of the pond, where they sink without trace, to join the shrapnel of somebody else's war.

It is after dark by the time I have trudged home. I appear sans bike, stinking, sodden and shivering. Mum stops dead in the doorway, the words 'where have you been' mouthing themselves silently. I burst into tears. Once bathed, dressed in paisley pyjamas, and ensconced on the couch in front of Doctor Who, I feel better. The policeman is taking down the bits of detail my parents are able to prise from my reluctant lips. PC Collins is a mate of my dad's apparently. He appears sympathetic. Not what I was told to expect from coppers, or pigs, as we'd grown up to call them.

Later my father explained to me PC Collins had said the boy was known to them, and was very much a subject of their attention. But he was too young still to be fully prosecuted. They would pull the father in for a chat, was how it was put. I was never to hear anything further of my first traumatic encounter with the one and only Jimmy Kavanagh.

33

It's Monday. The truck is due tomorrow. Text messages have confirmed someone will pick up the eggs as agreed. I'm antsy. Every unfamiliar sound makes me jump inside. If the Spanish police do get their act together, I have no idea still what form the action will take, which is excruciating. Need to know basis. I don't know if I will be able to get even the slightest inkling of impending action, I feel I should at least give Jonno a head start, a chance to get away. But it wouldn't be easy. Assuming that an intervention would use the access of the dirt track to us at the top of the hill, the only other escape routes are open country. Behind the villa, the land rises up, eventually becoming considerably hilly, with scattered pine and cork oak forest, deep gullies and steep sided hills, impenetrable to vehicles. Between us and the town is about half a mile of open scrub, a motorway that is a formidable barrier in itself, and then urban Estepona.

Scrub in southern Spain is vicious. Right now, it is resplendent in yellow. The gorse perfume is heady, and wafts in occasionally over the fumes of gas and metallic impurities burning off. Gorse is dense and prickly, but fairly forgiving, whereas the broom flower, equally yellow and pungent, is harsh and armed with thorns a full inch long. Lavender, rosemary, thyme and numerous species of orchids abound, all around the villa. Beauty and the beast. That's the nature of the Andalucian countryside. I don't see any obvious way out for Jonno. Collateral damage. I hope he's stashed the money I'm paying him carefully, so he can pick it up another day down the line.

There's the buzzing of a scooter. I jump.

'Hey, what's up?' asks Jonno. He must be picking up on my jumpiness.

'Scooter.' Pointlessly stating the obvious.

'Yeah, this is Spain. Lot of scooters. Chill.'

446

'Scooters. Yup, no shortage of them.'

We carry on, I am using the lathe to shave down the various chunks of scrap into smaller pieces, shavings and so on, so much the better to melt them down more efficiently. We spend inordinate hours battering bits of plastic, rubber and other metals off the scrap to keep it purer and avoid boiling, bubbling, spitting, plastics. With the temperatures involved, the paint, and impurities, the fumes are noxious, even deadly. Then the buzz returns, and a scooter inadvertently pulls up outside the locked gate. Even Jonno is spooked this time. We aren't expecting Darren, our eggs have all been delivered already. He retreats further into the garage, sheltering behind an old diesel tank. I walk gingerly out, staying about fifteen feet behind the gate.

'*Hola*?' Silence. '*Hola, quien es?* Who is it, what do you want? This is private property.'

'Fuckin' let me in!'

Jesus Christ it is only Darren after all. Jonno walks back out. 'What's this all about, we've had the twenty-four kilos.' He is understandably perplexed, as am I.

'Search me' I respond, shrugging. I walk over to the gate and resist the temptation to go for the rifle. That wouldn't look good, if it's a perfectly innocent visit, which it probably is, being Darren. It's possible his appearance might coincide with *the* raid, when, or if it ever comes. I'm pissed off and anxious, trying to get a handle on this. I open to let him in, and he whizzes through in his typical lairy way. He jumps off the scooter and struts about a bit in his usual bouncy gait, like some bizarre cross breed scouse poultry. I try to be composed, hide my irritation and angst.

'What brings you here, I didn't order a pizza.'

'Fuck you, Eugene'. Oh, that was nice, I hit the mark there.

'But seriously, what are you doing here? We are trying to keep movement to a minimum, keep things discreet, you can't just chug up here on a joyride. And no-one has texted me. That's not the protocol

447

and you know that.' Given the emphasis on the protocol, I'm perfectly entitled to talk this way. He goes over to his Pizza bike box and just pulls out another two keys of coke. I'm processing this. They would have had to put on the whole road clearance deployment. They did not warn me. It significantly affects our workload, creating a surplus ingot. Something definitely isn't sitting right, but I could be just paranoid.

'How come I didn't get a text message? I don't know if we can prepare an extra ingot in time.'

'How should I know, I'm just the pizza delivery boy. This is your show. Sort it out. Alright Jonno! How you managing to put up with this muppet?' Jonno doesn't reply. He's eyeing Darren uneasily, from inside the garage.

I take the two wrapped bundles of cocaine. At least I assume they are of cocaine. I decide as soon as Darren leaves, I will do something I have been expressly forbidden to do. I will check the content of the packages.

I am glaring at Darren, assuming he will leave directly, as he has always done thus far, presumably as he has been instructed to do. But he nonchalantly walks past me toward the open door of the garage. Too nonchalantly.

'Let's have a ganders at how you do this then, ay?'

I follow him, my mind racing, computing options and possibilities as to what this is about. If some kind of play is going down, I can't start on Darren, I have to wait for the main play. I allow Darren to stroll into the garage. Jonno looks at me quizzically, searching my face for some kind of indication, warning, who knows. A great herd of question marks stampedes at breakneck speed through my head. I am about to challenge Darren properly, when the mobile in my pocket buzzes. It's a text.

'Sorry, can you get us another couple of eggs, the recipe has changed.'

I read it, and then hold up the phone for Darren.

'Well what do you know, a text message.'

'Yeah, see, stop bustin' my balls, dickhead.'

I'm studying Darren acutely now. His passive aggressive name calling show he is stressed. There's genuine relief in his reaction to the text message, the usual Darren wouldn't give a shit. This is definitely not sitting right with me. He's peering around, but he's not taking in the details. He moves outside out the back. His gaze is taking in everything, like he's looking for something, or someone. Checking. Jonno is watching all of this, shaking his head, a pall of fear passing over his face. I grab one of the bindles of cocaine, and hack it open with a screwdriver. I ram a finger in and dab the powder that sticks to it onto my tongue and gums. Jonno does likewise. We stare at each other, the revelation making my stomach flip, and my thoughts race so fast I can't see the next step. I'm flailing, Jonno is looking around now like a cornered animal. We still can't figure out what is happening. I grab the pack and march out the back of the garage toward Darren who is by the pool, still peering around. His face changes abruptly now.

'This is not cocaine, Darren, it's baking powder. What the fuck is going on?' We stare at each other, each searching the other's face. Darren's breathing picks up, he's close to hyper ventilating, but holds my stare. I take a step toward him, and this is the trigger for his nerves to give. He sprints like a startled rabbit, heading to pass around the other side of the villa.

'Jonno we're blown. Run for it, go now, cross country out the back, don't use the lane.'

His instincts are pure, he drops the metal spatula and heavy gloves he has been stirring the molten metal with and sprints out of the garage toward the back fence, without a glance behind. I hurtle into the garage, pick up the spatula, and head back out of the front of the garage to intercept Darren on the other side of the house. The rush of adrenalin has not come with its usual associated fear. I know what is happening now, all my worst fears, all the possible deadly scenarios

449

that have stalked and battered my sanity, are now in play, unleashed, galloping toward me. It doesn't matter which one it is, or who. I only know it is now, and this is the definitive moment, the culmination of everything. I experience a clarity, a sense of purpose, a microscopic focus. My mental lens zooms in and I ramp everything down to super slow motion. This is the endgame, and the die is cast.

Darren is sprinting as best he can toward his scooter, I need to stop him. His route round the house is twice as long as mine. He's after something, his face says it. He gets to the box on the back and plunges his hand inside, but I'm on him. My first blow with the wrench lands on his shoulder. He screams and the reflexive yank of his arm out of the box flings a pistol out and onto the ground six foot away. Whimpering, he ducks away from me, swings around and dives toward the pistol. I go for a blow as best I can to stop him reaching it. As he is prone, the back of his neck is exposed and the spatula crunches into the vertebrae just below his skull, with all the force at my adrenalin saturated disposal. Darren's neck emits an audible, sickening, snapping sound. He falls forward, his body twitching and convulsing, the weight of his torso keeping the pistol from me. The blood rush in my head is getting louder, my self-control is crumbling, the herd of question marks break in panic in all directions. I'm gasping for breath through simple lack of fitness.

I run as best I can toward the locked gate and peer through the bars. My worst fears are confirmed. Dust is rising and the clear sound of an engine at full revs comes up from down the hill. And then I see it, rounding one of the bends about three hundred meters away. It's the tatty old Skoda we used that first night. It has to be Kavanagh. Dmitri. Both, surely. There's something right about it. There's that clarity again, that feeling of imminent release.

With renewed energy and wind, I start back toward the villa. Darren is still prone on the ground but I daren't try and get the pistol from under him. The body repels me. I get to the kitchen inside, and pull the rifle out from inside the empty chest freezer there. My hands tremble, but not so much I can't check the barrel. The cartridge is loaded. I put five more into my pocket from inside a kitchen drawer. Think think think. If I can get down the hill, into the scrub, it'll be harder to see me, and I may be able to keep them at bay, I'll have range, they'll probably have pistols. It's worth a shot. I can maybe make it to the motorway.

I head out the back, but an enormous crashing and scraping, the howl of a reluctant engine heralds their arrival. Jesus, they were fast. Sounds like they clean rammed the gate. I'm about to pass round the pool when my clarity draws me back. If I go for the fence now, I'll likely get caught trying to scale it, its covered in thorns, high, and there's little purchase while holding a gun. I'll be done. Voices make me swing around, my back to the pool, and raise the rifle at the empty French windows. Barely a second later they appear round the house at a run. I struggle to re-aim, but they are moving fast. The sight of me pointing a gun at them, which they wouldn't have expected, sends them scurrying for the interior of the villa. Kavanagh and Dmitri. I actually manage to smile to myself. I can't run for it, they'll shoot me in the back in two seconds. It's a bizarre Mexican stand-off.

Kavanagh is the first to speak. 'You fucking killed him, you cunt!' He sounds genuinely upset, wild with anger. I can hear his breathing from where I stand, fifteen meters across the scrappy garden. I shimmy quickly toward the olive tree to my left, gun trained on the window. It's not much cover, but, hope springs eternal. It's Dmitri who speaks next. The complete absence of emotion in his voice is a shocking contrast.

'Hey Gene. I'm going to put bullet right between your pig eyes. I'm going to spray your brains all over swimming pool. Just like I spray your brother's brains all over his nice car. I got you now. There's two of us and one of you, and I think you never fire gun in your life.' He's pretty much right.

I try to stay clear headed. I'm not processing anything he says. I'm just waiting for the first sign of movement. But I've only one real shot. Who do I save it for? Dmitri. It has to be him. He's done me a favour. He's made this easier. I know who did my brother now. What happens from here is all the same to me, if I can just take that bastard with me.

'Come on Genie boy, make your move,' says Kavanagh. He's recovered his composure. 'We've got all day. The cavalry aren't gonna be coming for you. Did you really think we wouldn't find out about your little scheme? You and that dumb-fuck copper? This is Marbella Eugene! The final frontier! From what I can see that's a bolt action hunting rifle. One chance. The odds are against you, especially as you've never even fired a shot, you useless fucking muppet.' And they both start laughing, but I can tell from the modulation of the sound that they are moving around inside the house. I listen intently, peeping either side of the gnarled trunk of the olive tree.

There's a loud pop from deep in the house and a bullet thuds into the trunk. Then three more. The impact on the tree is distinct. I squirm in its slender silhouette.

'Four down, how many to go?' yells Kavanagh. 'Do you even know how many bullets are in a Glock 19 magazine, Eugene?' I don't answer. I'm just trying to stay alive long enough to get a shot. Which means waiting until one of them breaks cover. 'Could be the ten-bullet version. Or the fifteen.'

Pop pop pop. More thuds, but this time in the grass close to my feet. They are trying to injure me, flush me out, whatever. They haven't rushed me yet, they're being cautious. There's a moment of calm, and I am straining to peep around the tree without them taking my head off. Contorting myself into the shelter of its form is starting to become painful. The law of diminishing returns dictates that while I keep safe, I am less and less able to function physically. Kavanagh suddenly pops in full view in the window. Tempting me to break cover, take a pop.

'Yoo hoo Genie boy, over here!'

I'm not taking that bait. I remain, hugging myself to the trunk, my resolve and equilibrium ebbing away with every second. There's another pause. Each one piles a bit more pressure on, allows them more time to plan and manoeuvre. Weakens my ability to hold myself behind the tree.

A volley of shots, from two positions rings out. I can't count. The trunk takes multiple shots and I feel stinging, biting impacts, on my limbs, whether from splinters or gravel I can't tell. Something lodges itself in my calf. It hurts, but not unbearably. I only know I can't keep this up. Must try to stay clear, focussed. I control my breathing, ignore the points of pain, the feeling of blood seeping. I listen. Listen for the final rush, it's the only tactic left they haven't tried. Listen. The screeching of an eagle high up, the occasional chatter of sparrows, green parakeets, the breeze rustling a nearby palm tree, the hiss of the gas heating the champagne bucket.

The gas.

Two six-foot-tall bottles of butane. Orange. Perfect. Gorgeous.

Clarity. One shot. Release…

'Hey Kavanagh' I yell. Wait.

'What do you want now, shithouse?'

'Fuck you, pizza face!' I swing the gun out, take aim, pull the trigger and instantaneously a vicious white jet of vapourising butane spurts out of the tank, and a split second later, a ball of flame erupts toward me. I instinctively make a break away from it, hear shots, the sound of projectiles sizzling through the air close to me. The force wave hits me, and I feel my clothes hot on my skin, my hair singe and I plunge headlong into the pool. The momentarily dark water is lit up orange and an audible hissing reaches me, even under the surface. Then the ground shakes as a proper, full detonation rocks the foundations of the earth. The second tank was still full. This time the shockwave is a hammer blow, even through the water. I feel a spike has been pushed through my left eardrum. I'm still under water, straining to hold onto my breath amid the pain and panic. Lumps of hot metal are falling into the pool, chunks of masonry. All is noise and flame and steam, even from within the green haven. I struggle, flailing to keep myself below the surface, as red-hot chunks burn me on their way to the bottom of the pool. As the orange glow subsides, I burst up to the surface, gulping and thrashing. The air is hot, full of fumes and smoke. Debris is still falling from the sky.

I pull myself onto the pool side and drag myself to my feet. I turn toward the house. The heat is fierce, and initially I struggle to see. My head is splitting and a high-pitched ringing plagues my left ear. I make my way round the pool side away from the house toward the fence. I'm limping for some reason. There's no escape to the lane. What blocks my path is an almighty inferno. The garage has completely disappeared, most of the roof and the right side of the bungalow has also gone. The opposite wing of the house is more intact, but flames shoot from the open windows. As I stand mesmerised, something, someone moves inside still. A figure staggers from the interior to the door post, the skin is blackened, hair gone, the clothing partly burnt off, the arms flail weakly, grasping at something. It staggers a few more steps, a vain attempt to make the safety of the pool. It is dumb. I don't know if it can see me watching it. And I am watching it. Which one of you is it? It pitches forward into a pile of burning debris. Gradually, the figure's movements lessen, until it is still, but for greasy blue smoke, rising up, sucked into the maelstrom of fire from the destroyed house.

Summoning the last dregs of strength and adrenalin, I turn and lurch off toward the fence. It is a nightmare to climb. Flimsy wire mesh attached to poles, submerged for much of its length under thorny bougainvillea. The abundant colourful flowers are out of keeping amongst the smoke and flames. The land immediately adjacent to the garage is already ablaze. I manage to pull myself up high enough to fling my body over the fence and come crashing down into the scrub on the other side. The throbbing in my head is causing me extreme nausea and I can't see. Something fades to black. Struggle, struggle for consciousness, escape. Fight or flight. Did the fight, now for flight. I open my eyes and stare upwards, hopelessly disorientated...

34

My eyes open. Still here. The room is painted in pale shades of orange and cream. The blinds are drawn so it isn't fully light still. A television high up on its bendy arm stares blankly. It is quiet. I slept very well. I think because of the morphine. Yes, the morphine. I look to my right and a bag and tube still drip fluid into my arm. Thank goodness for drugs. The pain is numbed. I am in discomfort but it's bearable, unlike yesterday. By the time the fire engine had taken me to an ambulance, I was coughing and crying with pain. By the time the ambulance dispatched me into the emergency room I was screaming. Much more than that I don't remember, other than nurses, doctors, picking and pulling at me, wiping and bandaging. It went on for a long time under the strong lights. Faces concentrated on my body, no-one talking to me or telling me what they were doing. The injections. They felt good, they made it all fade a few feet away until the blackness took over eventually. Now I appear to be fully back in the world. A room, some room, but hospital certainly. I reach my left arm up gingerly to feel my head, but it is completely covered in bandages. I lift the sheets up to try and survey my body. It has a thin hospital gown; underneath extensive further bandaging is visible. Fresh wounds, scratching, and dried blood cover much of that which isn't already wrapped in bandages. All have been covered in some kind of disinfectant which stains a bright reddish brown, giving the impression of an insane rash, skin like a cocker spaniel. I am in a bit of a state. I sink back into the bed. What happened? Then I remember the burning man. The twitching, watching the last shreds of life immolated before my eyes. I feel queasy. There's a glass of water by my side, but with the stiffness I fumble it and it falls, smashing on the tiles.

The door opens and a nurse bursts in with an alarmed face. *'Oh, estas despierto, bien. Vuelvo.*[36]' And she's gone again. As she leaves, I see someone outside the door looking over his shoulder at me. He wears a uniform. A policeman.

Some time passes, who knows how long. I drift in and out. A doctor enters.

'Hello Mr Phillips, how are you this day?'

I think for a moment. I want to sob, partly due to the horrors etched on my brain, partly through relief. I struggle for composure. 'All things considered Doctor, I think I'm pretty well.'

'Yes, because you are very lucky. Incredibly lucky, because you fell into a pool which saved you from being burned alive. You have suffered some burns yourself though, in spite of the water. Your hair is damaged but it will grow back. You have a perforated eardrum, and there was water invasion, but we have treated this and prevented major infection. But your hearing will be bad in this ear, I am sorry to say. We found a bullet in your leg. It was not deep, the tree probably saved you from serious damage, there was wood in the wound as well. You also have a compression concussion from the blast. This will lead to some nausea,' an expression which makes me snort at the irony. It's nice to feel nauseous for purely physical reasons, 'but in a couple of days this will pass. There are a lot of surface flesh wounds from the plants, and some metal pieces. You have *puntos*, erm, stitches, in many places. Really it is amazing how you can survive this kind of explosion. You were in a pool of very dirty water, and there is risk of infection with so many wounds, so you are on strong antibiotic. In four or five days you will be well enough.'

'So I can leave then?'

He looks embarrassed. 'When you are well, the police will take you. They are waiting for many questions, but only when I say

---

[36] Oh, you're awake, good, I'll come back

you are fit, they can talk to you. Enjoy your rest, until then.' He beats a hasty retreat, but is met at the door by someone in a more important looking uniform than the average copper. The conversation is in Spanish so I don't follow, but the body language is clear. This officer is desperate to get in to talk to me, but the doctor is not letting him at all. It is clearer now. A gas explosion. I laugh myself back to sleep.

Two days roll painfully and slowly by. Throbbing burns, itching wounds, headaches and bouts of nausea, but at least my mind feels considerably clearer. I am able to trace the steps and days back, trying to figure out where all the pieces are in this violent chess game. I took out two of them, a bishop and rook, and I murdered one of the pawns. I try to erase the sound of soft flesh impact and the snapping of Darren's neck, but I can't. It pokes at me, a shard of glass, scraping at my consciousness, making it bleed. The King, Lebid, is still free. Holme as well. My enemies are by no means defeated, and I have no idea if my allies have survived. I am desperate for news of Ana and Treece. But so far, all my requests for information have been fobbed off. I am totally incommunicado and the policemen never leave my door. I must be rather a special case.

~

A knock. It's not a medic. He doesn't introduce himself, but stands back for a further person to enter, who I do indeed recognise. It's the short Spanish drug squad officer who scoped out the villa that night with Treece. He looks serious. Pulls up a chair, and starts talking in Spanish. I cut him off, and shout,

'How's Treece? What happened to the Inspector?' The officer glances back at the other man who starts in English. He's the interpreter.

'Señor Phillips, this is Comandante Perez of the Drugs and Organised Crime Unit of the National Police. You are under arrest and will be detained in preventive custody pending the investigations into the events-'

'Whoah wait up, can you ask the Inspector this. What the fuck happened?!' and I spit the words into his face. 'We handed you this whole organisation on a plate, we put it under your nose, and you fucked it up! I nearly fucking died! Look at me!'

The Comandante remains calm and holds his hand up gesturing for me to calm down. Eventually I do. Then he starts talking rapidly again to the interpreter.

'The comandante recognises you have been through a traumatic situation. He needs your extensive help in this investigation, but he says you must be aware there were the bodies of three criminal suspects found at the house, after an explosion that caused widespread damage to surrounding property, and over four hectares of land were burnt, calling for the intervention of firefighting helicopters and ground units. This is a serious criminal incident in which you are an implicated suspect. Also, it is for your own protection.'

I sink into the bed. What did I expect? So fixated have I been on bringing the house down on our heads, I haven't given any thought ever to the implications of my own obsession, the inevitable ramifications, which, from what they just said, are considerable. The threat hasn't gone away, I've probably just signed my own death warrant in triplicate this time. The rest of Lebid's associates are all still out there, somewhere in the world, biding their time.

'What about Treece?' The Comandante shakes his head, the interpreter speaks.

'A further incident was the killing of the British citizen who had been collaborating with the Brigade. This crime is also part of the investigation.'

'Any idea who killed him?'

Comandante shakes his head, and puts his hand on mine and squeezes.

'He cannot say at this time' adds the interpreter.

'So' I continue 'you guys have got a mole, a grass. Treece died because your operation was, *is*, compromised. Ask the comandante what he's going to do about that!'

My question is translated, but the Comandante does not respond. He fixes me with an even stare. I search his face, but it's a wall.

'What about Ana?'

'We are not dealing with any suspects by that name. Who is she?'

This takes me aback a bit, but then I figure that bodes well. It means she is still insulated from all of this, she's not on the radar as such, probably. I decide to drop it.

'She's just my dead brother's partner, I just wanted to let her know I'm okay.'

'We can contact her for you if you wish and reassure her.'

'Thanks.'

They had little else to say and I'm left in the room mulling over my situation. I didn't expect to come out the other side alive, and such were the unknowns, I haven't been able to anticipate anything. Once given the all clear by the doctors here, I'll be interviewed at length and transferred to the prison outside Malaga city. Well, makes sense, I was destined to end up inside sooner or later. I need to see Ana, I will be entitled to a lawyer at some point, maybe she can help. I need also to check how much I can reveal of what she holds on Holme. My road looks like it's ending up in a Spanish jail, which at least will be a contrast to Strangeways. For how long? I am in the frame for conspiracy to traffic huge amounts of cocaine, and the violent deaths of three men. Whether that'll keep me out of Lebid's vengeful reach remains to be seen.

The closure I so dearly longed for is a poisoned chalice. I have the cathartic knowledge Dmitri has been repaid in kind. Kavanagh has paid with his life for his father's crimes. I feel no remorse for these men. The victorious elation I should be feeling is all but destroyed by the sight of Darren prone on the ground, his gun underneath him. Would he have killed me? Treece, bravely went down in the cause. I still have no details. It wasn't entirely his fight. I owe him everything, and his account has yet to be settled. Fate hangs by such weird threads. And what of the entire racket, the criminal nexus Treece worked so hard to deliver to the Spanish Police? My disgust and fury are bottomless. They have much blood on their hands, it wasn't meant to go down this way. It weighs so heavily. I feel crushed, when I should feel free. And I am headed back to prison once again. A very Gene way for things to end, I think.

Try to sleep. Sleep keeps all the noise in my head at bay, almost. I just have a few more horrific images to play with in my nightmares. What glorious combinations will they produce to torture my psyche? For how long? I yell for the nurses, feigning renewed agonies, and they duly turn up the drip rate, and I can slip, numbed and senseless, back to sleep.

35

My burns have passed the critical point, my concussion has subsided. I can breathe easily, and have been cleared for processing by the legal system. The lawyer I have been given is a stern, pinched faced, middle-aged Spanish woman. I am being held in Malaga town somewhere, an imposing building, some kind of police headquarters. I am informed that I don't have to make a declaration of any kind, it is my right. I tell them I am perfectly happy to cooperate, which they should know, as I was cooperating before this entire incident landed me here. The lawyer looks nonplussed and the short comandante doesn't elaborate.

'Are you prepared to make a full declaration' she keeps repeating, to which I keep consenting. We are properly set-up in an interview room. I must have watched too many films. There is no tape machine and video cameras. Just an assistant officer with pen and paper. It is curiously antiquated. The interview with Comandante Perez is interminable, due only partly to the tedium of working through the interpreter. Perez leaves no stone unturned. He has availed himself of my records from the UK. He goes through every detail of my movements and contacts the whole time I have been in Spain. If I was silent last time I was prosecuted, this time I am singing like a bird. Every suspicion, action, name, and possible avenue of activity I have observed and aided is detailed in full. Any attempt of mine to find out what has happened since the explosion, or indeed how our operation was compromised are met with aggressive warnings, reminding me of my situation and the likely sentence I am facing. I am likely to be charged with aggravated drug trafficking, murder and organised crime. Dramatic. Potentially up to thirty years. The fact I was cooperating with law enforcement doesn't appear to have been factored in. Any mention of Treece and the previous meeting is skirted around in the questioning. Only brutal insistence against a barrage of threats and obfuscation enables me to get the fact of our meeting and Treece's collaboration on the record. This sparring, with Perez apparently intent on me incriminating myself to the maximum, and me attempting to justify all my actions with the goal of bringing the wider conspiracy to book, is exhausting. Perez discounts my collaboration, claiming I was already fully involved in the trafficking conspiracy before I attempted to collaborate. One might concede he has a point. Not that I'm going to. He is trying to force me to confirm I was searching for a strategy to get me out of a situation I couldn't handle, that my motives were purely ones of self-preservation. I am being slowly crucified, just for being yet another *guiri* on the make.

Now that the state has decided to do some long overdue house cleaning, we appear to be all tarred with the same brush just by association with the country's most corrupt and venal politicians. The entire declaration is being written down in long hand by the assistant officer, and after what is several hours, I am offered a substantial sheet of papers to sign. Even now I only sign after checking, with the reluctant assistance of the lawyer, that my previous meeting with Perez and Treece is properly documented, that my intentions were clear. If that one shred of evidence dies, there is nothing to say I wasn't anything other than a convicted former trafficker engaged in some kind of turf war over an enormous drug deal with a well-known criminal syndicate. It is certainly some journey, from my first impressions of a benign, filmic dreamland, to this. All in less than two months. It weighs more than ever. All the endless, tortuous convulsions of my mental state that have wracked me since Gary's killing, and Mum's murder, for want of a better word, have given way to an inner deadness. My life slipping from my grasp, of being so worthless I can't find the means, the anger, the indignation, or even the self-pity to articulate a course of action, to find the wherewithal to convince myself it is worth holding onto. Self-preservation has finally deserted me. All I have left are the nightly visions of sprayed brains, twitching burning bodies, snapping necks and suffocated old ladies. Yes, my mother's image has joined the grisly line-up of my subconscious.

.

36

Preventative detention. That's what it's called. Remand, in *guiri* speak. Up to two years, renewable for two more, before trial, potentially. The case apparently has gone from merely being an investigation by the police, to a status of 'judicial instruction' where all further actions are informed by a judge or fiscal. This stage could be months, over a year. And a trial, potentially years ahead. From the police van, I can make out through the heavily tinted windows, a surprisingly modern jail. It looks similar to many of the schools I have seen around this part of the world. I start the long trudge through induction into the penal system of this still strange country. So many unknowns, so much time to kill. Now I am closer to the reality of incarceration again, some of the waking dread has returned, fearing not unreasonably, that associates of Lebid's organisation are ready and waiting to exact their vengeance. I'm a sitting duck. I snitched big time. So much for witness protection. The only person who could fight my corner would be Ana, and I have heard nothing of her. Maybe she's just moved on. Why attach herself to a hopeless cause. She has her own terrible battles to face and I am certainly the least of her problems.

Once processed, I am shown to a cell. The entire place is profoundly different to Strangeways, the two jails being from utterly different epochs. There is light here in abundance. There is art on the walls, murals, some visible patios with vegetation. It lacks the fortified aura, the heavy metal of incarceration so omnipresent in Strangeways. That's not to say there isn't a fair amount of razor wire in evidence. It's still a goddam prison. But there's a shower in my cell. I've seen student accommodation worse than this I think to myself. I wonder who my cell mate will be. He's not here. It's lunchtime. That moment, of when you first appear, the newbie, in front of the gathered cons, is still vivid in my mind from Strangeways. Everyone sees you, everyone assesses you, for all kinds of reasons, formulating all kinds of strategies, evaluating possibilities, dangers, opportunities. Will there be the same structure of competing gangs, controlling interests over desired merchandise; the drugs, telephones, and weapons that afford power and influence on the inside. How will I know who my enemies are, as I am sure there will be some, and they may already have been made aware of my arrival. And my status. Snitch. Grass. Supergrass in fact.

I walk into the refectory, and rather than the odour of stale cooking fat and cabbage I remember, it smells like a run of the mill cafeteria here. It smells of good ordinary Spanish food. I'm trying not to make eye contact, as I walk steadily along to join the food queue, nor trying to stare too obviously at the floor. My attention is caught by some laughter, above the usual din. Then whistling, then some applause breaks out. It's located in one area of the open space, but is quite distinct. A cheer or two. Someone starts up a chant, Eu-geeeen, Eu-geeeen, like in a football crowd. I dare to look up for a second. A significant section of the hall is looking at me. Over in the far corner, maybe twenty inmates continue to hoot and holler, clapping and beckoning me over. It is too surreal; I am extremely confused. I go along the line picking up elements of my food. Some wholesome lentils, fresh smelling bread, a custard dessert, could be worse. I'm still desperately trying to be invisible.

A voice behind me says, 'Go on, go and meet your reception committee then.' A Geordie accent. So there's Brits in here. Inevitable, really. I have my tray, I look up. Still men beckon to me, so I make my way over. I catch various glances as I walk, mostly curious faces, occasionally sardonic smiles, even amusement. At the corner of my vision I catch a pair of faces who show no amusement, just cold hard stares. Slavic faces, a kind of stare I recognize. It only takes minutes in a place like this to know who your enemies are. But who are all these friends?

466

For want of a better idea, I make my way over to the welcoming committee. The first person to speak to me does so in English, but the people gathered around are decidedly cosmopolitan. A very British face is laughing at me.

'Fuck me, you are not what I expected! Alright mate, how are you? Johnny's the name, Johnny Jones.'

'Hello Johnny, I'm Gene. What were you expecting?' I say, trying not to sound flippant. All eyes are on me as I sit, I am frankly, utterly bewildered.

'Well not you, the guy that took out Jimmy Kavanagh and the D machine! You're a fucking leg already mate!'

The babbled congratulations in various languages attest to my instant fame, slaps on the back, people introducing themselves, or just staring with admiration at me.

'Look, sorry, Johnny, I don't mean to be disrespectful, but what is this about? Who are you all?'

'Ah my son, we are what is informally known as the FBK.'

'FBK?'

'Fucked by Kavanagh.' No one laughs at this, Johnny means it, judging by the reaction.

'OK.' Now I am really intrigued. 'Do elaborate, please.'

As I eat gratefully through a meal of a standard that will brighten up the monotony of prison life, not reinforce it, I listen to a startling new insight into the wonderful workings of the Costa del Crime. Everyone here in this group, British, quite a lot of Moroccans, Spaniards, a couple of Frenchies, and a sprinkling of East Europeans have one thing in common. They are inside because they all got 'fucked' working on drug runs, about half of them working for the Kavanagh-Lebid operation. Over years it seems. Most of them were low rent drug runners, the decoys. The classic scenario was they'd be down on their luck and gratefully accept the opportunity to shift some hash, for a fistful of Bin Ladens, on a jet ski from the boat to shore, or drive a consignment along the coast in a stolen car. And they would get pulled. The Guardia Civil waiting for them, much to their horror. Meanwhile the big consignment has gone ashore elsewhere, as the Guardia have been preoccupied with several small fry. Or it may have been running small consignments to distribution points, storage places, all of it part of the sophisticated techniques of mis-direction and trial and error. Sacrificial lambs on the altar of serious narcotics trafficking. The pawns, dispensable in the larger chess game. And into this tight-knit club with a profound and bitter sense of grievance walks me, the man who took out two of the nastiest pieces on the whole board. I'm not only a celebrity, I am a living legend. But as Johnny Jones said so eloquently, nobody expected it to be *me*.

My gradual initiation over the coming days is surprisingly convivial. Thanks to the size and history of this group, they maintain a healthy independence from the many other narcos. By far the majority of prisoners here on drugs convictions are small timers, the foot soldiers, opportunists and losers that operations depend on to shield the people at the top more fully. The programmed in, cynical, collateral damage. I am informed and warned of which people to avoid. Elements of various British, Moroccan, East European and Albanian gangs cohabit here, who show clan loyalty always. The two people eyeing me on that first day continue to do so. They are from a Ukrainian gang of car thieves who specialised in ripping off high end motors and shipping them to the nether regions of Russia and Africa. They also supplied cars for drug runs of Kavanagh's. Their reason for being inside is not connected directly to Kavanagh. I also meet people who experienced Dmitri's role as enforcer. Beatings, humiliation, intimidation and surveillance. His nickname the 'D machine' derived from his completely expressionless way of carrying out all his duties. A veritable sociopath. The genuine gratitude and exaltation expressed to me for my actions is the most bizarre approbation I ever imagined. It goes some way to lifting my darkened spirit enough, so that I start to think constructively about my predicament. On my fifth day I receive a summons. I have a visitor. My heart leaps, as I can only imagine one person willing to make such a visit.

On entering the long room with rows of tables, I instantly spot Ana. Partly the clothing, partly the person accompanying her. Both are immaculately dressed in sharp business attire. But moreover, because she looks ravishing. Gone are the ruddy eyes, the gaunt sleepless face, the thousand-yard stare. Her face is flush, with freckles I don't remember seeing, her eyes twinkle, even from this distance. And her stomach, the baby is starting to show a little, her breasts are fuller, the rush of hormones creating a new creature, two new creatures.

I sit and clasp her hands, I can't contain my tears. The last shadows of depression slough from me, and a sense of optimism pokes, like green shoots of winter snowdrops, through the ice of my winter. I am introduced to the smart woman in her early forties.

'Gene, *te presento Doña Carmen Vasquez Ordoño*, your lawyer.'

I can't do anything more than just smile.

'*Hola, encantada, Señor Eugene.*'

'Please, call me Gene.'

'Of course.' A wash of relief, she speaks good English.

After the usual politesse of enquiring after my health, and so forth, Doña Carmen becomes serious. 'Gene, I cannot pretend the charges you are being held on are anything but extremely serious. If we go to trial, it will mean we have already lost the battle. You were clearly engaged in conspiracy to traffic the cocaine some time before Mr. Treece approached Europol. There is only one living witness to your participation in this collaboration of Europol and the ODYCO.'

'Perez. Shit. Pardon my French.'

'Perez was leading the investigation which was still young, and limited. It would normally have been a lengthy investigation of many months. It was not at the time a judicial investigation because there was so little evidence to put before a judge, enabling full police powers of surveillance, phone tapping and this kind of thing. The kind of intervention you and Mr Treece were hoping for would have required judicial authority, and this was not yet given when things went wrong.'

'Yes, evidently, and how did things go wrong? Is Perez corrupt?'

'No, we don't think so. He was in a rush to get the evidence together to enable a judge to grant powers of a judicial investigation. He maybe cut corners, made mistakes, maybe he was just unlucky one corrupt person was able to intercept the information, in the police or even the judiciary. We will probably never know.'

Great. Treece died for nothing. 'So, I'm basically screwed?'

'Pardon?' Ah yes, the vernacular.

'*Jodido*' translates Ana.

She pauses for a moment, regarding Ana.

'I think not. This lady is a very special woman, a very brave woman.'

'Well I know' I say, but I don't know what she's driving at in the context.

'And Mr Treece was a trained policeman. He kept proper records of everything he said, recorded his conversations, his emails, his movements, and left copies on a daily basis, where Ana could recover them.'

'Wow.' Light at the end of the tunnel maybe.

'If Mr. Kavanagh had succeeded in killing you, none of this would have been seen as anything other than yet another war between criminals. Europol would have had little information or any confirmation of what you were doing with Treece. Only Perez would know the truth. Now there are three dead gangsters, a villa destroyed, a big fire, and a lot of noise for Perez to deal with. Your statement is also a lot of noise. It is information that is now part of the case under full judicial investigation, as is the fact, on record, that you met with Perez and Treece. But it is maybe not enough to clear you of conspiracy to traffic, even if you can claim self-defence for killing the others.'

The weight is creeping back over me. It is all pretty damning. And I have admitted all of which I shall be charged with. To think I imagined I could engineer the downfall of such an organisation, just me and a retired copper from Warrington.

'But', she says, glancing at Ana again 'because of the information, the evidence that Ana has, thanks to your brother, we have hope.'

Ana looks uncomfortable, searching for the will to say what is on her lips. Something is wracking her thoughts. Her fingers fidget.

'We think Gary was killed for what he knew.' Ana is straining for composure. 'The evidence from the bank vault shows he knew exactly what was going on, precisely how Holmeland worked, the relationship with Lebid. It is all so detailed, going back for over a year. I have had to ask myself what is the truth about your brother. Did he collaborate with Lebid and Holme in the hidden side of the business? Was he simply collecting information to protect himself? If he knew so much, how could he have gone along with all of it.' Her eyes plead. These revelations will burden her for the rest of her life, questions whose answers are buried with Gary. Unless someone, somehow, catches up with Holme.

'He knew that was happening?!' I'm horrified by the compromises Gary must have knowingly made. How could he have carried on, knowing the degree of compromise involved in the entire edifice? Illusions about Gary are shattering like the windscreen of his car. Ana raises a hand.

'The evidence here is enough to put Lebid and Holme in prison for many years. I haven't seen anything that connects Gary to decisions made, to implicate him directly. And yet he knew all this, kept it secret from everyone, even me. Maybe I will never understand this.'

I am now thoroughly awed at what Gary undertook. What an immense burden. A torture. Did he discover his life's work to be a gigantic, corrupt, deadly lie? One that he certainly wouldn't have shared with his unpredictable, feckless brother. Or was he the liar? It is deeply unsettling.

'Well,' Carmen picks up the thread, 'the great amount of evidence Ana now has, connects all of Holmeland with the Lebid operation, Kavanagh, and what you have said to the police about it. A British policeman has been murdered, Gary also. They found many kilos of drugs, and dozens of girls kept for prostitution. A giant nexus. The big investigation of the Caso Malaya is linked and will cooperate with the judicial enquiry into your case, specifically. This is why Lebid has completely abandoned his interests here. He and Holme are the most important witnesses. Lebid is back in the Ukraine, hiding behind political friends. Interpol are working to bring them both to Spain, but who knows. We hope to be able to convince the fiscal your case is fundamentally compromised because of the leak, the very real failure to prevent a tragedy, and to take appropriate action against an extensive criminal conspiracy. That you are a victim, not a perpetrator.'

They both smile at me, smiles tinged with sadness. Two hugely intelligent, talented, beautiful women fighting my corner. Light. Tunnels. Who knows.

'So now what?'

'Wait. Things will happen more quickly if Holme and Lebid can be captured' answers Carmen.

'It could be months, even years' adds Ana. 'You are still a dangerous criminal in the eyes of the state until we can convince them otherwise.' This actually makes me laugh. It still sounds ludicrously hopeful.

'And what about Treece? What about his information, what can we do with it?'

'I looked at it. It is shocking,' says Ana, 'and has completely altered my idea of what British justice is. But it is the British legal system. It does not connect to this. And I fear, it is already history. So long ago, I do not know what could be done. But I contacted someone who might.'

'And?'

She shrugs. 'Wait.'

Mysterious. Distant hope.

'What happened to Treece?' I'm desperate to know, his death saddens me immensely, and I have no idea how to give him his due, to atone. He was sacrificed on the altar of my obsessions and compromises, not his.

'The investigation has thrown up little evidence. He was shot at home, drinking tea in his kitchen. It is entirely possible the people responsible were killed in the gas explosion. We will probably never know,' Carmen says apologetically. The assumption does tally with what Kavanagh hinted to me. Just before he was immolated..

It is excruciatingly hard to watch them go, although they leave me with a sense of optimism and purpose I had abandoned these last few days. Patience. All things come to those who wait. I smile. That was the oft quoted maxim lifted from my Mum that Doug and I would repeat, mantra like, as we waited for the sad little fish in those old bomb craters.

37

The months roll by. Routine routine routine. There is a marked difference in the level of casual violence between Alhaurín and Strangeways. Petty squabbles, racist slights and plain machismo provoke incidents, but by and large, life is peaceful. Only once does some newly admitted con pick on me, thanks to my reputation, to prove his worth. I take some thumps, and as I rally to defend myself, he is buried under a flailing mob of fists from the FBK. No one bothers to try that again. The FBK are just another part of the natural prison ecology nobody wants to disturb too much. Most of the remnants of other drug gangs regarded Kavanagh as a competitor, and one to be feared. Moreover, I get the overwhelming impression all of these people are glad, or at least hopeful their drug dealing days are behind them.

The prison offers a surprising range of courses and training within the walls. Those who want to be occupied, can be. As in the last time, I gravitate towards the library. Little of which is in English. I gradually learn Spanish, at least enough to curse and take the piss out of my fellow prisoners.

The nights vary in difficulty. I learn to turn down the offers of medication to control my occasional panics, my disturbed nights. I can't face numbing myself further to it all. I want to try and feel alive, in control, to look forward. Some nights I cry, for Ana, for Mum, for Treece, even for Darren. Sometimes, in my darkness, I have to seize on the flames, to relish and replay the delicious irony, of the purging fire of butane that roasted my enemies so brutally. It helps me balance the other horrors and regrets. It is a heavy burden, ever present during the hours of inactivity. I wonder how I will ever be able to find some kind of equilibrium that will allow me to function as a normal person. The odds of having the opportunity are slim. Even if I escape the clutches of Spanish justice, Strangeways beckons. My license is as burnt and destroyed as the villa back in Estepona.

Ana makes regular visits, up until she is too pregnant. It is an awe-inspiring experience, seeing her body change, grow. One day I will behold a new member of my family. Her news helps me maintain a focus on the future, still dreadfully uncertain. The British Home Office is fully aware of my location, and I will be expected to go back and present myself to the police, if I should be released from custody here. If I don't, they may try to issue extradition proceedings.

One morning I am summoned to visiting time, which puts a spring in my step, as only Ana can do. But it's not her. A cloud passes over my mind, fear and foreboding. A complete stranger, a tough looking character, a weathered face, wearing clothes from the colder climates of back home. I sit down, and he shakes my hand firmly, and takes out a notebook and pen. A journalist! I'm about to react, negatively, when he holds up a hand.

'Treece.' He says simply. The accent is distinctly Belfast. 'He was a good man. A real good man.'

'I know'. He regards me with a half-smile, getting the measure of me.

'You're not what I expected.'

'Oh, for fuck's sake, why does everyone say that?'

He laughs at this, heartily. 'Anthony Devlin, pleased to meet you, Gene.'

I'm getting impatient with the cryptic politesse. 'Look Devlin, I don't have anything to say to journalists, I'm sorry you've come all the way out here, but I've got nothing to tell you.' And I make to get up, but he cuts me off.

'Well, that's not what Ana said. We have a mutual interest. We've been victims of the same injustices, at the hands of the same people.' He doesn't elaborate, just fixes me with a clear blue-eyed stare, charged with that same steely determination that Ana possesses. 'I want you, to help me, to get the bastards who did your father in.'

'Well, I'm not much use to you in here.'

'I know. There's a few things I'd like to ask you. But mostly, I want to know, if you do get out of here, will you help me, back in the UK?'

'Back to Strangeways with a bloody great target on my back. You want me to make it even bigger?'

'I know people... who can talk to people, in the movement... you'll be safe. If you help me.'

I look at him, for quite some time, processing so many emotions, surveying the wreckage going back decades. And I start talking.

38

And just like that, one day, a month or so later, I emerge from the tunnel and I'm standing in the light. My lawyer has been successful. The prison governor has informed me I am to be released forthwith. The charges have been dropped; I am free to go. My first emotion is relief, quickly followed by fear. The British Home Office has my recall to Strangeways ready, and I am obliged to go back to Britain regardless. I am not really free.

My persecutors have, literally, been vanquished or have fled, and I shall not stand trial for it after all. From the news, to packing my sparse belongings, saying goodbyes to some strange but firm friends is but a few hours. Alarmingly precipitous. No time to prepare myself for the next step. And then I am standing out on the street in front of the sprawling modern institution, watching Ana step out of a taxi. She is carrying a small bundle of something.

She walks toward me. The air is cool and fresh, the sun still punishingly bright, all the more so for it being a late December day, as it is low on the horizon. The blue canopy hovers above me, framing the rows of palms and bright concrete. The bundle makes a squawking noise. A tiny hand flaps up. I stand rooted to the spot.

'*Hola Gene, como estas?*' Ana smiles. It is a smile that says nothing and everything. All that she has been through, all I have seen, what binds us together and what separates us.

'*Pues, muy bien, la verdad. No puedo quejarme.*[37]'

She raises her eyebrows.

'*¡Olé, como hablas, hijo mío*[38]*!*'

---

[37] Well, really well to be honest. Can't complain.
[38] Wow, how you are speaking, my boy!

She hands me the bundle, and I gingerly accept it. I'm shocked, by many thoughts colliding, but also simply because I've actually never held a baby before.

'Meet your niece, Rosa.'

The mini-human wiggles and waves, her dimly aware eyes search my facial features. I think she is beautiful, but I don't know much about babies. I haven't seen many. There though, in the shape of the brow and the nose, I recognise something, a hint of Gary. A distinct likeness. Maybe I'm remembering old family photos. Grainy snaps of babies in some long-forgotten album.

'Where are we going?'

Ana looks at me a while.

'Home. For a day at least. You can get to know Rosa before you go back to Britain. And then when you have finished that, maybe you can come back to see us.'

It's a long way away. Rosa grips my finger and gurgles. I smile.

'Yeah. Maybe.'

'Devlin wants to meet you as soon as you get back, he'll pick you up from the airport.'

Devlin, Jesus. The man who would raise up all the ghosts, the gatherer of skeletons from sundry cupboards. Ana eyes me, her look is pleading. 'For Treece. And for your father. For Gary. Devlin told me everything.'

Her face clouds. The baby in her arms is a living reminder of all that has befallen my family, and she is inescapably part of its tortured history. I am sorry she has to live with all of this knowledge, this legacy. But I'm also grateful to have one so strong, so determined and able, to be able to call her family. All I have left.

39

Descending yet again into the half-darkness of a North-West winter's day, my mind is a turmoil of speculation, paranoia, and fear. But that's not all. I feel charged by a visceral excitement. Ana had enlightened me during my brief stop-over between prisons, to the full complexity of Holme's compromised financial empire. The tight rope he walked, balancing his need for finance and influence, with the demands of his investors and their distinctly nefarious business model. Although still only speculative, Ana has formulated a theory that Gary was closing in on the truth of the relationship. Holme's promotion of him was expedient, making him too big to fail, too involved to be able to escape its concomitant liabilities. He was the protégé who would have been in so far, so compromised, so much a part of the corrupt edifice, he couldn't turn on his benevolent boss. He was also the perfect fall guy. Gary's veiled threat to expose everything may well have been what signed his death warrant. The Caso Malaya investigation set fire to the delicate fabric of Marbella corruption, detonating the finely wrought, Holme inspired symbiosis, of money laundering, property speculation, drug and human sex trafficking. Despite all of the detailed information Gary accumulated, nothing specific incriminated Holme in his murder. Ana is certain Gary was seeking to protect himself, but probably hadn't fully understood what he was dealing with. Or, as I suspect, he had only just realised. My discovery of the coke stash in the warehouse mirrored his own realisation, one we shared in those last moments of his life in his car that spring morning. It is cold comfort, and ironic, that Dmitri had a low enough opinion of me, to not shoot me at the same time.

Ana and I. Armed with our unique knowledge, our priceless, blood-stained troves of evidence. Ana pursuing Holme and Lebid, gathering her case, seeking reliable allies within the Spanish judicial system. And I, heading to a meeting, carrying Treece's trove, ready to collaborate with men committed to a cause so ancient and complex, I have only the most basic understanding of all involved. But at the centre of this small Warrington chapter of that vast Irish history, still walk the men who engineered the destruction of my family's happiness.

It's a bizarre pact, between two wounded survivors, bent on seeking justice, the lighthouse in the sea of filth and compromise. It may even go some way to stemming the nightly tide of images that still plague me, the cinema reel of blood, drugs and old ladies. But then again, it might not.

~

Anthony Devlin, investigative journalist, fearless pursuer of political and moral turpitude, meets me at Manchester airport. He has a colleague with him, a renowned civil rights lawyer. I am to turn myself over to the police tomorrow morning, and the recall to prison will be for a minimum of twenty-eight days, while the powers that be consider my case. A case that is creating some noise at both ends of the continent. The humiliating climb down of the Spanish prosecutors over my charge has been echoed by ancient reverberations in England. Inspector Geoffrey Treece's legacy is the waking up of slumbering animosities, bitter vendettas and career threatening rumours. The inability to solve his murder has set loose all sorts of tensions among former colleagues, and retired politicians. Revisionist journalists, expert at raking through the muck of the dormant troubles of Northern Ireland, are grubbing around, sharpening their knives. We have a good few hours still, before I surrender my freedom yet again. The three of us head for Warrington.

Devlin's car pulls up outside the little semi. On a December day it appears as miserable as it ever did, only more so. The myriad winking Christmas lights of the neighbourhood cannot compensate. The lifeless grey windows stare blankly out on the dank street. The

480

gloom of a mid-winter afternoon is descending rapidly. No wonder the damn place hasn't sold in nine months. Why would you endure living here? I yearn to rid myself of the building. I would have it demolished if I could. Its ghosts are too real. Too fresh. One of them will always be in there, waiting for me.

The estate agent pulls up, as I stare disconsolately at the house.

'Hello, Eugene isn't it?'

'That's me.'

'Well, here's the keys. I'm sorry we haven't been able to shift it for you yet, but don't worry, we fully expect the market to move a bit in the spring. Demand is low around here at the moment. We could talk about the price if you like. We've been trying to contact you for ever, you've been somewhat incommunicado.'

I laugh at this. 'You don't know the half of it.'

'Will you be staying long? Can we still do viewings while you're here?'

'Of course, I'm not going to be around really. I want it sold as soon as possible. Get whatever you can for it. I'll be back to Spain as soon as I am able to.' Whatever happens, however long this country, this history, will shackle my heels and my spirit, I will not live in that house again.

'That's great, that will help. Just over seeing friends then?' he says, eyeing my accomplices warily.

'No. Not friends, no.' I feel the weight of the heavy stack of documents in the rucksack over my shoulder. 'Just some unfinished business.'

FIN

About the Author

Roly Quesnel, born in 1960, grew up in Eccles, Greater Manchester, in a family of six children. Eldest son of Louis Quesnel, a senior lecturer in bacteriology and Dinah Quesnel, a teacher of English, he had a relatively comfy upbringing in a leafy middle-class suburb, attending a Catholic grammar school in Salford. After taking a wrong turn at 18, by choosing to work in a bank, he belatedly studied a degree in performing arts, becoming a further education lecturer in drama and dance. This career was short-lived, as he decided to study at the Jacques Lecoq school in Paris at the age of 29, with the aim of launching an acting career.

Together with colleagues from the school, he worked in their own theatre company up until 1998, touring various original shows and working as a freelance movement teacher and director. Working on a contract at the Seville World Expo in 1992, he met and later married Tracey Lewin, an English woman brought up entirely in Spain. Initially they settled back in London to continue theatre work. Tracey came from a film production background, working on location in Spain. The arrival of their first child in 1997 forced a change of perspective about his theatre career and living in the UK. In 1999, the family moved to the Malaga area, to work in a thriving family film service business.

Roly has worked widely in the media business in Spain ever since, as a production manager for film and televisión, as well as being a professional videographer and photographer. Having spent many years observing the life of the Costas through a camera, he finally felt inspired to write a novel mining his various perspectives and experiences of coming to the Spanish life from a very different background.

His passions are cooking good food, mountain biking, drumming and singing in punk bands, photography, Manchester United, fishing, and the Spanish countryside.

Roland lives in Mijas Costa, Malaga province, in Spain with his wife and younger daughter.

This is his first novel.

Acknowledgements:

Pooky Quesnel - for invaluable criticism and support.
Kev Heritage - for his indespensable 'Complete Indie Editor'.
Jane Love - for persepctives on the realty business on the Costa.
Johnny Gates and Anne Sophie Veronica Lyrefelt – for great anecdotes.
Fay Jones and Lee Collins – whose jobs gave me such an insight into the Marbella scene.
To friends and family for their feedback on the various evolving versions
To the people of Spain . for putting up with us all.

Further reading:

Much of what happens in the book is based entirely on the recent history of the Costa del Sol. The Caso Malaya is a well known and ongoing corruption scandal that detonated Marbella society in 2006. The main perpetrators are still in jail, and there are still trials pending in 2021. Marbella is as seductive today as it ever was. As part of my profession I am continually involved in making reality shows that celebrate the conventional and common perception of Marbella. This book is the flip side of that version so beloved of British television commissioners.

Below are links to further insights into this deceptive world.
This article in The Gaurdian was edited from an even bigger article in Spain's El Pais. It shows the continuing development of organised in crime, making the days of 2006 seem tame now.
https://www.theguardian.com/news/2021/may/20/a-united-nations-of-how-marbella-became-a-magnet-for-gangsters
Other local news outlets regularly publish updates on the trials and convictions.

http://www.surinenglish.com/20151116/news/costasol-malaga/true-story-operation-malaya-201511161056.html

https://es.wikipedia.org/wiki/Caso_Malaya

http://www.surinenglish.com/local/201803/16/juan-antonio-roca-mastermind-20180316093208-v.html

https://www.diariolibre.com/actualidad/the-marbella-or-malaya-case-IMDL262947

https://www.andalucia.com/history/people/jesusgil.htm

There is also an excellent documentary on Jesus Gil called 'The Pioneer' on Netflix.

https://www.netflixtvseries.com/tv/90913/el-pionero

Marbella is a great place to visit all year round. The stuff in the papers and this book rarely impinge on the lives of the fun-seekers. For the ultimate guide to all its wonders, go to the experts: www.myguidemarbella.com